BREAD AND SALT

Bread and Salt

Connie Biewald

iUniverse, Inc.
New York Lincoln Shanghai

Bread and Salt

iUniverse books may be ordered through booksellers or by contacting:

iUniverse
2021 Pine Lake Road, Suite 100
Lincoln, NE 68512
www.iuniverse.com
1-800-Authors (1-800-288-4677)

ISBN-13: 978-0-595-36267-7 (pbk)
ISBN-13: 978-0-595-67361-2 (cloth)
ISBN-13: 978-0-595-80712-3 (ebk)
ISBN-10: 0-595-36267-2 (pbk)
ISBN-10: 0-595-67361-9 (cloth)
ISBN-10: 0-595-80712-7 (ebk)

Printed in the United States of America

For my grandmother,
Wilhelmine Hulsken Biewald,
1905–1977
and my life partner,
Jeff Thomas,
two people who,
in loving me,
helped me learn to love myself

Narration is as much a part of human nature as breath and the circulation of the blood.

A.S. Byatt

PART I

▼

1914–1918

CHAPTER 1

▼

At the very beginning of the First World War, when many folk in Germany still had enough to eat, there lived three hungry sisters. Sofie, the oldest, had restless gray eyes, the color of the ocean on a stormy day. Amalia's eyes were the steady brown of newly plowed potato fields. Dora's shone blue as the Virgin Mary's robes.

At ages nine, eight, and seven these girls didn't have to be told the world was dangerous. They knew from their mother's worried face and how she said it would be only for a short while but they had to be good, no trouble to anyone, and spend their days locked safely in the room rented from Frau Becker—a tight white room with a bed, a chamber pot, some crates that served as table and chairs, one high shelf, a plain wooden crucifix, and the necessary nearness of sisters.

The coal darkened city of Tauburg, their strange new home, spread beneath their window. Sofie elbowed past her sisters and hung over the ledge, the morning air already thick and grimy. She watched their mother, Hanna, until she passed the butcher shop, until she disappeared around the corner to clean the factory owners' houses. The cobbled streets pulled Hanna away as surely as the current of the muddy river in which the girls had learned to swim, the river that cut across the far corner of their farm—the farm that wasn't theirs anymore even though it had belonged to Hanna Heller Bauer Kleinschuster, and three generations of Hellers before her. Behind Sofie, Amalia and Dora jostled each other. Each girl, buttoned and braided, clutched a hunk of bread their mother cut before leaving, the last of the loaf.

"Let me see," Amalia insisted.

"Mama's gone," Sofie said without relinquishing her spot.

Dora attempted to squeeze in beside her. Amalia pressed against Sofie's back. Sisters. Sofie longed to join the bustle in the streets, to have somewhere to go, dangerous or not. She might have followed her mother or even wandered a bit, in this crowded city tucked between the Ruhr and the Rhein, mighty rivers hectic with boat traffic, rivers she wouldn't dare to swim, even though her stroke was powerful and precise. Amalia and Dora would have made too much of a fuss— Amalia because she did what she was told and Dora because she was a scared baby.

Dora ate her bread and had only crusts left to chew. Amalia had divided hers, eaten one piece when the church bells rang nine and planned to eat the other at noon. Sofie stripped her crust and ate that first. With her thumb and fingertips, she pinched bits from the soft middle, rolled them into pellets, put half in her pocket and placed the rest in a row on the window sill.

"Birds will come and snatch those," Amalia predicted, hiding her own piece from herself among piles of clean clothes stacked in a corner, the clothes they'd helped each other into more than a month before, dresses over dresses until they couldn't bend at the waist. The outermost layer tore at the seams as they and their mother sneaked away in the night, past their stepfather, a tremendous mound of a man. The smell of stale beer rose from his mouth with every snore.

"If the birds eat all your bread," Amalia said, "you will have nothing." No one would catch her putting the last of her food out on a dirty window sill.

Sofie fingered the bits of gluey dough in her pocket. She liked the generous feeling that swelled inside her chest at the rustle of sparrows at the window. She knew how to take care of others and herself too.

At noon the church bells clanged for the longest time. Smells of cabbage and lard and sausage squeezed under the door. Amalia lifted a dark skirt to retrieve her bread. Sofie let a bread ball turn to mush in her mouth and gave another to Dora. The other boarders, all students at the mining school, streamed into the kitchen below for *Mittagspause* and consumed potatoes, soup and meat. The girls' stomachs ached and gurgled. They hoped that when their mother came home in the evening she would bring leftovers from the rich people. The day before, she had brought almost nothing.

"Let's do a story now," said Dora. It would help to pass the time until they could eat again. "'The Fisherman and His Wife.'" Her favorite. "I want to be the magic flounder."

"You always want to be the fish," Amalia complained. "It's the best part."

"I know." Dora frowned so hard that two wrinkles formed between her eyebrows. "That's why I always want to be it."

"Well, someone else should have a turn."

"But if you're the fisherman you can say the rhyme," Dora said and began, "Flounder, flounder in the sea..."

"All right," said Amalia. "As long as I don't have to be the wife."

Sofie put on their mother's apron. Amalia would never play a wicked part. Dora would, upon occasion, be an enchantress or witch, but an ordinary greedy woman or careless man? If Sofie didn't act those characters, no one would. She understood them to be as necessary to the story as the magic.

The fish was caught and released. Each time the fisherman approached the water with one of his wife's escalating demands, Amalia recited the rhyme, and they argued over the exact color and state of the sea.

"First it's gray and thick and then it's purple and bubbling." Dora stopped wriggling on the floor and stood up.

"No, it goes clear, green, purple, dark gray, black." Amalia ticked them off on her fingers.

"When she tells him to get her a hut, it's blue." Sofie knew she was right. "Then when she wants the castle it's purple and smelly, and when she wants to be the emperor—"

Amalia stomped her foot. "It doesn't go like that! First it's—"

"Gray!" Dora hollered.

"Get back in the water," said Sofie. "Fish don't stand up. You'd be dead by now."

"I'm a magic fish," Dora reminded her. She flapped her elbows like fins, opened and closed her mouth with a loud popping sound, and made her blue eyes huge.

"That doesn't mean you can do whatever you want." Amalia squeezed her arm. "Lie down."

"Will Mama be back soon?" Dora squirmed free of Amalia's grip and looked out the window.

Sofie untied her apron. She wanted to fling it onto the floor, but instead she matched the edges and folded it into a smooth white square.

At the window again, they waited for their mother as the day wound down, like most of their days, with Dora whining, Amalia worrying, and Sofie hating the rich people for making her mother work so hard.

Dora shouted, "I see her!"

"You do not," Amalia said.

Sofie stretched high on tiptoes and crammed her hands into her apron pockets to keep from shoving her sisters out of the way. Their mother would scold if she walked in to find them fighting.

They leaned out the window as far as they could and waved and shouted.

Their mother lifted her head in a nod and disappeared through the door beneath their window. She would stop in the kitchen to chat with Frau Becker, to see if the landlady's knees were aching. If so, Hanna would be paid a bit to help with the evening meal and washing up.

The girls waited, pressed close to the door—those last few moments as long as the whole day. They yearned for their mother's voice, the touch of her cool fingers, the cheese, bread, meat and cake she might unwrap, her brush strokes against their scalps.

"It's taking longer than usual," Dora said. "Isn't it?"

They waited, listening with their whole bodies, no sound of their mother's feet on the stair.

"Let's go see what's keeping her," Sofie suggested.

"How?" Amalia asked, pushing the locked door handle.

"There's a key."

"Mama has it."

"No, another one, in the blue bowl, beside the music box." Sofie pointed to the high shelf. They weren't allowed to touch the music box, a treasured gift from their father to their mother before he married her.

"Why didn't you tell us?" Dora demanded.

Mama had told Sofie about the extra key, trusted her with adult information not to be shared with her sisters, and instructed her not to use it except in an emergency. Sofie had never been tempted to tell, to ruin a secret shared with her mother. She suspected, too, that Amalia and Dora would expect her to use the key, to make good on her big talk about exploring the city, and she didn't want to be pressured.

"Why didn't you say anything before?" Amalia said.

"I forgot," said Sofie. She forced herself to look right at them.

Before they could challenge her further, before they figured out that her tendency to do things they wouldn't dare scared herself as much as it scared them, she stacked the packing crates they used as chairs and table and prepared to climb the wobbly tower.

"If Mama comes now, she'll be angry," Amalia said. "You won't know how to unlock the door anyway, even if you have a key."

"She'll come soon, Sofie," Dora added. "Get down. You're going to fall."

"Listen by the door and tell me if you hear her," Sofie ordered through clenched teeth as she gripped the edge of the shelf and reached.

The key was heavier than she expected, with a heart-shaped head, longer than the width of her palm. She leapt from the top box as the teetering pile crashed to the floor. Dora's hands flew to her ears. Amalia scurried to arrange the crates as they'd been before. Sofie picked herself up and waved the key over her head.

They stood still and waited for their mother or Frau Becker to holler or burst in, but no footsteps sounded on the stairs. No shouts.

Sofie fit the key into the keyhole as if she unlocked the door every day. She slipped the key into her pocket feeling important and told herself to remember to put it back.

"We shouldn't do this," Amalia said as she and Dora followed Sofie down the steep and narrow stairs.

Frau Becker was saying, "Over a month now...they're good girls. No trouble to me. I admit I was worried when you first came, but I couldn't say no, you were so...so tired. But look at you. Still tired. More tired every day and the girls...it's no good for them to be all day in a room. They should go to school. The oldest one anyway. But who knows what will happen now with a war starting."

Sofie flattened herself against the wall and motioned her sisters to do the same. They peeked around the door frame. Frau Becker, knees stiff, lurched around the large, low-ceilinged kitchen. Their mother sat at an end of the long table, just beyond the wide arch that divided the cooking and dining areas. They couldn't see her face. A cup steamed by her elbow.

Frau Becker stirred soup on the huge black stove. "With a war things will only get worse, even with a quick victory. The Kaiser says we will show our foes what it is to provoke Germany. I'm sure he should know! Isn't there someone who could take them, just for a while, until the war ends, to give you some time to make a home?"

Mama said nothing. Frau Becker went on. "They say the war will be over by Christmas. Somewhere in the country they might want help with the harvest while the men are fighting. Maybe my friend in Elsterdorf knows someone. That's not so far—less than a day's journey." She shook her head. "I keep a good, clean house, but it is no place for little girls."

No one had told Sofie about any war. Their mother had said they would start school here in the city before long. Mama taught them their numbers and letters. Even Dora could read the red covered, fairy tale book. For a few months, back home, Sofie and Amalia had gone to school to sit on benches in rows. Every morning Dora cried and their mother had to hold her hand to keep her from following. The scowling teacher with bushy black eyebrows only called them to the front of the room as examples of what happened to children who didn't bring their copybooks. They didn't know how to say their stepfather wouldn't buy their school supplies. Better the quick pain of the willow branch than the long humiliation of everyone knowing their mother's mistake in letting that man into their lives.

Their mother's shoulders slumped lower each time Frau Becker spoke. The old woman stooped to stir the fire in the bottom of the stove. Sofie wanted to kick her broad behind.

"Who could take all three?" their mother said. "I wouldn't want to split them up. Especially after all I've put them through."

"I want to go back upstairs," Dora whispered. "Please."

"Come on." Amalia tugged at Sofie's skirt.

Sofie slapped her hand away.

"You're going to have to do something. Look at you, you can barely sit up. And it isn't good for those girls. They should be outside. I know you worry about them, but children need to run. And God knows what will happen to us now. The young men will go to be soldiers and—"

"On Sundays, we spend the whole day outside," their mother said. In the shadows Sofie nodded. They went to church and to the park and Mama showed them the streets where the owners of the mines and factories lived in beautiful houses with gardens full of flowers. They collected the blossoms that fell onto the street from the bushes and trees. Just the Sunday before they'd filled their pockets with pink and purple petals. That evening, when they took the flowers out to look at them, the edges were brown, but they still smelled nice. They crushed them in a cup, added water, called it perfume, and they all, even Mama, brushed it into their hair.

"I can't..." Their mother shook her head. "Anyway." She straightened her shoulders and her voice gained strength. "War or not, people need coal. There will still be miners. You'll need help to run the house."

"At least think about it," Frau Becker insisted. "There must be someone."

"Come on, Sofie," Amalia said. "We're not supposed to be here."

Hanna rubbed her forehead with both hands. "My girls are waiting," she said. "I should go upstairs." She drank her cooled coffee in one long swallow.

Sofie spun around and led the way back, silent and quick. Moments later they heard their mother's key in the lock. She fingered its twin in the folds of her pocket. They sat in a row, on the one bed, the bed their mother slept in, watching the door handle move.

Their mother's face looked the same as always, pink and worried. She smelled like smoked meat. "I brought some wurst and apples." She put the basket on the largest crate and began to unwrap parcels. She noticed no difference in the arrangement of the crates, no clue that they had been moved and stacked and climbed upon. Amalia had done her work well. Bellies aching, the girls eyed the shriveled sausage and bruised fruit. Dora swung her legs and her heel hit the enamel chamber pot, but nothing spilled.

Mama sighed and said, "Help set the table. Aren't you hungry?"

The girls moved as a group to bring the dishes to the table. They crowded together on the same crate when it was time to sit.

"What's a war?" Dora asked. Sofie waited for their mother to realize they'd been spying.

"Nothing for little girls to think about." Mama put wurst on each of their plates. "Eat."

The meat filled their mouths. They chewed each bite for a long time. Only the apple stems and a few seeds remained on their plates, and they were still hungry.

"Will you play dice with us?" Amalia asked. "Will you help us with our numbers?"

Their mother shook her head with a weak smile. "I'm tired tonight. We'll wait until morning to brush out your hair."

"But what about a story?" Sofie dared to ask. While their mother brushed their hair, at night, that was when she told them their favorite tales. In the morning she was always in a hurry, rebraiding with a minimum of brushing.

"Please!" said Sofie. It didn't take strength merely to tell a story. "You can lie down and tell it."

"Mama, please."

"No!" Mama patted Dora's head, then Amalia's, then reached toward Sofie as if to soften her refusal. Sofie ducked, but they all stopped begging. They didn't want to hear her say no again. They rolled out their blankets and tried to sleep.

"People get killed in wars," Amalia whispered.

"Only soldiers," Sofie whispered back. "And the Kaiser will win. Frau Becker said." Outside, the sky stayed light for too long, the air still and sweltering.

The next morning their mother gave them their bread and kisses but told them she mustn't be late for work. She had no time to fix their hair.

Sofie left the window first and picked up the bread knife. Her braid hung down her back, long and fuzzy from her restless night.

"We can brush our own hair," Amalia said. "I can do yours, Sofie."

"You don't know how to braid tight enough," Sofie told her. "All the hairs slip out. Even I don't know how."

"We could try. We could try on Dora. I'll bet we could do it."

Amalia waited. Sofie knew her sister wanted her to nod and say, go ahead and get the brush. Sofie slapped the long blade of the knife against the flat of her hand.

"Watch out," Dora said. "You'll cut yourself."

Sofie lifted her braid off her neck and reached around with the knife. Her shoulders ached.

"What are you doing?" Amalia whispered.

"Cutting my hair. To make things easier for Mama. You're next."

"Oh no!" Amalia said backing away. "Not me."

Sofie sawed at her rope of hair. The knife seemed to chew through one tough strand at a time. Her neck grew stiff and her arms burned, but if she stopped she might not be able to start again. She pulled the braid tighter. She thought she could hear the severing of individual hairs and was surprised it didn't hurt. "There." Sweating and breathing hard Sofie held her braid in one hand, knife in the other—her head light.

"You look like a boy!" Amalia cried. "Mama will be so mad." She pressed her hands against her temples and whimpered.

Dora inched closer to look at the braid. "It looks dead."

Sofie wiggled it at her. "It is dead," she said in a spooky voice.

Dora squealed. Amalia laughed nervously.

"All right," Sofie laid the braid on the table. It stretched all the way from one side to the other and dangled over the edge. "Amalia?"

Amalia folded her arms in front of her. Dora shivered and shook her head.

Sofie pointed the knife at each of them. "Mama is tired. Do you think it's easy braiding all our hair?"

"But she can teach us and we'll practice until we can do it ourselves," Amalia said. "I'll ask her tonight. We should have thought of it a long time ago."

"She'll be too tired to teach us." Sofie knew she was right. She shoved a crate over with her foot. "Sit here in front of me, Amalia."

"But...she won't like it. She'll be mad that we—"

"Sit." She pointed the tip of the knife at the crate, and with a fierce look pulled Amalia toward it.

"I'll do it," Dora said, slipping between them, sitting before Amalia could. She bowed her head.

Sofie picked up one of Dora's two scraggly braids. Wisps of hair fringed her pale, bent neck. Sofie's hands shook.

Dora's breathing sounded loud and fast. Amalia made no sound at all. Sofie pressed her index finger against the knife point and felt no pain. When she saw blood, she stopped and stuck her finger in her mouth.

"We'll wait," she said finally and put the knife away in the box with the dishes. It looked sharp and mean beside the innocent spoons and smooth, round plates. "We'll see how Mama likes my haircut first."

"Maybe she won't be tired if she only has to braid two of us," said Dora.

Amalia pulled her braids to the front and studied them. "I know I can learn to do it right."

Without looking at her sisters, Sofie picked up her braid and crawled into their mother's bed. The key in her pocket pressed against her thigh. She rubbed the frayed end of the severed hair up and down, up and down, against her cheek.

Dora and Amalia sat beside her, their weight pulling the covers tight.

"Sofie?" Dora's breath smelled like bread. "Tell me about when we had milk every day. Tell me about the apple pancakes with butter and the trees full of cherries and peaches. Are the cherries small and red or are those the peaches?"

"Cherries," Amalia said. "Peaches are big and the color of...the sun late in the day, when Mama comes back. Come on, Sofie." Amalia poked at her shoulder. "You tell it best. Once upon a time..."

If Sofie lay still, with her eyes shut, maybe they'd think she was asleep and leave her alone. She held the braid under her nose and breathed in the smell. The hairs tickled.

They couldn't fit side by side in the narrow bed but somehow Amalia and Dora pretzeled themselves around her, sticky in the heat. Then the giggling began. They couldn't tell who started it. Every time one of them caught her breath, the sister beside her dissolved into helpless laughter. They laughed until they were limp.

"Now tell the story," Dora said gasping. "Once upon a time..."

"Once upon a time," Sofie began, eyes closed. "There were three sisters and a mother and a father. When the girls were babies the mother took care of them and the garden and the animals. Their father worked in the coal mine and came home all covered in black dust. He'd act like a stranger and make funny faces to get the girls giggling until the mother brought him soap and water and rags for washing. The girls watched him turn from black to white. After they all ate supper, a lot of supper, and, when he wasn't too tired, the father played his violin. He told the girls stories and taught them prayers. They had everything they wanted on their farm."

"Now comes my favorite part," said Dora. Sofie began the list of all they had. "Big feather beds, a swing in the pear tree—"

"The chickens!" Dora shouted. "Don't forget the chickens."

"I was just going to tell about them," Sofie said.

"Tell about the pigs," said Amalia. "The big one. I used to scratch its back with a broom."

The list took a long time. Then the sad part. In real life, the sad part happened earlier in the story, long before the pig. But the satisfaction of pushing the broom across the sow's bristly back belonged in the beginning before things turned bad. Just as in real life Dora had never even seen their father, but in the story she knew him as well as Amalia and Sofie pretended to.

"Then the father died. And the men from the mine told Mama."

In the same way they understood the passing of time until their mother came home, the church bells ringing longer and longer then suddenly short and longer again, the angle of the sun across the floor, the swell and fade of the smells of *Mittagsessen*, they knew about stories. Sofie knew there were limits. She knew, without knowing she knew, that she could reorder events, add detail, leave things out, but without trouble there was no story at all so she always told the part about the father dying. She didn't relate every little thing she thought she remembered, but might have been told, as she'd been barely two years old when it happened. She didn't tell about Mama dropping the eggs she'd held in her apron, the funny and terrible plopping sounds they made hitting the dirt. The yolks oozing yellow among shattered brown shells while Mama screamed. That night a cold, hard rain washed away the yolks, but the empty shells stayed where they had fallen until Sofie made Amalia, who had just learned to walk, help her, their small black shoes grinding the egg shells to dust that blended back into the earth.

She didn't tell about Amalia's brown eyes, so wide she could see the whites all around, and Amalia never chimed in with a description of Sofie's, wild as the sea when the fisherman's wife first wants too much. Neither of them mentioned clinging to their mother's legs, her pregnant belly looming over them. Dora must have heard the screaming too, but muffled, through a cushion of muscle and water and blood. Sofie left out the hard fingers that peeled them off their mother and the days they spent at the neighbors'.

Their mother went to bed and didn't get up until Dora was born.

She was happy again for a short while after meeting and marrying Herr Klein-schuster. *Teufelmann*, the girls came to call him, the Devil man who in four long years, little by little, gambled away their land and livestock. They laughed about the time that Sofie rolled his wad of chewing tobacco in horse manure. They'd hidden behind a wall and watched him put it into his mouth.

"He never even noticed!" Amalia still marveled.

They skipped over the beatings with the belt and the broomstick. Instead, they told about helping their mother in the garden. They told about playing cards and dice and learning their letters in the evenings when *Teufelmann* was out. They left out the many nights they trembled in bed, pretending to be asleep, twined around each other—waiting for him to stumble down the walk, listening for the sizzle of his piss against the house, his lurching and crashing past their door, his mutterings.

They told about sneaking away: how they walked and walked, like scarecrows with their arms stuck out, stuffed into all their clothes; how a farmer gave them a ride along with his baskets of strawberries to the market in the city; how they knocked on Frau Becker's blue door, and she answered fat and smiling and let them stay even though she normally didn't allow children, just because they seemed like such good girls.

"Now the girls are safe and happy," Dora said, ending the story the usual way.

Sofie wrapped her severed braid around her hand. She felt like she was wearing someone else's head. When Amalia and Dora helped each other with their hair, she covered her face. Her worry about what Mama would say grew as the hours passed.

She could unlock the door and run away, but where would she go? She could put on a scarf. She could say she thought she had lice. She couldn't tell the truth, with its implied accusation that Mama couldn't take care of them.

When their mother's footsteps sounded on the stairs, Sofie was still in bed. Amalia and Dora stopped playing. The door opened.

"Is Sofie sick?" Mama asked. Her bundles rustled and thunked. No one answered. She pulled the covers from Sofie's head.

"What happened?" their mother wailed. "Oh, my poor girl. You look like a hedgehog."

"A hedgehog!" Dora shouted. She and Amalia began their hysterical giggling. Sofie lay rigid.

Mama stroked Sofie's short hair. "What happened?" she asked again softly.

"She cut it," Amalia said. "She wanted to make things easier."

"No!" Mama said.

Amalia and Dora stopped laughing.

Mama's sigh filled the room. "I don't deserve such girls." The silence that followed seemed to last for a long time. "Thank you, Sofie," she said. "Maybe it will. Besides, hair grows. It will get long again."

"I'm keeping it short forever," Sofie said. "I'm tired of long hair."

"Amalia, Dora, bring me the brush and a ribbon," their mother said. She nudged Sofie. "Sit up; let's see what we can do. It will be fun."

"No, I don't want to make trouble for you." Sofie snuggled close to her mother. She rubbed her head against Mama's shoulder.

"There are times when small troubles are a blessing," Hanna murmured. Amalia and Dora clambered onto the bed, hands full of brushes, ribbons and bowls of petal-scented water.

Sofie returned the key to the bowl. She knew enough of what was happening outside their room to know she, Amalia, and Dora might be better off locked in. Rivers of soldiers in spiked helmets flooded the streets, pushing the carts and people to the edges. Parades of horses requisitioned from farms clomped through the city. Amalia wondered aloud if the animals had any idea they were going to be part of a war. She didn't want them hurt.

In late October, after many days of mashed turnip and watery cabbage soup, Tomas Blau, a friend of Frau Becker's cousin who had already gone to fight for the Kaiser, came in his wagon to take the girls away.

"It's the war," their mother told them the night before, as she tucked them into bed. "You know I've tried to keep us together. The city is growing too dangerous for children and there's nothing to eat. With the men gone to fight you'll be able to help on the farms. Frau Becker has found places for you."

"Places?" Sofie sat straight up on her blanket.

Hanna took a deep breath. "No one had room for three. You'll be near each other."

Dora began to cry.

"Stop it." Amalia pinched her.

"You won't be there long," their mother said. "The war will be over and you'll come back. It's little more than a half a day's journey away. We'll visit."

None of them slept well that night.

Hanna stayed home from work the next morning to wait for Tomas Blau. The weekday room felt wrong with her there. She fussed with Dora's hair, straightened Amalia's collar, looked through Sofie's little sack of folded clothing. If there had been anything to eat she would have fed them. What could be worse for a mother than having no food for her children? The girls were quiet. Sofie paced back and forth to the window. Amalia paged through the fairy tale book. Dora sat on the edge of the bed, hands folded, her gaze fixed on their mother fluttering around the room.

"I think he's here," said Sofie finally. Beneath the window a thin blond man climbed down from his wagon. The brown horse shook its head and snorted.

"I don't want to go," said Dora.

Sofie stared at her. How dare she say those words? Just because she was the youngest she thought she had the right to blurt out whatever stupid thing came into her head. Their mother's forehead creased. She pinched the bridge of her nose. Anyone could see she was trying to be strong. They were all trying to be strong. Dora had to try too.

"Come on," Sofie grabbed Dora's hand and pulled her to her feet. Amalia took the other hand. Each picked up a bag. Hanna followed them down the stairs. Outside the front door she leaned on Frau Becker's muscled arm, her face stiff. Tomas Blau lifted the girls into the back of the wagon. None of them wanted to sit up front. They huddled together in a nest of hay.

"I'll see you soon," Mama said. Sofie knew her words were more hopeful than true. "Be good girls."

The wagon jerked forward; Dora wept. Sofie picked hay from her stockings. Amalia shaped a pillow for herself. Tomas Blau gave them all peppermints, which burned their tongues and made their stomachs growl. They fell asleep to the squeak of the wheels and clop of hooves and didn't wake up until the sun was setting and they'd arrived at the Neufelds' farm.

A stooped and smiling old woman wrapped in a shawl of fluffy pink wool emerged from the well kept house. "And which of you is Dora?" she asked.

Dora clung to Sofie and Amalia's hands and sat motionless. Tears slipped silently down her cheeks.

"Go on," Tomas urged from the wagon seat. "We've got to move along here."

The old woman took the crocheted shawl from her shoulders and held it out like a blanket. Sofie stared at the feathery patterns. "Tomas, help Dora down," Frau Neufeld said.

Tomas clambered into the wagon bed and swung Dora over the side. Sofie and Amalia watched Frau Neufeld envelop their sister in rosy wool, arms tucked into her sides so she couldn't wave good-bye.

At the Muellers' a crowd of chattering blonde children tumbled out the door behind their grandmother. Amalia squeezed Sofie's arm and, with a resigned sigh, stepped down to greet Frau Mueller. Surrounded by plump-cheeked, laughing faces, Amalia looked bony and sad. Sofie, on her way to the Blaus', grew cold without her sisters in the hollow their three small bodies had made in the hay.

CHAPTER 2

▼

In the city and on the farm the year passed; the war continued. Miners mined coal, factories operated at full capacity, food riots raged—throngs of desperate women in city streets shouting for the fair distribution of bread and turnips and cabbage. Hanna cleaned and cooked in wealthy homes and the boarding house. In the country the girls learned new words: air raid, poison gas, bayonet, zeppelin, massacre, demonstration, socialist, *Kriegsbrot* or K-bread, names of towns and fields in France and Belgium and countries in Africa.

Amalia, the shovel standing as tall as her nine-year-old self, pried potatoes and turnips from the rich Elsterdorf ground, careful to collect even the marble-sized ones. She missed her mother and sisters, yet had grown used to standing on dirt instead of cobblestones, to seeing fields and sky instead of buildings, to smelling earth and manure and growing things.

Dora still cried at night at the Neufelds' farm seven kilometers down the road to the east. Sofie lived almost the same distance away to the west. Amalia, the middle sister in the middle, where she belonged. The girls saw each other only on Sundays in church, and afterward, while the adults, mostly women with just a few old or wounded men, stood in tight circles talking and shaking their heads, the children looped and darted through the goldenrod and thistle in the fields behind the church, tagging and hiding and finding each other. Sofie knew the best hiding places. She wasn't afraid to hide in the graveyard even though it was forbidden. Crouched next to her behind a gravestone, Amalia's worry about punishments or ghosts disappeared in stifled giggles. Since most of the other children were afraid to follow them, the Bauer sisters always won.

Five long days until Sunday. Amalia rubbed dirt from a little potato and held it in her palm, missing her mother. The mother she lived with on the farm, Frau Mueller, was kind enough but never had time for stories. Her grown daughters worked at the munitions plant and her sons-in-law were fighting on the Eastern front. Frau Mueller spent the day chasing her four small grandchildren who always needed food or a cuddle or a spanking. When Frau Mueller braided Amalia's hair her hands worked quickly, pulling so hard that she stretched the corners of Amalia's eyes.

"Hey!" Someone shouted from the road. Amalia raised her shovel, ready to scare off a scavenger from the city. The Muellers had traded all the food they wanted to, had more than enough silver and jewelry. When the scavengers were turned away, in their desperation they'd try to steal, so everyone, even children, had to guard the fields. Amalia felt sorry for the city folk, but the Muellers wouldn't make it through the winter unless they kept the food for themselves.

She was trying to decide whether or not to tell the person to come back the next day—perhaps there would be a few eggs to trade—when she recognized Sofie, small against the big pink sky, the green of the potato fields blackening around her in the setting sun.

Still clutching the potato and shovel, Amalia ran, calling to her sister.

"I can't stay there any longer," Sofie blurted out, apron muddy, hair tousled, gray eyes sparking. "I went to bring in the cows and Gustav followed me."

"He always follows you," Amalia said. "He follows everybody."

Gustav was fourteen, the youngest of the four Blau boys. All the others, including Tomas, had gone to fight. Gustav was strong and did the work of a man; he shaved the dark beard from his square jaw, but he had the mind of a small child. People said he would never get any smarter, even if he spent every day in school and lived to be old. Over and over he sang *Ich und du Muellers Kuh, Muellers Esel, Das bis du,"* pointed and shrieked and pulled at the crotch of his pants.

The children said the song had nothing to do with the Muellers, that was how it happened to go and it was true that he sang it to everyone, even himself. When Amalia clapped for him at the end, he beamed and clapped with her. She always had the urge to pat him on the head.

"He grabbed me," said Sofie. "He squeezed my arm and pulled me and rubbed against me, like a dog."

Gustav's huge hands were always clean, even though he worked in the dirt and with the animals. People said his mother beat him so hard for having dirt under his fingernails or on his clothes that he became terrified of the dirt itself. He never touched Amalia or any of the other children in their games at church.

"He's like a dog, with his big teeth and his drooling mouth. And his tongue, always hanging out." Amalia did her best imitation, expecting Sofie to laugh or at least smile. "Order him to heel. He'll obey."

"I stepped down hard on his foot. Surprised him enough he let go and I ran, but he chased me. When I climbed over the fence I hurt myself." Sofie's arm was tucked to her side like a broken wing, her index finger wrapped in a dirty, blood-soaked handkerchief.

"Maybe you can stay here tonight."

"I have to," said Sofie. "I can't go back." She sank to the ground in an oddly graceful motion, landing cross-legged.

Between the rows of potatoes, Amalia crouched beside her. She took Sofie's wounded hand, unwrapped the handkerchief. A yellowish substance oozed from a hole in the middle pad of Sofie's index finger. Amalia's knees quivered. "It looks deep."

Everyone knew what could happen when you were stabbed by something rusty and sharp, just as everyone knew what happened when you were bitten by a mad dog or drank bad milk. Amalia rewrapped the finger, wanting to shake Sofie. Why hadn't she been more careful? If only Sofie would say something, make a joke.

They sat surrounded by acres of potato plants as the twilight turned to night. Amalia imagined herself a soldier in a trench beside her wounded comrade. She wasn't sure she knew exactly what a trench was but it sounded like a row in the field, only deeper. The handle of the shovel she'd stuck in the ground slanted over them against the sky.

"We'd better go in. The Muellers will let you stay. It's too late to walk back now."

"I'm never going back," Sofie pronounced through chattering teeth.

Amalia wrapped an arm around her sister's shaking shoulders and pressed close until one of Sofie's jutting shoulder blades jabbed her in the armpit. She couldn't squeeze tight enough to stop Sofie's trembling. Amalia wished for Dora. She would wrap her other arm around her younger sister and both of her sides would be warm and protected; both of her armpits would hold her sisters' firm bones.

"That's where your wings will grow," Mama had told them, touching their shoulder blades when she tucked them into bed at Frau Becker's. "When you turn into angels."

"I don't want to be an angel," Sofie said.

"Why not?" Dora asked. "Angels are near God in heaven."

"I like it here," Sofie said. "The only places on earth I've ever seen are our farm and Tauburg and the road between. I want to see America and China and lots of other places on earth when the war is over. To be an angel you have to die."

"Angels see Tauburg and China and everywhere else from up above," Dora said.

"Angels wear white dresses that never get dirty." Amalia didn't want to be an angel either. "I never heard of one digging in the dirt or feeding a pig or climbing a cherry tree."

The farmhouse was far across the field. If they were angels, they could have flown and been there already. "Can you walk now?" Amalia asked. The light in the window shone warm. Frau Mueller wouldn't turn Sofie away.

"I want Mama," Sofie whispered.

Silence surrounded them, too close to winter for crickets or frogs.

"I'm supposed to bring the potatoes back." Amalia pointed into the darkness in the direction of the basket. "And the shovel, but I can come back to get them if you can't walk by yourself."

"I can walk," said Sofie, straightening. "My finger is hurt. Not my legs." She held her injured hand under her chin. They marched through the dark between the potato plants toward the Muellers' house.

"Is it bad?" Amalia asked.

"It feels like it has its own heart pounding. It feels like it'll burst." A sob slipped through Sofie's tight lips. "It feels hot. I wish Mama were here."

"Frau Mueller will help." Amalia hoped that was true.

She leaned the shovel against the side of the house before they entered the low-ceilinged kitchen. Amalia smelled Herr Mueller's tobacco and knew he was in the front room smoking his pipe with his eyes shut. She heard Frau Mueller singing the grandchildren to sleep.

Embroidered tablecloths, napkins, silver candlesticks, and porcelain bowls covered the sideboard and counter, like shelves in a well stocked store—all the possessions people had traded for food: a watch for three turnips, a silver baby rattle and teething ring for a jar of plum preserves. Herr Mueller's war map showing German progress on the eastern and western fronts decorated the wall over the sideboard. The Ten Food Commandments were posted over the counter near the stone sink. Even the littlest grandchild could recite them. *Number Three: Be economical with bread in order that the hopes of our foes may be confounded. Number Seven: Do not cut off a slice more than you need to eat. Think always of our sol-*

diers in the field, who, often in some far-off, exposed position, would rejoice to have the bread which you waste. Amalia cleared a space under the Food Commandments for the basket of potatoes. Sofie dropped to a bench and rested her head on the table.

The kitchen was just like the one in the house where they were born, before their mother married *Teufelmann* and everything went wrong. Frau Mueller had set out a white bowl of three hard-boiled eggs and war bread. The dirty dishes waiting near the sink indicated that Frau and Herr Mueller and the grandchildren had already eaten.

"I'll peel you an egg." Amalia touched Sofie's shoulder. She rapped one against her forehead to make her sister laugh. Sofie winced. Amalia picked off the shell and tried to hand the egg to her. "Aren't you hungry after that long walk? Come on, eat." Sofie closed her eyes.

"What is this?" Frau Mueller's cheerful voice startled Amalia. She hadn't noticed the silence in the children's room, the sound of approaching footsteps.

"My sister." Amalia squeezed the egg until it began to crumble in her fist. "She's hurt."

Frau Mueller asked no questions. She unwrapped the finger. "Get a bowl of warm water. There should be some still in the kettle." Amalia rushed to the stove, relieved to have someone, an adult, telling her what to do. Frau Mueller dumped in the bowl of salt and stirred. Sofie's wound was serious or Frau Mueller wouldn't have used so much salt at once. She always cautioned Amalia not to waste. She took Sofie's hand and placed it in the salty water. Sofie groaned, half asleep. "This may keep infection from setting in. Do the Blaus know she's here?" Amalia shook her head.

"If they don't come looking tonight, we'll have to let them know in the morning." Frau Mueller poured a splash of schnapps into a cup. "After the salt water, soak the finger in here."

"Hilda!" Herr Mueller called. Amalia jumped, afraid he'd sensed his wife's squandering his liquor.

"She can sleep with me," Amalia said.

"Of course," Frau Mueller nodded. She patted Amalia's cheek. "Let her finger soak a while. Herr Mueller needs me. *Schlaf gut.*"

Their own mother would have tucked them in.

In the morning, the Blaus wanted Sofie back. They needed her to help Gustav pick the last of the apples. There was nothing Frau Mueller could say to prevent it. Gustav came to fetch her in the wagon, laughing, patting the boards of the seat beside him.

"My finger's heart is still beating so hard I can't think," Sofie whispered as she hugged Amalia good-bye. "If I could think, I would find a way not to go back."

"I'll see you at church," Amalia said. "Four days."

On Sunday, hiding in the graveyard, they told Dora about Gustav and the finger. Sofie's eyes shone too bright. Her face burned hot. "They tried to make me stay home," she said. Sofie unwound her bandage and Amalia screamed. Frau Mueller's salt water hadn't helped. The finger swelled big, tight and red like a *blutwurst*. Dora touched the pale skin of Sofie's forearm, tracing faint red lines toward the soft place in the bend of her elbow.

They didn't know what to do. Sofie began to cry. "I can't milk the cow. I can't work in the field or even the orchard. Everything hurts. I'm not lazy like they say. Everything hurts. It doesn't matter if it is dangerous in the city. I'd rather be all together even in the middle of the whole war. Even in the middle of the worst fighting. Even if we are all killed. I want Mama."

"Me too," Dora said.

Amalia knew just what they meant, but Sofie, who never cried, was crying, and someone had to be strong, brave like the soldiers. "Frau Mueller will get the doctor. I'll ask her if you can come home with us today. If you can't work, the Blaus will be glad not to feed you."

Frau Mueller, her soft white hair swept up especially for church, chatted with the other women. Amalia pulled the skirt of her green Sunday dress. Frau Mueller cupped the back of her head with her big callused hand and said to the circle of women, "Such a good girl. I never have to remind her to do her work. I'll miss her when she starts school."

Amalia would have enjoyed the compliment but for remembering Sofie and Dora huddled behind the leaning tombstone, waiting for her. She tugged Frau Mueller's skirt one more time, the fabric rough and heavy in her hand.

"Yes, Amalia, what is it?" Impatience dimmed Frau Mueller's smile. "Go play with your sisters. We'll be leaving soon enough. Where are they?" She shielded her eyes and scanned the fields surrounding the church.

"My sister, Sofie," Amalia began. "She needs a doctor." Amalia nodded toward the graveyard where the children were playing and Sofie sat on the ground, cradling her injured hand.

Frau Mueller was a softhearted woman. The sisters all agreed that Amalia had ended up with the best family. Dora lived with a very, very old couple and their very old son. They were kind but slow-moving and partially deaf and she missed being around other children.

Frau Mueller bent and wiped Amalia's tears. "I'll talk with Herr Mueller. Has the doctor driven off?" She looked over the lot for his buggy.

Amalia edged away to the cemetery where Sofie lay on the ground, Dora on her knees, hands pressed together, praying beside her. Ever since her First Holy Communion in May, Dora had taken to praying when she needed something. She was learning to trust God. People meant well, but their power was limited.

Sofie looked dead, stretched out, and Amalia began to scream, "Get up! Get up! Get up! Get up!"

Dora leapt to her feet. Amalia kicked at Sofie. "Get up!"

The priest hurried toward them, flapping his arms. "Out! Out of the cemetery. This is not a place to play."

Then he noticed Sofie, her breath spasmodic and shallow. His eyes flickered with uncertainty.

The very old doctor, working only because the younger doctor had gone to war, was picking his way through the churchyard, urged on by Frau Mueller. The priest waved him over. As he examined Sofie, a crowd gathered. "Blood poisoning," he pronounced, exhibiting the red lines running up her arm. "Very bad."

Frau Mueller whispered to Frau Blau. Frau Blau scowled and gave a disgusted, backward wave of her hand, as if she didn't want to be bothered. Gustav paced back and forth behind them, shoulders hunched, wringing his hands, muttering to himself. Dora gripped Amalia's fingers so tightly the tips turned purple.

Frau Mueller approached the doctor. Amalia heard snippets of conversation. "Soak it…poultice…must drain…nothing else to do…notify the mother."

"Maybe Mama will come now that Sofie's sick," Dora whispered. "Ask Frau Mueller if I can come with you too. To help take care of Sofie until Mama comes."

The waxed ends of Herr Mueller's long mustache hit Sofie's face as he lifted her up. Amalia felt the tickle on her own hot cheek. Afraid to ask for too much, she pushed Dora ahead of her into the line of children following him like ducklings. Maybe in the confusion no one would notice. Frau Mueller stepped toward them, then seemed to change her mind. She approached Dora's farm family instead. Because she had to shout to be understood, the girls heard every word. "If it is all right with you, she can stay with us while her sister is sick. They're so close it might do them good to be together. It shouldn't be more than a week either way. She'll get better or she'll…" Frau Mueller stopped, aware of the silence in the churchyard. The old people nodded their consent, and Frau Muel-ler hustled all the children into the wagon.

Sofie lay on a potato sack, her body so scorching Amalia could feel the heat without touching her. She leaned against Dora, relieved and frightened at the Blaus' and the Neufelds' easy acquiescence. The wheels creaked. Dora cradled Sofie's head in her lap; the grandchildren sat strangely quiet and still. Frau and Herr Mueller whispered. Amalia strained her ears hoping to hear the word *mother* again.

For the next two days Dora and Amalia spent every free moment in the attic, where Sofie lay on her cot, burning, sleeping and not sleeping, muttering crazy talk about Gustav and *Teufelmann* and witches and Mama. They took turns plac-ing cool cloths on Sofie's forehead and cheeks. It seemed as if Sofie had been sick forever. They wondered when their mother would come, but were afraid to ask. She had been sent for. The doctor and Frau Mueller talked in terrible whispers about cutting off Sofie's finger.

Then she was there, stooping to keep from hitting her head on the slanted ceiling. Amalia and Dora flung themselves at her. Their mother's sleeves still held the smells of Frau Becker's, the mining students, the coal dust, baking bread.

Her arms reached around both of them, but Amalia felt her stretching toward Sofie. She and Dora moved along with their mother to the cot where Sofie lay. Worry pinched Mama's face more than usual, so much that she looked like some-one else. Sofie could die, Amalia thought. Dora believed that God would save her sister. He'd brought their mother. He'd let her be with her sisters at the Muel-lers'. She squeezed her eyes shut and prayed as hard as she could.

Mama placed a hand on Sofie's head, and Sofie didn't even notice. Amalia would have noticed. She wanted to be the one Mama looked at, heavy dark eye-brows coming together over her nose, eyes full of sorrow and love. Sofie, with her eyes shut tight, didn't even know Mama was looking only at her. Amalia grabbed Dora's hand and hung on.

Their mother sat in the low, armless rocking chair beside Sofie's pillow, her bag on the floor nearby. While Mama examined Sofie's ugly finger, Amalia tried to guess what was inside the lumpy paper-wrapped packages. She wanted to rip them open.

Sofie winced, then opened her eyes. And smiled. "Mama," her lips moved soundlessly.

Amalia released a long breath—the breath it seemed she'd been holding since before their mother came, since before Sofie stumbled toward her across the potato field with her ruined finger—a long, long exhalation that left her deflated and limp.

"Will you stay here?" Dora asked.

They waited for the answer. "I'll stay a few days," Mama said. "Until Sofie is better."

Until she is better. Amalia liked the sound of it.

As long as Amalia didn't look too closely or too long at Mama's face she could believe Sofie would get well.

"What did you bring?" Dora eyed the bag.

"Bread Frau Becker made this morning. She insisted I bring it. One loaf all for you and one for the Muellers." Mama pulled it from her bag and gave it to Amalia. She and Dora tore pieces from either end. She ate so fast she hardly tasted it. Mama unwrapped another package. The music box. She turned the key and set it on the small table beside them. The sad song wound around them like a long dark shawl.

"Tell us a story," Dora said, settling onto Mama's lap, though Amalia thought she should know that eight years old was too big for laps. Even if Amalia were the youngest she wouldn't act like such a baby. She'd know better. Dora pushed against the bed frame, her scuffed boots rocking in time to the slow music. Amalia sat stiffly on the edge of the bed.

Their mother acted like she hadn't heard. "A story?" Dora urged. "I think a story would make Sofie feel better. You want a story, Sofie, don't you?"

Sofie moved her head. "See, she does," Dora said.

Their mother lifted Dora from her lap to adjust the bed sheet. She brushed the sweaty hair from Sofie's flushed face, tucking a short curl behind an ear. She stared at Sofie as if Dora and Amalia weren't there.

"Tell Hansel and Gretel." Dora patted Mama's shoulder. "Sofie likes it best."

"I don't know," Mama said. "A story? Now?"

"Please…Hansel and Gretel…for Sofie."

Mama arranged Dora's long braids so they lay straight and flat.

Could Sofie even listen? Amalia wondered. She was so still, asleep or…sometimes Dora could be so stupid, a pest. Sofie didn't need a story.

"Once upon a time there was a poor woodcutter…" Dora prompted.

At first their mother's voice sounded flat and unfamiliar and Amalia wanted to tell her to stop, but then, after rushing through the part in which Hansel and Gretel overhear the parents' plan to leave them in the forest, she sounded like herself again. None of them ever liked that part and now they liked it even less.

But whether Sofie could hear or not, Dora seemed to need a story and, now that Mama had started, Amalia needed it too.

When their mother told about the trail of bread crumbs, Amalia studied Sofie's flickering eyelids, remembering her feeding the birds. She was glad she had a smart sister instead of a foolish brother who thought he could throw out crumbs to a hungry world and have them remain untouched. The trail of stones had been a good idea, she'd give him that, but bread? If Dora and Sofie and Amalia were lost in a forest, Dora would tell them to pray, Sofie would make plans, and Amalia...she supposed she would look for edible plants and wood for a fire. She would build a shelter, not merely lie exposed to the night the way Hansel and Gretel had done. And if they found a house made of bread and cakes with sugar windowpanes, she would know not to trust it. She'd tell Sofie and Dora to break off as much as they could, to fill their pockets and run away.

Mama sat silent. Amalia had missed the happy ending. Dora scrambled off their mother's lap when Frau Mueller entered with a kettle of hot water. Mama held the bowl while Frau Mueller poured. A look passed between the women that Amalia didn't understand and Dora didn't notice. Frau Mueller steadied the bowl while their mother immersed Sofie's swollen hand in the steaming water. They all leaned close to watch. Sofie's forehead wrinkled, her lips twitched.

The water clouded. "It's draining," Frau Mueller announced. Her tone indicated good news, but the clouded water looked scary.

Their mother lifted Sofie's hand from the water. Pus oozed from the bent finger. A rotten smell filled the room. Amalia tried not gag, remembered finding the putrid, maggot-riddled body of a dead crow near the barn and the stench that rose up when she touched it with the toe of her boot. Mama and Frau Mueller conversed in excited whispers. Frau Mueller left to heat more water. Mama sank into the rocking chair as if her legs couldn't hold her.

The next morning Sofie awoke, her gray eyes sunken but silvery and clear. She laughed as she tried to straighten her finger. The doctor came and pronounced her better though everyone could see that for themselves. He said the finger might remain bent. Sofie seemed to like that. "I'll use it to frighten Gustav," she said. "I'll tell him I'm a witch with powers in my crooked finger."

"I wish we could all stay here," Dora sighed. "Mama, too."

"Not possible." Sofie sounded like an adult. "Mama said this morning I'll have to go back to the Blaus'. She has to return to the city. You to the Neufelds'. We have no choice."

"I'll pray, then." Dora's lip trembled. "I'll say the rosary fifty times a day. More even."

"You should tell Mama about Gustav," Amalia said. Their mother should be told about Sofie's panic in the potato field, the strange substance leaking from her finger, her shivering body pressed against Amalia's as they stumbled toward the house, Sofie's shaky determination never to go back. "Tell her you can't stay there."

"No." Sofie sounded like her own tough self. "If my finger doesn't work to scare him, I'll throw dirt. If that doesn't work I'll wrap the rusty fence wire around his throat and I won't care if I go to hell for it, either. I can take care of myself."

Amalia's own straight fingers rested in her lap. Even with all the dirt under her fingernails they wouldn't scare anyone. They wouldn't pray either. She couldn't remember where she'd put her rosary beads. Sunday. She'd see Dora and Sofie on Sunday. They'd see Mama at Christmas. Winter came after fall. Sunday came after Saturday. Over and over, round and round. Amalia picked at the dirt beneath her thumbnail. Stories began and ended and began again. Some things took longer—potatoes—planted, harvested, planted again. Like a wheel turning. She would use this new idea to put herself to sleep at night when she was afraid, to comfort herself on Sunday nights when it seemed forever until they'd be together.

"Don't you go and tell Mama either," Sofie warned. She pointed her bent and bandaged finger at Amalia, eyebrows raised, waiting. Secrets, shared and unspoken, whirled through Amalia's mind: their mother's clothes they'd worn and carefully put back, the key they used to sneak downstairs, the secrets they kept to make it through the days without adding to their mother's burden.

"We won't, will we?" Dora whispered, poking Amalia with her bony elbow.

Sofie had been hurt and healed—not Dora, not her. Like poison gas a vague loneliness filled Amalia's chest. She looked at Sofie, fierce and frowning against the pillows, then at Dora, both waiting for her answer. She heard their mother's step just outside the door. She wanted to tell. She was sure she should tell, but Sofie didn't want her to. If she told, she'd be telling Sofie's secret. By not telling, the secret would belong to all three of them. She heard Mama laughing with the Muellers downstairs. Laughing—when, in just a few minutes, Herr Mueller would be taking her to the station. "No, we won't," Amalia said.

CHAPTER 3

▼

Home. A word with a shape that feels good in the mouth.

"How much farther?" Dora rocked with the sway of Tomas Blau's wagon. "Don't you feel like a turnip rolling around back here?" On hands and knees she crawled in a tight circle. "Or a pig. I'm a pig." She snorted. When Amalia, hunched in the rear corner of the wagon bed, didn't laugh, Dora sat still and picked at one of the patches holding the scraps of her coat together. None of them had bundles. Everything they'd used for the past four years of their lives belonged to the families that had taken them in.

Dora wished Amalia would talk to her, but her sister sat silently staring at the road unrolling behind them. Dora snuggled close to her to keep warm, but faced forward to keep an eye on Sofie, perched high on the wagon seat beside Tomas, Gustav's only brother to return from the war. Sofie seemed much older than her thirteen years. She leaned too close to Tomas, listened too hard to all he said. Dora wanted to sit up high on this long ride home, craning her neck for the first glimpse of Frau Becker's blue door, only it wasn't Frau Becker's anymore. The blue door and the whole boarding house belonged to their mother now.

Last Easter, Frau Becker rushed around the kitchen on her bad knees, complaining in a hearty voice, "Ach, my bones, the pain will kill me! Ach, these prices, and for what? Who can live on this? These students, they are always hungry. I shop and cook all day and it is never enough." It was their uncomplaining mother who seemed shaky and fragile. Sofie scared Dora, and Amalia, too, by wondering out loud if their mother were sick, or just hungry and tired of the war like everyone else. Now Frau Becker was dead, though it wasn't work that killed her, and Germany had suffered defeat, but joy bubbled through Dora's whole body, and songs and laughter threatened to spill from her lips every time she opened them. The war was over. They'd survived the *Steckrubenwinter*. They would be together, with Mama. Tomas Blau would drive back to Elsterdorf and they'd never have to see him or Gustav or the Neufelds or the Muellers or cranky Frau Blau or anyone else from there ever again.

They passed the mine where grimfaced men stood smoking outside the gate. They held signs Dora could read if she'd had time to sound out the words. Most of the men looked tired. A couple of them talked in loud, angry voices. One yelled at them as they passed. "They're striking for better working conditions," Tomas told Sofie. "Sometimes they go too far. If the bosses don't agree, there'll be violence. Times are tough."

"Like the Spartakists rioting in Berlin?" Sofie asked. "Will they come here?" Berlin was many kilometers away, on the other side of the country.

"They're here already. Spartakists, Communists—it's all the same thing." Tomas slapped the reins against the horse's back. "Making trouble everywhere. Crazy Liebknecht. And Rosa Luxemburg. What's a woman doing trying to make a revolution?" His voice grew so loud, Dora didn't have to strain to hear. He ranted as if expecting to be contradicted, but for the moment even Sofie sat cowed and silent. "The *Freikorps* will squelch this rebellious Russian nonsense before it goes too far. More good citizens are volunteering to take up arms every day."

"I wonder if the miners at the boarding house are striking," Dora whispered to Amalia. "Are they violent?" She was afraid to even think about the Communists. Frau and Herr Neufeld and most of their Elsterdorf neighbors talked about them with a hatred they used to reserve for the French. "The reds," they'd say, "always stirring things up, especially in the cities." Dora imagined men with angry, red faces, devils in scarlet suits, stirring a smoldering cauldron with their enormous spoons.

Amalia pointed at the gray and ragged group of men growing smaller with every clop of the horse's hooves. "Some of those miners probably live at the boarding house," she said. "They look too tired to be violent." She sounded tired herself. And sad. Dora realized that Amalia would miss the country.

The wagon rattled over the icy cobblestones and they were back among city buildings. Sofie and Tomas began whispering again. Steam poured from the horse's nostrils and from Sofie's mouth as she laughed at Tomas's jokes.

When Tomas leaned close to Sofie and turned his head, Dora tried to see behind the edge of the patch covering his right eye. Sofie said it covered an empty socket; the eye itself was gone. But when Dora asked if you could see the inside of his head, his brains and bones, Sofie said she didn't know. His cheek thinned when he clucked to the horse, and a gap appeared between the patch and his skin. But behind was only darkness. Dora winked one eye, then the other, then both together, glad she had them.

On the corner, a one-legged man leaned against the bakery. So many men with empty trouser legs and shirt sleeves. Where did all those legs and arms and hands and feet go? Maybe they roamed the earth looking for the bodies they belonged to, even though Sofie and Amalia told her they had to be buried some-where. She saw them sometimes; squinting, she could see an arm floating, finger curved and beckoning.

"So many men coming back, not enough work. You could say those miners are lucky to have jobs," Tomas said.

Sofie seemed to have stopped paying attention to him. "Almost there," she shouted. There was the butcher shop. Last Easter the window was full of dead crows, hanging by their skinny feet. Now it was empty.

Amalia whirled around. Dora hung over the side to see. Tomas slowed the horse. Before the wheels stopped creaking, their mother burst from the door, thin but whole, dark eyes laughing. She tried wrapping her arms around all three of them, but they didn't fit the way they used to. Dora wriggled her way to her chest, pressed her nose against her mother and breathed in the salty, warm smell until she felt as light as a zeppelin, so full of feeling she would float into the clouds if it weren't for the sweet weight of Mama's chin resting on her head.

"Amalia, you're tall as I am. And already twelve!" Mama admired Sofie and Amalia at arms' length. Cheek against her mother's chest, Dora felt the sad regret beneath her laugh. "I think Sofie's even taller! So much time...so many changes...come inside, everybody." They jostled each other through the door, Tomas following.

"Sit here, by the stove," Mama said, pulling up a circle of chairs; filling a kettle with water; patting their heads, cheeks, knees. Dora prayed for somebody, some-thing to stop Mama's smooth efficiency; to make her stop, sit, hold her on her lap, forever.

"Will the students be here soon?" Sofie asked.

The wooden benches, polished over the years by the seats of so many pants, glowed in a pale shaft of sunlight.

"To travel back and forth mid-day wastes time and the country must produce all it can to recover from the war, the blockade," their mother quoted bitterly. "We have our meal in the evening now." She seemed to study Sofie, who since

Easter, had developed the body of a woman. Her dress pulled tight across her breasts and bottom.

"The students aren't striking?" Tomas asked.

"From day to day it changes," she answered. "Tomorrow they may be. It's chaos here. Not the best time to come back from the country, but I missed you all." She looked at Dora curled in Frau Becker's rocking chair.

Dora wished the chair were Mama's lap. She was sad about Frau Becker, but it was nice having the warm, familiar kitchen to themselves. The only thing out of place was Tomas, blowing his nose on a smudged handkerchief and asking questions.

"Come," said Sofie. "Let's look around. Everything's the same but different, smaller."

"Because you're used to all that open space in the country." Mama unwrapped the end of a loaf of bread and waved the white cloth at Sofie. Crumbs fell onto the floor. Dora wanted to wet the tip of her finger and pick them up, the way she'd devoured every bit of crust from the front of her sweater after carrying Frau Neufeld's bread home from the bakery on Saturdays.

"Or," Mama added, "because you're bigger now."

Dora remembered the very chair she was sitting in and how her legs used to dangle. "I'm bigger too," she said, pressing the soles of her feet to the floor.

Amalia found the broom in the closet where it had always been, and swept up the crumbs. The look of appreciation Mama gave her made Dora wish she'd thought of cleaning them up instead of eating them, but she was so hungry.

"The upstairs is the same as always," their mother called as Sofie dragged Amalia toward the stairs. "No need to be bothering the students' things."

Dora wanted to follow them but she couldn't leave Mama, not yet. And part of her kept waiting for Frau Becker to burst through the door, hands covered in flour.

"So finally it's over," Mama said, slicing the bread, arranging five thin pieces in an overlapping circle on a plate, like petals on a daisy. Dora remembered Sofie plucking a flower behind the church: *He loves me, loves me not.* Sofie wouldn't say who 'he' was. At the time Dora hadn't cared a bit, but now she did and wondered why she and Amalia didn't make Sofie tell. Dora glared at Tomas as he took a slice, ruining Mama's design. The fourth food commandment ran through her mind—*Respect the daily bread, then you will have it always, however long the war may last.*

"Who can tell when we'll have butter again?" Mama sighed. "But maybe you have some, out there in the country."

"No milk to spare for butter," Tomas said, mouth full. "Long ago the government in all its wisdom," he swallowed, "ordered our livestock slaughtered—not enough fodder, they said. Keep the city folk happy, they said. No one thinking, where will the next generation of cows come from? All those workers making guns and ammunition. All those soldiers. Give them meat!" He wiped his lips with the back of his hand. "I can tell you any meat I saw on the front didn't come from Germany but from French and Belgian farms of people like us. More like us than these rich industrialists who call themselves good Germans as they grow fat on war profits and make deals with the enemy. Sometimes the farmers even gave the meat. Sometimes we took it. Sorry...people tell me I go on too much. I haven't seen butter in years. Have you?"

"I am proud to thirst and hunger for the Fatherland." Mama's eyes were hard, her voice sarcastic. She held out the plate of bread with its missing slice. Dora took one, trying not to disturb what was left of the pattern. *Food commandment number eight—Eat War Bread. It is recognizable by the letter K. It satisfies and nourishes as thoroughly as any other kind.*

"I can tell you." Mama perched on the edge of a straight-backed chair. "Here in the city it was no party either. Strikes. Shortages. Influenza. We've all suffered."

Dora thought of the men with the signs they'd passed on the road, the near-translucent slices of bread arranged on the plate, the ersatz coffee made from roasted acorns. There were still strikes and shortages and suffering.

"I've been lucky. I have the boarding house. I have my daughters back."

Tomas ate two more slices of bread.

"Look," Amalia ran into the kitchen, waving Sofie's shorn braid like a whip. "It was still in the blue bowl, right where we left it."

Their mother shook her head. "It's Sofie's."

"You could have sold it," Sofie said. "Used the money for food."

"I thought about it. But then I always decided to keep it a little while longer. We never knew if things would get worse." They all stared as Amalia stretched her arm so that the tip of the hair just brushed the floor.

"Let me see that." Tomas extended his hand. "It must be a meter long." Blushing, Sofie grabbed it before Amalia could pass it to him and held it behind her back.

Tomas winked at Sofie, then shrugged. Their mother filled his cup. Dora watched him drink, three long swallows. He wiped his lips with the back of his hand. "I should be going," he said.

Dora nodded but Sofie said, "Stay. Rest a while. It's a long trip back." Sofie looked toward their mother. "Have more to eat." She tossed Dora her braid.

He's had enough to eat, Dora thought. More than his share. He should leave, then she and her sisters could play Rapunzel, the way they used to. Amalia would tie the braid to her own. Sofie with her short hair made a perfect prince. Dora would be left with the role of wicked enchantress. "Rapunzel, Rapunzel, let down your hair," and Amalia, standing on a stack of crates, would release the braid balled in her hand, letting it tumble down.

Sofie held the coffee pot near Tomas's cup and poured carefully. They smiled at each other for a long time; too long, Dora thought. She coiled and uncoiled the braid in her lap. Embarrassing tears burned her eyes. Could an empty eye socket cry? She pulled at her lower eyelids.

"Stop making ugly faces," Amalia said.

"Do you want your eyes to stay that way?" Sofie asked, laughing.

Don't pretend to be so grown up, Dora wanted to say. You're only thirteen. She picked at Sofie's braid and considered unraveling it but then they wouldn't have it to play with later. Maybe this time Sofie and Amalia would let her be Rapunzel.

Finally Tomas said good-bye. Their mother walked the few steps to the door with him and pressed some coins into his hand. He looked back at Sofie. "We'll miss you," he said. Then, reddening, he added, "All of you. Come visit when you can."

Sofie watched out the window. Amalia refilled the kettle. Dora stuffed the braid into her apron pocket. She'd never get to see behind the eye patch.

"Well, here we are, thank God, and Frau Becker, may she rest in peace," said Mama. "And we'll all have to work hard, starting in just a few minutes. The students will sit down to supper and we'll feed them. Then we'll wash the dishes. I've been doing it all myself since Frau Becker took sick."

"Did she suffer long?" Sofie asked.

"The Spanish influenza is terrible and quick. In the morning we were making bread; in the afternoon she was in bed with fever, gasping for breath, like a fish on the beach. She knew she could die; so many others have. She signed papers leaving the house to me. Said she had no relatives she wanted to leave it to. She knew I could run the business as well as she had, better, with you girls helping. So here we are."

Here we are, Dora thought. God must have wanted them to be together again because here they were—none of them in heaven. "Is the influenza gone?" she asked, but no one answered.

Sofie was already slicing turnips. Amalia set the table for sixteen. Their mother stirred something that smelled vaguely of potato peelings. Dora hunched in her chair, fingering the bumps in Sofie's braid, wrapped round and round her knuckles and wrist. No one told her to help.

The mining students shouldered through the door, loud and black and hungry. They showered at the pithead, but scrubbed faces and hands again at home. They crowded into the small dark washroom off the kitchen. One by one they came back in, damp and clean. Even without the coal dust it was hard for Dora to tell them apart. There were so many. They patted her on the head and nodded to Amalia but it was Sofie they watched move about the kitchen.

Sofie mashed the turnips at the counter and every man around the table leaned toward the wide arched doorway to watch the wiggle in her hips as her arm moved up and down pounding in a bit of lard for flavor. They looked starved. Dora felt small, lost, like a bead from a broken necklace left in a corner after the rest has been swept up. The war was over and she was home, yet anger burned in her throat. Mama stopped on one of her trips between the stove and counter and table to ask if she felt sick. She shook her head.

"It's only a matter of days, Frau Bauer," one of the students said. "We'll all be on strike."

"I've been a Social Democrat all my life," said another. "But that's over now. Where has it gotten us? Independent Socialists have the right idea. Who has ever given power away? It must be taken."

"To change things around here, we need more than the Independent Socialists are willing to do with their endless negotiating, compromising. We need a Red Army of our own."

"They'll send in the *Freikorps*," someone else said. Everyone talked and pounded the table. Occasional phrases reminded Dora of things Tomas had said, or at least the words he'd used. The miners sneered when they said *Freikorps*. Tomas had seemed to approve of them. She wasn't sure, but the miner with the big nose talked as if he might be a communist. He seemed to like them.

"Then we'll have a mess," said another in a rasping voice. "Haven't we had enough warfare?"

"You don't get anything unless you fight for it."

The men flung disgruntled mutterings and angry exclamations back and forth across the table. Sofie and Amalia leaned into the thick of it to fill a cup or clear a plate. They fluttered around the table, faces beaming and flushed. Near the stove Dora rocked her chair and resisted the urge to hide her face in her hands.

"We have to make the owners see it's in their interest to make us happy. Fighting won't work when they have everything. I'm no crazy communist."

"Haven't you heard of revolution? They are successful sometimes!"

"Just make sure you pay your room and board." Their mother's higher-pitched voice cut through the din.

Big Nose laughed. "Don't worry, Frau Bauer. We'll pay. You take good care of us."

"We know you have to feed these growing daughters of yours," said the one with hunched shoulders.

Dora didn't like the way he said *growing*, but Sofie and Amalia exchanged glances and smirks.

Her mother bent over her. "You must be tired. Do you want to go lie down?"

She would feel worse upstairs alone while people talked, laughed, argued, and ate below. She didn't answer.

"Amalia, run upstairs and get a blanket for Dora." Mama stroked the back of Dora's head. "We'll wrap you up right here."

Amalia returned breathless, and threw the blanket at their mother. She widened her eyes at the mining student with the blond hair and the crooked tooth.

Mama squatted beside her, tucking the blanket around her shoulders, and put a hand on her knee. "Will you look at your sisters?" she said. "What a big help!"

"Frau Bauer," the mining student with the biggest grin called above the clatter of dishes. "You can retire now. Let your girls do the work."

"I suppose you're right," Mama said. She lifted Dora enough to slide in beneath her. Finally. Dora snuggled between her soft body and the scratchy blanket, glad she still fit on her mother's lap. Sofie and Amalia wouldn't fit. Well, maybe Amalia, but not Sofie.

"Hey, lazy," Sofie said, pinching Dora's cheek. "I hope you're planning to help with the washing up."

"She will." Mama answered for her.

Dora squished the braid in one hand. "Let's do Rapunzel later, okay? Before bed."

Sofie rolled her eyes. "Maybe we can tell it," she said. "If we're not too tired."

"Help clear the plates." Amalia, hands full of dishes, nudged Sofie with an elbow. "They said they play music in the other room later. Mama, can we listen? We're invited."

"I don't want to tell it," Dora whined. "I want to do it. Like we used to. With the braid."

"Can we, Mama?" Sofie asked.

"Please," Dora said.

"Please," Sofie said.

Amalia balanced stacks of dirty plates on her hands and forearms and jiggled her foot.

"You too, Frau Bauer. What do you want to hear?" called one of the students. "Any requests?"

"No," Dora whispered.

"I suppose so," said Mama. "For a little while, after we eat and the dishes are done." She stood Dora on the floor and moved to help. Dora's legs wobbled. The blanket fell in a heap.

Amalia and Sofie beamed. Neither of them paid any attention as Dora slumped back in the chair and tried to pull the blanket tight around her. She might as well have been locked at the top of a tower with no way in. Why didn't they want to play? In the few visits home during their four years on the farms, she, Sofie and Amalia had found refuge upstairs whenever they could. They hardly noticed the miners except to say thank you for a sweet or to laugh at a joke.

With a shuffle and a scrape of benches some men headed out for beer and some climbed the stairs to their rooms.

In the sudden quiet Mama, Amalia, and Sofie all stood still, looking at Dora—Sofie at the sink, Amalia by the stove, and Mama in the middle of the room. Dora knew that without even trying she had on her saddest face.

"I think you girls have time to play upstairs for a little while before music," their mother said. "Just start these dishes and I can finish. You've helped so much already. Tonight feels like a vacation." Mama said *think* but Dora heard the nudge underneath it, the message to Sofie and Amalia. They would play. She leaped up and began to clear cups and cutlery from the table.

Upstairs in Frau Becker's well-furnished attic apartment that now belonged to them, Dora snapped the braid into the air. "Let's do Rapunzel." She twirled around a few times while waiting for Sofie and Amalia to argue or agree.

Amalia found a soft red dress in their mother's wardrobe and held it in front of her. "Sofie, should I wear this instead?"

Sofie leaned close to the mirror nailed to the wall and pinched her cheeks. "Do you think I look pale?"

"Who will be what?" Dora said, ready to fight for the Rapunzel role.

Sofie shook her head and combed her fingers through her short curls. Amalia stood behind her on tiptoe, trying to peek into the mirror full of Sofie's reflection. "Move over, let me see."

Once, when they were acting out the story, the two of them dangled the braid from the window arguing over whether or not there were princes in Tauburg and whether the braid would be strong enough to hold one should he decide to climb it. Dora had begged them to stop, sure a strange man would be hanging from the end if they left it out there any longer. Sofie and Amalia, often quick to comfort her when she was afraid, had ignored her and laughed.

Dora rummaged in a drawer for a clip and attached the braid to her own. "Look, I'm ready." She stood on the bed. "I'm Rapunzel first."

"My eyebrows are too thick," Amalia complained. "Like Mama's."

"I'm Rapunzel!"

Amalia and Sofie turned from the mirror. Their lips twitched. If they laughed, Dora would kick them. She swallowed but stood tall.

"Fine," Sofie looked at Amalia and shrugged. "You're Rapunzel. Who do you want me to be?"

"Who do you want to be?" Dora asked. This wasn't the way it was supposed to go.

Sofie raised one shoulder in response.

"I'll be the witch," said Amalia.

Dora breathed deeply. "You're the prince then, Sofie."

Sofie was back at the mirror, standing on tiptoe. Hands on hips, she twisted her shoulders.

Dora tightened her grip on the braid, rolled and ready to drop the moment Amalia chanted, "Rapunzel, Rapunzel, let down your hair." Sofie knew there was nothing in this story about the prince admiring himself too long in the mirror. Dora wanted to complain—really she wanted Amalia to complain—but she could tell Amalia wasn't going to. She adjusted her stance, noticed her feet buried in the bedclothes, and knew that Mama would not approve of her standing on the bed. She was old enough to know better, but she didn't climb down.

"Sofie," Dora said. "Be the father in the beginning because the prince isn't in it yet. Be the father getting caught stealing the witch's rampion. Promise to give her your daughter."

"You know," said Sofie. "One thing the story never tells is how that wife feels when she has her baby and has to give it to the witch. All I've ever heard is that the baby is born, the enchantress appears and takes her, and she grows into the most beautiful child under the sun. It never says anything about the father being sorry or upset. Too much is left out."

Dora was trying not to cry. "Just do it, Sofie. Be the man. Please."

"Why do people in these stories just let their children go? Think about it—they leave them in the forest, hand them over to witches. At least Hansel and Gretel's father is sorry, but in Rapunzel it's as if it doesn't even matter."

"It matters," Dora said. "They just don't tell that part. You can't tell every little thing—right, Amalia?"

"Come on, Sofie." Amalia said. "Let's start. The students will be back soon."

Dora plopped down onto the bed. Another look passed between her sisters. "Stop it," she said. "I don't want to play anyway." She pictured Sofie giggling and blushing with Tomas, Amalia leaning over the blond mining student as she took his plate. She would have to play all the parts herself. It wouldn't be as much fun, but she could do it and it would be better than all this talking and looking at each other and not paying attention.

"Come on, Dora," Sofie grabbed her elbow. "I said I'd play. I'll be the father." She crouched down. "Look, here I am, picking the rampion. Amalia, come on, be the witch."

"How can you dare?" obliged Amalia. "Descend into my garden and steal my rampion like a thief? You shall suffer for it!"

Sofie put a scared look on her face that almost satisfied Dora.

Downstairs an accordion wheezed. Someone tuned his violin. Amalia and Sofie delivered their lines too fast and with no real feeling. Dora could tell they played it through until the end to give her the chance to drop the braid, have twin babies, be found in the desert by the blinded prince, wet his eyes with her tears so they grow clear again, find the way to his kingdom, and live happily ever after, but it wasn't satisfying the way she remembered it.

"The end," Sofie declared. The violin, mandolin, and accordion merged and swelled into song, pulling Sofie and Amalia, already dancing, away from her.

Dora sat on their mother's bed, arms wrapped around her skinny legs. Applause sounded as the song ended, then their mother's footsteps on the stairs. She counted them, listening as they grew closer. She would ask for a story—two stories—to keep Mama with her until Sofie and Amalia came too. She yawned, then decided never mind the stories, she didn't want to risk falling asleep without her sisters, not on their first night together again. Sofie and Amalia laughed so loud she could hear them two floors down. They didn't sound tired. The music started up full force. Dora pulled her knees in closer to her flat chest and refused to hear it.

PART II

▼

1923–1924

CHAPTER 4

▼

Amalia couldn't avoid the French soldiers standing guard on windy street corners. They brandished horse whips and bayonets and leered at her whenever she passed. They were everywhere in the weeks since January 11th when the occupation began, but she would never accept their presence. No loyal German would. Everyone, from the rich factory owners to the mining students, participated in the passive resistance. They would show the French and Belgians; they couldn't be pushed around. The glow of the blast furnaces and coke ovens no longer lit the early dark of winter. Work at the mines stopped or slowed. The French had no right to take over the coal fields and the rivers and rails just because Germany couldn't fulfill impossible reparations payments. They had no right to turn schools into barracks, arrest mine owners, expel loyal German railway workers and police, or create their artificial borders around the *Ruhrgebiet* complete with customs posts where they collected taxes and hounded honest German citizens for their passes.

Amalia and Dora arrived back at the boarding house with five rotting potatoes, two cabbages and a piece of salty meat the butcher called ham. Sofie sat at the kitchen table whispering with Lorenz, Amalia's favorite mining student. Long ago, nine years now, when she and her sisters had watched the men from the room upstairs, the students had all looked the same—faces and clothes black with coal dust, shuffling home in a tired group. Every other summer, one class graduated and a new one came; the miners stayed the same age while Sofie, Dora and she had caught up. Amalia noticed differences now—a mole on a muscled neck bent at grace, a blackened thumbnail on a hand holding a cup she filled from the heavy coffee pot, a blond cowlick her fingers itched to smooth after setting down a plate of soup. She thought she might love Lorenz with his idealistic ranting, his ready smile and laughing eyes. Sofie said she liked Oskar, so why did she have to flirt with Lorenz too? Twinges of jealousy merged with hunger pangs in Amalia's empty stomach.

Dora set the cabbages near the sink. Amalia put the rest of the food onto the table. Lorenz glanced up.

Sofie examined a potato. "This is all? How are we supposed to feed fifteen men and four of us with this?"

"That's for you to figure out," Amalia said. "Tomorrow you go to the market, see if you can do better, and I'll cook." Let Sofie suffer the indignity of waiting in endless lines, herded like an animal by soldiers who touched her at every opportunity on the shoulder or the bottom.

"Tomorrow you might not need to go to the market," said Lorenz, widening his eyes, then winking.

"Why?" asked Amalia. "Are you going scavenging? Looting the shops? Invading the kitchens of the French army?"

"Shh." His finger brushed her lips, a quick tickle, gone before she could respond. "I was just telling Sofie. Karl overheard a railway worker talking about a boxcar full of lard, abandoned on a spur near the coke ovens. Just sitting there. I'd say it's our patriotic duty to liberate that lard. Tonight. Before it goes bad, if it hasn't already."

"It's dangerous," Dora said chopping cabbage.

"What isn't these days?" said Lorenz.

Sofie cut the ham into slices thin as playing cards and forked them into the frying pan. The smell flooded the kitchen; shreds of meat doing their best to pose as a meal.

Amalia stayed up long after Sofie and Dora had gone to bed. Hunger and the rumble of the men's talk kept her from sleeping. She sat with a basket of mending in the warm corner of the parlor, her feet pressed against the tiled stove. The mining students managed to smuggle enough coal in their clothing and lunch pails to keep the house warmer than the night outside. A circle of men played cards around a small table. Oskar Schmidt, the quiet one Sofie wondered about, plucked his mandolin.

Amalia poked her needle through the worn fabric of a blouse she and her sisters and their mother all shared, planning to go to bed when she felt tired enough to ignore her aching belly. She stared across the room at Lorenz, willing him to put down his cards and talk to her, touch her lips again, smile.

He stood suddenly, as if he'd received her silent message. She pricked her finger in her excitement, leaned forward, preparing herself for his approach. When he and Karl passed her by without a word and slipped from the room, she flung the blouse on top of the mending basket and followed. The outside door closed just as she entered the kitchen. They'd gone out.

She grabbed her coat from its peg, sliding her arms into the sleeves as she hurried after them into the street. When they got to the boxcar and were wishing for help to carry the spoils she'd reveal herself, a heroine. Lorenz would see her as distinct from her sisters, daring, self sacrificing, tough as Rosa Luxemburg. He'd beam at her—her, not Sofie—across plates of fried potatoes, crisp and dripping with the fat they liberated. Even Sofie wouldn't dare to go out in the wintry night after curfew.

Lorenz and Karl turned a sharp corner, and Amalia lost sight of them, but she knew the way through the tangle of cramped streets to the railway spur they'd mentioned. The more hands available, the more lard they could carry. She wondered what the soldiers would do if they noticed two mining students and a girl. She could be shot or stabbed, or worse.

They avoided the main, dimly lit streets with soldiers posted at regular intervals and wound through tight alleys where they ran into no one. Amalia had no difficulty keeping up, and the mining students were easy to identify, even in the murky dark, Lorenz tall and lanky, Karl blocky and slow.

A soldier on horseback guarded the approach to the silent coke ovens. Karl and Lorenz faded back into the shadow of a building. Amalia squeezed into a narrow space between two houses and waited, waves of anxious fear filling her empty belly. No doubt the men were strategizing the next move. She'd wait.

The horse whinnied. Amalia flinched and almost wet her bloomers. When the guard clomped away along the perimeter of the yard, Karl and Lorenz made a quick break across the open area, running hunched and low. They flattened themselves to the ground near the boxcars lined up on the track. She couldn't see them even though she'd watched them dive. She'd have to make her own dash to the tracks, soon, before she lost the men, before the guard returned. Holding her skirt bunched tight in her hand she scampered across, landing breathless beside Lorenz on the cold ground.

It all happened so quickly. A hand over her mouth kept her from crying out as her arms were twisted behind her back and her body crushed beneath the weight of a man. Another hand at the back of her head pressed her face into the gravel.

Karl's urgent whisper: "Wait. It's Amalia."

"Quiet."

She was released. No flicker of admiration on either man's face, only fear turning quickly to anger and then to resignation. No more words passed among them—too risky. Hoofbeats drew near; she could feel them through the length of her stiffening body, then silence but for their breathing—rough and hushed. Hoofbeats again, fading.

"Let's go." Karl scrambled and rolled over the tracks, under the boxcar, Amalia and Lorenz right behind him. She bumped her knee against the rail. Her fingers and toes burned with cold. Lorenz's disapproving glare hung in her mind, shaming her.

Shielded by the motionless train cars they stood. Lorenz counted silently and pointed to a car a long way down the track. They crept toward it. Amalia tried to walk lightly, tried to feel as bold as she had before.

Karl took a felt packet of tools from his pocket and unrolled it. Amalia watched as, without a word exchanged, Lorenz and he sawed and pried their way into the locked boxcar. The grating rumble of the door sliding open ripped through the quiet night, and they hit the ground again, under the train, between the rails. The splintery railroad tie scraped her cheek. Stones bit into her knees. She listened for the guard and his horse, every nerve attuned to sound and vibration. She felt Lorenz, tense alongside her. Sensitive to every tremor she anticipated the moment when he and Karl were about to act, and she stood when they did, lifted herself into the narrow opening, loaded her arms with heavy tins of lard.

"Don't take so much," hissed Lorenz. "We can make another trip. Bring more men."

"Take all we can carry now," Karl argued. He stacked another tin the size of a wash bucket on top of the two Amalia held in her arms.

"We have to be able to move," Lorenz said.

The fat was heavy. If only the tins had some kind of handle to hold, but they were cylindrical and smooth. Amalia's back hurt, and she hadn't walked a step toward home.

The top canister thudded to the floor. Karl leaped from the car. "Toss them to me," he said.

Amalia dropped the lard down to him. He set it on the ground near his feet.

Can after can she rolled them out the door into Karl's waiting arms. Lorenz put a hand on her shoulder. "Enough."

"A couple more," Karl urged.

Gravel crunched under quick hooves. A beam of light swept over the boxcar opening. They froze.

"What have we here?" said someone in French-accented German. Amalia shrunk back against the piles of lard cans. "A thief." The guard dismounted, pointing his gun at Karl, the bayonet sharp and threatening. Come forward with your hands in the air."

Karl, surrounded by the stolen containers, raised his arms carefully.

"You could be killed for less than this," the guard said. "You're a fool." He kept his bayonet pointed at Karl, and held his lantern toward the boxcar door. Amalia and Lorenz held their breath. "Are you alone?"

His face, illuminated by the flickering lantern, was young.

Lorenz leaped from the opening, tackling the soldier. Karl grabbed the gun and smacked the guard into unconsciousness with the butt of the rifle.

"Don't kill him," Lorenz said. "The reprisals wouldn't be worth it. Amalia, hurry!"

Amalia held a tin of lard under each arm. Lorenz and Karl made sacks of their coats and managed more. They hurried back through the same winding passages, feeling lucky, made careless and invulnerable by their narrow escape. A soldier passed the mouth of an alley without seeing them, and Amalia almost laughed out loud. They merely paused for breath and to wrap their arms more tightly around their loot, and continued home.

At the boardinghouse, everyone slept. The canisters lined up on the table gave silent testimony to the success of the mission. Amalia considered waking Sofie who wouldn't, couldn't, sneer at this bounty. She ran her hand over the cold metal lids, grinning with pride. "Maybe we should make another run," she said.

Karl and Lorenz had already pried open a can and were eating lard from a spoon.

Lorenz swallowed and looked at her for the first time since entering the house. "She wants to make another run," he said, voice full of contempt.

Amalia, about to sink her own spoon into the glistening white fat, stopped.

"Karl, should we tell her what the French have been known to do to women with their bayonets? Should we spell out exactly how lucky she was?"

"We were all lucky." Karl patted her hand. "Amalia, eat."

She didn't think she could swallow past the lump in her throat, but she plunged her spoon into the lard with a defiant thrust and, dry-eyed, met Lorenz's narrowed gaze.

The household ate well for many weeks. Sofie, Amalia and Dora even gained weight. The mining students leafleted and picketed with renewed vigor. Every potato or turnip Amalia bargained for at the market tasted good soaked in grease.

Full bellies, however, didn't change the fact that others starved. The mayor, police, and many more railway workers and their families were accused of insurgency and expelled, allowed only to take what they could carry. The mining school closed indefinitely, and fuel was more scarce.

One snowy Wednesday in early March, Amalia, Sofie and Dora huddled near the stove in the kitchen, wrapped in a threadbare blanket, as the last scrap of wood and bits of coal disappeared. They spent part of every day in the meadow on the edge of town or by the river gathering reeds and branches to burn, but hesitated about going so far in the snowstorm. The city park had already been stripped bare.

"If we go out, we'll just get colder," Dora said. "There must be something to feed the fire."

"Yes," said Sofie. "But if we wait until closer to *Mittagsessen* I can cook at the same time."

"Don't burn the rocking chair," Dora said.

They agreed it made sense to burn furniture but argued over which piece.

Hanna burst through the door in a swirl of snow. "It's finally happened." She put her dripping rag of a coat in the sink and removed a sodden document from the pocket. "I didn't think they'd billet a soldier in a house of angry miners, but the housing shortage is so serious now, we've been assigned a French captain." The wet paper tore when she tried to unfold it.

"Never mind. I can tell you what it says. We're to prepare the attic apartment, our apartment, for Captain Luc Didier. He's arriving later today."

The girls were too cold to care. The attic was the coldest place in the house, well furnished, but they hadn't slept up there since winter began. "We can burn the armoire," Dora said. "And the dressing table. We can burn everything except the bed. Chop it all into pieces before he comes."

"Yes," their mother agreed. "Let me warm up bit first." She lifted the edge of the featherbed from Amalia's shoulder and squeezed in next to the girls.

Amalia recoiled from her mother's chilled body even as Hanna snuggled close.

"The sooner we smash the furniture, the sooner we'll have heat," Sofie said. "You stay here, Mama, until you're thawed. We'll start."

Amalia hopped up, away from her mother's icy skin.

Sofie emerged from the storeroom with an ax and a sledgehammer. Dora followed with a crowbar. Empty handed, Amalia climbed the stairs behind them and the next set of stairs to the attic apartment where the innocent furniture meant to last for generations waited in air so cold the girls could see their breath.

Captain Luc Didier arrived late. He swept his kepi from his head, bowed to Hanna and the girls and, in perfect German, apologized for causing any inconvenience. Everything he'd brought hung from his knapsack and belt. When Hanna refused to accept his outstretched hand, it dangled with nothing to hold onto.

The miners in the parlor stopped their music and swarmed the doorway to the kitchen.

"Together, can we make the best of this awkward situation?" the Captain asked them.

Karl Braun stepped forward. "It's not enough you take our food and coal, put us to work at gunpoint? Now you have to live with us too?"

The men clustered behind him jeered.

"I'll take meals in my room, if it's not too much trouble." Dark circles surrounded the Captain's brown eyes like a mask. His cheeks, already chapped from the cold, flushed an even brighter red.

"Come with me," said Hanna—brusque, businesslike. "Karl, you'll remember this is a civilized house. No need to let what's happening out there, affect us in here."

"Mama!" Amalia spoke up. "That's crazy! He's the enemy. Outside or inside—"

Hanna stopped her with a look and turned back to the Captain. A muscle in her neck twitched.

Amalia regretted her words until Lorenz nodded and raised a fist in solidarity.

The Captain didn't flinch. He didn't swell with anger. He merely stood his ground, waiting for Hanna to lead the way to his rooms.

Oskar Schmidt motioned the students back into the parlor where they resumed their music, a loud medley of patriotic songs that lasted far into the night.

Amalia, arms aching from wielding the ax, gathering and carrying the broken boards, sweeping the splinters, felt no compassion for the Captain, even when he smiled gently in her direction.

As the hours and days passed Amalia discovered that red was the Captain's natural color and that Luc Didier, with his impeccable manners and perfect self-containment, needed no pity from her. When he had to pass through the house, he did so with quiet grace, ignoring the mining students' whispered insults.

Passive resistance, officially still in effect, turned more active. The girls went out to the market but bypassed city hall where rioters and soldiers clashed. They knew better than to walk near the train tracks or cross bridges, where saboteurs set their explosives.

By mid-spring, they'd eaten the last of the stolen lard, and Hanna insisted they sit for a photograph before they became thin again. "Call it a necessary extravagance," she said. "I want a picture of my girls with meat on their bones."

On the way home from the photographer in their best dresses Amalia, Dora and Sofie passed the train station where groups of skeletal children with name cards pinned to their tattered clothes waited silently.

"They're too hungry to cry," said Dora.

"Or even jostle each other," Sofie added.

Amalia couldn't speak. She knew they were being sent to the country for their own benefit, to fatten them up so they wouldn't die. Farmers had agreed to take them in, just as they had taken her sisters and her during the war. This evacuation program was touted by some as an innovative, life saving measure. Others worried about ulterior motives—were the French planning something especially diabolic for the rest of the population once the children were gone?

She felt ashamed of her own plump cheeks. She ached for the little boy clutching his big sister's hand and wondered if they'd live on the same farm or be separated.

She walked faster to keep up with Dora and Sofie. "Promise we'll stay together," she said. "Whatever happens." She grabbed their hands and inserted herself between them as they rushed down the street, putting the children behind them.

The photographs were delivered, and they gathered around the table to look at them. In the three weeks since the picture was taken they'd gotten thinner again.

"I have something to tell you," their mother said. "It's not good news."

"It never is," said Sofie.

"Things keep getting worse," Hanna agreed. "The Captain heard about an opportunity for two of you to work in a hospital in Gunstadt, outside occupied territory. He tried to procure three passes, but only managed two."

Amalia exchanged a glance with Sofie. When had their mother taken to scheming with the Captain? When she brought him his lunch? What had she given him in exchange for such a favor?

"I'm sure there are other girls who would be happy to go," Amalia said.

Dora looked stunned. Sofie stacked and restacked the four photos in their thick cardboard frames. Amalia banged her fist on the table. "This is our home," she said.

"In Gunstadt there's food," Hanna said. "Food. No soldiers. No terrorists. You won't be there long. Just until the occupation ends."

"I have to start the soup," said Sofie.

"Don't make us leave again," said Amalia. "You need help here." *It won't be for long.* The last time their mother had made that promise, four years had passed before they came home again.

"The Captain went to a great deal of trouble to get these passes, and two of you will use them."

Amalia studied her sisters' faces. Passive resistance. None of them would go.

"Why would he go to so much trouble?" Amalia asked. "Why would he care?"

Her mother ignored Amalia's purposeful smirk and broke three straws from the broom. "If no one wants to go," Hanna persisted. "We'll let the broom decide. The shortest straw stays."

The straws bristled from her closed fist. "Agreed? Now choose."

Dora pulled one. It was impossible to tell how it compared until others were drawn.

"Why does anyone have to go?" Amalia said. "We don't want to."

Hanna's eyes flashed. She seemed to grow taller. "I hope you never have to be a mother who can't provide for her children. I've found a way to save two of you. For now. You will take advantage of it."

Amalia turned away from the two straws in her mother's hand and began to set the table. She pushed the pictures aside with her elbow. "Someone please get these photos out of the way."

"Please," Hanna said. "If not for yourselves, for me." She sounded tearful.

Amalia clenched her jaw and tightened her shoulders. She set forks beside the plates. Out of the corner of her eye she saw Sofie reach for a straw. Dora held hers beside it. Sofie's was shorter, but without Amalia's they still didn't know for sure who would stay in Tauburg.

"Amalia?" Hanna held out the last straw in a steady hand.

Amalia told herself to resist, but her mother's eyes shone wet and pleading. She snatched the straw. Sofie and Dora moved in close, and they all placed their straws on the table side by side. Sofie, Amalia, Dora. Three sisters. Three straws. Sofie's was the shortest. She would stay behind.

CHAPTER 5

▼

In the last moments of quiet before *Mittagspause,* Sofie stirred the watery soup with a long wooden spoon, covered a simmering pan of mushrooms and cabbage, and listened for the mining students. She liked them all, but the man she memorized was Oskar Schmidt, the short one, who at breakfast, smelled of pine sap and wet leaves. After dinner she listened to his mandolin. As other students sang, Sofie hovered at the edges of the room, outside the circle of light, waiting for his voice, but the sounds came only from his fingers. She felt a sudden and unexpected shyness with the miners. With Amalia and Dora she hadn't hesitated to join the men, but after they left for jobs in the Gunstadt hospital, she kept to herself and wrote letters that had small chance of reaching their destination. Loneliness spilled onto the pages between descriptions of the terrible summer heat, the curfews that required closed windows, the miners' demand for increased wages and her decision to raise the price of room and board. She needed buckets of paper money to buy even one cabbage. She wrote to them about the end of the resistance, the miners' return to steady work. She wrote about the farm they'd have someday when they could be together again. She didn't write about their mother's persistent cough or the time Hanna spent in Captain Didier's room. She didn't write about her desire to have them back home.

She considered writing about her growing fascination with Oskar but hadn't yet. When she pinned wet sheets to the line and pressed her body into their cool, flapping wetness, as she shook out the feather beds and hung them over the windowsills to air in the October sunshine, she imagined his fingers on her skin.

Just that morning Sofie lay in the windowless room off the kitchen, the one she now shared with her mother, and, eyes wide open in the dark, listened for the particular squeal and sigh of Oskar's door. She imagined his whispers in her ear, his calf against her foot, his fingers pressed to the neck of the mandolin. With racing heart she thrilled to the thump-tap of his feet descending the stairs, knowing he'd be back before breakfast to present her with a basket of mushrooms, damp and sweet. He'd name them, but she never listened, distracted by his fingers against the fleshy stems, the pictures in her mind of him crouching to pick them for her. She ached to go with him to the meadow or the woods or wherever it was he wandered.

The door slammed. Hanna appeared, hat askew, coat unbuttoned, with a bag of turnips and cabbages. "I know I'm late," she said. "The lines were even longer than usual. But I managed to buy these before the noon dollar quotation. Fifty million marks a cabbage; now it's double that." Her chin and cheekbones jutted disturbingly from her thin face. She fell asleep often and suddenly during the day, whenever she sat down; some nights she kept Sofie awake with her coughing.

"Is Luc—Captain Didier—back?" Hanna blushed and stuttered over his name, unpacking vegetables with unwarranted attention. Sofie wondered, not for the first time, about her mother's fascination with this enemy in their home. He sensibly avoided the kitchen and the parlor when the mining students ate, played cards, or made music. Their mother brought meals to his attic room. Sometime during the spring, after he'd obtained the passes that sent Amalia and Dora on their way, she began staying while he ate.

"He's here." Sofie stopped a turnip from rolling off the counter and stowed the bag in a drawer of the sideboard. "Waiting for you, no doubt."

"Waiting for his dinner, you mean." Hanna put a soup plate on a painted wooden tray. Sofie knew her mother couldn't admit to loving another unsuitable man, even to her daughter. Especially to her daughter. Sofie plunged the ladle into the soup pot splashing precious broth over the sides. She glared at her mother, daring her to criticize, but Hanna looked away.

The students pushed through the door, Oskar among them. Sofie ladled soup into the Captain's bowl and her mother hurried toward the stairs with the carefully balanced tray. She never looked back. If she had, she'd have seen twenty-four hungry miners clamoring for food and Sofie rushing around to fill their plates. There weren't enough seats at the table. A shaft had to be repaired, they needed everyone back at the mine—one long shift today for everyone. That the men got a break at all was a miracle, or perhaps evidence that the strikes had accomplished something.

If Mama would stop for even a moment, thought Sofie, she'd know she belonged in the kitchen helping to feed good German workers. Did she spread the lard on this enemy's *Schmalzbrot*? Did she wipe crumbs from his chin? For months Sofie wondered what they talked about but hadn't the courage to ask. She told herself her mother felt compassion for the Captain, alone in a strange country, and Tauburg, no less—such a provincial city when he was used to the glamour of Paris. She told herself to be glad her mother had a friend. With Frau Becker dead and visits from her only other friend in town, Frau Grunberg, the dressmaker, all too rare, Mama needed the distraction. *Two businesswomen*, she and Frau Grunberg laughed and called themselves. *Two businesswomen too busy for fun*. Mama wasn't too busy for fun with the Captain. Sofie couldn't help thinking about *Teufelmann*, supposedly dead in France—maybe Mama felt she owed the French army a favor in return for his demise.

When Sofie finished serving soup, conversation stopped: Karl Braun always insisted upon a quick blessing. For a moment there was only slurping and the scrape of spoons. They tried to have meat for the soup two times a week; today there was none.

Sofie hefted the iron skillet and scraped the mushrooms and cabbage into a serving bowl. "Ahh!" Karl leaned back and waved her toward him. "Come here, darling, and put a little of that on my plate." He made pointing at his plate an obscene gesture.

Sofie stood by Oskar. "He brought the mushrooms. He'll be served first," she said. A flush started up Oskar's neck, visible even through the gray veneer of coal dust. His clipped brown hair smelled like the woods. Sofie hadn't meant to embarrass him.

Karl hooted. Oskar's lips twitched. Sofie managed a cool smile as she spooned a large helping onto Oskar's plate. He nodded his thanks and stared into her eyes until she blushed too and had to look away.

"Where do you find these things?" someone asked. "When I go outside all I see are cobblestones, trolley tracks, and trampled dirt."

"I'll find Sofie a mushroom," Karl teased. "A nice big one."

"Shut up, you big lout," laughed Lorenz.

"Will you show us where you find these?" Another voice joined in. "These are even better than last week's."

"*Boletus badius*," mumbled Oskar. "And *boletus aereus*." Sofie wasn't used to hearing Latin outside of church.

"Delicious whatever they're called," Lorenz said. "Sofie sure knows how to cook."

She glanced at Oskar, busy eating. She served Karl last and whacked the plate with the edge of her spoon. He drew back in mock fear.

"Mushroom hunters are a strange lot," Lorenz added. "I've known a few. Their best spots are closely guarded secrets. Right, Oskar? Bet you've never shown anybody where you found these."

Oskar gave an ambiguous shake of his head.

"As long as you bring them home to us," Karl said. "Next thing you know we'll be eating grass. Unless we get some strong leadership in this country, we'll be eating what's left of our shoes."

Oskar swallowed and wiped his mouth with the back of his hand. "This inflation has to end. The government will find a way. Smart men thinking together. People must be patient."

Around the table men shifted and muttered. Opinions erupted.

"Hungry, unemployed people can't be patient. Smart men thinking? This government can't do anything right. Too many voices talking, talking, talking. Nobody doing," announced Karl over the noisy conversation. "The one man speaking sense, if anyone would listen, is Adolf Hitler. I know this room is full of Social Democrats and Communists…" He gave Lorenz a pointed look. "You don't pay attention to him, you think he's a crackpot, but when I read that piece about him in the paper last April I thought maybe—"

"Anything but the Communists," another man said with his mouth full.

"The republic is still new," said Oskar. "It takes a while." He chewed every bite for a long time. Sofie had perfected the art of watching him with sidelong glances as she stirred and served and washed and wiped.

"Nothing wrong with the Communists," Lorenz said. "You'd all be Communists if you stopped to look at who's getting rich from this occupation. Not just the French. You won't see Hugo Stinnes and Fritz Thyssen eating grass."

"Talk, talk, talk," Karl said. "When the French overrun our borders and take over our mines and factories. When we can barely afford a pig's ear for the pea soup in the morning and can't afford it at all by afternoon!"

"No one gives up power," Lorenz said. "It must be seized."

They argued all through the meal, agreeing only that times were bad, until they left for work, leaving silence and a table cluttered with dirty plates. On his way out, Oskar brought his dishes to the sink.

"Thank you," he said.

Sofie nodded. When he left, the kitchen seemed to tighten around the mess and quiet. She opened the door to breathe in the sulfurous outside air. Her limbs felt like water-soaked rags, heavy and limp. If she tried to lift a plate she'd drop it. If she straightened a bench or chair she'd collapse. Her mother would have to help with the cleanup. She wouldn't do it herself. She dragged herself up two flights of stairs to end the private lunch with the Captain. Just outside the door she stopped. Someone was crying. She knelt to look through the keyhole; all she could see was the end of the daybed. When she shifted a bit to the left she could see the hem of a brown skirt and the sharp bones of her mother's stockinged ankle. An isolated fragment, it seemed unfamiliar, even exotic. The crying continued, steadily pulsing sobs from deep in a chest. It sounded like a man. The Captain's boot appeared beside her mother's foot. Her heel left the floor. Was she kissing him? This was nobody's business, certainly not a daughter's business, but the crying…how could she ignore that?

The feet tripped together across the room. Hanna and the Captain's faces appeared, framed by the keyhole like photos in a locket. Tears on the Captain's cheeks, Hanna's braided crown lopsided.

"Luc," Mama said, her face full of need, ugly need that Sofie wished she'd never seen. She knew she'd never look at her mother without remembering. She vowed she'd never wear that expression herself.

"We cannot be together," Sofie heard her mother say. "This has gone too far. You must tell your superiors you need a different place to live."

Sofie turned from the door and ran downstairs.

The Captain slipped through the kitchen and out the door while Hanna tied on an apron. "No second shift?" she asked.

"They all came together today," Sofie muttered, wanting to add, 'If you hadn't been so eager to get upstairs you would've noticed.'

"You must be exhausted. I'm sorry I wasn't here to help." Hanna began to clear the table.

When had she been there to help? When their father died, she went to bed; when she got up she married *Teufelmann*. Sofie heard Dora arguing, *What about the years in between? When we were together on the farm.* What about the days locked in the room, the months in Elsterdorf? Amalia's voice: *She did the best she could.*

Her mother stood stacking dishes in the sink. From the back she looked like a girl. *Why am I the only angry one?* Sofie asked her sisters. *If you saw her with the Captain, what would you think?*

She wiped the wooden table with a damp cloth. *She's lonely for a man,* Amalia said. *It's natural.*

You're jealous, Sofie, said Dora. *Because you don't have a boyfriend.*

"Shut up," Sofie muttered.

"Did you say something?" Hanna turned from the sink.

Sofie pressed her lips together and shook her head.

"Was Karl giving you a hard time again?"

"I can ignore Karl," Sofie said, but she couldn't help thinking of that big mushroom he teased about. The men alluded to sex almost as much as they talked politics, though usually not when they remembered her presence. She'd seen plenty of animals mating on the farm, the horse's phallus huge as he chased the mare. She'd heard about the improprieties of the soldiers. She'd never seen a man naked. Perhaps she should be shocked or disgusted, but she was curious and wondered how she'd ever find out more than the little she knew. She should ask her mother, or peek through the Captain's keyhole some evening when Mama hadn't yet come to bed. She shuddered at the idea of Mama and a naked Captain. Her mother's ankles looked sturdy again, standing in the kitchen connected to the rest of her body, no boot nearby to dwarf them.

"Are you going to dry these?" Hanna asked.

Sofie picked up a dish towel. Her mother handed her dripping plates faster than she could wipe them. Why had she never noticed the energizing effect of time spent in the Captain's room? So often her mother appeared exhausted and spent.

"You know, Sofie, I think Lorenz might be sweet on you. Oskar, too." Hanna's voice bubbled. "But whatever you do, don't fall in love with a miner."

"What other kind of man do I see?" Sofie slammed a plate onto the counter with a fury that startled them both. "Crazy, worn out war veterans? There's nothing wrong with a miner. I'm used to coal dust. A German miner is better than a French captain."

Hanna stiffened, hands deep in dishwater.

"What do you see in him, anyway? He's not even a real soldier. Just sits at a desk all day."

"Would you rather he be out killing people, or forcing miners back to work with a gun at their backs?" her mother replied. "He saw enough violence in the trenches. He was shot and would have died, but a dog led the medics to his body."

"You know a lot about him, don't you?" Sofie sounded terrible even to herself. "What did you have to do to get those passes? What kind of a deal did you make?"

She glared as her mother bent over in a burst of coughing. Hands dripping, Hanna covered her mouth with the hem of her apron. She gasped for air; her shoulders jerked. Sofie watched, helpless and guilty, as her mother, thin back heaving, bent over, coughed and coughed, folded almost in half. Then it stopped.

The first moments of quiet were the worst, the moments before they could slip into pretending it hadn't happened, the moments when the echoes hung over their heads. They avoided each other's eyes.

Hanna balled up her apron and threw it in the laundry basket by the door. She washed her hands and armed herself with a knife and a turnip. "He's a good man," she said.

"You know we can't afford to waste the peels," said Sofie. "Here." She held out the scrub brush.

Hanna hesitated. "Thank you." She accepted the brush and turned on the faucet. Water rattled into the metal pan. Sofie watched her mother's thin hands as the stiff yellow bristles gnawed the skin of the tough root.

"Why don't you go upstairs and rest?" Sofie asked.

"I'm fine," her mother said. She set the wet turnip beside the sink and picked up the next one.

"You should eat more," Sofie said. "Did you eat any dinner?"

"A little." Anyone could see she was lying.

"Where was your plate? Did the Captain share his soup with you?"

Hanna whirled to face her. "I'm not hungry, Sofie. Why should I take food from someone who is?"

"You're too thin." Sofie's lip trembled.

Her mother dried her hands on her skirt. "No thinner than everyone else," she said. "Don't worry about me. I'm fine."

"But the coughing…"

"The air is bad. We all cough."

"You should see a doctor."

"What for? To pay a lot of money and be told I have a cold? Stop worrying. So, who do you think is more handsome, Oskar or Lorenz?" Her voice was suddenly light and girlish. "I know you wouldn't say Karl."

Sofie didn't answer. She dumped the risen bread dough on a board and began kneading it, pushing so hard that the heels of her hands hurt.

"Lorenz reminds me of your father—quick to laugh and cry. Passionate."

Sofie looked up. She couldn't feign indifference to stories about her father, no matter what the circumstance.

"I never cried; I was known for it. Even at my brother's funeral. But your father believed in crying. Unusual, especially for a man."

Sofie pounded the bread dough, but she was listening.

"When he laughed or cried his neck turned red. I loved that about him."

Is that why you like the Captain? Sofie wanted to ask. *Because he's red and cries?* She thought of Oskar's neck and Karl's teasing and felt her own face grow hot. She folded the dough and smashed it down.

"He gave me the music box, that Christmas before we were married. My parents had gone to bed. He wound it with its little gold key and set it on the table. We sat side by side, so stiffly on the sofa. The music began to play. The saddest sound. As though all the sadness of my life was drifting from that little box into the air. The music stopped and he didn't let me wind it up again. He said nothing and held me and held me while I cried for Georg and all my mother's other children who died before they could crawl, brothers I'd never let myself love. I cried for Frau Hagen, the old lady who slaughtered our pigs and made sausage for the whole village and told me stories while she smoked her pipe. I cried for every time I'd lost something that mattered, every time I'd been hurt. I thought I would never stop crying, that we'd have to sit there for the rest of our lives. I never doubted he would do it, sit beside me and hold me forever."

Sofie felt her eyes fill as she listened, drops that fell and dampened the dough. Sofie formed the bread into loaves and covered them to rise again, wondering if anyone would be able to taste her tears at supper.

"I'll rest now," her mother said, patting Sofie's arm on her way to bed.

Sofie snatched the broom, a handful of rags, and a bucket from the closet. Cleaning settled her.

She'd been in all the students' rooms many times to dust and sweep, and change the linen. She and Amalia and Dora would strut around, reading the students' mining journals and evaluations aloud in funny deep voices, "In the month of September, I worked pushing coal cars in the area of the explosions on the ridge of the sunshine stratum." She couldn't do such things by herself. She wouldn't want any of the young men pawing through her possessions. She didn't think she would, anyway. She shivered, imagining Oskar smoothing her pillow. Why did she always think of him? Lorenz was funnier, more passionate and outspoken, but Oskar made her wonder, left more to her imagination. Would he know the braid in the blue bowl was hers? Funny that Dora and Amalia always used it to play the princess role and she, whose braid it was, never did, as though by cutting it off she'd lost any claim to it.

Most of the students were tidy. They all had clothes and shaving kits and their blue work journals. Karl had a locked box. Lorenz had a bible. Oskar had his mushroom guide. She flipped through the small green book, admiring the illustrations. The first few pages were filled with recipes which she tried to memorize.

The rest of the book had colored illustrations and told which mushrooms were edible and which would sicken or even kill a person. Without careful study, it was nearly impossible to tell many of them apart.

That night Sofie dreamed about following Oskar. In the dream she is bare-foot, with the long hair she had when she was a girl. It hangs loose to her waist. She hides behind streetlamps until they reach the edge of town, then behind tree after tree as she follows him through a gray, Tauburg morning. She loses sight of him, then he reappears. He is naked but always hidden below the waist by dis-creet wisps of fog. She realizes she is naked too and can't go any farther.

Sofie woke and felt the short ends of her hair, heard his step on the stair—the pull to be near him real and irresistible. If she were late getting back to prepare breakfast, Mama could handle it alone. After yesterday's lunch, her mother owed her a little time off. If Hanna could spend time with her man, Sofie deserved a chance too. She slipped into a dress, tugged on her shoes, and caught up to Oskar before he reached the corner, before she could tell herself to stop.

She tapped his shoulder. He startled. "Is it true you won't show your secret places to anyone?" she asked.

"I'll show you," he said with a slight smile. She thought his eyes looked pleased. You. She felt chosen, even though she had followed him, even though she had to ask. "You," he said.

He offered his arm. She felt grown up walking through the streets with a man, though there were few people to see her, some French soldiers and a woman on a bicycle with a basket of bread.

Beside him, not talking, her skin sang. She didn't wonder what he was think-ing.

They walked through the early-morning streets, past the yard where the street-cars parked, a long, long way, to the edge of town where they left the road, passed through a misty, yellowing meadow, and entered a narrow wood where, in the winter, she'd collected branches. The leaves at the top of the beech trees sparkled in the rising sun, the leaves half-way down glowed. A breeze scattered light and shadow across the spongy ground. All of this was here all the time, every morn-ing, every afternoon, while she was in the kitchen or cleaning the upstairs rooms.

Oskar squatted in the midst of the beech trees. He called her over. The mush-room was brilliant red, speckled white.

"*Amanita muscaria*," said Oskar, pointing. "Very dangerous."

"But beautiful," Sofie said, crouching beside him. Her thigh brushed his. He stood quickly; she fell over onto the damp leaves.

"I'm sorry," he sputtered. He took her hand and helped her to her feet.

"We could pick it for Karl." With her free hand Sofie brushed muddy leaves from her skirt.

"What? Oh. Yes." He laughed. She was still holding his hand. His fingertips were callused from playing the mandolin, his palms from handling shovels and picks.

"How come you never sing?" she asked.

"I can't." He looked at their clasped hands and let go. "I expect there are some edible types over there."

"Anybody can sing," Sofie said. Had she offended him?

"We should pick some and get back. I can't be late." Oskar walked more briskly, bent over to examine the ground.

Sofie thought of the coal in the kitchen stove burnt down to ash; Dora might call her a sinner, sneaking out to the woods with a man, chores undone. Sofie wanted to be kissed. She'd wanted it for weeks.

They walked on separately, her fingers itching.

"The light," Sofie prattled. "The birds."

"Underground it's so dark," Oskar nodded, finally pausing to look at her. "That's why I come most days. The mushrooms are an excuse. Out here..." He extended both arms in an uncharacteristically grand gesture, pompous and generous at the same time, as if the day and woods belonged to him, and he was offering it to her. "I could almost believe in God."

"Almost?" Sofie frowned, incredulous. She'd known Oskar wasn't Catholic. Their mother had told them that Tauburg, like several other *Ruhrgebiet* cities, was primarily Evangelical. If a person wasn't Catholic, he was Protestant. A few exceptions were Jews. She was fairly sure Protestants and Jews believed in God. The only people who didn't were Communists, and even Lorenz had a Bible.

Oskar sat on his heels to study a patch of moss.

"Almost?" Sofie prompted. "What do you mean?"

"Nature has a rightness about it, don't you think?"

"Yes, but about God?"

He pointed to a ring of white mushrooms. "They call that a fairy ring," he said. They picked them, filling the bottom of the basket.

"What are you?" she persisted.

He looked puzzled.

"Evangelical?"

"Oh." He laughed, then stopped when she didn't join in. "I'm not a religious man," he said.

"You don't believe in God?"

"No," he said.

Birds tittered. A breeze rustled the highest leaves. The earth didn't shake, no booming voice shouted from the clouds. The shady clearing resonated with watery light and quiet possibility. Oskar knelt on the ground beside her, a man for whom the miracle of mushrooms was enough.

"My father died in the mines," Sofie said.

Oskar studied the mushrooms in the basket. "It's dangerous work. No room for mistakes."

"They happen anyway." Sofie drilled the soft ground with the toe of her shoe.

"Lorenz is in love with you," Oskar said suddenly.

Sofie placed a mushroom in his basket the way he showed her. "Really?" Why did he bring up Lorenz now? Was Oskar trying to let her know gently that he himself wasn't interested?

"He's a good man. Radical politically but, who knows, maybe he's right. He contributes more of his salary to the strike fund than anyone I know. He doesn't just talk. A man like that can be trusted."

"I trust you," Sofie said. "You can be trusted, can't you?" Who was this girl, saying these things? Small splashes of light flickered over his face. She could be home in bed or stoking the fire, but she'd come here. She was a girl who could travel, learn new things. A girl who would dare to love someone who didn't believe in God.

Oskar nodded, fingering the mushrooms.

"I thought you said you weren't supposed to handle them too much."

"Lorenz thinks times will get better."

"So do you," said Sofie. "I heard you. The republic is still new, you said."

"Yes, but I think things will get worse before they get better. When we're hungry and afraid, we think of our bellies, our own locked doors, not about models of government and what's best for most people. When we're hungry all the rest is abstraction."

If she agreed with him would he kiss her? What would he do if she kissed him first?

"Hunger and fear turn quickly to anger and rage. Look at the veterans—missing arms and legs, unable to breathe right from the poison gas, and still they march—on crutches—protesting their meager pensions. Look at the workers—striking. The housewives rushing to buy food, running each other down with wheelbarrows and bicycle baskets full of worthless money. What will happen when marching does no good? People with nothing to lose are the most dangerous. Lorenz looks forward to the revolution." He stopped, scuffing his boots in the layers of damp leaves.

Now, she thought. Kiss me now.

"I don't. When I finish at the mining school I'll go to America and find work. There is nothing to keep me here. My family is all dead."

America! Far away across the ocean. Rich people lived there. Cowboys and Indians. Wild women. Annie Oakley.

"Lorenz likes you," Oskar said. "He told me."

Lorenz didn't seem shy. Sofie wondered why he hadn't told her. And why Oskar kept bringing it up.

Oskar stood before her, looking at the ground. She'd rarely heard him laugh. She couldn't imagine him crying. But there was something about this man, so compact and careful.

"Do you know anyone else who might…like me?"

He met her challenging gaze, then nodded.

"Who?"

They were almost the same height. He stepped forward. She lifted her lips just the tiniest bit and then he was kissing her. She was being kissed, and it was all she'd hoped for. She wondered what her sisters would say when she told them.

CHAPTER 6

▼

In just two weeks, Dora and Amalia would go home for the Christmas holidays. Amalia couldn't wait to sing and laugh with the mining students. In the dormitory, in the hospital run by nuns, she was surrounded by women. The doctors never stopped long enough to notice them, and the jobs the girls did never involved the few hired men. Sofie's letters had changed. They were all about going to the beer garden, falling in love with Oskar. Maybe Lorenz and Karl still needed girlfriends, and all of them could go dancing.

"The nuns want to keep the men for themselves," Amalia whispered to Dora as they gave the babies in the infant ward their morning feeding, even though she knew Dora would disagree and maybe take offense. Amalia's baby had a purple birthmark spread over his face like a mask. She ignored the name written on his card and called him Little Blackberry. He was her favorite.

"Nuns are married to God!" Dora's shocked voice startled the baby she was holding; they called him Cowboy because of his bowed legs. Everyone knew about cowboys in America. Sofie had talked about wanting to meet one, but now she had Oskar; maybe she'd forgotten. The baby's whimpers came faster and faster, rising to a howl. Dora jiggled him. "With God for a husband why would anyone want a regular man? Men smell like beer and sweat. They swear and they listen only if they feel like it, if something else doesn't have their attention. Why would the nuns want that when Jesus is always listening? Any time you speak to Him, He hears, even when you talk only with your heart."

Amalia almost laughed. Did Jesus kiss them until their toes curled? Did God hold them tight and whirl them across the floor? Did the Holy Ghost buy them dinner at the beer garden as the lights twinkled on and the pink-streaked sky turned to velvet?

"At Christmas we can get to know Oskar," Amalia said. She and Dora hadn't been in Tauburg since before summer, when strikes and sabotage had stopped train service for weeks. Afterward, new passes were required to cross the border of the occupied area. Thankfully, things had settled now that the resistance had officially ended. Amalia ached to be home, even for just a few days.

Dora didn't answer. She slipped the empty bottle from Cowboy's slack mouth and stared at his face.

"Well, don't you want to be there to see our sister falling in love?" Amalia leaned forward. "What's wrong?"

Still looking at the baby, Dora asked, "Don't you wonder what Christmas is like here? With the nuns? Jesus's birthday. Wouldn't it be fun to be here at Christmas time? I miss Mama and Sofie but…"

"Fun? You'd rather stay than go home? You'd rather eat what these nuns call soup than Mama's sauerbraten? You'd rather sing in church than in the parlor with the mining students?"

"The soup is watery everywhere. Mama won't be able to afford sauerbraten." A shaft of pale light fell across Dora's shoulders. Above it, her face was in shadow. "The mining students will go home for the holiday…"

"Not all of them. Sofie said Oskar will be there." If Amalia hadn't been holding Little Blackberry she would have grabbed Dora by the chin and forced her to look up. She wanted to squeeze her jaw until she admitted she was joking. "You'd rather sleep in the dormitory, when everyone has gone home except for the girls with nowhere to go, than sleep at home in our own—"

"Girls, girls, how are the babies today?" Frau Hollicher, the wet nurse, washed her hands at the small sink in the corner of the ward. "Who is hungry?" she sang, consulting the small white card Sister Monika filled out in handwriting so cramped Amalia and Dora could never decipher it. Frau Hollicher walked with great purpose, flat shoes slapping the black and white tile. Almost everything in the hospital was white or black, even the uniforms the girls were required to wear and the babies' blankets, but Frau Hollicher's dress was a faded, restful blue. She softened the sharp hospital air with the homey scent of lard and onions.

Amalia glared at the top of Dora's bent head, willing her to look up. Dora's lips moved as if she were praying. Yes, under Cowboy's thin blanket Dora was fingering her rosary beads. Amalia tilted Little Blackberry's bottle at such a sharp angle he spluttered.

The smallest, sickest babies got the breast. Frau Hollicher took tiny Liesl—Amalia called her Mouse—from her bassinet and settled in the rocking chair. Amalia sneaked looks at Frau Hollicher as she unbuttoned her dress and freed her swollen breast from a complicated undergarment. She wiped her huge brown nipple with a cloth soaked in disinfectant while cradling Liesl, whose entire body fit between elbow and hand. Frau Hollicher's breast was bigger than the baby's head and lacy with pale blue veins the color of her dress. Little Blackberry drained his bottle. Amalia burped him against her shoulder. Watching the wet nurse, she felt a tug at her own nipples and a pang between her legs.

Frau Hollicher paid no attention to the baby sucking at her breast. She talked to Amalia and Dora. "My husband is man enough to make babies; nothing wrong down there." Her hearty laugh made Amalia blush, though she enjoyed it. "But up here..." Frau Hollicher tapped her forehead. "He is ruined. 'They owe me a suit,' he says. All he can think about is that suit."

Amalia liked her talk. You never knew what would come next. Most people repeated themselves, but Frau Hollicher told different stories every day. She wanted to hear more about 'down there.' "What suit?" she asked.

"His discharge suit. They stopped giving them when they ran short of material. They owe us more than a suit. No veteran can live on these pensions. I have to eat to make milk. I feed these sick babies, who knows if they will even live, and my own get less. Customers swarm our shop the moment we have a delivery. They know that later in the day things will cost more. They'll buy anything we have and he lets them. He sells what I've put aside for the family, all the while moaning about his suit. I tell him, be quiet; concentrate; this box of food is for our children. 'You want too much,' he says. 'If I had my suit, the suit they promised, life would be good.'"

"I thought the *Rentenmark* ended the inflation," Amalia said. "People say it's over now."

Frau Hollicher shook her head and clicked her tongue. "People are used to hoarding. They can't stop overnight." She sighed. "They've learned how to make artificial legs and arms, but they can't fix a mind. I want him whole again. I want food for the family. All he wants is a suit."

Amalia thought of the fisherman's wife. All that wanting. For such a strong woman Frau Hollicher had a soft face. Maybe it was her nose, more round than long. She wore her hair like Mama, coiled around her head. Her eyelids never seemed to open all the way.

"The world demands reparations from us. Why? They fought the war too. We need what we have to feed our own people. Two hundred thousand meters of telegraph poles. Twenty four million gold marks worth of coal. This is what they say we're to pay. Then, when we can't, they move in."

Frau Hollicher talked on until a shadow fell over them.

Sister Monika, the unsmiling nun with the sharp, red-tipped nose, loomed over them. "No need for this chatter," she snapped. They'd all forgotten to watch for her.

Amalia, Dora, and Frau Hollicher bowed their heads to the babies in their laps.

"Silence is best for the digestion," Sister Monika said. "These are sick babies. When you girls are finished here, Sister Julian needs your help in the kitchen, Amalia. Dora, today you'll help Sister Raphaela in the laundry. Frau Hollicher, you'll manage the afternoon feedings yourself. The girls will be free after vespers to help you with the last feeding."

"Yes, Sister," Dora said for all of them.

Amalia wished Sister Monika away and worried that even if a nun couldn't read her thoughts, God might be able to. God might know how much she detested Sister Monika and how she longed to know how it felt to let a baby suck her breast. When Amalia held Little Blackberry against her, wiggled the rubber nipple into his toothless mouth, and felt his squirming desperate need settle into a complete and satisfied sucking, she forgot home and Sofie and their mother and the mining students with their music and jokes. Amalia couldn't imagine anything better than providing that total satisfaction with her own body. Dora would say it was a sin to even think like that.

Sister Monika glided away through the quiet ward, checking on the few sleeping children as she went.

"What does she know?" Frau Hollicher asked. There were no other babies who needed the breast that morning so Liesl got both sides.

"She knows God," Dora said, scolding as if she were a parent and Frau Hollicher the child.

Frau Hollicher's lips tightened into a smirk. She met Amalia's eye. "I mean about babies," she said. "What could she possibly know about babies? They like the sound of people talking. Liesl likes the sound of our voices. Don't you, little one?"

Liesl stopped sucking and stared up at Frau Hollicher.

"See? People, even babies, need conversation as well as food. You like my stories, don't you?" she cooed to the baby. "Look, she's smiling."

Amalia knew Frau Hollicher was right. Maybe Dora did too because she didn't argue. Little Blackberry was sound asleep, and it was long past time to put him in his bassinet. Sister Monika would be back, and they'd better be elsewhere as she'd directed.

"Dora wants to stay with the nuns for Christmas," Amalia said.

Dora bristled. "I didn't say that."

"She doesn't want to see our sister or our mother. She wants to stay here and pray."

"No," Dora said. "I just wonder what it's like. I heard that Sister Raphaela sets up the nativity outside the nuns' chapel and puts the three kings at a distance so she can move them closer every day."

"It might be funny to see the old nuns lugging plaster cows around," said Amalia.

Frau Hollicher looked from Amalia to Dora and back again. Amalia wanted her to speak up and take a side, her side.

"I want to see Mama and Sofie as much as you do. You're always telling me what I think."

Dora moved to put Cowboy to bed. She had lost her bouncy step. She skimmed across the floor and was gone, following Sister Monika's order. Dora seemed to like being told what to do. Amalia suspected Dora would rather be with wrinkled old Sister Raphaela in the steamy laundry room than in the ward with her, her real sister.

Just the night before, as they turned down their beds, Dora, with a ridiculous smile on her face, said, "Sister Raphaela's face glows. She must be the happiest person I know."

"She's just nice compared to Sister Monika and the others." Amalia tried to plump her flat pillow and waited for her sister to argue. Dora's pitying look infuriated her. She climbed into bed, pressed her face into the pillow, and clenched her fists under her chest.

"What's the matter?" Dora had asked, perched on the edge of her own cot, separated from Amalia's by a small nightstand and less than a meter of polished floor.

Amalia listened to the rustling, giggling, and hushed conversation of the other girls getting ready for bed. What exactly was the matter? She waited for Dora to ask again, practiced an answer. *I'm afraid you're serious about joining the convent. I'm afraid of losing you.*

After a long time, quiet settled over the dormitory, and she heard Dora's whispered prayers. Disappointment filled her body, so heavy that she despaired of ever climbing out of bed. Yet, in the morning, she woke and ate her portion of bread at breakfast. She had even smiled at her sister.

"Christmas…" Frau Hollicher mused. "A family should be together at Christmas. Your sister should go with you."

"I don't think she wants to," Amalia said. She pressed Little Blackberry to her shoulder.

"Even the nuns see visitors at Christmas. Tell her that."

"She'll come home. She's my little sister. She does what I say."

Though Sister Julian, in the hospital kitchen, was probably at that very moment complaining to Sister Monika that Amalia hadn't arrived to deliver trays or wash the pots, Amalia had no intention of hurrying. "Dora acts like she belongs here. And I don't."

Frau Hollicher's sleepy eyes and wrinkled forehead showed concern. She patted Liesl's back, both breasts still exposed. "You're both good girls. Anyone can see that. With the nuns she will never have to worry the way we do about streetcar fare costing two thousand marks or men and their suits or caring for babies."

Amalia hadn't said Dora should join the convent. She looked behind her, suddenly afraid Sister Monika might be within earshot.

Frau Hollicher followed her gaze. "It's a crazy world. Do you know, just this morning two women came into my shop arguing about whether or not veterans without arms or legs would father deformed children?" She buttoned her dress. "People are ignorant."

Ignorant herself, Amalia waited to hear more, but Frau Hollicher sighed heavily and pushed herself up from the rocking chair. "If I go home I'll have a couple of hours to work in the store. I need to be there for the afternoon delivery if I want something for supper. It will take time for people to trust the new mark. And why should they when a lifetime of savings won't even pay for a cup of coffee?" She smoothed her hair and retrieved her worn coat from the coat rack. Her footsteps echoed.

Amalia stared at Frau Hollicher's empty chair until it stopped rocking. Married to God. How different was that, really, from the fisherman's wife who wanted to be God? If she'd settled for being the wife, would she have ended up back in that pigsty? But she'd never asked to be the wife. How did it go again? Little hut, great stone castle, king, emperor, pope, and God. If the fisherman's wife had asked to be God's wife, would she have ended up a nun? Would she be as satisfied as Sister Raphaela was folding linens?

Sister Monika should have been back long ago. Maybe she'd seen Dora in the laundry and was satisfied that Amalia, too, had obeyed. Someone was sure to come around soon. They didn't leave the babies for long.

Little Blackberry stirred. She moved to lay him down, instead settled in the rocking chair, and started it moving again, creating shadows in the puddle of light on the floor. The poor baby. No one knew who his parents were. He had been left at the hospital, nothing wrong but a birthmark. Was that why his mother left him? If it had been on his legs or back, would he be part of a family right now? His thick purple eyelids opened and he looked at her with liquid eyes. She willed him to remember her face. She hummed the music box song. She hummed it every time she held him. If she had a magic fish she'd wish his birthmark away. No, she'd wish for his mother to love him, for Dora to walk bouncy again, for a boyfriend for herself. She'd wish for a farm where she and Sofie and Dora and Mama could work and live happily ever after. Was she too greedy? Wishes were tricky things.

Little Blackberry gurgled. His mouth opened and closed and opened again. Even in the relentless cleanliness of the hospital, dust danced in the sun. Amalia fingered her buttons. Her breasts ached. It would surely be a sin to do what she was thinking of, but she wanted to—just for a moment, to see how it felt. She looked at the black crucifix hanging on the clean white walls, a lot like in their room back home, but this wasn't their room. That wasn't their room anymore either, now the boarding house was packed with miners. Where would she and Dora sleep when they went home? She could pray for Little Blackberry, for Dora, for herself, for Mama and Sofie and her boyfriend, for Frau Hollicher and her husband. Her nipples burned. Wishes, prayers, sin, satisfaction—she didn't know the difference. Who did? Dora?

The baby rested in the crook of her arm, heavy as a loaf of war bread made with sawdust. Awkwardly, with one hand, she tugged at her blouse. A white button skittered across the polished floor. Heart pounding, she took one more look behind her, then lifted her camisole. Her breasts were small in comparison to Frau Hollicher's, but bigger than her sisters', bigger than was fashionable. Usually she tried to hide them, but right now, in the sunny quiet, she liked their rounded whiteness, her nipples rosy and tight. She checked over her shoulder again for approaching nuns then, cupping the baby's little bottom in one hand, pinched her nipple with the other and tried to insert it between his lips. His hard gums clamped down. Wincing with pain, she fought the reflex to pull free. She'd never expected it to hurt. The soft spot in the middle his head pulsed in and out alarmingly, in rhythm with his fierce sucking. When he realized she was giving him nothing he let go, stared into her eyes with a long indignant look, then, tensing with fury, started to howl. Several other babies responded with cries of their own. Their wailing filled the ward, rising up to the high ceiling. It reminded her of the neck-prickling yells of desperate cats that wove their way into her nightmares before waking her, on hot summer nights at the Muellers' farm. She'd lie awake listening to their strange yowling, missing her mother and sisters too much to sleep.

With her free hand Amalia hurried to straighten her camisole and button up before Sister Monika arrived to quiet things down. Her blouse gapped between her breasts. She had lost the most necessary button, her punishment for tricking an innocent baby to satisfy her own sinful curiosity.

She put Little Blackberry into his bassinet and patted him a few times. When he continued to cry, she moved on to the next baby, jiggling the crib, and on to the next, frantic. Only the pitch and rhythm of their cries varied. The volume couldn't be louder. Tempted to run for Sister Monika, she decided instead to head for her assignment in the kitchen. Sister Monika would hear the cries and come soon enough.

First, though, she should find her button. If she had to ask the nuns for a replacement she would be made to pay somehow for her carelessness. Sister Monika would have her washing and ironing and mending until her hands bled. On her knees, heart pounding, she ran her fingers over the smooth floor.

"Amalia!" Sister Monika scolded, then stopped, taking a backward step. Confusion twisted her face. Amalia realized that the nun thought she was praying. Praying—for what? As if anything but a careful systematic search could locate something lost. She saw the white button where it had come to rest, under Liesl's crib, at the edge of a black tile.

"Help calm them," Sister Monika said in a matter-of-fact voice, leaning over Little Blackberry.

Amalia slithered across the floor, slid her arm beneath the baby's crib, stretched her fingers as far as they could reach, and just managed to touch the smooth, cool edge of the button. She concentrated to keep from pushing it farther away, wiggling it toward her with her fingertips. The babies screamed, even Little Blackberry. Sister Monika's attentions couldn't appease him. Amalia captured the button in one movement, slipping it into her pocket, rising, and picking up Liesl, the closest baby. She turned to face Sister Monika. The little body, hot and quivering, hid the gap in her blouse.

CHAPTER 7

---▼---

Dora closed her eyes and, to the sound of the train's steady clacking, went over and over yesterday's conversation with Sister Raphaela. The old nun had lifted Dora's chin with her finger. She could still feel the spot, felt there should be a mark as visible as the priest's thumbprint in the middle of her forehead on Ash Wednesday. She was surprised that Amalia, sitting on the edge of the seat facing her and pressing her nose to the window, didn't notice anything. Stooping slightly to look deep into Dora's eyes, Sister Raphaela had said, "Keep praying, dear. He'll let you know."

But I do know, Dora wanted to say. *It's my mother and sisters who don't. I can't tell them. I can't make them understand. Maybe Mama would, but Sofie and Amalia—never.* "He'll help," Sister Raphaela said as if reading her thoughts, her smile serene and sure. "Pray."

Amalia tapped her knee. "Can we switch places? I'm getting a stiff neck trying to see what's ahead. Can you see the mine yet?"

Dora stood, stooping to peer out the window. They had passed several mines and the towns around them, everything black with coal dust, smokestacks and dark metal chutes, their shafts reaching toward the colorless winter sky. "Not the one we're looking for," she said as she sat down, facing the way they'd come. In the dark space of her pocket she fingered her smooth wooden rosary, a present from her mother on her first Holy Communion. Her thumb caressed the tiny Jesus nailed to His cross. She squeezed Him so tightly that His sharp little feet pricked her palm.

"If it weren't so cold, I'd open the window," Amalia said.

"You're going to break it with your face, you don't watch out." Dora folded her hands in her lap.

Fog bloomed on the pane around Amalia's mouth and nose. She smeared it away. "I just can't wait to be home and see Sofie and Mama. I hope Lorenz stayed for Christmas. I want to run and scream and sing and go to the market and buy sweets. I feel like I've been locked up somewhere, with the witch—that's it, witches—without even a house made of sugar to nibble and make the suffering worthwhile."

"Don't talk about the nuns that way," Dora said. "It's not their fault you're homesick." Amalia looked at the nuns and saw witches. How could that be? Why would God let her see the beauty of religious life and not make it clear to Amalia or Sofie? Dora prayed they be forgiven for their careless and critical remarks about the nuns. She tried to minimize her pleasure at being the chosen sister. She tried to squelch any sense of superiority, knowing it was wrong. Sofie had been blessed with the ability to manage anything, and Amalia's sense of humor and curiosity about people drew them to her. It was hard not to bask, a little bit, in the sense of finally having been recognized.

Amalia jumped up, pressed both palms against the window, then struggled with the latches. "Dora, help me. There's the station, coming right up."

Before Dora could respond, Amalia had the window open. She shouted, hanging half out of the train, the wind whipping away her words before they could be heard. Dora wobbled to her feet, her heart and body lurching at the same moment, just as the train screeched to a stop.

Amalia had already gathered bundles and bags and was racing down the platform before Dora regained her balance and bent closer to the window, squinting. Sofie ran toward Amalia, smiling wide into her cheeks. Arms outstretched, they flew at each other. Following Sofie at a steady lope was Oskar with a calm expression a lot like Sister Raphaela's. He moved quickly, and yet his coat didn't flap, his hat stayed on his head, the newspaper folded neatly under his arm didn't flutter. Amalia and Sofie bounced up and down in each other's arms. Oskar waited, smiling, until Sofie released Amalia and dragged him forward. He removed his hat and nodded. Looking down on them, Dora had a perfect view of the bald spot on top of his head. She hadn't expected Oskar Schmidt to meet them at the station. She'd expected her mother.

The three of them turned toward the train window looking for her, wondering. People were beginning to board. Amalia pointed right at Dora.

"Come on, you little fool!" Sofie hollered, grinning. Dora knew she should wave or call back, but she stood where she was, frozen, scanning the platform for their mother. Where was she?

If their mother had come to meet them instead of Oskar Schmidt, Dora would have hurried off the train. She would be hugging Mama right now instead of letting herself be trapped in her seat by the frowning woman who shoved a bulging suitcase ahead of her and dragged a thin boy with a runny nose. In a moment the woman would settle in beside her.

Sofie yelled again. Amalia and Oskar beckoned. Dora grabbed her small valise and tried to squeeze around the boy and the suitcase and the unhappy woman. In the time it took them to stow their luggage, then back out of the compartment so she could pass, the desire to hug her sister and to demand the whereabouts of their mother, burst in her chest making breathing almost impossible.

Cold air stung her face as she climbed down from the train. Sofie wrapped strong arms around her, lifted her from the step, valise and all, and twirled her around before her feet had even touched the platform. When they finally stood side by side Dora noticed, with some surprise, that she was taller than Sofie.

"God in heaven, what took you so long?" Sofie didn't wait for an answer.

"Where's Mama?" Dora asked.

"Can't you say hello?" Sofie beamed and threw one arm around Amalia and the other around Dora. "I'm so glad you're home!" Her smile dimmed. "So glad."

Oskar removed his hat again and nodded. He grinned with his eyes as much as with his lips. Dora decided to be happy that Sofie loved him; only the eyes of a genuinely good man would crinkle like that. "So where's Mama?" she asked looking from Sofie to Amalia and back again. Sofie swallowed and smiled wider than before.

"Sofie said she had to stay home to take the bread out of the oven. She'll have the table ready and the food hot when we get home." Amalia glanced at Sofie for confirmation. Sofie nodded like a puppet. Oskar looked down at his hands on the brim of his hat.

Their mother had known what time to expect their train. She would have started the bread baking earlier, or more likely after the girls arrived so they could help. Worried, Dora trailed behind. She tripped on a curb, caught herself, and hurried after Oskar and her sisters toward the trolley stop.

They stood close together in the crowded car. People could afford to ride again, now that the mark was stabilized, and the streetcars were safe, now the resistance was over and an uneasy peace reigned. When the trolley squealed around a curve Oskar stepped on Dora's toe and apologized. Sofie linked her arm comfortably through his, as if she often stood that way. Amalia's eyes widened as she nudged Dora with her elbow. But Dora had already noticed how they fit together. Her squashed toe throbbed.

Easier to look at strangers. Gunstadt, a mere day's journey by train, had none of the coal miners and factory workers, and no French soldiers. Tauburg had a gritty vigor that it had taken time away in Gunstadt to appreciate or even notice—a simmering tension, frightening and exciting at the same time. Amalia kept bending to peer through the windows and sneak peeks at two men arguing beside her. Sofie and Oskar seemed to take all the energy, the bustle, for granted. Oskar looked at his folded paper. Dora squinted at the article. *Adolf Hitler, jailed and awaiting trial after his failed November putsch, is gaining support among the Bavarian middle class. Furious over loss of life savings they look to*…She came to the fold in the paper.

"Is the Captain still billeted at our house?" Dora asked.

"Yes." Sofie said, voice flat. She hadn't mentioned the Captain in any of her letters. Dora couldn't read her expression or her tone.

"Is it hard, still, between the students and him?" Amalia asked.

"What do you think?" Sofie asked. "Of course."

Amalia rolled her eyes. "You don't have to snap at me. I thought everyone might have gotten used to the situation, that's all." She glared at Sofie. "We're not even at the house yet. It's Advent. You could be nice."

"You weren't here during the summer when the soldiers would shoot at anyone out after 8:00. They made us keep the windows closed. It was impossible to sleep in that heat—"

"I know," Amalia said. "I read your letters."

"You don't know!" Sofie's voice was loud enough that the arguing men both stopped talking to listen to her. Dora tried to make herself small behind Oskar, but she was taller than he. She bent her knees a little and ducked her head.

"And the retaliation after the smallest acts of sabotage…they'd search houses, arrest people, even kill them. You can't pretend everything is all right! They stormed the beer garden and smashed some of the band's instruments. Oskar just managed to save his mandolin."

"Sofie," Amalia voice rose too. "I read the letters. I know. You told me."

"It's a miracle the letters made it through," said Oskar.

"You don't know," Sofie said. "You think you do, but you don't."

Over Oskar's shoulder Dora noticed Sofie seemed to fight tears. Oskar patted Sofie's arm.

"Sofie," Dora whispered. "Why didn't Mama come? We can't know what you haven't told us."

No one responded. Perhaps with the noise of the streetcar and the loud conversations, no one heard.

"I hope you got the letters we wrote." Amalia sounded conciliatory, but her attention seemed focused once again on passing buildings. The streetcar squealed to a stop. "We're here! You painted the door! It's so shiny."

Illuminated by the setting sun on that shortest day of the year, the blue door was as radiant as the Virgin's robes in the chapel's stained-glass window.

"Sofie and I painted it yesterday." Oskar held Sofie's hand up high so Dora and Amalia could see it. "She still has blue under her fingernails. We painted it for you, to welcome you home."

Sofie said nothing but gave Oskar a weak smile.

Dora imagined Sofie and Oskar side by side, dipping their brushes into a bucket of blue set between them, stroking the glistening wet paint over the old scraped and faded surface. Did they work their way out to the edges or start on opposite sides and meet in the middle? Either way, she could only imagine their bodies moving in some synchronized rhythm—though Sofie would be quick and efficient and Oskar slow and careful.

Oskar tucked Sofie's hand back under his arm and shepherded all of them off the streetcar.

The moment their feet hit cobblestone, Amalia clamped her sweaty fingers around Dora's hand and yanked her past Sofie and Oskar. Dora thought her arm would separate from her shoulder. Her suitcase banged against her leg.

"Wait!" Sofie's voice sounded strange. "Mama...Mama might..."

Amalia threw down her armload of bundles to open the door. Her grip on Dora stayed firm. "We're home! Mama, we're home!" Amalia dropped Dora's hand, plunged through the door, and disappeared into the dark of the kitchen. Dora bent to retrieve her sister's things.

Oskar stooped over the pile. "Permit me," he said.

Sofie pushed past them. "It's freezing in here." She hurried to the stove. Amalia stood near the table, looking around as if answers were written on the ceiling or the floor or the walls.

Dora blinked. Something was wrong besides the cold. There was no smell of bread baking, just stale traces of yesterday's cabbage under the sharp Christmas scent of evergreen. The table was bare but for the traditional wreath Mama always made—a circle of needled branches, simple and reassuring, with four candles evenly spaced, one for every Sunday of Advent.

Oskar delivered their bags to the small room off the kitchen. "I've been sleeping there," Sofie said. "You'll stay with me."

"What about Mama?" Amalia had stopped moving, her gaze fixed on Sofie's bent back. Dora watched the worn shoulder seams on Sofie's old coat strain as she poked around in the stove. She listened for their mother walking overhead, but all she heard was Oskar's firm step on the squeaky stairs.

"She sleeps up there." Sofie scratched around in the cold ashes. The clock ticked. Dora's head pounded. "In her own room. I'll get this started up in a minute," Sofie muttered into the belly of the stove.

Amalia stamped her foot. "What's going on?"

"There." Sofie closed the stove, stood and faced them without meeting their eyes. "It's getting dark. Turn on a light, Dora. I can't see you. We'll have to keep our coats on for a while. I'm sorry…"

"Sofie!" Amalia fumed. "Why isn't Mama here?"

"She's here." Sofie said, voice weary. "She's in her room, resting."

Amalia moved toward the stairs, Dora so close behind that when Amalia paused, Dora stepped on her heel.

"What's going on?" Amalia asked again.

Dora waited; Amalia blocked her path. She wanted to answer for Sofie. She knew the answer. Amalia knew it too, or she should, even a stranger could tell something was wrong, yet still Amalia seemed to be waiting for Sofie to lie again, to protect them for another few minutes. Dora didn't know which sister made her madder.

"She has a little cough," Sofie said, rattling pans. "She's just resting. Maybe I should go wake her up. Or maybe we should wait until I've got supper on the table. Karl and Lorenz are the other two mining students who stayed over the holiday. They said they would be back for—"

"Mama won't mind if we wake her," Amalia said. "While you make supper. Then we'll do the washing up. I'm sure she missed us." She pounded up the narrow back stairs, Dora one step behind. Sofie's "Yes, but…" faded behind them.

As they approached the closed bedroom door, Amalia slowed. Instead of bursting through, she stopped and, with raised eyebrows, looked at Dora. When Dora nodded, Amalia nudged the door open. The shuttered window kept out all light but for a few strips of late sun.

That woman in the bed, so fragile and still, had not baked any bread that day or the day before or last week. It was hard to imagine her on her feet. One didn't become a skeleton that fast, not even during the worst times of scarcity and hun-

ger. Dora and Amalia held hands and stood where they were, just inside the doorway.

Eyes closed, their mother leaned against a stack of pillows. On the table near
the bed stood an empty drinking glass, a brown ceramic bowl, and a crumpled
mass of handkerchiefs. Even in the dimness, the stains on the handkerchiefs were
visible.

"She looks terrible," Amalia whispered.

Dora breathed in a thick odor of rotting plums, rusty and sweet. During these
cold, short days of December the smell didn't come from decayed fruit.

Mama's eyes opened. They filled her bony face. "My girls." Her voice, familiar
and strong, pulled Dora toward her. She and Amalia bumped against each other
in their rush to touch her.

"Wait." Mama stopped them a half a meter from her bed with a lifted hand.
They froze midstep as if under a spell. Everything stopped except their thumping
hearts.

"I'm not feeling well today," their mother said. "I don't want you two getting
sick. I don't think you should come any closer. I'm sorry."

"Not even to hug you?" Amalia sounded starved.

Dora wanted to hug their mother too or be hugged by her, but she wouldn't
pout like Amalia. *God, make me strong*, she prayed. *Help me understand what's
happening to Mama, to us.* The smell, the cough, the bloodstained handkerchiefs,
the luminous eyes, the skin stretched tight over bones. Tuberculosis. Amalia had
to see it too.

Sofie bustled in with a cup and approached their mother. Mama waved her
away.

"Dora, you've gotten so tall," their mother said. "Let me look at you both. I'll
be better in no time with you home to cheer me up."

Amalia brightened.

Dora wasn't so easily fooled. Tuberculosis was not cured in no time. Perhaps
if they could bring their mother to Gunstadt, to the hospital…

"Has the doctor been here?" Dora asked.

Sofie moved her mouth as if to speak, then closed it. She held the cup before
her like a priest consecrating the wine. Dora wanted to shout at her to put it
down. Their mother systematically squeezed each joint from index finger to pinkie, moving back to do the thumb. She repeated the process in reverse on the
other hand, while the girls gazed fixedly at her pale knuckles. Bones, all that was
left after souls went to heaven and the body rotted away. Bones. Dora thought of

witches' bony fingers; the chicken bone Hansel used to trick the witch, to save himself from being roasted.

"Has the doctor been here?" Dora said again, louder.

Their mother folded her hands on the covers, fingers locked together. Dora thought she heard them click. "No."

"No?" Dora and Amalia said together.

Sofie tossed them a look, wild and wordless, and set the cup on the table, beside the bloodied handkerchiefs, before scurrying from the room.

They had never seen their sister scurry. "All we're seeing of Sofie since arriving home is her back," Amalia muttered.

Their mother shrunk into the pillows, tucking her head down between her shoulders. "I told Sofie no doctors," she whispered like a chastised child.

Amalia shook her head, disgusted. Dora wished Sister Raphaela were there. She would know what to do. From the hospital they sent TB patients to the sanitorium. Many recovered. But it probably cost more money than their mother had.

Sofie clattered and banged in the kitchen below. Someone slammed a door. Loud men's voices traveled up the stairs. Dora couldn't make out the words, but the tone was boisterous and jolly. Across the hall Oskar's door opened and closed. His footsteps faded as he descended to the kitchen. No doctor? Dora didn't know what to say. Amalia appeared at a loss for words herself.

Finally it was their mother who spoke. "I know what's wrong with me. All a doctor will tell me is to rest and eat well. I'm resting and eating as well as I can. I don't want to go to a sanitorium. I don't want anyone nosing around this house, saying we can't have boarders. I stay out of the kitchen."

"Sofie lied," Dora said.

"She told us you were home, baking bread." Amalia's face crumpled and her shoulders slumped.

"Don't cry," their mother said, her voice weak and commanding at the same time. "Sofie needs your help. She's been doing the work alone for too long."

"But what's wrong with you?" Amalia asked.

Dora rolled the rosary beads between her fingers. She said three Hail Marys as the slice of light across the bed reddened and faded. After a decade of the Rosary, Mama hadn't answered.

"If you're so sure you don't need a doctor, then you must know what's wrong. So tell us," Amalia demanded.

Their mother didn't even react to the rudeness. It was as if she hadn't heard. Dora wished she were back at the hospital, her mother with her. Doctors and nurses did help. They would have taken one of those X-rays when their mother first coughed. They would have found out the cause and they would have made her rest. Mama had tuberculosis. Amalia must know that too; they'd both seen cases at the hospital. There was even a surgery that could be done to relieve the pain but, now, with Mama so frail, it was sure to be too late. Downstairs a wave of laughter swelled and crashed. Their mother smiled in response.

Rage surged through Dora's body. "Why didn't you let us know?" she spit out. "Why didn't Sofie tell us?"

"I would have come home," Amalia said. "I would've come right away. You could've rested sooner. It's tuberculosis, isn't it?"

Sofie stood in the doorway in a white apron, gripping a long wooden spoon. "We're almost ready to eat. Mama, do you want to come down?" Dora hadn't heard the stairs creak. Sofie had appeared as silently as if she'd flown.

Mama opened her mouth to respond and started to cough instead. Dora grabbed Sofie's shoulders. "Are you crazy?" she asked.

"You're the crazy one." Sofie tried to laugh and shrug her away. "Let me go."

Mama's racking cough filled the room.

"Why didn't you tell us she was sick?" Dora yelled.

Sofie looked from Dora to Amalia and back to Dora. Her frightened expression startled Dora into releasing her grip. Their mother's painful cough braided them together, but there was no comfort in shared fear; it only grew larger. Finally Mama stopped coughing, but her labored breathing in the sudden quiet sounded worse than before.

"We're not going back," Amalia announced. "I think we can be more useful here than at the hospital."

Sofie bowed her head, her determination dissolving into silent tears. Amalia put her arm around Sofie's waist. Dora longed for the dim peace of the chapel, the comforting glow of the rack of candles. She wanted X-ray machines, doctors, Sister Raphaela's serene face. She moved closer to her mother and tried not to judge Sofie, or be angry with her for not telling. Sofie hid her face on Amalia's chest.

"Sofie will be glad for the help," Mama said.

"I hated it there anyway," Amalia said.

Was she imagining it or were they all waiting for Dora to say something? All she could think of to say was that Amalia hated Gunstadt, and she liked it, but that didn't seem right. Downstairs, a man laughed and another joined in.

"They're waiting for their supper," Sofie said.

"You all go on," said their mother. "Please, I should rest now, but seeing you girls together again makes me feel better. Come back to say good night."

Dora adjusted the covers as Mama sank back against the pillows, eyes closed. Sofie and Amalia whispered their way down the stairs; Dora trailed behind stopping on the bottom step to pray some more.

Surrounded by the silence of the rest of the house, the kitchen burst with light and noise. Oskar carried a stack of plates. Two other miners sat at the table across from each other, a pitcher between them and glasses in their hands. Their loud, good health was startling. They smelled of earth and sweat and snow as it begins to fall. Someone had lit three of the four red candles in the advent wreath.

Lorenz poured Amalia a glass of beer. Karl patted the bench beside him, but Amalia squeezed in by Lorenz, seemingly encouraged by his welcoming grin. She rubbed one teary cheek then the other with the back of her hand, and emerged smiling. She swallowed the glass of beer in two long swigs. Sofie and Oskar worked together putting dishes on the table. Everyone seemed to be trying to forget that above them, Hanna struggled to breathe, yet the awareness lay like a persistent hum, beneath the talk, the laughter, and the clatter of dishes. Dora closed her fist around her rosary beads, praying without moving her mouth.

"Little one," Karl called out to her. "Dora. Your sisters call you little but you're not, are you? You're taller than either of them. Come, sit here. Talk with me."

Dora couldn't move.

Everyone looked at her. Sofie and Amalia urged her with their eyes.

"She's been with the nuns too long," Amalia said. "We're not used to male company."

"Don't be afraid," said Karl. "We're like a family here."

Dora watched Sofie unwrap a blue and white cloth from half a loaf of bread and hand it to Oskar who set it on a board in the middle of the table. She handed him the bread knife. It would have been just as easy for Sofie to put things on the table herself, but she placed a heavy white soup tureen in his waiting hands as if handing him a baby. And the way he looked at her; they acted as though they were the only two people in the room. Too bad they weren't, since there appeared to be only enough food to fill two bellies. Dora's stomach ached.

"Sit down, silly girl," Amalia ordered. "Sit by Lorenz and me, if Karl frightens you!" Karl refilled Amalia's glass.

"Sit, Dora," Sofie said. "Everything's ready." Her smile was apologetic. "I hope the nuns fed you better than this."

"Looks like they did!" Lorenz pinched Amalia's rounded cheek and grinned.

"We'll be eating well again soon," said Oskar. "We're back at work and the mark is stable now. It's only a matter of time until we have meat at every meal."

"Stresemann and all his talking to the French," Karl complained. "Why work just to send German coal out of Germany? Glad to be rid of him, but he's already done his damage."

"The strike went on long enough," said Lorenz. "The French won't leave without their coke and coal. I'm just glad to be working."

"I'm glad to be working again, too," Karl agreed. "But I want the fruits of my labor to stay home, to keep these German girls warm." He grinned at Dora frozen in the doorway. "A man like Adolf Hitler talks a bit of sense and they put him in jail for it. Do you think the rich industrialists, those rich Jews, have suffered like we have during the strike? They don't care. For them a deal with foreigners is as good as a deal among countrymen. Not for me." He held up his glass. "Make a deal with a foreigner, but only after your own have enough to eat."

"Enough to eat," echoed Lorenz. "I'll drink to that."

"Me too." Amalia raised her glass.

Sofie stood in front of the soup tureen with Frau Becker's silver ladle in her hand. Dora was surprised they hadn't sold or traded it. "Sit," Sofie said again to Dora and to Oskar.

Dora sat next to Karl to prove she wasn't afraid. Oskar was on her other side. She edged closer to him. Across from her, Amalia actually grinned. Her face flushed a healthy pink; her eyes were bright. Again Dora felt a strange longing for the hospital laundry room, the clanking machines, the hissing steam, the running water—no needless conversation, no dire talk about the fate of the country, no lewd comments to make her blush. And upstairs from the laundry, in the wards, only sick strangers, no one she knew.

Sofie ladled thin potato soup into bowls and passed them around. "Don't expect a main course," she said. "This is it. Dora, why don't you say the blessing? You're the one God is most likely to listen to." Sofie smiled. Dora replayed her words, listening for sarcasm, but there wasn't any. She licked her lips. There was so much to say, she didn't know where to start.

Amalia snickered. Sofie jabbed her with an elbow. It was so quiet Dora could hear stomachs gurgle.

Dora squeezed her eyes shut. She tried to recite the blessing she'd murmured before so many meals. But around the table sat strange men and Amalia seemed drunk. Sofie was in love. Upstairs her mother was fading away. She could feel everybody waiting, thinking that the soup was getting cold.

"Amen," Oskar said. "Sometimes silent prayers are the most eloquent." She gave him a grateful smile as spoons clicked against bowls.

"Tonight we'll have music," said Lorenz.

"Of course," Karl agreed.

"We'll go up and see how Mama's doing first," said Sofie. "Maybe she'll come down, if she's rested enough."

Dora caught Amalia's eye. How could Sofie think there was a chance of Mama's joining them? They looked toward Oskar. He rubbed the heel of bread over the bottom of his soup bowl. Sofie broke the silence by hopping up to clear the table.

"Who wants to go tomorrow to cut a Christmas tree?" she asked.

"We can all go," said Karl. "Make an afternoon of it."

"Yes." Amalia brightened. "With all of us, we can haul a big one!"

Dora had forgotten all about Christmas, the birth of Jesus. If God's own son had to bear the weight of the cross, the pain of crucifixion, why should she expect to suffer any less? She would have to try harder.

As hungry as she was, Dora had barely touched her food. She started eating before Sofie could try to clear her plate. The lukewarm soup slid past the lump in her throat.

"I have a radical idea," said Lorenz. "We men will wash the dishes tonight, while you girls visit with your mother. Then we will have the music sooner."

"Yes," Oskar agreed, stacking soup plates. "Go on." He stopped work to touch Sofie's arm and Dora saw the heated excitement of their bodies meeting, even in that one small spot. Amalia looked toward Lorenz with a naked longing that embarrassed Dora, even though the miner was too busy talking with Karl to notice.

They stood around their mother's bed. "Do you think we should wake her?" Amalia asked.

Mama's uncoiled hair, full of snarls, made Dora want to reach for the brush.

"No." Sofie's voice was sharp. "She loses so much sleep coughing, we should let her rest. That's what she needs." She threw open the window.

"What are you doing? It's already freezing in here." Amalia said.

"The fresh air and the cold are good for her," Sofie said. "That and feeding her the best food we can. That's all we can do. That's all they'd do at a sanitorium."

"So you admit that it's tuberculosis," Dora said. "How long have you known?" A cold breeze blew through the room.

Sofie hustled them out into the hall and closed the door. They huddled in the narrow hallway.

Amalia glared. Her breath smelled like beer. "What were you thinking? You let her stop you from getting a doctor? Why didn't you call for us?"

Dora examined Sofie's anxious face. Amalia should be less harsh.

"Think," Sofie said. "However little food you get there, it's more than you would have gotten here."

"You don't know that," Amalia said. "The inflation hit nuns and hospitals just like anywhere else. You don't know what we've been eating. A loaf of bread cost two hundred billion marks in Gunstadt, just like it did here."

"Well, it doesn't cost that much anymore." Sofie leaned against the wall, hugging herself, one hand over the very spot Oskar had touched. "Things will get better now. Everyone says so."

"If I'd been here, I would have forced her to see a doctor," Amalia said.

"Well, you weren't," said Sofie. "Remember. I was the one with the short straw."

"We would have been here if you'd sent for us."

We. Us. Dora let Amalia argue and accuse. It freed Dora to be the forgiving one, the understanding one. She'd pretend, even to herself, that like Amalia she would have wanted to come home, if only she'd known. Poor Sofie had done her best so, of course, Dora understood. And as for returning to the hospital after Christmas? Caring for strangers when her mother was sick? Her mother had people to nurse her. The hospital was understaffed. Dora would be making a sacrifice, doing what was most right.

"Listen," Sofie said. "There is no money for a doctor. The miners earn nothing with the occupation and the strikes. Money is still almost worthless, even when we do get it. We know what a doctor would say—rest, good food, fresh air. I try to give her those things. It's not easy." She lowered her voice. "People do get better. She will get better. She will." Dora was glad Sofie's angry glare was directed at Amalia and not at her.

Whether it was the beer she'd drunk or the depth of her anger, Amalia would not be silenced. She leaned toward Sofie. "I want her to get better too. We all want her to get better. She looks like she's dying, Sofie. You should have called us."

Downstairs, the clatter of dishes stopped and the sound of instruments being tuned began. Sofie sat on the hallway floor. Her legs stuck out in front of her. She hid her face in her hands. "It happened so fast," she whispered. "She didn't cough so much before."

Amalia stood, eyes closed. Dora slid down next to Sofie, and prayed silently. *Dear God, Please give my sisters and me the courage we need to do Your will. You never give us more than we can bear. Help us, help us. We need Your help.*

A determined strength flowed through Dora, beginning in her hungry belly. She placed a hand on Sofie's thigh. "We weren't here," she said. "We don't know what it was like for you. We're just shocked to see how sick she is."

Sofie's shoulders shook. "The Captain will tell you. When Mama said she didn't want a doctor he argued at first, then said we should respect her wishes. We hoped for the best." Amalia sat on Sofie's other side, all three of them lined up, legs bridging the narrow hallway.

"We're back now," Amalia said. She took one of Sofie's hands from her face and held it. Dora considered doing the same, but the hand closest to Sofie was deep in her pocket holding her rosary and she couldn't let it go. Why had God made Mama sick? *Meditate on the joyful, sorrowful, and glorious mysteries of the rosary to immerse yourself in the mysteries of your faith.* Sister Raphaela's words rang in Dora's mind. Too bad Amalia understood mysteries as something to be solved rather than something to be appreciated. Sofie denied their very existence. One shouldn't ask questions the way they did. They would be happier—more able to accept what life held if they accepted God as she did and developed their faith in Him through prayer.

A head appeared at the top of the stairs, then the rest of the French Captain. They began to scramble to their feet, but he motioned for them to be still. They pulled in their legs to let him pass.

"Sofie, it is good your little sisters are home, no? Dora, Amalia, I am glad to see you again." His welcoming smile, gentle, accented voice, and friendly red face made him seem more like a kind uncle than an occupying soldier. "And your mother, how is she tonight? I tried to come home earlier to feed her supper, so you could enjoy your first night together, but work prevented me. I'm here now. Go sing with the men. Have fun." He rested a hand on Sofie's bent head. She responded with a grateful and unsurprised smile.

"She hasn't eaten anything," Sofie said. "I didn't want to wake her."

He stepped past them into their mother's room. Dora and Amalia both turned to Sofie. This man was an enemy, a usurper, a stranger, yet he entered their mother's room like he had every right to, like a husband, and Sofie showed no surprise.

"He loves her," said Sofie before they could ask.

"What?" Amalia sprang to her feet.

Sofie closed her eyes.

"It's clear that he's a good man," Dora said. Not only did her mother have Sofie and Amalia to nurse her, she had the Captain. There could be no doubt Dora belonged back at the hospital with those less fortunate.

She would miss her sisters and her mother, but it would be wrong to ignore God's call. The girls' dining room at the hospital suited her better than the boarding house kitchen. The chapel there welcomed her any time she needed to pray. But she knew better than to speak these thoughts aloud. No matter what she said, Amalia and Sofie would accuse her of running away.

Their mother started to cough, softly at first, then louder. Downstairs the men began to play—mandolin, violin, and concertina blending together. Captain Luc Didier attended their mother behind the closed bedroom door. Amalia looked about to say something, but seemed unable to find the words. Sofie stared at the wall. Dora prayed. Why couldn't they understand that with enough faith in God everything begins to make sense? What breathing was to the body, prayer was to the soul. Dora squeezed her eyes shut and prayed as she'd been taught until her mother's cough became part of the music, rising up.

CHAPTER 8

▼

Sofie wobbled across the river on ice skates, sandwiched between Oskar and Lorenz. They kept her upright with her arms tucked through theirs, gloved fingers interlaced. She bumped against one warm side then the other, threw her head back and laughed—a clear, careless sound that sailed away through the frosty air. She ignored Amalia standing alone on the bank under the low, tarnished sky. Even when Amalia yelled, "It's my turn for the skates!" Sofie pretended not to hear.

The last time she'd had this kind of fun was before Dora went back to Gunstadt, the day they cut down the Christmas tree, another wintry afternoon. They'd had a snow fight—Sofie, Amalia, and Dora against the men. The three sisters ganged up on Lorenz and sat on him all at once, rubbing his face with snow until he struggled free, knocking them every which way. Sofie smiled, remembering that she was the one he'd grabbed and tickled. He could have caught any one of them. Even though he knew she was Oskar's girl, he chose her over her sisters.

Back home they'd drunk schnapps with their coffee and decorated the tree with cut paper ornaments and candles. Sofie carried Mama downstairs to see it. She weighed so little Sofie hadn't had to ask the Captain or anyone else for help. Almost two months ago—Mama hadn't left her room since.

Few people would have braved the wind this frigid Sunday afternoon, but after dinner, when Lorenz said they were heading down to the river and Oskar pulled the extra pair of skates from his bag, Sofie knew she'd always wanted to ice skate and had to try it right away. Wordlessly, Amalia pulled on her coat and wrapped her scarf over her ears. The angle of her chin and set of her shoulders made it clear she wouldn't be left behind, one pair of skates or not.

"We shouldn't leave Mama alone for long," Sofie said.

"She isn't alone," Amalia answered, pulling the door shut behind them. "The Captain is with her. He said he had paperwork he could do beside her bed."

Paperwork. They knew he sat holding their mother's hand, humming French lullabies. When she was well enough, he spoke to her of Paris and private things.

If Amalia had stayed home to listen for their mother instead of waiting in the cold for a turn with the skates, Sofie would be having a still better time. Did Gretel ever think of leaving Hansel behind, in his cage in the house of cake, running while she had the chance? Did he ever think of leaving her in the woods?

"Sofie! Come on!"

Amalia's insistent voice triggered a rush of rage.

"Wait a minute," Sofie hollered. "Just wait!" With her whole body she pushed against Lorenz and pulled Oskar so they skated away from the shore.

"She's probably freezing," Oskar said.

Could a man be too considerate? Sofie suddenly thought so. She leaned closer to Lorenz. He pressed her arm tighter against him. Through their coats she felt his muscles moving and a tingling warmth. Oskar was the man she loved, the man she thought she would marry, but the arm he held was just an arm, while the one entwined with Lorenz's was beginning to burn with a slow heat.

"Sofie!"

She could see Amalia stamping her feet and blowing on her fingers. Oskar steered them back.

"Just a short turn for her." Lorenz's whisper tickled Sofie's ear. She shivered, neck prickling. Oskar should have been the one to say that. She glanced at him, but he looked straight ahead. Lorenz peered down at her from the corner of his eye. When he caught her looking up, he winked.

They glided across the bumpy ice and stopped. The wind rattled and scraped through the rushes.

Amalia, boots unlaced, sat on the frozen ground with her skirts wrapped tight around her stockinged legs. Sofie sat beside her and began to undo the skates with numb fingers. Amalia didn't have to stay at the boarding house. She could have gone back to Gunstadt. Oskar and Lorenz stood watching, lit from behind by the afternoon sun. Lorenz spun in a lazy circle as Sofie wiggled off the skates. Amalia wore a larger shoe; she would be lucky if she could even squeeze into them.

Boots felt strange and low after the ice skates. Sofie walked a few steps. She watched her sister loosen the skate laces and try to jam her foot inside. Amalia stripped off the thick socks she wore over her stockings. She wouldn't last long out there before her toes froze. Oskar helped Amalia lace up. Sofie knew her sister would prefer that Lorenz help her and in less of a brotherly manner, but Lorenz, a few meters out on the ice, skated back and forth smoking a cigarette. Sofie almost felt sorry for Amalia. How awkward and eager she was!

Oskar helped Amalia teeter to her feet. She squealed like a baby pig as they pushed off onto the ice. Lorenz attached himself to her sister's other side, and Sofie settled in for a long, cold wait. Out on the ice, trying to keep her balance, she had been able to forget her mother for a few minutes. She should go home and check on her, but something kept her at the river's edge, thinking uncharitable thoughts, her feet flat against the cold earth, watching Amalia skate. Their mother, so sick she could hardly lift her head from the pillow, was having a grand love affair with an attentive man full of secrets he shared only with her. Sofie, in robust health, thank heaven, and the right age for romance, stood freezing by herself. Her nose and cheeks burned with cold and a hard lump of resentment caught in her throat.

Amalia let go of both men and jerked along on her own. She tipped forward at the waist with her knees bent and her arms out at her sides, silly and graceless at first, but Lorenz and Oskar clapped and shouted encouragement as she straightened up and took longer strides. She was skating! Lorenz and Oskar sailed alongside, whistling and clapping.

"Just call me Sonja Henie!" Amalia hollered. Since the January radio broadcast of International Sports Week, everyone was intrigued by the spunky eleven-year-old skater from Norway. She'd placed last, but it didn't matter.

Amalia extended a leg out behind her, spread her arms, and glided on one foot for a moment before falling in a laughing heap, her skirt twisted around her legs. Both men helped to pull her up.

"Hey, Sofie! What do you think of that?" Lorenz yelled.

"Look at me!" Amalia called out. She wobbled, then straightened her ankles, arms wide open for balance. "Quick, Sofie, before I fall!"

Sofie gave her an indifferent wave. Before Amalia could feel disappointed, Lorenz smiled. She swooped forward, basking in his encouragement. If Sofie wanted to stand on the bank with a sour face, let her. She'd had her turn. Ever since Dora had gone back to Gunstadt Amalia had sensed Sofie's resentment, as if the boarding house and Mama belonged only to her. If Amalia were Sofie, she would be glad to have a sister to share the work and worry, but Sofie talked more with the Captain about Mama than with her. Lorenz skated up behind her and grabbed her waist, propelling her forward. She glimpsed Sofie, shadowy and far away, among the broken winter reeds. She shifted her weight, dug the blade of her skate into the ice, and angled toward the opposite bank, pulling Lorenz along. Sofie had Oskar. She didn't need Lorenz too.

Sofie clenched and unclenched her fingers deep in her coat pockets. Oskar skated toward her, but she was watching Amalia skate away from Lorenz, tumble, and struggle to her feet. Sofie wished she had thought to let go of the men, but she felt so good there between them. Now she wondered if she'd have another chance. Instead of being happy that Lorenz and Oskar found a pair of ice skates, she was furious that rich people had skates enough for everyone in the family. She could be out there with her sister, spinning and twirling, drawing intricate figures on the surface of the pond. She thought of Dora, imagined her skating across the polished floors of the hospital, head tipped back, staring through the ceiling toward the heavens.

Sofie tried to ignore Amalia's happy chatter and cheerful complaints as they undressed for bed in their crowded and cold bedroom.

"My knees ache," Amalia said. "Makes me think of Frau Becker. Look at this bruise."

Sofie nodded.

"Are you angry about something?" Amalia asked.

Sofie shook her head and fluffed up her pillow. She crawled under her covers. "I'm tired."

"I know you're mad," Amalia said sitting on the edge of her own bed to brush out her hair. "You hardly talked the whole way home and at supper, when that big argument broke out about the dissolution of the *Reichstag*, it was like you weren't even there. I thought there would be a fight. Lorenz and his buddies against Karl. Anyone else so outnumbered would shut up. Oskar kept looking at you to see what you thought and you didn't even notice. I know you're mad. You might as well tell me why because, I swear, I have no idea."

Sofie's feet were still cold from all that standing beside the pond. She rubbed them together instead of answering. The Captain told them their mother had slept all afternoon, waking only to cough. If she said to Amalia, our mother is dying, would that shut her up?

"You're not jealous because Oskar's nice to me? I'm the one who should be jealous. Oskar's your boyfriend, but anyone can see that Lorenz wants to be. The only one interested in me is Karl, and he'd like anything in a skirt." Amalia brushed her hair with long, steady strokes. "He even likes you better than he likes me, but he doesn't want to be third in line. You're much luckier and prettier than I am. At least you don't have this dark eyebrow stretching all the way across your face." Her voice cracked.

Sofie told herself to be generous; it wouldn't cost her anything to give a little laugh in return. She knew better than to coddle her resentment, but she turned toward the wall, curling knees to belly. She heard Amalia set the brush down and envisioned her expertly braiding her own hair, faster than their mother ever had. Sofie felt snarls down the length of her own absent locks like the itchy phantom limbs of the amputees. Her fingers ached to comb through the imagined knots and pick out the tangles.

"Sofie, please," Amalia said. "Tell me why you're mad at me. I won't be able to sleep, and I'm tired."

"I'm tired too," Sofie managed to say. Amalia's feet were quiet crossing the floor, but Sofie felt her approach.

"You and Dora left me here," Sofie whispered.

"It was Mama. It was the straws." Amalia sat on the edge of the narrow bed, her weight pulling the covers tight over Sofie. "Besides, you were lucky. If you knew what it was like with the nuns…"

"I didn't know Mama was so sick," Sofie swallowed. "I didn't know I'd be here trying not to notice her disappearing little by little every single day." The words flowed faster. "Where does a person go—the muscle and fat? The spirit? The energy? It has to be somewhere. Does that wasted body feel like our mother to you?"

"Sometimes." Amalia rested her cheek on Sofie's back. "She's just sick, Sofie. When people are sick—"

"She's dying." Sofie began crying, silently and hard. Amalia crawled under the covers beside her, wrapped an arm around Sofie's waist.

"When Frau Grunberg came by last week with that satin bed jacket for Mama, I was working in the kitchen, and I heard her and the Captain talking on the stairs," Amalia whispered. "Even he doubts she'll get better. He told Frau Grunberg he would pay for a doctor, but it was too late to be much help. He was crying. After Frau Grunberg left, I saw him sitting in the shadows near the top of the stairs, his face hidden in the bed jacket. I couldn't tell anyone. I try to forget I've seen him like that. Someone has to believe she'll get well. Nothing good ever comes of expecting the worst."

Sofie pretended to fall asleep under Amalia's heavy arm, but when Amalia got up, she was still awake and her feet stayed cold all night.

In the deserted parlor, Amalia turned on a lamp. She picked up Lorenz's news-paper from the sideboard where he'd carelessly left it, sat in the most comfortable armchair, and began reading.

"You're interested in that communist nonsense?" She felt Karl close, standing behind her, hands on the back of her chair, peering over her shoulder at the page. His breath smelled of beer and onions. Hunger pinched her belly. Her mouth watered.

"Can't sleep?" he asked.

"No." Eyes fixed on the smudged type, she thought about smoked ham and black bread warm from the oven.

Karl placed a heavy hand on her shoulder and rested his chin on the back of the chair. "Amalia, you want the wrong man," he said.

"What?" She swiveled her head around to look at him. "Ow, I think I hurt my neck." She rubbed the muscle hard with the flat of her hand.

"Here, let me." Karl gently took her wrist and moved her hand away. With his thumb and broad fingertips he found the tight spot and worked it until it soft-ened. She remembered his kindness after the night they stole the lard, when Lorenz had been so angry for so long. Nothing moved except Karl's fingers. The room held its breath. "How's that?" he asked.

Amalia didn't know what to say. Her calves ached. He could rub those next, and then her thighs and then…He knelt on the floor before her, Karl Braun. She shouldn't be allowing him such liberties. No one would blame him if he demanded more.

"Lorenz—" he began.

"Lorenz is interested in Sofie." Amalia hid behind the newspaper. "I can see that. I'm not stupid."

"Lorenz is married to his politics," Karl said. "He dares to flirt with Sofie because she's taken. God forbid a woman would require some of his precious time. He's at a meeting right now, stirring up trouble. Maybe if you were another Rosa Luxemburg he wouldn't be able to resist you, but look what happened to her. Put the paper down, will you?"

She turned a page. She should get up and go to bed, but she wasn't tired.

"Are you going to put the paper down?" Karl folded back the top so he could see her. She couldn't look at him. "You don't even know how pretty you are."

He was a sweet-talking liar; she was dark, hairy, and short, with breasts too big for her body.

"Amalia, I could make you happy," he whispered.

She folded the paper deliberately. "No you couldn't," she said. A healthy mother would make her happy. A home. A kitchen full of food. A garden. Sisters who cared more for each other than for miners or nuns." "Good night."

Karl dropped his forehead to the arm of the chair and didn't look up as she stood and clambered past his slumped body. On her way out of the room, she stopped to check the dirt in her nearest potted geranium. Dry.

The next morning passed like any other Monday. Then at 11:23, the church bells clanged madly, an insistent, wild alarm that wouldn't stop. Sofie was mopping the kitchen floor. Amalia came downstairs with a tray of food their mother hadn't touched.

"Something happened at the mine," Amalia said.

Sofie heard echoes of their mother's screaming the day their father never came home, the day the group of serious men came instead, hats in their hands. She tried to remember if Oskar was scheduled underground today. He usually was. Lorenz and Karl too. It was what they did, mined coal, but sometimes they did classroom work too, as part of their training. Today could be a classroom day. Chances were it was nothing, a practice for an emergency or some silly whim of the French. Accidents didn't happen too often.

Amalia ran to the door, and Sofie dropped the mop and joined her. All along the street heads poked from open doors and windows. People gathered outside. Several truckloads of men sped past, French and German together. Police cars and an ambulance raced by. The streetcar headed toward the mine was jammed so full the doors wouldn't close.

Sofie started after it, Amalia right behind her, sprinting through the cold, dodging the crowd.

"Wait!" Amalia grabbed Sofie's dress, but Sofie didn't stop or even slow down, and the waist seam tore halfway around.

"Look what you did," Sofie screamed over the sirens. She tried to gather up the fabric and keep running, but Amalia held tight. Sofie had to stop or lose her whole skirt. Around them people surged forward toward the streetcar stop. A group of aproned women blocked a passing wagon heaped with rags and leaped into the back.

Amalia's frightened face reminded Sofie again of that day when they were both small, staring at each other in the shadow of their mother's pregnant belly. Now, instead of clinging to her mother's skirts, Sofie was holding her own. She and Amalia scrambled into the back of a truck packed full of standing men with picks and shovels. The girls squeezed in, pressed up against the side of the truck bed. Sofie tried tucking her skirt into the waistband of her drawers. The men's hard silence prevented her from asking for the information she craved. She and Amalia were unnecessary, an afterthought; they should be home where they belonged, taking care of their mother instead of crammed in with muscled men who spent days and nights underground lifting tons of rock by the shovelful, the whole world pressing down on them. She'd never been down in a mine, though she'd tried to imagine it. She wanted to go down now and search for Oskar. Anything would be better than waiting.

They reached the gates near the pithead. She and Amalia were lifted down into the midst of a clamoring crowd of women. The truck passed through and the gates swung closed with a loud clang.

They pushed their way to the locked fence and wrapped their hands around the cold iron bars. Sofie tried to make sense of the bustle in the yard. Her wide eyes watered and stung in the frigid air.

"What happened?" Amalia asked a tall, gray-faced woman beside them. "Does anybody know what happened?"

"Roof collapsed in the Lorelei stratum, trapping some men. I'm sure that's where my husband's been working."

"Do you remember where Oskar was working today?" Amalia asked.

Sofie winced and shook her head.

She remembered Saturday night, the music, the cozy warmth of the parlor full of rowdy mining students; Lorenz and Karl urging Oskar to dance with her, Karl's concertina and Lorenz's violin calling as Oskar held her close, fingers wrapped around hers, hand pressed against her back so firmly she thought she could feel every callous and ridge and whorl on his thumb and fingers. He couldn't die and leave her with no one to touch her like that. She adjusted her torn skirt and rubbed the small of her back with her own inadequate, icy fingers.

"I can't remember anyone mentioning where they were working," Amalia said.

"Me neither." Sofie shook her head. It had been years since she had sneaked looks at anyone's mining log. She knew exactly where Oskar kept his, on a small writing table in his room, but she never bothered opening it. They were boring, the same entries over and over: worked pushing coal cars, replaced some timbers, built a floor section, removed timbers, on and on. If he had a book in which he wrote about his feelings for her—that would be worth looking at.

An ambulance separated the crowd and forced them back from the gate. They lost their front-row spots and Sofie stared into the patched back of an unfamiliar brown coat. She barely glimpsed her sister over a strange woman's shoulder. She pushed toward Amalia, but then the gate opened; the ambulance horn blared, and they were pushed back again, separated by the moving vehicle.

"Did anyone see who that was?" the women asked. It could be anyone.

"There was more than one man put in there," someone said. A child shrieked, a sharp sound that cut through the murmuring, frightened hum of the waiting women in a way that even the ambulance horn had not. It triggered a sudden unraveling—wails, screams, lamentations. Would someone tell them what was going on? Sofie pushed back to the front, past women equally determined to see. Numb, she used her frozen body as a weapon, a battering ram. She clung, squinting, to the bars of the fence. Groups of black, slump-shouldered men emerged from the mine shaft. She could see someone being carried. The only way to recognize a loved one from such a distance was by his walk. She hung onto the cold iron and wouldn't be moved.

"Do you see anyone?" Amalia asked, right behind her, breath hot on Sofie's neck. "Sofie, that looks like Karl!"

It was Karl, carrying one end of a makeshift stretcher. There was no mistaking that swagger. Sofie screamed, Amalia with her. "Karl! Karl! Over here. Over here!"

He didn't seem to hear them, intent on his task. Sofie and Amalia kept shouting his name.

Sofie half-climbed the fence, so as not to lose sight of him as he brought the injured man to a spot on the ground near the sorting sheds. She glimpsed other men lying there and strained without success to see who they were or if they moved.

She yelled and waved at Karl as he hurried back across the yard with the empty stretcher. She wouldn't let him disappear without telling them something. Slipping down the bars, struggling to hang on amidst the pushing, screaming his name, she wouldn't give up. Finally, he turned.

He shaded his eyes with a hand, then, to her relief, seemed to recognize her. She gripped the fence with her feet and one hand while wildly beckoning him toward her. He waved her away.

"Karl, where's Oskar?" She could barely make herself heard above the crowd of clamoring women. "Oskar?" she hollered again.

He waved again with his whole arm, dismissing her, no mistaking it. Still she yelled.

Karl transferred his section of the stretcher to a man beside him and loped over to the fence. Sofie tried to reach for him, but he didn't come close enough. "Go home," he said harshly.

"But—was Oskar down there? Is he all right?"

"I said go home. There's nothing you can do here. Go home." She couldn't read any facts in his forbidding expression, other than the lack of any good news. She couldn't keep her hand and arm from straining to grab at him; if only she could reach his belt or shirt collar, she'd latch on, pull him toward her with all her strength, and force him to tell her all he knew.

"I don't know anything now," he said. "I don't want to make guesses. Go home. Amalia, take her home."

He turned with a finality that silenced Sofie. Amalia steadied her as she slipped down into the panicked throng.

"Let's go home and wait where it's warm," said Amalia.

Sofie scanned the men milling about the pithead, studied others moving purposefully between the machine house and the office, looking for Oskar's neat walk and his small man's way of standing tall. She wouldn't budge. Once she lost her spot she'd never get it back.

"We're going home." Amalia pried Sofie's fingers from the fence and dragged her toward the street.

Hanna called to them the moment they entered the house. They exchanged guilty looks. Half an afternoon had passed without a thought given to their mother. No worry about her condition, no concern over whose turn it was to care for her. It was like the joke about the doctor prescribing a blow to the head for the person with the aching toe.

"I'll go," Amalia said. "You rest."

"How do you expect me to rest?" Sofie followed her sister up the stairs.

"What happened?" Mama formed the words with dry, cracked lips.

Amalia offered a sip of water which their mother waved away.

Sofie answered in a whisper. "An accident at the mine."

"Oskar?"

"We don't know."

Mama breathed and coughed, so weak she could barely hold a handkerchief to her mouth. She wiped away a strand of bloody saliva.

"Open your mouth." Amalia brought the cup to Mama's lips. Water dribbled down her pointed chin. She didn't swallow. Sofie met her sister's eyes, those clear brown eyes so much like their mother's. Mama's stared feverishly from her bony face. When Sofie offered to brush her knotted hair, she refused by opening and closing her eyelids. Those huge eyes were the only part of her that moved as she looked from Sofie to Amalia and back again.

"I loved your father," she said after a long silence. "Then he was killed."

"We know," Amalia said. "We loved him too."

Sofie collapsed into the rocking chair and pressed her head into her hands to stop the throbbing.

"Maybe you should go lie down," Amalia whispered.

Sofie couldn't bear to be alone with the images tumbling through her mind—Oskar trapped behind a wall of rubble, crushed under a slab of stone, gasping poisonous air; Oskar in the greeny light of the morning woods kissing her; Oskar reduced, as her father was, to a tragic story, but unlike her father, with no children to hear it or care or remember.

"We would still be on the farm if he'd worked above ground," Hanna whispered on. "The farm would be yours. All of it."

"Shh," Amalia said.

"I wanted to be a grandmother on my farm. Collect eggs with my grandchildren. Make sausage like Frau Hagen's. All my dreams dead, with him. Miners." Derision ripped through her weak voice.

"Mama, it's okay," Amalia couldn't stop their mother from talking. The words spilled over Sofie like boiling water.

"Now, Frau Hagen, she did it all, slaughtered the pigs, ground the meat, filled the casings. A pipe—she smoked a pipe and told stories."

Hanna had talked about Frau Hagen so many times before that Sofie had a vivid picture of the old woman, washing blood from arms thicker than most people's thighs, filling her pipe, putting her feet up and, with eyes half closed, telling little Hanna whatever stories she asked for and many she didn't, the smell of blood and tobacco and old-woman sweat weaving through the stories' wishes, punishments and rewards.

"I loved him," Hanna said. "He gave me that music box."

"Yes," Amalia said. "We know."

Sofie couldn't bear to hear the music box story again, her mother's ridiculous pride in only crying twice in her life, how even as a baby Mama never fussed in church, and even when her brother drowned, she remained dry-eyed. The only times she shed tears, she'd told them, was when the men from the mine told her that her husband had died and when the music box made her weep—the combination of the sad song, her future husband's easy company, and the love driving him to work the many hours necessary to buy such a gift for her. "Just listen," he had said, winding the key, lifting the polished lid. "And watch." They'd bent their heads close together as the small, studded cylinder rotated, notes filling their ears. Sofie couldn't bear hearing how her father had held her mother while she cried and didn't take his arms away until she was finished, hours later. Oskar hadn't had the chance to care for Sofie in such a way, and now, it seemed, he might never have one.

A careful knock at the bedroom door and Captain Didier appeared, disheveled and concerned.

"Any news?" Amalia asked.

"Four men killed so far, many still trapped."

"This is your fault," Sofie said. It felt good and right to blame him. "You don't belong here forcing men to work night and day to repay a debt we don't even owe, to keep your greedy country going. "Why don't you go back to France where you belong and leave us alone?"

"Sofie," he said. "You're upset."

"Yes, I am. Of course, I am."

Hanna coughed long and loud. Captain Didier rubbed her back as she leaned forward, gasping, choking, and spitting into the jar he held for her.

"Stop it, Sofie," Amalia warned in a whisper. "He's just one man. He's good to us. To her."

Hanna caught her breath. "Don't marry a miner," she said. "Either one of you. I mean it."

When the men came back, and some of them surely would, they'd be hungry. Sofie left her mother in the hands of the enemy and went to make potato soup.

Sofie and Amalia dozed at the table, heads resting on their folded arms. Just before midnight Karl arrived with the news, too hungry and exhausted to wash away the layers of dirt and coal dust.

"They're on their way home," he said. "Oskar and Lorenz. I helped to dig them out. We'd almost moved on to another spot when I heard a tapping. It was them."

Sofie leaped to set the table and heat the soup. She wished she had sausage, apple pancakes, eggs. She wanted to feed Oskar and all the rest of them well, these men, these warm, breathing bodies with enough strength and determination to dig their way to fresh air through a wall of rock.

She hovered just outside the door, on the stoop, peering down the dark street, waiting. She didn't see him until he was there right beside her, pulling her close, covering her clothes and skin with dirt. They kissed and she laughed out loud at the grit between her teeth.

Lorenz told her the rest of the men would be along later after a stop at the beer hall. "Oskar insisted we come straight here," he said and tweaked her nose.

In the kitchen Sofie ladled her share of the potato soup into the three bowls she filled for the men. Amalia caught her eye and with a nod gave permission to do the same with hers.

The men slurped their soup. If it weren't for the dirt and the late hour and the thick relief in the air, it could have been any evening meal. Sofie sat next to Oskar and put a hand on his knee. She wanted to touch him all over, make sure he was whole. Karl, quieter than he'd ever been, chewed each bite of gristly meat for a long, long time. Lorenz spooned soup into his mouth and stared at one spot.

"Was it terrible?" Amalia asked.

Sofie wanted to ask the same thing, but the words sounded so naive she was glad she hadn't spoken. Still, she waited for the answer.

Karl continued chewing and shook his head. Lorenz looked to Oskar.

Oskar said, "It's hard to think about going back down after something like that. I don't know if I can do it."

"Don't!" Sofie squeezed his knee. "Don't, there are other jobs."

"You're a miner," Lorenz said. "You'll go back."

"What other jobs?" asked Karl. "This is all we know."

Oskar pulled a coal-streaked rag from his pocket and blew his nose.

"We thought you died," said Amalia. "We thought of our father. I was barely walking, but I remember that day." Her lip trembled.

Sofie glared at her. If Karl and Lorenz and Oskar weren't crying, what right did Amalia have to weep?

"All I could think about was blasting through it all. I wasn't going die, or let my friends die, mining coal for the rich people to share with the French. Bad enough that's how we have to live," Karl muttered.

"The whole time I dug, I thought about my mother being notified of my death," said Lorenz. "I figured the company would let her know, but I wondered exactly who and how. I tried to imagine you girls at her table and over coffee and cake telling her about my last days. About dancing in the parlor, skating."

Everyone waited for Oskar to speak. "My parents are dead." Under the table his hand covered Sofie's. But I have you, she imagined his fingers telling her.

She heard echoes of Hanna's coughing. Soon, she, Amalia, and Dora would be saying the same thing. *Our parents are dead.* Then Amalia would have something to cry about. They all would.

They ate from Frau Becker's dishes, served soup from her tureen with her silver ladle. Frau Becker was dead, but her things remained. They used them every day. That's how it would be when their mother was gone. Soon. Sofie thought they should call Dora home, though Amalia wanted to wait. She would have to insist.

"Hell couldn't be worse than being trapped in a mine," Karl was saying.

"Hell *is* being trapped in a mine," said Oskar. "Hell is unemployment and hunger and war. Hell is right here on earth. All anyone can do is try to make it better."

"How?" Karl asked, interested and mocking at the same time.

"Be kind. Be fair." Oskar shrugged. "What else?"

"What about angry?" Lorenz asked. "Has any big change happened without anger? Someone has to be angry."

Karl and Lorenz leaned in toward each other, over the empty plates, as if eager to get back to everyday conversation.

Lorenz slapped the table, rattling the dishes. "Oskar, people like you keep voting for your Social Democrats, be kind, be fair, talk, talk, talk, let everybody else do the dirty work, leave it up to everyone else to get angry for you. Where is your passion, man?"

"Oskar must be saving it for the bedroom." Karl grinned.

Sofie bit her lip, trying not to smile.

"You don't have to be angry to speak up or act," Oskar said mildly. He squeezed Sofie's fingers.

Lorenz sighed and hit his forehead with the heel of his hand. Amalia tried to stifle a giggle or a sob; Sofie couldn't tell which.

"What are you laughing at, little girl?" Lorenz leaped at the chance to lighten the atmosphere. He pinched Amalia's cheek and tickled her under the chin. She laughed out loud.

"So what will you do if you don't go back to the mine?" Karl asked.

"I'll go to America," Oskar said quietly. The hairs stood up on Sofie's arms and the back of her neck.

"You need a sponsor," said Lorenz.

"I've got one," Oskar said.

Amalia's mouth dropped open. Sofie kept her face blank.

"Yeah?" Karl shook his head. "Who is this mystery sponsor and why have we heard nothing about him before? Or it is a her?" He elbowed Lorenz and they both grinned.

"An uncle of mine," said Oskar. "A sailor who jumped ship in America. When they wouldn't let the men leave the boat he left his gold watch for collateral. No one could believe someone would give up a watch like that. But he did. The papers are approved on the American side of things. I found out a few days ago. I just have to get them stamped here."

Lorenz and Karl stared, speechless. Sofie glanced at Amalia, who chewed her lip and blinked.

"Sofie," Oskar said. "I planned to tell you as soon as we had a moment alone. I didn't mean to say it like this. The accident...I wanted to..."

"That's all right." She stood up and gathered plates.

Frau Becker's ladle gleamed in the empty tureen. Amalia sat silent, eyes full of questions. Sofie willed her to just go ahead and ask, then hoped she wouldn't.

"I'll help with the dishes, Sofie," said Oskar. "Why don't you all have a little music? It's still early."

"Too tired for music," said Lorenz. "Good night."

"Tomorrow," said Karl and followed him from the room.

Sofie's empty belly ached. She lifted covers from the pots and pans on the stove, estimating the amount of food left for the other mining students and the Captain. Maybe there was enough for Amalia and her to have something. But the other men would have worked as long and hard as Oskar, Lorenz, and Karl. They would be just as hungry or hungrier. Food wouldn't ease the spasms in her stomach anyway. The pains hadn't started until Oskar mentioned America.

"I'll check on Mama," Amalia offered tentatively but made no move to get up.

"Have some soup," Sofie said.

Amalia hesitated. "No."

"They'll each do with one less mouthful. Who will notice?" Sofie filled the ladle without looking at her sister.

"You have it, then," Amalia said.

"No, I'm fine."

Oskar filled the dish pan. "Eat something," he urged. "Both of you."

"I'll check on Mama," Amalia said again, voice firm, and hurried off.

"We'll eat later," Sofie told Oskar. At the sink she soaped a soup plate, rinsed it, and passed it over. He dried it thoroughly and was ready for the next one just as she handed it to him. Working in perfect rhythm, neither spoke. The small splashes of the water, the little clicks of the stacking plates, the soft flap of the dish towel. Oskar's steady calm soothed her.

Oskar dried the last dish. "Sofie?"

She didn't answer, just clenched her hands in the soapy water. From behind he wrapped his arms around her waist. "You'll come to America with me, won't you?"

She stiffened.

"You'll marry me? My uncle will sponsor me and my wife," he said, holding her tighter.

This was a marriage proposal, an event of huge significance, yet Sofie liked the moment she put a clean dish into his ready hand better, and thought the wet plate, dripping and warm, was what she'd remember later. She wondered how she could leave Amalia and Dora for a whole new country—all the while knowing that she would. She saw herself and Oskar on a boat staring back toward Germany. The wheels of a wagon or an automobile left a track in the earth, a road you could follow and find your way home. If she threw out pebbles from a ship to mark the path, they'd sink.

"We can send for Amalia once we're settled," he said. "Dora, too."

He didn't mention Mama. Oskar knew Mama wouldn't live long enough to see them go. He would take care of himself and her, and her sisters if they'd let him.

"Sofie?" She still hadn't answered. His tone hinted at an impatience she'd never heard in him. She liked it. Say you love me, she thought. If you say you love me, I'll have to say yes. He was kind. He helped do the dishes. His warm body fit nicely against her back. Her mother was dying. It was only a matter of time before Dora was locked behind convent walls. And Amalia...they'd send for her. It would be easy to earn enough money in America. It wouldn't take long. "Will you come with me?" he asked. She turned around, the sink edge digging into her back. She concentrated on the blue lines of coal dust tattooed into scars on Oskar's neck, the steady pressure of his fingers on her shoulder blades, the tingling all over her body. Kiss me hard, she thought. Kiss me really, really hard, so that my lips bleed. She pressed her mouth against his. Her breasts pushed against his chest. If he tore open her blouse and kissed her all over, she'd forget she had sisters and a dying mother. Marrying him, sailing to America—it would all be as easy and right as handing him a clean, wet plate.

He pulled her closer. He kissed her face, her throat, held the curve of her bottom in the palms of his hands. "Yes," she said. "Yes." She opened her eyes to Amalia's startled and embarrassed face in the doorway, then closed them. When she opened them again, Amalia was gone.

CHAPTER 9

▼

Amalia jerked awake, snapping her head back, and setting the rocking chair in motion. She looked around the dimly lit room for whatever had startled her, at her mother lying quiet, eyes closed, thank heaven, after a rough night. Sofie, Amalia and the Captain, bless his strange French heart, had taken turns staying with Hanna through the night during the past two weeks. Amalia was sure her nights were hardest, filled with exhausted coughing—coughing that went on until all of Mama's insides seemed to gush from her mouth. Both Sofie and the Captain said they were able to lie down and sleep occasionally, but Amalia never managed more than dozing in the rocker.

She listened hard for the sound that must have disturbed her. It hadn't been a cough or her mother would still be coughing. She never coughed just once anymore. It couldn't have been a footstep; the house stood silent. No wagons or automobiles passed outside at this odd hour, when both those who stayed up late and those who woke early slept. She strained her ears. No sound, nothing but the deep, thick quiet. The room smelled like the latrine, but Amalia knew the chamber pot was empty. Mama couldn't use it without help.

Mama's ragged breathing, steady as a heartbeat or the thump of dough against the bread board, where was it? Amalia leaped up, and the blanket slid off her lap, onto the floor tripping her as she rushed the three steps to the bed. The empty rocker thunked behind her.

She touched her mother's sunken cheek with the tip of her finger. Its coolness surprised her, even though in the stumbling moment between chair and bedside, she'd realized her mother was dead. Amalia had never tried to picture this moment, expected for so long. She never wondered if she, Sofie, or the Captain would be first to know Hanna had passed on, never imagined how still the body would be, no more coughing or twitching or shifting of shoulders, lips shut tight. No more answers or advice, no more stories.

Lately, washing blood or watery feces from the nightdress Amalia had cut up the back into a hospital gown—a trick learned from the nuns, life seemed an unending routine of work and dirt, work and dirt. As she rubbed her mother's back with its protruding spine or rolled her gently to arrange the pillows under her—Mama sometimes recognizing her, sometimes not—Amalia had wished she'd hurry up and die.

She wished she'd never wished it. No more phlegm and excrement. No more life. Hanna Heller Bauer Kleinschuster had survived war, a flu epidemic, the deaths of her parents, her brother, her husband, the loss of her farm, only to die sick and exhausted at thirty-seven years old. No more mess. No more trouble. No more pain. End of story. And they hadn't told Dora.

Maybe they should have forced their mother to see a doctor, Amalia thought for the more than hundredth time, but there was no money and, as Sofie said, they'd done most of what would have been done for her in a sanitorium. Most, but not all. They had so little food. But she wouldn't eat even the food they'd brought her. The Tauburg air, full of smoke and coal dust—she might have gotten better in the mountains.

Amalia couldn't find her tears. She ached for a hug, for her mother's fingers on her face. One of her mother's thin hands rested on the blanket, just centimeters from Amalia's hip, but she was afraid to touch it, afraid the cold would freeze her fingers, chill her blood and force her to believe she was an orphan now. She had her sisters, but they were leaving. Sofie was Oskar's. They would be Americans. Dora was God's and would be a nun. There would be no farm with all of them together the way they were meant to be, the way they'd promised. Their mother was dead.

She had to tell Sofie—Sofie sleeping soundly, dreaming of America. Just the day before, she and Oskar had come home triumphant, late for supper, with their stamped papers from the emigration department in Koln, the blanks all filled in. Heads bent close together, they practiced the English phrases spelled out on the back of the pamphlet. They showed off to Amalia, Karl, and Lorenz: "Where is the baggage examined? Where can I change German money? Does this car go to the German Consulate, Battery Place, Whitehall Building?" They laughed and laughed. Karl and Lorenz laughed too, in spite of Lorenz's indignation over Germans and their money abandoning Germany. Everyone forced tongues around English vowels and consonants. Amalia and Sofie avoided looking at each other.

"Amalia," Oskar said more than once, during the hilarity. "You'd better practice. We'll be sending for you before a year goes by."

"Here." Sofie held the pamphlet in front of Amalia and pointed to a phrase halfway down the page. "Try this one." Amalia wanted to snatch their precious paper and tear it up. Instead she reached for it, held it before her with two hands, like a hymnal. The words, even the column written in German, blurred.

"We should all practice this one," Sofie said. "'Where can I get something to eat?' That's the first question I'm going to memorize."

The crisp paper rattled in Amalia's shaking hands. Sofie took it back. Oskar slid it together with his into an inside jacket pocket, close to his heart.

Amalia should have shredded those papers. Replacing them could have taken weeks, slowed everything down.

She collapsed onto the edge of her mother's bed. If Sofie had told their mother she was leaving, Amalia could blame her death on the shock of the news. But Sofie hadn't told her. Oskar had figured they wouldn't sail until October. They all knew Hanna couldn't live that long.

Amalia told herself to wake Sofie. They'd call Dora from the telephone in the mining supply store two doors down. She rose to open the shutters and looked out the same window from which they'd waved to their mother all those years ago. The sky shone metallic gray. Night would be over soon. If only she could see the sun rise, but buildings blocked the horizon.

She stared over the empty street and instead of racing downstairs, hollering for Sofie, leaned over the sill, and remembered dangling her sister's braid over the street. No passerby had ever stopped to ask what they were doing. Rapunzel's mother craved rampion from the witch's garden so intensely that she threatened to die if her husband didn't steal it for her. Amalia, tired of breathing soot-filled air, suddenly wanted to plant things, pick fresh apricots, feed her garbage to hungry pigs. She wanted to be in the country with her sisters collecting eggs and her mother in the kitchen canning beets or beans or peaches, face sweating, not from fever, but from the heat and work, steam frizzing the tendrils of hair that escaped from her neatly pinned up braid. Amalia's eyes stayed dry, but her throat ached, and her mouth watered.

After eating a salad of witch's rampion, Rapunzel's mother longed for it three times as much as before. Her husband, caught, made a deal with the enchantress—all the rampion he wanted in return for the child when it was born. The witch took the baby and no more mention was made of the parents. They must have grieved. They must have argued. Of course, they eventually died, but before they did, had they seen their daughter again? Had they known of her rescue, their royal son-in-law, their twin grandchildren? A wisp of pink streaked the sky, over the shops and houses across the street. Amalia longed for the days when waiting for their mother eventually brought her home.

The bedroom door opened a crack. Sofie whispered, "Amalia?"

"You don't need to whisper," Amaila said. "She won't wake up. She's gone. Dead."

Sofie's knees hit the floor. She sobbed into the deep folds of the featherbed. Amalia wished she could cry as easily, with such utter abandon. Wherever their mother was now—and Amalia really didn't believe there was such a place as heaven—at least her worn-out body could be buried, at least there was an end to pain.

"We never called the priest," Amalia said, when she couldn't listen anymore. "Dora will never forgive us."

Sofie stopped crying long enough to look stricken. "Mama's soul is wandering in purgatory!" Her tears started again. "She would have wanted the priest."

"You don't really believe that. Mama hadn't been to church in ages," Amalia said.

"Only because she was sick. She always liked to go."

"She went with Dora," Amalia said. "You told me yourself she stopped right after we went to Gunstadt."

"She was sick."

"Not right away. Not too sick to go if she wanted to. Anyway," Amalia said. "We can't tell Dora. Even if she asks."

"We should have called the priest. Oh! Such a terrible mistake!" Sofie wailed.

"The real mistake is that our mother is dead."

"We can't tell Dora," said Sofie. "About not calling the priest."

"The other mistake was not calling Dora home," Amalia said. "She would have wanted to say good-bye."

"Did you say good-bye?" Sofie asked. "I didn't."

In the brightening room they looked helplessly from each other to their mother's body. Too late. Too late. The words hammered in Amalia's head.

"We have to pray," said Sofie.

"I don't believe in purgatory," Amalia whispered.

"Even so," Sofie said.

The Captain charged past them in his nightshirt. Amalia had never seen him out of uniform. He stood over the bed, shoulders sagging, bony wrists and ankles exposed. Sofie and Amalia hung back near the foot of the bed.

"Rest easy, Hanna," he murmured. He clutched her hand and kissed it. "No more pain." He caressed her cheek, cupped her chin, and tucked a piece hair behind her ear.

"We knew she was dying?" Sofie said. "Why didn't we call the priest?"

The Captain arranged their mother's hands, one on top of the other and covered them with his own. Amalia watched, ashamed of her own reluctance to touch the body.

"I called," he said without looking at them. "She had her last confession. She received the sacrament."

"When?" Amalia asked. He might be making it up to comfort them.

He slowly straightened and turned away from the bed. "Yesterday."

Sofie threw her arms around him. He awkwardly patted her head.

"Hanna asked me to. Sofie, you and Oskar were in Koln. Amalia, I don't know where you were."

She'd been less than a kilometer away, at the market, haggling over a scrap of dry ham. She'd talked the woman down to half her original price and felt she'd accomplished something until she got home and discovered how shriveled and tasteless it was.

Sofie stood close to the Captain, too willing to let him share their grief. He'd known their mother for just a little over a year. He'd barely spoken to Sofie and Amalia the whole time he'd occupied their home. Amalia had to admit he'd tried, but they'd done nothing to encourage him. They didn't even know him. Captain Luc Didier. He didn't look like a captain now, this grieving man, skinny and red, in a night shirt that revealed his knobby knees.

"I loved her," he said. "I wanted to marry her and take her home with me when this occupation ended. She was the strongest woman I ever met. Why couldn't she beat this sickness? She was so young. We might have had a child."

What? Their mother, old enough to be a grandmother, with a baby, a little brother or sister with French blood in its veins? A high-pitched whimper escaped the Captain, and Sofie mumbled something meant to soothe.

"I'll get dressed," he said. "And call the undertaker."

"Thank you," said Sofie.

"She wasn't strong," Amalia said, after he'd left the room. "She chose one lousy man after another. She couldn't even take care of us."

"How can you say that?" Sofie's eyes blazed. "With her lying right here."

"She can't hear me. She's dead. Dead. Dead. Dead." Even as she said it, Amalia wondered. Maybe she wanted her mother to hear. Everybody leaving. France, purgatory, heaven, America, convent, hell. What difference did it make to the one left behind? "A baby?" Amalia couldn't stop. "He wanted her to have a baby. With him!"

"I'll call Dora," Sofie said. "We should do it right away."

"She was too old to have a baby, wasn't she? But then she was too old for a love affair and that didn't stop her."

"I admire her for that," said Sofie. "A person can be too practical."

"I don't think so."

Sofie winced. "I'm going to call Dora."

Amalia waited until the door closed and approached her dead mother. She wanted to scream or to slap her awake, but stood trembling with clenched fists, hating herself.

Their mother's body lay in the low white building near the cemetery by the time Dora's train thundered into the station and shuddered to a stop. Overwhelmed by noise and dirt and people, Amalia let Sofie scan the windows for Dora, while she stared up at the gold-tinged clouds scudding across the early evening sky. She thought she smelled traces of thawing earth, even through the stench of burning coal.

People descended from every car. "Look at her. She's so thin!" Sofie said. She pulled Amalia by the crook of her arm toward the front of the train. Amalia still couldn't see Dora. She felt dizzy, tripping along, shoes scraping concrete.

Sofie waved frantically with her free hand, yelling Dora's name above the rumble of the waiting train and the shuffle of the crowd. Dora stepped from the train into the throng of passengers moving toward the station, and Amalia lost sight of her until she stood right before them, face oddly tranquil, holding her small brown suitcase. Her placid smile didn't change to acknowledge them; it seemed sketched on. Her huge blue eyes didn't blink. Amalia wanted to pinch her, but Sofie had already wrapped her in a hug.

"Why didn't you call me before she died?" Dora asked. At close range her calm seemed too deliberate to be real. The hysterical quaver of her voice gave her away. "I wanted to say good-bye."

You should have stayed home when I did, Amalia thought. *If people stayed where they belonged there wouldn't be a need for good-byes.*

"I'm sorry," Sofie said, beginning to cry again.

"There's nothing to be sorry about," Amalia said. She had yet to shed a tear. "We didn't know she was dying. We would have called if we'd known."

Dora's nostrils quivered. Her eyes widened with hurt.

"Maybe your prayers could have healed her." Amalia took pleasure in her meanness; it felt good even as she knew she'd regret her words within moments. "God might have listened to you. He likes you more than he likes us."

Sofie elbowed her hard in the ribs. Dora's lip trembled. Amalia felt strong in her refusal to pity anyone but herself. "But then, our mother was having a love affair with the enemy. God wouldn't have approved of *that*, would he?"

"Shut your mouth!" said Sofie. "What's the matter with you? You know we would've called Dora if we'd known how close Mama was. Just be quiet."

Amalia opened her mouth to say more. When she heard herself, she'd know what it was.

"Don't talk," Sofie ordered. The train whistle screeched. "Let's go." She grabbed Amalia's forearm so hard that her fingers were sure to leave bruises. Amalia tried to shake her off and couldn't, so she let herself be pulled toward the streetcar.

"She died peacefully," Sofie told Dora.

"You don't really know that," said Amalia. "You weren't there. And I was sleeping at the time she finally died." Dora said nothing. Sofie threw Amalia a look of contempt and yanked her arm again as they hustled to catch the streetcar.

All three of them squeezed onto a seat wide enough for two, Amalia in the middle.

"What will we dress her in for the funeral?" Dora asked.

"I gave the funeral director her good brown dress," Sofie said.

"What?" Dora said. "We aren't going to wash her body? Prepare her to meet God?"

"The Captain called the funeral director right away. They took the body. It's their job to prepare it."

"That's our job," Dora said. "She's our mother."

Their words flew back and forth, whispered and urgent, before Amalia's face.

"Just stop it. It's taken care of. Be grateful," Amalia snapped.

"Why did you let him do that?" Dora's voice rose.

"I didn't *let* him," said Sofie.

"She's our mother. I thought we would be with her, one last time, all together." Dora sounded about to cry, right on the streetcar in front of strangers.

"We can't be with her," Amalia said. "She's dead. You're too late."

"Amalia," Sofie said. "I told you. Stop it."

Amalia pressed her lips together; Sofie didn't have the sense to appreciate her support. Around them people went on with their lives—women shopped for soup bones and swept the sidewalks, children flocked home for supper, men on bicycles carried newspapers, talked politics. Amalia wanted to scream, "Our mother is dead." She wanted the streetcar to squeal to a sudden halt between stops, the conductor to express his condolences and try to compensate them with a free ride, no, a lifetime of free rides. Amalia's unshed tears filled her chest and throat. They pressed against the backs of her eyes, and even her teeth ached. She held herself straight between her sisters as the streetcar rattled on.

At the house Amalia wandered into the parlor as Sofie busied herself in the kitchen, and Dora disappeared into their mother's bedroom upstairs. She sat down, stood, sat down again. She could help Sofie, but nothing needed doing. They didn't expect many people. Frau Becker was dead. Aside from Frau Grunberg, the dressmaker, and the Captain, Hanna hadn't made any friends in Tauburg. Some of the miners they'd boarded over the years would come, if word spread fast enough.

Oskar, then Karl and Lorenz, arrived with some of the others from work. She heard them greet Sofie, then water running and snippets of conversation from the washroom as they scrubbed and shaved.

Karl's voice, "Will they keep the place?"

Splashes of water, mumbling. Amalia heard someone say her name.

She sat on the edge of the worn love seat. She and her sisters would have to talk about what to do next. They knew what *they* were doing. America, Oskar. The convent, the nuns. Only she had nowhere to go, unless she went along to America. She was too mean to be a nun. Then she remembered Sister Monika. No, she didn't want to be a bad-tempered nun, even if they did exist. But she didn't think she wanted to go to America either.

The house would be theirs now, the three of them. The scratchy love seat beneath her was theirs. The faded green-and-pink flowered wallpaper, the two oversized ceramic beer steins no one ever used, the very floor under her feet: all belonged to her sisters and her. A home and a means of making a living. They were very lucky, practically speaking.

Amalia circled the perimeter of the darkening room, touching everything, and stopped by the window where the fading March sunlight fell across her table of flowerpots. Sofie didn't approve of indoor plants. She didn't understand why one would purposely bring dirt inside, when she spent so much time trying to rid the house of it, though she did appreciate fresh mint and parsley in her food. It took great effort and attention to keep plants alive in the winter. They needed both warmth and light; Amalia was forever moving them from east-facing windows in the morning to west-facing windows in the afternoon to a shelf beside the green-tiled stove at night. She always remembered. Even today, before they left to meet Dora, she'd found comfort in moving her geraniums, the reds and pinks brighter than anything inside or out at this bleak time of year. Sometimes she wished she were a plant, rooted in the soil with nothing to do but soak up sunshine and water. She broke off a sprig of mint and smelled her fingers.

She waited a long time in the parlor. No one, not even Karl, came looking for her. She told herself she was practicing being on her own. Amalia tried not to think about Sofie and Dora sleeping together in the room off the kitchen, too crowded, she told herself, for the three of them.

The funeral service was scheduled for first thing in the morning so the men could go to work afterward. Amalia climbed the narrow stairs—Frau Becker's stairs, now theirs—to put on her dark dress. All her clothes, and Sofie's too, were in the large armoire in their mother's room.

She dreaded facing Sofie and Dora. Downstairs, they would be waking up. Had they talked about her meanness? Had they missed her last night? They could have persuaded her to come to bed. She would have followed. She would have slept better crowded in with them than on the parlor loveseat with her knees folded. Her whole body felt cramped, as if she'd spent the night tensed, waiting for something terrible to happen.

She passed Oskar's closed door, then Lorenz's. Karl's hung open a crack. He stood before his small mirror, adjusting his tie. The strange intimacy of the moment stopped her until he noticed her reflection behind him in the mirror and winked. Blushing, she nodded and hurried on.

Amalia stopped at the closed door. More than she needed her dress, she needed to see her mother's empty room. Dora was right. They should have prepared the body themselves, then she'd believe Mama was really gone. Had anyone fixed Mama's tangled mess of hair? With one swift motion she stepped into the room where she'd spent so many hours doing what she could to make her mother comfortable. She stared at the naked mattress, the bare surface of the night table.

A throat-clearing noise, then the Captain's voice. "Amalia."

He sat in the rocking chair in the corner of the room. "I didn't mean to scare you," he said. "I needed to sit here a while, to convince myself she's gone." His hat and coat and their mother's music box rested in his lap. "Is it time to leave?"

Didn't he even notice she wasn't dressed? Amalia crossed her arms over her breasts, barely covered by the worn fabric of her nightgown. The floor burned cold under her bare feet. She wanted to snatch back the music box and order him out of the room, but he had as much right to be there as she did. He, at least, had cried.

"You have no idea what she meant to me," he said.

He was right. She didn't. He seemed about to tell her, and she wasn't sure she wanted to know, not right now. Whoever knew what really existed in that charged and invisible space between two people? Even their mother had seemed bewildered by it sometimes. He wound the music box and placed it on the table by the bed. The familiar notes tinkled. He closed his eyes and rocked. She thought she should leave, she wanted to leave, but she couldn't walk out on her mother's sad song, so she stayed where she was.

As the music wound down, the Captain opened his watery, red-rimmed eyes. "She'd almost agreed to move to France once you girls were settled, but if she hadn't, I would've stayed here. She thought I was crazy. Once the occupation was over, Germans wouldn't tolerate my presence, she said. But I wouldn't have been strutting around in uniform. I told her I'd help her run the boarding house."

The stripped mattress gave the room an abandoned feeling, as if the occupant had run off. Amalia would never know if her mother would have agreed to the Captain's plan or if he was deluding himself.

"What made you fall in love with her?" she asked.

"She had a beautiful laugh," he said. "She laughed at the inflation, the occupation, and, for as long as she could, her illness."

"I didn't hear her laugh much," Amalia said. "To me, she seemed tired." Of course she was tired, always working, having to feed and care for three daughters. With the Captain she was just a woman—not a mother or the industrious proprietor of a busy boarding house, or even an invalid. He'd made her mother happy. For a moment Amalia felt real sorrow for him.

But the Captain had merely lost a good friend, an almost-lover. Maybe an actual lover—but even so, she'd lost her mother, her only living parent.

"I need to get my dress." She gestured toward the armoire.

"Your mother worried about you," he said.

"Me, why?" How dare he tell her what her mother thought of her?

"She talked about Sofie's adventuring spirit. She thought Sofie wouldn't stop long enough to let pain in. Haven't you noticed that to be true?" Without giving her time to think he went on. "She talked about Dora's unquestioning faith—that Dora would count on meeting her in heaven and would be glad that Hanna was at peace with God."

This was the longest conversation the Captain and she had ever had. Did he dare to think he knew her? She couldn't help waiting to hear what her mother had said about her.

"'But, Amalia,' Hanna would say, and shake her head. 'That girl. What does she believe in? What does she want? Always playing in the dirt. Eighteen years old and no man, no faith. What will happen to her?'"

She'd never talked with her mother about a lack of faith. How had she known? Amalia needed her sisters. She needed to get away from this weepy stranger, too tall for the rocking chair. He looked all wrong. Yanking both her dress and Sofie's from the wardrobe and hurrying from the room, she ignored a twinge of worry that she might be offending him. He hadn't worried about her feelings.

Dora's black dress hung loosely over her thin frame. Sofie stood behind her adjusting the sash. They both stopped talking when Amalia came in. She held out Sofie's dress.

"I was just going up to get that," said Sofie.

They don't know Mama talked to the Captain about us, Amalia thought. *They don't know anything.*

Her back to them, Amalia dressed quickly. Maybe they watched her. Maybe they didn't. Either way, she didn't care. Her dress fastened in the back. She reached around, the fabric tightening over her bosom. She managed the first button, but the ones between her shoulder blades eluded her. She grabbed at the fabric, pulling it up toward her neck.

"Let me help," said Dora. She smoothed the back of Amalia's dress. Her deft fingers moved down the row of buttons along Amalia's spine.

"We need to hurry," said Sofie. "I'll make coffee." She exchanged a few words with someone, maybe Oskar, as she entered the kitchen.

"Are you all right?" Dora asked. "Sofie thought we should leave you alone last night. I wasn't sure. Did we do the right thing?"

Dora's arms crept around her waist. Amalia felt her sister's cheek press against the back of her head—her little sister who was taller than she was.

"I have to brush my hair," she whispered past the ache in her throat. "We're late."

"Sofie won't let us be late," said Dora. "Pray with me, Amalia. It helps."

"It helps you." Amalia pushed the words out while swallowing a sob.

"It helps me," Dora agreed. She released Amalia. "Let me do your hair," she said. The bristles of the brush stroked her scalp, more comforting than prayer.

Dora whispered words about God and infinite mercy, but Amalia heard their mother's voice begin a story, *Once upon a time...*

When the casket had been lowered into the hole, each daughter threw in a handful of dirt. One, two, three, pebbles skittered across the polished lid. Amalia wished she could finish the work, fill in the rest herself, but over by the small tool shed, uniformed men waited to do the job.

She licked the dirt from her fingers, cleaned under her nails with her teeth. If she left for America a paid stranger would tend their mother's grave, just as a stranger had prepared the body, just as those men no one knew would fill the hole. As their mother's flesh began its gentle transformation back into the earth that held it, Dora would be locked in a convent, Sofie and Oskar would be somewhere in America, as impossible to find as Hansel and Gretel in the woods. And she would be...? Before she went anywhere she'd plant some bulbs, so that whatever happened, a year from now the raw earth covering her mother, Hanna Heller Bauer Kleinschuster, would be covered with flowers. Crocuses, Amalia's favorite, those tenacious blossoms that brave the coldest days of spring, shouting yellow and purple even through late blanketings of thick, wet snow.

CHAPTER 10

▼

Within just a few short weeks of Hanna's death the Captain hesitated in the doorway of the kitchen, his coat buttoned, his bags packed. He'd found a new place to live, closer to his office, he said. The mining school wanted to purchase the boarding house. He'd be foolish to stay in a place inhabited by a pack of hostile miners, with no woman to bring him his meals or to buffer him from their rage.

Sofie, Amalia and Dora paused in their breakfast cleanup.

"I'll be going now," he said.

Sofie stepped forward wiping her hands on a towel, face full of feeling. They hadn't discussed how they would say good-bye to the Captain. It came so suddenly, along with all the other changes. To Amalia and Dora the relationship with him felt insignificant really, except in this moment of leave-taking, when his importance to their dead mother shimmered around him.

Sofie extended her hand. He took it. They stood unmoving and wordless until Sofie half-spoke, half-sobbed her appreciation for his help during the past hard months. They didn't notice Dora disappear and return with the music box.

"What are you doing?" Amalia whispered.

"We have to give him something of hers," Dora said.

"Not that!" Amalia said, but Sofie, beaming at the rightness of the gesture, had already taken it from Dora and thrust it at the Captain. He held it in both hands, as if it contained gold, frankincense, or myrrh. After a long moment, he managed a hoarse thank you, unpacked a folded shirt from his bag, wrapped it carefully, and tucked it into the leather pouch strapped over his shoulder. Amalia couldn't very well snatch it back.

"Bless you for your help with our mother," Dora said. *Our mother*, not *your friend, your sweetheart.*

He disappeared, and their mother belonged to them again.

And, suddenly, there was money. Oskar, Sofie at his side, led them through the legalities, the reading of the will at the *Notar's* hushed and polished office, and the sale of the boarding house to the mining school. Dora thought of the fisherman's wife and tried to grow used to the idea of having so much. Months before it would have been nothing; it wouldn't have made sense to sell the property, but with the economy on track again, the marks mattered. Times were still hard, and some of the miners, Karl especially, thought the girls foolish to give up the steady livelihood the boarding house provided. Karl tried to persuade Amalia to stay in Tauburg and run the place, but she'd have none of it. Of course, they'd divide the money from the sale into thirds. Dora would have a more-than-generous dowry to bring to the convent.

Dora thought about the money as she picked her way through the parlor full of crates and settled on the floor beside the china cabinet. They'd spent the past week sorting through Frau Becker's kitchenware and knickknacks, the household items they hadn't traded away for food. Strange, how she and her sisters still thought of most everything in the house as Frau Becker's though she'd been dead for six years. Their mother had owned almost nothing. It had taken less than an hour to sort through her personal effects.

Dora stopped thinking about their mother—too sad—and thought about the money while wrapping Frau Becker's good coffee cups, the ones they'd never used, in paper. She imagined the black ocean, churning and wild with waves when the fisherman goes to the flounder and asks that his wife be made emperor. Rich people had money, not the Bauer sisters. Hands shaking a little and slippery with sweat, Dora almost dropped a cup. Still, the real coffee they could now afford to buy smelled of heaven and tasted even better. They'd each ordered a new dress from Frau Grunberg for Sofie's wedding and their new shoes fit just right.

Dora stuck her foot out beside the box of cups and wiggled her toes inside the solid, unscuffed shoe, admiring the polish and the stitching. Sofie and Amalia had put their fancy shoes away to save for the wedding, but Dora bought hers to be used—practical, comfortable, black with a low heel. She'd never had brand new shoes before. Before her feet stopped growing, shoes came to her already stretched to fit Amalia's wide feet, worn down on the outsides of the heels. In these last hard years they kept paper patterns of their soles and, from cardboard, cut out several at a time. With holes in their shoes and puddles in the streets, the cardboard innersoles didn't last long, so they carried replacement liners in their pockets and bags. In her new shoes Dora had skipped home from the store, even though she was far too old for skipping, and had crumpled up her paper pattern and burned it in the stove. The rest of her share of the money would go to the nuns. God couldn't find fault with that.

Sofie bustled into the parlor, all business, followed by Amalia, and grabbed one of the heavy, colorful beer steins from its shelf on the wall. "What should we do with this?" she asked. "It's old. I bet it's worth quite a lot."

"We should give one to Karl and one to Lorenz," Amalia said. "To remember us by. It would've been traded for potatoes months ago if a farmer had any use for it. What good are fancy steins when there's nothing to put in them?"

Amalia seemed to blame Dora, not Sofie, for giving the Captain Mama's music box. Amalia acted more interested in wedding preparations than Sofie herself, ignoring Dora except to order her to pack or clean or sign a paper.

Dora remembered the night after their mother's funeral when Amalia joined Dora and Sofie in the little bedroom as if she'd never spent the night before sleeping in the parlor. Dora prayed that God would forgive her for the pleasure she'd felt having Sofie's confidences to herself and then, for being the one to comfort Amalia at the funeral. For a short while she'd been the one they both liked best, instead of the odd baby sister who didn't want to get married and prayed too much, whose deepest regret was not having the chance to tell her mother she was joining the convent.

"What about Oskar?" Sofie opened and closed the stein's silver lid. "Doesn't he deserve something?"

"He's got you." Amalia said. Her grin didn't cover the resentment edging her voice.

Sofie swatted her with a dust rag. Amalia swung back with hers. They laughed and shrieked and ducked behind the stacked crates, flapping their rags in the air.

Dora tucked a cup in a box of straw, next to the others. If the steins were worth a lot, they should sell them and do some good work with the money.

"Maybe you should put down the stein," Amalia said. "So I can clobber you without breaking it!"

"Clobber me?" Sofie leaped onto a chair. She held the stein high and the dust rag over her arm. "Look, I'm the Statue of Liberty! You can't touch me!"

Amalia snapped her rag against Sofie's legs.

Sofie wasn't even planning to have a church wedding. Dora had assumed they'd do what most people did and have both the civil and religious ceremonies.

But Oskar would have nothing to do with church, Sofie told her, not seeming at all upset. In fact, she'd sounded almost proud, like a mother whose child would rather study than play outside. If Sofie weren't married in the eyes of God, would she really be married? It didn't seem to matter to Amalia either.

How could they play like that? In a few weeks they'd be separated, maybe forever. Sofie and her ridiculous Statue of Liberty. Amalia acting wild and rowdy, as if they were still children out on the farms during the war when all Dora had wanted was to go back to the city and be together.

Dora fingered the gold edging on a thin saucer. "We should use these," she said loudly. "We should have used them for the lunch after Mama's funeral."

Her sisters stopped. "I didn't think of it," said Sofie.

"Let's use them for your *Polterabend*," Dora said.

Sofie hadn't even wanted a *Polterabend*. She'd told them she'd rather spend the night before her wedding quietly, but Amalia had ignored her and was pushing ahead with plans for a wild celebration, enlisting everyone's help. Thanks to the miners there would be plenty of guests breaking crockery on the doorstep, plenty of food collected over weeks, and music.

"These dishes are too fancy for a *Polterabend*," Amalia said.

"I didn't mean smash them," Dora said. "How about for the luncheon after the wedding?"

"We need to finish packing everything," Amalia said. "We need to decide what to sell and what to keep."

"We have time," said Dora. "We have time." The words burst from her with unexpected force. Sofie and Oskar would be married, if you could call it that, next week. Their tickets to sail were for the week after that. With money from the house they'd upgraded their fares to second class. Oskar's Onkel Schultz in America had written that it was worth it. With second-class tickets, their travel would be comfortable, but more important, their examinations to enter the country would happen on the boat. They wouldn't have to disembark and wait in crowded lines. They'd wanted to save every *pfennig* for their start in the new country, but decided that Onkel spoke from experience.

"Not much time," Amalia said. "We have to be out of this house by the first. That gives us…" She calculated on her fingers. "Just about three weeks."

Even the lawyer had urged them not to sell the house. Few were lucky enough to own property. Everyone knew land to be far more valuable than money. But Sofie couldn't bring land to America and Amalia was tired of the thick, smelly air of the city. Dora would go back to the nuns, this time for good.

"Amalia?" Dora asked. "Do you want to keep any of this?" Her gesture took in the contents of the room.

"I've been wanting to talk about the money." Amalia sat next to Dora, tying knots in her dust rag as she spoke. "Dora, if you're really going to join the convent, I don't think you should take a whole third. You don't need it. They don't expect a dowry that large. All you need is a couple of years' worth of personal supplies, things like soap and stockings, maybe an extra pair of shoes."

Dora heard Sofie come from behind. "What do nuns need with money?" Sofie said. "They live a simple life. God provides."

Sofie's face stayed serious, but Dora thought she heard a mocking tinge in her voice. Their sidelong glances proved her sisters had discussed this before. How could they think she didn't see them silently urging each other on? Their collaboration surprised her; Amalia seemed so angry at Sofie for choosing America over a shared farm, Oskar over a sister.

She opened her mouth to speak, but no words came out. She tried not to think that they laughed at her prayers and her dreams. She told herself it didn't matter if they did, but Amalia's flushed face really did remind her of the greedy fisherman's wife. Dora felt outnumbered. Maybe Oskar put them up to it.

"We know you need some of the money," Amalia said. "It's just that… well…a third seems so much more than the nuns would expect."

"Don't they take girls even when they have no money at all?" Sofie asked. "Even with no money for supplies. Even if they arrive with nothing they're accepted as lay sisters." She opened the lid of the stein and gazed into it.

Dora's stomach ached. Her sisters knew that a third of the money was hers. She knew that giving the money to the nuns to do God's work was the best possible use for it, but she hadn't presumed to tell Sofie or Amalia what to do with their portions. Sick of being the youngest, she stared at the floor. With her toe, she probed an edge of the box of packed china. Her sisters sat waiting. How could they do this to her? She felt their impatient stares.

Amalia cleared her throat. "You know that nuns can't own anything. Even your washrag belongs to the community. If the money really were going to be yours, we wouldn't think of trying to talk you out of it. But the minute they take you in, it wouldn't belong to you anymore. We could really use it. Think of Sofie all the way over there in America. She'll need it. And what about me? How am I ever supposed to establish myself?"

Sofie broke in. "Be practical, Dora. Amalia will never get a piece of land without marrying into a family that owns some. *Teufelmann* took care of that. She's the one who needs a good dowry."

Dora chewed the insides of her cheeks. "She has a dowry. We all do." Something burned behind her eyes.

"We would make good use of it, Dora," Sofie said. "Don't you think Mama would have wanted us to have it?"

Dora kicked the box of china. She'd packed it so well it didn't even rattle. Sofie and Amalia jumped back as she leaped to her feet and faced them. They stood there, those fishermen's wives, wanting more and more, not satisfied with their thirds. Dora could feel a storm crackling in the close, dusty air of the room.

"You want too much!" she whispered. "Be careful. You're trying to take money away from God."

Sofie laughed. "God doesn't need money as much as we do."

"You're trying to take it away from me!" Dora shouted. "From me!" Her head filled with voices, and she didn't know whose they were. *You greedy girl. You undeserving girl. Give your sisters the money. You don't care about the work of God. You care that your two sisters are leaving you out, that they've made plans without you. They're selfish. They're trying to take money that rightfully belongs to you. Don't let them win. They're your sisters. They need the money to make their new lives. You don't.*

She pressed her hands against the sides of her head and squeezed her eyes shut. Pray, Dora, pray. That always helps. God will help you. Pray.

"Shh. It's okay." Sofie's voice on her left. A hand on her arm.

"Calm down." Amalia on the right. Another hand. "We can talk about it later."

"Frau Grunberg said our dresses would be ready this afternoon." Sofie glanced at the clock. "We should take a rest from all this packing and go to pick them up."

"You go," said Dora. The argument wasn't over.

"We all have to go. We have to try them on in case she needs to make any adjustments."

"Why bother with fancy dresses when you're not even having a church wedding?" Dora said.

Sofie laughed dismissively. "Are you still worried about that? Come on."

Dora let herself be maneuvered toward the door. Amalia thrust a sweater at her, and she wrapped it around her shoulders, too defeated to push her arms through the sleeves.

The streets swarmed with people making their way back to work or out to shop after *Mittagspause*, enjoying the pale sun filtering through the coal dust and smoke from the steel mill. All the trees that could bloomed with white or pink flowers; the ones that couldn't sported wet-looking yellowy-green leaves.

"Let's walk," Amalia said, as the streetcar rattled to a stop.

"But it'll take longer," Dora said feeling disagreeable. "And we've got all that packing to do and supper to make." She moved to follow the knot of people toward the door of the car.

Sofie yanked her back. "Let's walk; how long does it take to slice bread and arrange some cheese and meat on a plate? As for the packing, we still have time. When have we ever bought new dresses?"

"Never," Amalia answered. "Never, that's when. And not only are these our first new dresses, but they're for a grand occasion, our sister's wedding."

Dora would have to pray hard for her sister and her godless man. She'd pray for God and the Virgin Mother to bless their marriage and Saint Christopher to give them a safe journey to America. Her sisters pulled her away from the streetcar tracks, through the busy streets, toward the fancy dress shop. Sofie, laughing recklessly at something Amalia said, needed prayers more than ever, but didn't realize it.

A news boy waved papers at her, yelling, "Miners refuse eight-hour-day. Owners threaten lockout!" His cries faded as they passed. "Dawes Plan presented!"

A plan. A Sofie and Amalia plan presented to cheat her out of her money. To cheat the nuns and God. Amalia, at least, should understand all the good the money could do at the hospital, the babies it could feed. They thought they could get away with it, two older sisters ganging up. Just like the owners of the mines. Just like those greedy French and English and Americans ganging up on Germany with their terrible reparations payments.

She scraped her new shoes against the street, resisting her eager sisters and, with dismay, noticed the white scuff marks. Her anger at Sofie and Amalia swelled to include herself.

A bell chimed their entrance into Frau Grunberg's shabbily elegant shop. Their mother told them Frau Grunberg had purchased the shop at the worst possible time, during the Great War, but the opportunity had come, and she'd seized it. She lived in the shop through the war and afterward, to protect it from looters and save rent money. Karl said she'd survived through Jewish cunning and greed, but shut up when their mother ordered him to. Dora wasn't sure if Frau Grunberg really was Jewish; she'd never asked.

In the window two intricately beaded and pleated dresses shimmered in the shadowy light. The hushed stillness reminded Dora of church. Sofie's voice fell to a whisper. "I can't wait to see how they look."

Summoned by the bell, little Frau Grunberg bustled in from the back, cracking the quiet with a delighted clap of her hands. "Oh, it's the bride and her sisters. Girls, girls, these dresses would make a princess envious, if I say so myself. Come, to the fitting room." They followed her through a worn velvet curtain into a mirrored, well-lit room, bigger than the front room of the shop.

"Sit down." She motioned to a plush bench. "I'll bring them out one at a time. Sit."

Sofie sat, foot tapping. "Amalia, Dora, come on. Sit down."

Amalia sat beside Sofie. Dora wedged herself into the small space remaining. They shifted to make room for her, but she had to sit with shoulders scrunched forward. She folded her arms across her chest. She hoped Frau Grunberg wasn't waiting for her to smile, because she couldn't.

When they seemed settled, Frau Grunberg disappeared back into her workroom. Sofie's jittery leg jiggled them all. Amalia gave an indulgent laugh and rested her hand on it. Frau Grunberg poked her head out from behind the curtain. "I can't decide whether to start with the bride or save her for last. What do you think?"

"I don't think she can wait another minute," said Amalia. "You'd better start with her."

Sofie hadn't wanted a white wedding dress. She said her romantic side wanted something special, gorgeous and expensive too, now that they had some money, but she wanted to be able to wear it again. She'd chosen a pale, blue-gray panne velvet from the bolts of fabric Frau Grunberg had purchased on the black market and hidden, carefully wrapped, in her basement. Frau Grunberg brought the dress out on a hanger. It was low-waisted, in the latest style, with a beaded bodice and pleated skirt. She had to hold her arm up high to keep it from dragging on the floor, she was such a tiny woman.

Sofie gasped. None of them had ever worn anything so new, so elegant.

"Do you want to try it on now, dear?" Frau Grunberg asked. There was room on the bench now that Sofie had leaped up to meet her dress. Dora nudged Amalia over.

Sofie had already stripped to her undergarments. Her everyday frock lay in a heap at her feet. Frau Grunberg helped her step into the new dress. Amalia perched on the edge of her seat, hands pressed together near her chest, looking almost like she was praying except for the silly grin on her face. All this excitement over some clothing.

God, forgive my foolish sisters, Dora thought. Forgive me for judging.

Frau Grunberg buttoned Sofie up the back. Sofie's eyes glittered as she stared at her reflection in the mirrors. Front, back, sides, going on endlessly, an infinite number of gray-eyed, glowing, about-to-be-married, about-to-sail-away Sofies in soft velvet. Dora and Amalia's reflections went on forever too, together on their island of a bench. But Sofie and Amalia both beamed huge smiles and Dora's repeating reflection looked grim and scared. Her attempt to smile looked like a wince.

"She's lovely, eh?" Frau Grunberg, eyes damp, adjusted a pleat. "If only your mother had lived to be here. The mother of a bride deserves a beautiful dress. I would have made hers rose, like that curtain. But what am I saying? I don't mean to make you sad. This is a happy occasion." She ran her hands along Sofie's shoulders and straightened a sleeve. "Perfect, don't you think? All I have to do is mark the hem. Sofie Bauer, you will be a beautiful bride." She sighed. "I do wish your mother could see you." She looked up. "Maybe she can. Hanna, look at your beautiful daughter."

Their mother would have insisted that Sofie have a church wedding. Then again, maybe she wouldn't have. They'd never know.

"For your hair, no veil? Just a wreath of flowers, you said?"

Sofie nodded and twirled in her stockinged feet, arms raised.

"Shall I mark the hem now, or dress your sisters, then mark them all?"

"Dress the sisters!" Amalia called.

Sofie stood back next to the loveseat. Frau Grunberg brought out Amalia's dress of pale yellow-orange. It looked like peaches, Amalia had said when she chose it. She insisted the silky velvet even felt like peaches, just picked and warm from the sun. "Remember how you'd tease me for rubbing them against my cheek before biting into them?" Sofie nodded. Dora didn't. Only a year they'd had together before she was born, yet they pretended to share a lifetime of memories.

Frau Grunberg fastened Amalia's hooks and buttons. "The bodice is a little snug. You must be eating well. We're all eating a little better these days." She patted Amalia's cheek. "I will let these seams out a bit, and it will be fine, don't worry."

"It's beautiful," Sofie whispered. "That color is perfect for you." She stood next to Amalia. Their eyes met in the mirror. "We should go out dancing in these dresses." Dora had liked dancing in the beer garden with her sisters the time she'd gone. Were they including her, even though they'd been transformed and she wore her drab, everyday clothes?

Sofie took Amalia in her arms and they danced a few steps, laughed and stared into the mirror again. Amalia fussed with her hair.

"You would create a sensation." Frau Grunberg nodded. "Now yours?"

Dora had a dress too. Lost, grieving for their mother, worrying about the inadequate civil wedding, watching her sisters turn into fancy ladies giddy with their beauty and good fortune, Dora had almost forgotten.

"Don't you worry for a minute," Frau Grunberg said. "Your dress is every bit as lovely."

For Dora, Frau Grunberg had suggested a rich green fabric, the color of the stained-glass leaves in the apple tree in the Garden of Eden when the sun shone through the chapel window on Sunday morning. Amalia and Sofie had chosen the style when Dora had trouble deciding.

Frau Grunberg reappeared with the dress. Sofie and Amalia stopped admiring themselves and looked at her.

"Do you like it?" Sofie asked. "Why are you waiting? Try it on!"

Frau Grunberg stood before her, holding the dress. The glass beads around the neck caught the light and sparkled. The velvet hung in soft folds. Sofie's fingers brushed her neck as they unbuttoned her. She remembered the time Sofie threatened to cut her hair, then stopped and chopped off her own instead. Amalia tugged at her sleeves.

She stood shivering in her ragged cambric chemise. Her elbows and knees still looked knobby. Sofie and Amalia had seen her undressed many times, yet it couldn't be Frau Grunberg's neutral gaze making her feel as exposed as a tree with the bark stripped away.

They had stopped smiling. A moment ago the room had been full of grins and high spirits. Where did all that go? Did happiness and sadness drift around the world like weather, move from place to place?

No, people, with God's help, spread happiness and joy. People spread despair too, when they'd lost faith. Dora hadn't lost faith, but she was sure it was her angry hesitation and sad face that had driven the joy from the room. It couldn't have been real joy then, just worldly joy. Dresses—what right did they have to waste money on these dresses, even with Frau Grunberg's generous discount, when many people still had so little to eat? When they were trying to cheat her out of her rightful inheritance? Sofie and Amalia knew as well as she did how it felt to be hungry. How it felt to be wronged. *Teufelmann* had cheated all of them. How could they forget?

"Come, come," Frau Grunberg said. "Lift your arms."

Dora couldn't look at herself, bony and white, angry and sad. She closed her eyes and tried to pray but she didn't know what to pray for.

"That's it," Sofie said. "Keep your eyes shut a minute more."

The dress settled on her shoulders. Please, God, Dora prayed, help me appreciate what I have. Help me not to judge my sisters. Hands smoothed, tugged, pressed, arranged, and straightened her as if making a sculpture. Her sisters' hands, and Frau Grunberg's, good women, all three of them. Why did it feel so hard? Having a beautiful dress couldn't be a sin.

"Dora, open your eyes," Amalia said.

"Look at yourself," Sofie breathed.

"Look at all of you!" said Frau Grunberg.

The shop bell chimed. "I'll be back in a moment." Frau Grunberg went to wait on a customer.

Dora willed herself to raise her eyelids. Color flooded her eyes. Deep green, pale gray-blue, and sunny orange-yellow.

"We're beautiful and glamorous," Sofie said. "Don't you think?"

"Funny how we can see our backs in these mirrors," said Amalia. "I've never seen my back before."

"We can see how we look from behind, walking down the street," Sofie said. "We can see ourselves the way other people see us."

"Dora, lift your chin; stand tall." Amalia elbowed her. "You look like you're wilting."

"Come on, Dora, straighten your shoulders. Look at us!"

"Remember that photograph we had taken for Mama, before you two left to work at the hospital?" Sofie said.

"We should take another at your wedding, Sofie. I want to remember us like this." Amalia ran a hand over the beaded pattern looping across her chest.

"We will." Sofie said. "These dresses are prettier. Though we had more meat on our bones then. Before the inflation. I'd rather remember us like that—looking so healthy with our plump cheeks. Dora, what's wrong?"

"She's still mad about the money," Amalia said. "Right?"

"I want my share to go to the nuns," Dora said. "It's only right. You do what you want with yours." She stood a little straighter.

"But—" Sofie began.

Amalia interrupted her. "It's just that we thought you wouldn't need it as much as we do. We thought you wouldn't mind. We didn't want to cheat you or anything. Really."

"You're plotting together against me," Dora said. "It's not fair."

"We're not plotting. We just don't see why the nuns should get Frau Becker's, I mean, Mama's—our—money," Sofie said. "They have the whole church backing them."

"It's her share," Amalia said. "She should be able to do what she wants with it, really Sofie."

Sofie, perhaps made magnanimous, momentarily anyway, by Frau Grunberg's generosity, the rich folds of velvet, the infinite reflections, didn't argue.

"I'll give you this dress," Dora said. "I wouldn't have any occasion to wear it. Easter just passed."

"It'll fit Sofie better than it would me," Amalia laughed.

"And any of Frau Becker's things that either of you want, you should have. I don't think I can bring any of it with me."

The china cups, soup tureen, silver ladle, embroidered tablecloths, featherbeds—Amalia and Sofie would get all of that and more. They were just things.

In the cathedral in Koln rested bones of the Magi, matter made holy. Dora imagined the Captain listening to the music box, the song made holy by their father's and mother's love and the whole sad truth of life. Whenever they'd opened the lid and listened they remembered. Things of this world helped her, everyone, to connect to…what? Memories? God? She couldn't have brought the music box to the convent.

"Sorry for the interruption." Frau Grunberg hurried back with her tape measure and pins. "I told that customer she'd have to come back later but she was full of just-one-more-questions."

Dora stared into the mirror—Amalia, rosy and smiling; Sofie, gray eyes looking into the distance; and herself, still the gangly little sister uncomfortable in her new dress, taller than both of the others, tucked between them. Three girls in soft velvet. Remember. Dora studied her sisters and herself, their faces and her own, memorizing every curve and fold, and the exact way the light illuminated their features and brightened their hair. In case nuns weren't allowed to have family photographs.

CHAPTER 11

▼

In the late afternoon light Sofie knelt before the three open suitcases she and Oskar had begun to fill. Humid air, thick with coal dust and tinged with the scent of blossoming trees, drifted through the open window. Tomorrow was her wedding, their wedding. Oskar wasn't home yet from the mine. Tonight their *Polterabend*—food, music, drinking, dancing, cards perhaps, a good time—yet the future spread before her like the vast, heaving ocean she was about to cross. She longed for her mother to help her dress for her wedding, to cry a little, to wish her farewell.

She slid a photograph of Hanna from the pocket inside the lid of the largest suitcase. It had been taken in front of the boarding house, just after Frau Becker's death. The blurriness of the door behind her hid the peeling paint. How, unless you'd seen it in life, could you ever know that door was blue, not gray? You could guess that the dark-browed, serious woman had suffered—most people had—but how could you know she'd lost her brother, her parents, a good husband, and then, to a bad one, the farm and her home? You'd imagine she must have laughed sometime, but you wouldn't guess how her thin cheeks dimpled and her eyes gleamed. You wouldn't know she loved music, or how her baking skill made even warbread full of sawdust edible.

Don't marry a miner. Her mother's words echoed in Sofie's head.

Sofie wanted Oskar to quit the mines before their wedding. She'd wanted this shift to be his last. He'd argued sensibly that he should make all the money he could.

"He won't be a miner much longer," she told her mother's picture, to still the whispers in her head. *Remember the fisherman's wife. Be satisfied. Stop tempting fate.* She stuck the photo back out of sight. Oskar would have other work in America.

He should be home soon. All day Amalia and Dora scurried around preparing for tonight's party and tomorrow's celebratory luncheon. They wouldn't let her help. She needed to help. She was happiest working. Too much to think about sitting still, especially now.

"I'm not really marrying a miner," she said, louder, out the open window. She leaned over the sill, squinting into the hazy distance, toward the mines. She checked the clock—another hour and thirty-nine minutes of his shift. Then there was next week and the week after. If something happened to Oskar, would she go to America alone?

Tomorrow she would be a wife—Frau Oskar Schmidt. What would happen to Sofie Bauer? Frau Grunberg had offered a choice of nightdresses as a wedding present. The one she wanted was of a silk so sheer she had been embarrassed to try it on in the shop, embarrassed to want it, too self-conscious to accept it in front of her sisters. Dora and Amalia had already boarded the streetcar when Sofie heard herself mumble she'd forgotten to ask Frau Grunberg about a corset, and they should go on ahead. She had run back to the shop.

She still blushed thinking of Frau Grunberg's knowing smile as the woman took her time wrapping the nightdress while Sofie arranged herself to block the view of any prospective customers. The whole way home on the streetcar she felt men looking at her as if they knew she had a secret and were trying to guess what it was. She felt naughty and pleased with herself.

Oskar's clothes and possessions, including his mandolin, filled only one of the open suitcases. He thought it silly to pack things he'd be needing during their last days at home, but Sofie persuaded him they had to see how much space things used, how much of their lives they could take with them.

She snapped open Oskar's mandolin case. Running a hand over the polished wood, she felt a quiver between her legs. She held the instrument across her lap and pressed and plucked the tight strings. They cut into the pads of her fingers, leaving pairs of red lines. On Oskar's callused fingers they left no imprint. She ran her fingers over her cheek, remembering his touch. She tucked the mandolin into its case. She'd never learned to make music. Maybe in America.

She closed the shutters and locked the door before reaching way under her bed to retrieve Frau Grunberg's wrapped package. She let the paper drop to the floor. The nightdress spilled, cool and liquid, over her hands before she could unfold it. She held it against her cheek and closed her eyes, imagining Oskar's lips on the back of her neck. She fingered the bit of pale blue ribbon threaded through eyelets at the scooped neckline. She slipped out of her clothes and into the wisp of a dress. On tiptoe at the small mirror, she admired her dark nipples shadowy and tempting under silk.

She held her breasts in her hands, pulling the fabric taut against them. Still on her toes, eyes closed to better hear the swells of music filling her head, she waltzed lightly around the room, stepping and spinning until she fell dizzy across the bed.

"Sofie!" Amalia called from downstairs, back from her errands.

Sweaty, with a pounding heart, Sofie lifted the nightdress over her head, stuffed it back into its paper wrapping, and shoved it deep under the bed. She struggled with her clothes, her sisters' footsteps mounting the stairs.

The door handle rattled. "Are you in there?" Amalia's voice, annoyed and surprised to find it locked.

"Yes, yes, wait a minute, will you?" Sisters didn't have to know every little thing. Sofie believed in secrets. She hoped the nightdress wouldn't be a mess of wrinkles, and wished she'd taken time to fold it.

Finally, she unlocked the door. Amalia burst in, Dora right behind her. "Are you all right, Sofie? You look flushed. What are you doing in here?" Amalia looked past her, as if scanning the room.

"I'm packing." Sofie gestured to the suitcases.

"Oh." That stopped her. Sofie had broken the unspoken agreement not to mention anything about the trip.

"Sofie," Dora piped up. "Are you ready for tonight? Because we…"

"Come see what we've done!" Amalia interrupted. "The men will be home soon." Dora grabbed Sofie's hand as Amalia shepherded from behind.

The sitting room, almost empty of furniture, would be perfect for dancing. The kitchen had never been so full of food. Dishes covered every surface—bread, rolls, wurst, ham, cheeses, jams, yogurt, fruit, pickles, potato salad—and in the center of the table a plum cake glistened red and purple.

Sofie felt Amalia and Dora on either side of her, waiting. "God in heaven!" she said. They'd gone to so much trouble. In America no one would love her enough to give her a party like this.

"Let's hope there's something left for you and Oskar when you finally finish sweeping up the mess we make for you out on the street," Amalia laughed. "Lorenz told me that so many people came to his cousin's *Polterabend,* the bride and groom were out there all night. He took pity and kept bringing them beer."

"This is going to be a big one," Dora took off her apron. "All the mining students are coming." She pointed to the brooms standing in the corner. They'd tied rose colored ribbons around the handles. "Maybe we'll sneak you food, if it gets late."

"I'm hungry now," Amalia said. "Let's eat something. We'll rearrange the plates and no one will ever know."

When Oskar arrived home they were back upstairs, full of party food, dressing for the evening in their now-second-best dresses, the ones they'd been wearing to church. With Dora home, they went every Sunday to keep her company. Sofie liked the virtuous feeling she got after communion, though she'd told Amalia she wouldn't go in America.

"All by yourself?" Amalia called down from the window. "Have your friends deserted you?"

Sofie rushed to join her and hung over the sill. Oskar looked up, squinting, hand on his hat, small and vulnerable from above. Amalia's chatter rang in her ears. Sofie couldn't make out the words.

Dora placed a hand in the middle of Sofie's back and leaned close. "Are you all right?" Sofie shrugged her off, steadying herself on the windowsill. Her stomach felt queasy. They shouldn't have eaten so much, so quickly.

Amalia hollered, "We'll be right there." Sofie let herself be escorted down the stairs again, more sedately this time. They met Oskar just inside the door. Amalia and Dora disappeared with a quick *Auf Wiedersehen*, off to round up the guests.

Sofie and Oskar stood close together in the dim entryway. He hung his hat on a peg, set down his lunch pail, and wrapped her in a hug, a nice hug, but she couldn't help thinking she would have liked it if he'd been in more of a hurry, if the lunch pail had bumped against her back and his hat fallen to the floor.

They heard the banging of pots, the clanging of pans, the yelling of their friends and then, just outside, the smashing of crockery. Sofie flung the door open to a parade of some fifty rowdy miners and their girls, led by Dora, Amalia, Lorenz and Karl. They blocked the street. The trolley screeched to a standstill. Passengers leaned from the open windows into the warm evening light and shouted, joining in. Horns blared.

"Get your brooms, you two!" boomed Karl, pounding on a metal washbasin with a huge wooden spoon. "Let's see how well you work together!"

Amalia pushed past Sofie and Oskar to fetch the brooms. She handed one to Sofie. At least the handle was intact. There were stories of jokers slicing into the wood so it split when the bridal couple began to sweep. The crowd cheered and yelled. More people joined. Karl and Lorenz pounded Oskar on the back. He studied the growing pile of broken dishes, as if figuring the best way to approach the problem. Sofie wished he'd look at her instead. She touched his arm. He looked at her then, the flicker of panic in his eyes reminding her how much he hated to be the center of attention. He needed her. Work would help. Work always helped.

"We'd better get started," she said loudly, close to his ear. "If we ever want to make it to the party."

The mining students cheered them on for a few minutes, then streamed past, packing into the house to make music and eat. More people came, Frau Grunberg, even Oskar's supervisor, to smash more dishes and join the party—people they knew and some they didn't. People passing in cars and carts and on bicycles honked and rang and shouted encouragement. Strains of a polka and snippets of talk drifted from the open windows.

Oskar leaned on his broom listening to the shreds of political argument he could hear. "These *Reichstag* elections mark a desertion of the reasonable center, Sofie," he said. "The radical left, the radical right, it doesn't matter. It's a mess."

Sofie considered the spread of shattered crockery. Always politics. This was their party. "I know that!" she said. "I've heard it countless times. I don't care."

Oskar looked about to say something, maybe scold her, contradict her, tell her she should care, people had to care, but then he pressed his lips together and seemed to be thinking hard as he studied the bristles of his broom.

"They're having fun," Sofie said.

Oskar placed the broom against the house and sat on the stoop. "Are you?"

"Can you forget politics, just for tonight?" Sofie tried for a light, teasing tone, but her words sounded harsh.

"Politics can't be left to the politicians for even a moment. You know that!" he said. She told herself his voice held a hint of playfulness.

The sky had turned dark blue at the top, purple over the rooftops. The cobblestones, the shards of porcelain, the brooms, and Oskar, too, glowed in the changing light. The parade of guests appeared to have ended with everyone in the house having a good time. The smell of sweat, beer, and smoked meat mingled with the hearty accordion music.

It felt like days since she, Amalia, and Dora had sneaked food off the platters inside, laughing as they spread the slices of meat thinner and stirred up the bowls of whipped cream to hide their fingerprints. Sofie had to get away from Oskar, just for a minute. He wouldn't know what to do if she started to cry. "I'll slip in and bring you some food. I ate earlier, but I would like to try some of that cake before it's gone."

"Don't let them see you!" Oskar wrapped a hand around her stockinged calf. Tingles of warmth raced up her leg. When she came back out, she'd kiss him, feed him fingerfuls of cream.

Inside, she pressed herself against the wall, peering around the doorway into the kitchen. Lorenz sat on one of the benches with Amalia on his lap, eating cake. He wasn't haranguing her with his communist views. They were laughing, so intent she doubted they'd notice if she marched right in and took her time arranging a plate of food to bring to Oskar. Karl followed Dora in from the parlor.

"Dance with me, little one!" he pleaded. "Are you afraid to know what you'll be missing when you lock yourself away in the convent. An evening with me might change your mind! Your sister, there," he said to Dora in a loud voice Sofie at first assumed was directed at her, then realized his words were meant for Amalia. "A pity she's such a poor judge of men."

"You're drunk!" Dora said without even a trace of the critical tone Sofie would have expected.

"He is," Lorenz laughed. "He's not the only one!" Sofie watched as he lifted Amalia's hair and nibbled at her neck.

Dora spun around, and Karl caught her wrist and whispered something that made her smile and shake her head. Sofie thought of Oskar, patient in the dark, mourning the state of the republic. She stepped into the kitchen.

Amalia leaped to her feet. Karl released Dora. "What are you doing?" Dora cried. "You're not finished yet, are you?"

"Not finished?" Karl feigned horror. "Outside with you then!"

"No, we're not." The cold edge to her voice surprised Sofie as much as it did everyone else. This was her party, hers and Oskar's, the night everyone's good-natured rumblings and racket drove away any bad spirits threatening them, the bridal pair, the guests of honor. She and Oskar were the only ones moping. Her bad humor silenced her sisters. No one dared chastise her further for sneaking in early. Even Karl said nothing as Sofie circled the table collecting a plate of food. She sliced off the piece of cake stripped of its plums and made a show of pushing it to the side before cutting a new piece. Plate in hand she flounced out. Lorenz would have given up sweeping long ago and joined the party. Karl would have bullied people into helping. She and Oskar should leave the broken mess. The guests were drunk enough that they wouldn't notice or judge for longer than a moment, whatever she and Oskar did.

She thrust the plate at Oskar, sitting in the dark. "Thank you, Sofie," he said. She didn't answer. They sat side by side on the hard stoop. "I finished sweeping it all into heaps. We'll just dump these piles in a rubbish bin," Oskar went on after swallowing. "Unless more guests arrive to make more work. But everyone we know and it seems even everyone we don't is already here. The sitting room must be packed. Did you get a look at it?"

"No."

He cut into the cake with his fork. Sofie tried to imagine his reaction if she suddenly picked off a plum and tried to feed it to him. A laugh caught in her chest.

"What?" He wiped his mouth on his handkerchief.

"We're getting married tomorrow!" she said. "We're sailing to America. Sometimes I can't really believe it, even though we've been planning for so long."

"I'll be glad to leave all this behind," Oskar said. She knew he meant the violent politics, the shaky economy, but someone walking by would be likely to think he meant the party going on behind them—her sisters, their friends. "We'll be able to make a better life there. For our children."

Children. Of course. Marriage, then children. Children whose aunts would never hold them in their laps, teach them to cook, tell them stories, braid their hair. Sofie feared she'd cry, right there on the stoop between a neatly swept pile of broken dishes and a wild party in her honor.

Oskar put down his empty plate and wrapped an arm around her. He kissed her ear. "I love you, Sofie Bauer," he said. Finally! She turned toward him and kissed him so deep she felt a pressure in her toes.

Karl poked his head out the window and hollered at them. "You'll never get anywhere in life fooling around like that! You're missing the party."

Oskar took a hand from Sofie's back long enough to wave Karl away, as if he were a pesky fly. Sofie kissed him harder.

"Come here, everyone!" Karl thundered. "Look at what we have here!"

Sofie glimpsed an array of heads above them. She held Oskar tight; she wouldn't allow him to let go. Let people see them kiss! They were young and in love. She had no concerns about their ability to work together. Oskar needed a little practice being passionate. She'd give it to him.

The party continued until almost dawn. The music died down. The remains of the food had been pushed to the middle of the table.

"I have to go to sleep," Sofie announced to the few people left. "I'm getting married tomorrow, I mean today."

"I'll come with you," Amalia stood from her seat beside Lorenz, who was winning his card game and showed no signs of tiring. She tapped Dora, who sat with her head down, asleep at the table. "Time to go to bed."

"We'll clean the place," said Karl looking up from his hand. "Don't worry about a thing."

Oskar put down his fan of cards and walked Sofie to the foot of the stairs.

"Hey, are you trying to look at my hand?" Karl pulled his cards against his chest. "That's a good one. Act like you're going to say good night to your girl so you can see what I've got here."

Oskar cheating was so preposterous that everyone laughed. Sofie kissed him again in the shadowed entryway, even though her lips felt raw from practicing passion on the stoop. She dragged herself up the stairs after her sisters.

"I hope you liked your party," Amalia said as they undressed. "I did. I'm going to miss Lorenz and even Karl. Sometimes I wonder if we did the right thing selling this place." Her earring slipped from her fingers and skittered across the floor under the bed where Dora sat. Amalia reached under to feel for the earring. "I can't…" She slithered half under the bed. "Where is it?" Her voice came back muffled.

"We had to sell it," Sofie said. "Unless you wanted to live here and you said you didn't. You'd better not be changing your mind about that now." She leaned close to the mirror to examine her lips.

"There's something under here!" Amalia said. "A package."

"Leave that alone!" Sofie whirled around. "Just don't touch it!"

"Why not?" Amalia emerged from the under the bed, package in hand.

"Did you find the earring?" Sofie snapped.

Amalia perched next to Dora with the package in her lap. "What is it?" Dora asked suddenly awake. "Sofie, is it yours?"

"Of course it's hers," Amalia said. "Or she'd want to know what's in it. Nice paper. I've seen paper like this somewhere before."

"Give it to me!" Sofie stood over them and grabbed at the package. The paper tore. She let go. "Please give it to me. Please."

"What do you think?" Amalia asked Dora, holding the package tight against her belly. "Let's take a vote!" She laughed.

"I vote we keep it!" Dora leaned into Amalia's lap for a better view.

"Me too."

Sofie tried to snatch it from them but fear of damaging the fabric, and her sisters' kicking legs, kept her back.

As the nightdress fell across their laps Dora and Amalia's voices blended into a musical sigh of admiration, devoid of the mockery Sofie feared.

"Frau Grunberg's...that's where I saw the paper!" Amalia said. "Sofie, this is beautiful. Why are you hiding it?"

Amalia held up the dress. It wasn't wrinkled.

Dora fingered the lacy hem. "It's very romantic," she said.

Sofie busied herself removing her shoes and stockings. She felt the strange expression on her face, couldn't imagine what it looked like, and didn't want her sisters to see. She undressed, her back to them.

"Oskar will like it," Amalia teased. "Try it on, Sofie. Let's see how it looks on you."

"I'm too tired," Sofie said. "I have to get some rest." She took out her flannelette sleeping suit.

"Sofie, let us see!" Dora started up.

"No." Sofie put one foot into a leg of the suit. Dora and Amalia took advantage of her precarious position and dragged her to the bed. They tugged the sleeping suit from her foot. Amalia held her around the waist, while Dora tried to fit the dress over her head.

"Come on, lift your arms," Dora coaxed, laughing. "Come on, be a good girl!"

Sofie, hampered more by her fear of tearing the dress than by her sisters' clumsy efforts, lifted her arms. The silk felt different over her cotton camisole and bloomers, but Dora and Amalia stood back and stared at her, impressed. "Turn around," Amalia said. "Oooh, Oskar is a lucky man."

"Sofie's blushing," Dora said.

Sofie slipped off the nightdress and tossed it toward the nearest suitcase without looking to see where it landed. "I really have to get some sleep," she said. "And so do you."

"We should sleep in the same bed," Amalia said. "One last time. Tomorrow you'll be sleeping with Oskar."

"Are you scared, Sofie?" Dora asked.

"No." Sofie buttoned her sleeping suit and climbed under the featherbed. "What is there to be scared of? Husbands and wives have been sleeping together since Adam and Eve." She rolled onto her side, crossed her arms, and drew her knees up against her chest. She heard the rustle of Amalia's and Dora's skirts.

Her sisters readied themselves for bed. Sofie tried to imagine Oskar beside her. She would discover scars in places on his body she hadn't yet seen and kiss them. He would lick her ears and caress her breasts. The light clicked off. The bed sagged as Amalia climbed in, then sagged again. Dora scrambled over her to the side near the wall whispering, "I want to sleep next to Sofie too; let's put her in the middle."

"She's not asleep yet?" Amalia asked. "Sofie?"

Sofie, in that fuzzy in-between state, made a sound through her nose.

"I wish I were getting married too," said Amalia. "I want to find out what it's like."

"Who would you marry?" Dora yawned.

"That's the problem. I think I want a farmer. I know I want a farm, and I'm not going to find one here. Still, it seemed as though Lorenz liked me tonight, didn't it? And you and Karl? What about that?"

"He was drunk. You know I'm not interested in a husband."

Sofie felt Dora's involuntary shudder and wondered if it was meant for Karl or marriage in general.

"How can Sofie lie there sleeping? I'd be too excited. Look, I *am* too excited and it's not even me who's going to be married, who's going to find out what it's like to be with a man. All I can picture are horses and dogs. Do you think it's like that?"

"I hope not," Dora gasped. "I hope it's more...restful, more romantic. I'm sure it is. Horses and dogs don't kiss or hold each other."

"Yes, but the part I'm wondering about is the part where they stick it in. Do you think it hurts? I can't imagine it could feel good."

"I don't think it does," said Dora.

"I heard women just do that part because it feels good to the man," Amalia said.

"Will you be quiet?" Sofie pressed her palm against her crotch, which had begun to ache listening to her sisters. Prickles of apprehension ran through her body, waking her completely. Their mother shouldn't have died and left them with such important questions unanswered. As the oldest, she would have to find out and prepare her sisters, Amalia anyway, before she left for America.

"She's awake!" Amalia flung an arm over her.

"I'd rather be sleeping," Sofie grumbled, but she let Amalia's arm stay where it was.

"Dora?" Amalia wouldn't be quiet. "Really. Don't you think you'll miss men? Don't you at least want to know what it's like? I saw you flirting tonight."

Dora rolled onto her side, curling her back into Sofie's belly and pulling Sofie's arm over her. "No," she said.

"What about children?" Amalia persisted.

"Go to sleep," Sofie said. "Stop talking." Dora's neck smelled like vanilla cake and her hair fell soft against Sofie's forehead. Amalia's body lay firm and familiar along her back.

Amalia lifted herself on an elbow and leaned over Sofie. "Dora, don't you even want to see what being with a man is like before you run off to join the nuns?"

"What man?" Dora said facing the wall. "You don't choose someone 'just to see what it's like.'"

They shifted and settled. The house creaked. Sofie released a long breath and slipped toward sleep.

Amalia whispered in the dark. "This is the last time we'll share the same bed. The last time we're just sisters, no husbands, no brothers-in-law."

"Shh," Sofie mumbled. "You'll wake Dora."

"I'm sorry." Amalia's voice was small, unsure.

Sofie purposefully kept her breathing even and slow. She couldn't let herself start thinking about good-byes.

"I'm sorry," Amalia whispered again.

Sofie rolled over to hold her sister. She willed herself to sleep as the light of her wedding day began to fill the streets outside.

Dora was right, Amalia thought as she looked around the bare magistrate's office. Sofie should have had a church wedding. Their colorful dresses seemed out of place in the dingy little room. Neither the cheerless bureaucrat nor his cranky secretary thought to raise the shades more than halfway. Instead of stained glass behind an altar, a shadowy rectangle where a portrait had hung darkened the wall behind a massive wooden desk. Sofie and Oskar stood side by side in the soupy light. The magistrate muttered a few words. They signed their names in a thick book, and it was done.

Amalia wondered what their mother would have thought. According to family legend her wedding to their father had been a grand affair, so crowded they couldn't close the doors of the church. Afterward there had been a party at the farm, with long tables covered in white cloths set up in the freshly mowed field and strings of lanterns hung between the trees. All the neighbors brought chairs and planks for the dance floor.

Hanna had married *Teufelmann* in a ceremony similar to Sofie's. A portrait of the Kaiser hung on the wall; the desk had been smaller, the office brighter. Amalia remembered *Teufelmann* scolding her for fidgeting, and her mother's apologetic smile. Afterward, they'd gone to the pub for lunch. *Teufelmann* joined his cronies at the bar, Hanna flitting back and forth between him and her daughters at their table. Dora, only three years old, fell asleep on the hard wooden bench of the booth. Sofie built houses with the coasters and silverware. Amalia devoured the small golden potatoes cooked in bacon that Dora had left untouched on her plate. She stretched on tiptoe to peek over the back of the wooden booth to watch their mother at the bar. *Teufelmann* kept a proprietary hand on Hanna's bottom, an ominous look of dissatisfaction clouding his face when she moved to check on the girls.

In the airless magistrate's office, her woman's body draped in folds of soft peach velvet, as she watched Sofie marry Oskar, Amalia's mouth suddenly filled with the taste of Dora's potatoes. She was struck by the sensation, astonishing and strange, of tasting something perfectly delicious while outside her skin, the decisions of people she loved most destroyed the familiar pattern of her days.

CHAPTER 12

▼

Amalia stopped at the side of the rutted road to the Muellers' farm and waited for Sofie and Dora to catch up. They'd insisted on joining her in her quest for paying work and a place to live; in less than a week Sofie would be leaving on the boat from Bremerhaven, and God only knew when they'd be together again. Amalia supposed she was glad to be with them, though they seemed to think of the day as a lark in the country rather than a serious pursuit of employment.

Maple trees in full leaf along both sides of the road shaped a tunnel of cool green shade. Cows and sheep grazed in the bright fields beyond. Sofie and Dora sauntered toward her, Dora swinging the bag containing their picnic, Sofie talking, her gestures sculpting the air.

Frau Schmidt. Frau Oskar Schmidt. Amalia tried thinking of Sofie that way and couldn't, even though they had smashed plates at the raucous *Polterabend*, witnessed the quiet wedding, eaten at the festive luncheon afterward. They'd been there, seen it all—Oskar and Sofie standing steady, side by side before the magistrate; Oskar's hand against Sofie's back as he raised his bubbling glass in a toast to his wife; Sofie's fingers curled around his on the handle of Frau Becker's silver knife as they sliced the plum cake; their laughter, the kisses Sofie planted on Oskar's face and neck when she thought no one was looking—yet Sofie still seemed more theirs than Oskar's.

Amalia breathed the smell of warm earth, grass, and manure. Across the field a magpie swooped down from its round thorny nest, its wings and tail flashing blue-black in the light. A man on a squeaky bicycle appeared in the distance, behind her sisters. She squinted, trying to recognize him. Sofie and Dora stopped and looked too.

Sofie seemed the same to Amalia, yet in the dark, with Oskar, she'd done what married people did at night before sleep. Oskar would have unbuttoned the little pearl buttons, cupped Sofie's breasts in his hands, stroked her bare thighs. There, Amalia's imagination stopped. She pictured animals again, the snorting bull, desperate and silly on two legs behind the cow, and couldn't relate it to humans though common sense told her it had to be somehow the same. How could Sofie walk and talk and act the way she always had when she knew what Amalia only guessed at, when she'd done what all their lives they'd been cautioned never to do, spread her legs for a man? Amalia had to stop thinking. She felt crazy, restless, like she had to relieve herself.

Sofie and Dora answered the rhythmic squeal of the bicycle with cries of recognition as the man reached them. He removed his cap and wiped sweat from his forehead with a large white handkerchief. From this distance he looked a bit like an older version of Lorenz: tall, blonde, and lanky.

"Amalia!" Sofie beckoned. "It's Tomas!"

Tomas Blau, the man who had driven them back home after the war, Gustav's older brother. But Amalia could see from where she stood that this man didn't have an eye patch. She retraced her steps.

Tomas sat grinning astride the bike, feet flat on the ground. A strap across his chest held a rifle to his back. He greeted Amalia. "Surprise, surprise—the Bauer sisters, And Sofie tells me she's a married lady about to leave for America! I never would have recognized you. Remember the wagon rides, back and forth to Tauburg for Easter and Christmas? You rolled around in the back squealing like little piglets. Not you, though." He pointed at Sofie. "You were always the lady, sitting up nice and proper on the seat beside me. Remember?"

Sofie blushed. "I was, what, thirteen years old? A little girl."

"And how old are you now? Let's see." He made a big show of calculating on his fingers.

"She's nineteen," said Dora.

"You don't say? That means you must be about seventeen? And you..." He turned to Amalia. "Eighteen. Right?" One blue eye glittered bright with questions; the other stared blankly over her shoulder. "Sofie tells me you're looking for work here in Elsterdorf."

Amalia studied his face, realizing too late he was waiting for an answer.

"I already told your sisters—it's a glass eye. Better than a patch, don't you think? So..." He leaned forward, over the handlebar basket that held two dead rabbits. "I happen to know that the Neufelds are looking to hire a girl. I work there myself late afternoons and evenings."

"Can you believe it, Amalia?" Dora asked. "God is really looking out for you. We haven't even made it to the Muellers' door yet and already you might have a job."

"I'd say you do have a job, if you decide to take it." Tomas pulled up on the handlebars of his bicycle, raising the front wheel a few centimeters and letting it bounce down. The lifeless rabbits twitched, then settled. "The Neufelds need the help and haven't been able to find anyone."

"They were so old back during the war when I lived with them," said Dora. "I'm a bit surprised to hear they're still alive." She paused. "That didn't sound very nice, but you know what I mean."

"Herr Neufeld passed on," Tomas said. "His wife can't do much outside the house and her mind wanders. Heinrich, their son, never married. He's getting on in years himself. You know, it's not easy to find a woman who wants the farm life." He pinned Sofie with his living eye. "I'm almost twenty-seven and I haven't found anyone myself. Like you, everyone wants something better, America, the city." He paused. "Come for dinner." He gestured to the rabbits stiffening in the basket. "I shot these this morning. Mother will skin them and we'll have fresh rabbit and potatoes by the time you're finished at the Neufelds'. Tell them I sent you."

"The Muellers are expecting us," Sofie said. "We have to catch a train back to the city."

Amalia touched the brown fur. When she looked closely she could see individual black, white, and yellow hairs. The top rabbit lay on its side, soft belly exposed. Tomas had shot it in the head. All the meat would be good.

Sofie took a step in the direction of the Muellers'. "They're expecting us," she said again. Dora moved to follow.

"The fur will make a nice pair of mittens," Tomas said. His gaze moved from Amalia's fingers in the fur, along her arm to her face. "I was lucky today. Most days I go out and get nothing. With one eye, it's difficult. To judge distance is nearly impossible."

Tomas—twenty-seven? An old man. He'd always had an interest in Sofie. She'd lived with his family. He knew her best. Yet Amalia wanted to tell Sofie and Dora to go on without her. Tomas could take her to the Neufelds' on his bicycle, and she could get the job matter resolved quickly.

"How is your mother?" Sofie asked.

"Tough as ever." He laughed. "You have to be to survive all these shortages and drops in prices. Terrible times for farmers. Gustav, well, he's the same too. A little thinner, maybe. Does his share of the work, but could never figure out what needs be done or exactly how to do it without Mother or me telling him."

"Give them my best," Sofie said. "We really have to be going," she added in her bossy oldest-sister voice. Sofie the leave-everybody-behind-and-go-to-America, fancy-nightgown, touch-her-man-whenever-she-wanted sister. And right behind her, ready to echo the need to move along, no doubt in the same self-righteous tone, Dora the future nun, bride of Jesus, helper of the sick and weak.

Amalia imagined her own hands around Tomas's waist as she sat on the seat of his bicycle and he stood pedaling. She could be the one to ride away leaving no trail but dust settling on the road. Tomas was a one-eyed old farmer with an idiot brother and the most merciless mother in Elsterdorf. Why was she picturing herself gutting the rabbits, preparing a stew, sewing mittens, and wearing them during a long, dark winter? At night, under the covers, she'd learn what wives and bad girls and Sofie knew.

"Should I tell the Neufelds to expect you?" Tomas lifted a foot to a pedal.

"Yes. In about two hours?" Sofie consulted Dora with a look.

This is my life, Amalia wanted to shout.

Tomas's tires crunched and the squeak resumed. "Nice to see you again," he called back.

"Do you think he takes that eye out?" Dora asked.

Sofie laughed. "He might have to, to wash it, or sleep."

"What's so funny?" Amalia said. They could see the Mueller's tidy little house on the other side of the potato fields. The prospect of a visit exhausted her.

"What's wrong with you?" Sofie asked. "You just heard there's a job. Maybe the Muellers know of something better. But if not…I'd still say you're lucky."

Lucky. They turned up the Muellers' drive and the sun fell hot on their heads. Frau Mueller rushed to the dooryard of well-swept, hard-packed dirt to welcome them, exclaiming how big they'd grown, how they were women now. The chickens fluttered, squawked, and pecked in the chicken coop beside them.

Frau Mueller looked the same as she had almost a decade ago. The smell of boiled eggs wafting from the house mingled with the scent of straw and chicken shit, traces of Herr Mueller's particular pipe tobacco and the fatty scent of soap making. The aroma of separation and not quite belonging, and of hair braided too tight.

Sofie asked Frau Mueller about her grandchildren, chattered about meeting Tomas, the job. They had just begun talking about America when Dora sidled up to Amalia. "Are you all right?"

She was, but could only manage a nod. Frau Mueller and Sofie laughed together. For the first time Sofie seemed like a Frau Schmidt. Frau Mueller and Frau Schmidt—two wives laughing hard. Frau Mueller wiped her eyes with a corner of her apron and rested a hand on Sofie's arm. Sofie, hand on hip, shook her head.

Amalia knew they weren't laughing at her but, even knowing it, felt as though they were. Dora whispered in her ear. "You'd think Sofie was the one who had lived with the Muellers."

"I don't care about that," Amalia said.

"You got the best family," Dora said.

Amalia tried to picture the Blau's house where she'd visited Sofie several times. More often Dora and Sofie had come to play with her right here at the Muellers', where they were used to children underfoot. Frau Blau allowed visiting children into her house only grudgingly and on special occasions, like the time she'd given a party for Gustav. The cake had marzipan icing; no one knew where she'd found almonds and sugar during the war. Amalia, Dora, Sofie, and other children from nearby farms sat around the table trying not to spill, swing their legs, or clatter their silverware. They didn't have to be told. The scowl permanently etched on Frau Blau's face; her hands, quick to slap and correct; her whole shrunken body emanating disapproval—all made scolding unnecessary. Each child had received a sliver of cake and was glad to have it. After everyone was served, most of the cake remained on the plate. Amalia could see it now, shining like a three-quarter moon on its way back to kitchen, the door slamming before anyone could think to want seconds.

Dora swung the bag with their lunch. "I'm hungry. We should have eaten this by now. We'd be full and I wouldn't have to carry it."

"Remember how stingy Frau Blau was?" Amalia asked.

"Everyone was stingy," Dora said. "Times were so hard. No one had much. As bad as things are, they're better now, not just for us, the whole country. Things are better." She nodded toward Frau Mueller still deep in conversation with Sofie. "You really did have the best family, though, that's true."

Sofie—Frau Schmidt—gestured toward the chicken coop. Frau Mueller nodded and they moved toward it, still talking.

"Do you think Sofie likes being married?" Amalia asked Dora.

"I still wouldn't call that a wedding—a stamp, a pile of official documents, and a big book to write their names in. Where's the altar, the priest? Where's the communion, the blessings, the prayers, the music? Where's God? Sofie would have had a church wedding if she'd married someone else."

"But do you think she likes being a wife?" Amalia said.

"It's only been a couple of days." Dora stamped her foot at an inquisitive chicken. It skittered and clucked.

"And nights. That's the part I'm wondering about. We see them in the day. It doesn't seem all that different from before."

"Has she said anything to you?"

"No, and I don't know how to ask."

Frau Mueller held Sofie's crooked finger and leaned over to examine it.

"Well, it is a private matter between her and Oskar," said Dora.

"But she's our sister. If we can't ask her, who can we ask?"

"They're looking over here." Dora nodded at Sofie and Frau Mueller. "They're going to think we're rude."

I am rude, Amalia thought as she followed Dora across the yard. *I'm nosy and I'm rude. But I have to know.*

Frau Mueller fed them salty smoked ham and apricots she'd canned last summer. They contributed their loaf of bread and hunk of cheese. They told more about their mother's death and Sofie's wedding and Amalia's desire for a job in the area. Frau Mueller mentioned the Neufelds again. Amalia let them all talk. She swallowed an apricot slice without chewing, spooned the sweet syrupy juice, realizing the dress she'd worn at Sofie's wedding was more the color of apricots than peaches.

All the way to the Neufelds' she listened hard for Tomas's squeaky wheel and tried to think of a way to ask Sofie about married love. She studied her sister, looking for signs of disappointment or satisfaction. Sofie seemed sure of herself (but she always had), determined (but she always had), and bossy. Nothing new.

"We turn here," Sofie said.

"I lived with them for three years," Dora reminded her. "I know the way."

"Sofie," Amalia began, after one last look down the road to see if any bicycle rider made a moving speck on the horizon. "What's it like, being with Oskar?"

"Being with Oskar?" Sofie stared over the field where some men stooped, working in rows. "It's hard to put into words. It's like having a railing to hold onto on a rickety staircase. It's like…having a seat in a crowded streetcar. I feel safe and taken care of. He's with me. He's there." Her forehead wrinkled as she met Amalia's eyes.

"That's exactly how it is with Jesus!" Dora cried.

Sofie laughed. Amalia shook her head. That wasn't what she meant at all.

Heinrich Neufeld, looking a lot older, bald, more like his father than the way Amalia remembered him, emerged from the barn carrying a pitchfork and blinking in the light. He shaded his eyes and stared at the three girls. Flies buzzed around his head.

"Dora," he said. "Tomas rode by and told me to expect you. Amalia, Sofie." He extended a huge, rough hand. They each shook it in turn. He leaned the fork against the barn, then led them to the house. Chunks of plaster were missing from the outside walls. A shutter hung from a broken hinge. At the doorstep they waited while he methodically scraped the mud and manure from his boots. A few of the flies settled on the manure. No one spoke. Amalia remembered Dora's complaints about how quiet Heinrich had always been, how whatever he was doing required his full attention.

They waited for Heinrich to clean his shoes. Amalia listened to sound of the flies and watched thickening clouds fill the sky. Sofie tapped her foot.

"How is Frau Neufeld?" Dora asked anxiously. The woman she had lived with would never have permitted the house to fall into such a state of disrepair.

After a long silence while Heinrich inspected the soles and sides of his boots, he answered, "Come see for yourself."

Frau Neufeld sat, tiny and wrinkled and almost bald, at a table covered with an intricately crocheted cloth. Once famous in the town, her original patterns crocheted in plain white thread could be read like stories. The Muellers had a Neufeld tablecloth they used on special occasions. Amalia remembered how afraid she'd been of spilling on it, until Frau Mueller taught her the many ways to remove a stain.

Frau Neufeld held a leather dice cup in her hand instead of a crochet hook. She rattled the dice, poured them across the tablecloth, studied them, her lips moving. Strips of fly paper, speckled with flies, dangled from the ceiling in the corners of the room.

"Mother," Heinrich said. "We have visitors."

Her lips continued to move with no sound. She didn't look up from the dice. "*Schweinhund! Scheissekopf!*" she screamed. Dora gasped. They all jumped. With a sudden sweep of her scrawny arm Frau Neufeld scattered the dice through the air. They clattered against wood and glass while she slumped silent in her chair, staring at her gnarled fingers as they worried the cloth.

"Bad roll," Heinrich explained before falling to his knees to search for the dice.

Sofie, Dora, and Amalia dropped to the floor, glad of a reason to hide their faces. Amalia chewed her lip to stifle panicky laughter. She wanted to ask Heinrich how this had happened, how had the village's most respectable *Hausfrau* had turned into this demented dice player. Had the change been gradual or sudden? The Frau Neufeld they knew during the war had never cursed. She would be horrified to see herself. Amalia wanted to lie down under the table and close her eyes. Instead she felt under a chair and brought up a dustball. Cleaning she wouldn't mind, she'd expected it, but caring for a crazy old woman didn't fit her plan.

One by one Heinrich found all seven dice. Clearly, he'd had practice.

Sofie stood, brushing off her skirt. "Tomas Blau told us you were looking for help," she said. Dice all back in their cup, Frau Neufeld shook them contentedly.

"Yes," said Heinrich. "We can give room and board and a small salary."

"How small?" Sofie asked. "It doesn't seem like an easy job. I would think the salary should be big."

"No one has much money," Heinrich said. He placed a hand on his mother's arm to keep her from flinging the dice. She hissed, then began to shake the cup again.

Amalia struggled to her feet. Her knees hurt. She should tell Sofie she didn't want the job, at any salary.

"What would the job involve?" Sofie asked. "We should be clear about that."

"Mainly caring for my mother, cooking, housework," Heinrich said.

Amalia cleared her throat. She had to say something. She thought of the roll of money back home tucked into an envelope in the corner of her pillowcase. She would use it to buy a ticket to America. The fly paper flapped in the breeze.

"With Tomas Blau's help," Heinrich said, "I can take care of the farm. He comes every afternoon. Amalia wouldn't have to do the outside work."

"But that's the work I like," Amalia protested weakly. The whole day had begun to feel as though it were happening to someone else. It couldn't be her future Sofie was discussing. She tried to remember the chain of events linking the day they left Elsterdorf in Tomas Blau's wagon six years ago as girls going home to this moment, when they had reappeared in the Neufeld's livingroom as homeless young women, but memories flashed and tangled and wouldn't be organized or connected in any way that made sense.

"That sounds fair," Sofie said, as if Amalia hadn't spoken. She began negotiating a salary. The dice clicked. Sofie talked. Heinrich murmured agreement. Dora hummed and peered out the window. She seemed unable to look at the old lady. The sky had filled with rain clouds.

Amalia sank into a chair at the table beside Frau Neufeld. She wouldn't have to stay forever, only until something better came along. There would be other jobs, other possibilities, once she was settled in the area. She decided to try to feel loved instead of angry, to let Sofie make all the arrangements. Without a hus-band, Sofie was her railing on rickety stairs and Dora, her seat on a crowded bus. The skin on Frau Neufeld's's neck hung in small wrinkled folds. She'd spilled something yellow on her collar, boiled egg maybe. Next laundry day Amalia would scrub that out.

Frau Neufeld pinched her sleeve. "Do you feel lucky?" she whispered. "Are you ready to play?" Her rheumy blue eyes focused on Amalia's face. The old woman smiled, revealing all five of her teeth. "I'm lucky," she said and continued to grin.

"We have to be going," Sofie said. "We have to catch the train and I think it's about to storm."

Dora edged to the door.

"Rain is good right now," said Heinrich. "I would give you a ride in the wagon, but I don't like to leave her long. If it thunders, she'll be frightened."

"Frightened. Frightened. Stay, please stay." Frau Neufeld clung to Amalia. "I'll be frightened. So frightened. It's not safe. The Communists. The terrible French. They'll shoot you no matter who you are. They don't care."

Heinrich held her hand, the one clutching the leather cup, and shook it gen-tly. She smiled at the familiar sound, released Amalia, and concentrated on the dice. "I'm lucky," Frau Neufeld said.

"Amalia," Sofie said. "He wants to know when you can start."

You decide, Amalia wanted to say. *You've decided everything else.*

"After I've gone to Gunstadt," Dora said. "Please. I'm counting on you to go with me."

They'd take Sofie to the boat and see her off. Amalia would take Dora to the convent. No one would be left to say good-bye to her. "All right," she said. "After Dora goes."

"Okay," Sofie told Heinrich. "Two weeks. She'll be here in two weeks."

The old lady rolled and cursed again.

Heinrich followed them to the door.

Amalia dreaded the walk back to the station through such thick and steamy air. A warm wind rustled the leaves in the trees along the road, but did nothing to cool her sweaty skin.

"That was easy," said Sofie. "I feel better leaving, knowing you're all set."

"That's what this is to you!" Amalia stood in front of her, stopping her mid-step. "That's why you came. Not to help me. Not to be together, to have a picnic, a nice time in the country before you go. This is all for you. To make it easier. So you don't feel guilty leaving poor Amalia all alone."

"We did come to have a nice time," Dora said. "Please, Amalia, we came to have a day together. A picnic."

"And we didn't have one!" Amalia shouted. Rage, menacing and thick, like the clouds in the sky, rage that had settled in her chest since Sofie decided to go to America threatened to liquefy into tears.

"Come on," Sofie pushed Amalia's shoulder. "We're going to miss the train. If you have to yell at me, do it while we walk."

Amalia wouldn't move that easily. "So now I won't be alone, will I? I'll be feeding and cleaning up after a crazy old lady and her silent son."

"You were the one who wanted to be in the country," Sofie said. "You could have kept the boarding house."

"The boarding house belonged to all three of us and we needed to split the money! And I do want to be in the country but outside or in the barn. I don't want to crawl around on the floor looking for lost dice."

"You can start looking for another job right away," Dora said.

They'd come this far together, Amalia thought, but just she would be staying. It wasn't fair. It wasn't right. Instead of saving her, rescuing her, showing her the way, it was as if Sofie had a made a deal with the wicked witch, sacrificing her so she could escape.

"I did you a favor!" Sofie shouted. "You should be thanking me. If you'd spoken up, I wouldn't have had to make all the arrangements. I did it to help you. Stop crying."

Amalia, about to protest, realized she did have tears on her cheeks. At that moment very large rain drops plopped onto the road, splattered their skin and clothes, and then began to fall seriously.

"Look," Sofie yelled. "Now it's raining."

"Is that my fault?" Amalia yelled back. "Now the weather is my responsibility?"

"We would have been a lot closer to the station if you'd kept walking," Sofie snapped.

"Why did you let me stop you? I thought nothing got in the way of Sofie Bauer—excuse me, I mean Schmidt. Frau Oskar Schmidt leaving for America."

"You can come to America!" Sofie screamed. "I want you to come. I told you that. I thought you would."

"Why? Why did you think I would?"

"You still can, when you get tired of living here. We'll help pay for your passage."

"Stop fighting!" Dora pleaded.

Amalia's hair hung plastered to her head. The road had dissolved into mud.

"I don't want to go to America!" she shouted. "This is my home. It's your home too. We belong here. If Mama hadn't married that devil man we'd have our own farm. That's what was supposed to happen."

"That's silly." Sofie rubbed her forehead. "Who's to say what's supposed to happen?"

"Who, besides God," Dora said. "You know, we're going to miss the train. And I'm cold."

The mud sucked at their shoes as they trudged along. *Maybe I should go to America*, Amalia thought. They had a lot of land there. She could have an American farm, with cowboys. She could own it herself without marriage or an inheritance.

No. People weren't meant to move all over the world. People should stay with what they knew, where they belonged, with their own kind. She belonged here—German rain on her face, German mud under her feet. She could never learn the strange sounds of English, the green paper money that all looked alike. Sofie belonged here too. If she hadn't married Oskar she wouldn't be leaving.

She caught herself, blaming Oskar, sounding like Dora with her church wedding. Dora must have known Sofie wouldn't have especially wanted one, Oskar or not. Part of the reason Sofie chose him had to do with his lack of religious beliefs. Sofie would have wanted to go to America, anyway. Oskar's plans to go were, most likely, part of why she chose him over Lorenz.

Amalia shivered in her wet dress, wishing she'd brought a sweater, but the day had started so clear and sunny. There was no other train today. If they missed this one, they'd have to find a ride to Kirchstadt and catch one there, or sleep at someone's house. Amalia didn't want to go back to the Neufelds'. She'd be back there soon enough.

Behind them, through the beating of the rain, came a squelching, rattly sound. Amalia turned—Tomas Blau with his cart.

"I came to find you!" he shouted. "I'll take you to the station."

"Thank heaven!" Sofie yelled.

Tomas climbed down to help them. Surprisingly, Sofie scrambled into the back with Dora, leaving Amalia the seat up front. Happy not to have to look at her sisters, especially Sofie, Amalia stared ahead through the curtains of rain. Let the two of them whisper about her. She inhaled deeply in an effort not to cry in front of Tomas Blau. All around them Amalia could smell the rain, the mud, the young plants, wet and lush. She thought she could hear them absorbing water, growing, pulling all they needed from the earth.

"Will you be working at the Neufelds'?" Tomas asked.

She nodded.

"The old lady can be difficult," Tomas said.

"That was clear." She wiped raindrops from her eyes.

"You'll need a break sometimes," he said. "You'll need to have a little fun."

"Fun?"

"Cards, dice…on Saturdays there's dancing in town."

"I love to dance," Amalia said.

Rain blew against her face. Sweet rain. Free of coal dust and ash.

"You can teach me," he said. "I'm not very good."

"You can teach me *skat*," she told him. "I just learned to play and I forget a lot of the rules."

"It takes time," he said. Behind his words hung the hint of a question.

"Were the rabbits good?" Amalia asked.

"Meat that fresh, prepared well, is always good," he said.

"I'm sorry we couldn't join you. My sister—"

"Under your seat there, that bowl's for you to take home."

She bent to see a large white bowl with a plate on top, tied in a towel. Had Frau Blau prepared it so quickly? How had he persuaded his mother to share? Had she become more generous? Or was this all his doing?

"You can bring the bowl back with you when you come," he said. "Let me know how you like it. It's my specialty. It contains a secret ingredient. See if you can guess."

During their whole conversation he looked ahead, over the horses. Maybe he had to, with only one eye.

No one else waited at the little station. At first Amalia thought they'd missed the train, but they were a few minutes early. The roofed portion of the platform was hardly big enough to shelter the four of them. They stood near the wagon in the rain, so wet already, that a few more minutes made no difference.

"Better be ready to board," Tomas said. "It never stops long here."

They heard a distant rumble from down the track, too steady to be part of the storm.

Sofie and Dora thanked him for the ride and climbed the few steps to the platform. "Good luck in America, Sofie," Tomas called. "Dora, pray for me, poor sinner that I am!"

He handed Amalia the warm bowl. "I'll see you when you come back." She felt his smile all over her wet skin.

They found seats in the empty car. She settled with the stew in her lap, where she could see Tomas wave good-bye. Sofie and Dora sat on either side.

Their breath and soaked clothes steamed the windows. The train jerked, the plate slipped, and gravy dribbled over the lip of the bowl. Amalia caught it with her finger and tasted it, rich and spicy on her tongue. The secret ingredient could be anything.

The conductor punched their tickets. They rocked through the countryside, the three of them together.

"Thank heaven Tomas came along. We would have missed this train. How can such a nice man be cursed with such a terrible mother?" Sofie asked, wringing water from her skirt. It rolled down the floor of the car in a little rivulet. "Everyone was afraid of her. Even Herr Blau. Most times people did what she said, no questions asked, Gustav especially. I remember how he was fascinated by the barn cats. When they'd have kittens he'd carry them around, bring them inside to his room. A normal person would just bring the cats back outside or to the barn where they belonged."

Amalia's shoulders tensed. Her feet rested in the puddle from her own dripping skirt. She didn't even try to dry off.

"The first few times it happened Frau Blau made her husband or Tomas remove the cats. Then, one day, neither of them was around, and Gustav had done it again. It was like she went crazy, in a scary, silent kind of way." Sofie shuddered. "I was terrified of her angry face. I offered to carry the cats out but, no, she wanted to teach Gustav a lesson. Enough was enough."

"Do we want to hear this, Sofie?" Dora asked. "I don't think so."

"Go on," Amalia said. "What did she do?"

"She made Gustav put the kittens in a grain sack. There were three of them, three little black and white cats, eyes just open. Afterward, I told myself they might have died anyway after all Gustav's handling. The mother might not have taken them back. Frau Blau stood over him—strange, he was so big and she was so small but it did seem like she was standing over him—as he dropped them in. You never heard such a mewling. You would have thought it was twenty cats crying. She ordered me to knot the top, but I wouldn't do it. It was the one time I defied her."

Sofie had never told this story. Amalia would have remembered. How had she kept it to herself all these years? What else about her sister didn't she know?

"That's enough," Dora said. "We can figure out what happened next."

"When I refused, she began yelling, 'Gustav doesn't know how to tie a knot. The least you could do is help. What are we feeding you for? You worthless parasite.' She'd never said such terrible things before."

"Was this before your finger or after?" Amalia asked, not sure why it mattered, only knowing it did.

"You know, I don't remember," Sofie said. "I really don't." She looked forlorn. Amalia regretted asking.

Dora coughed and bowed her head.

"She made Gustav drown the kittens. I still don't know if he knew what he was doing."

The train passed through the next small village without stopping.

"She told me to get rid of them," Sofie went on. "I buried them behind the pigpen. I'll never forget their soggy little corpses. Matted fur."

A flock of sheep grazed in a passing field, oblivious to the rain. Amalia wished she hadn't encouraged Sofie to tell this story.

"I tell myself with all the terrible things that have happened and are happening—riots, accidents at the mine, Mama's death, the casualties of the war, all the people who died of influenza—the drowning of three kittens is not a big deal. But it was. Using poor Gustav that way, and me. She's a disturbed woman. I'd stay away from her, Amalia."

"Maybe she's changed," Amalia said. "People do."

"Not that much," said Sofie.

The train clacked along.

Frau Blau wouldn't live forever. Amalia saw herself on the wagon seat beside Tomas, with the sun shining, or maybe in the dark, cycling home after a dance— the sky thick with stars, the air saturated with the music of insects and squeaky bike wheels. "Sofie, what is it like with Oskar? You know, at night." Amalia studied their muddy feet lined up on the floor.

Dora stifled a giggle.

Amalia didn't think Sofie was going to answer, so much silence passed, but then she said, "I vowed I would tell you exactly what it was like. I never missed Mama so much as on the night before my wedding." She paused again.

Amalia's whole body waited for her words, like one big straining ear. Tomas's bowl warmed her lap. She held it steady.

"Then I found I couldn't tell you," she said. "I had this feeling it's different for everyone. I really didn't know what to say about it. And I still don't know."

"Did he like your nightgown?" Dora asked.

"I think I liked it more than he did. He just asked me to take it off." Sofie lifted the shoulder next to Amalia's in a shrug.

"Did it hurt?" Amalia asked.

"Not so much," she said. "I think that if the man is gentle and patient, it doesn't hurt."

Gentle and patient was not what Amalia expected to hear. She pictured a wild struggle and hot, hard kisses that filled her mouth. Sofie's feet, crossed at the ankles, swung a little. Dora's rested close together on the floor. Amalia flexed her toes up and down. With her thigh she tilted the bowl, deliberately filled her cupped palm and licked it clean.

"What are you doing?" Sofie asked. "Can't you wait until we get home?"

"No," she said, and spilled some more.

CHAPTER 13

▼

Before dawn on the day of Sofie's departure, Dora gave up trying to sleep. She slid out of bed, leaving Amalia sprawled out and snoring, and knelt to say her morning prayers, asking God to protect Sofie and Oskar as they crossed the ocean. She would have feared less for their safety if Oskar weren't a skeptic; she couldn't even bring herself to think the word *atheist*. Maybe her prayers, combined with those of the good Catholics on board ship, would keep it afloat.

One class of miners had graduated, and with the house already sold and emptied out, Dora and Amalia shared a room on the second floor, though each of them could have had her own. Sofie, Oskar, Karl and Lorenz—the six of them formed an impromptu family that wouldn't exist tomorrow. Dora made a last request for God to bless all of them and decided to make breakfast so that Sofie, on her last morning in Tauburg, wouldn't have to. A parting gift.

From Sofie and Oskar's room next door came shuffling sounds and footsteps. With a quick *amen* she tugged a dress over her head, buttons catching in her hair. Slowing enough to untangle herself, she imagined Sofie on the other side of the wall, stepping into her dark tailored skirt, twisting a little to button the waistband, the tip of her tongue poking from her lips until she glanced in the mirror and pulled it back in. She'd frown at her reflection as she adjusted the collar of her blouse and use just her fingers, no comb or brush, to fix her hair. Dora could see her sister as if the wall were glass.

In America Sofie would buy new American clothes and Dora wouldn't know what they looked like. She'd speak English and Dora wouldn't understand what she was saying. Maybe she'd even have a baby. Of course she'd have babies, and

Dora would never know them—her own nieces and nephews. She had to sit down on the edge of the bed.

Amalia rolled over and yawned. "What time is it?"

"Early," Dora told her.

"Wake me up for breakfast." She covered her face with the featherbed.

Just because Sofie always made breakfast Amalia expected her to make the last one. Dora felt like the more considerate sister because she didn't. Then she felt guilty for being proud. Nuns were humble. Murmuring a string of Hail Marys, she practiced her humility on the way down the hall.

On her way past Lorenz's slightly open door she heard voices, angry whispers. She stopped.

"I don't care." She thought it was Karl's voice. "You can't take money from your best friend, and from girls whose mother never overcharged us."

Lorenz answered. "It's for the strike fund."

"Put it back. Put it back now before they wake up. I can't believe you'd steal from Oskar, from those girls."

Stealing! What money? From where? How much had he taken? She had to do something. If they walked out and caught her eavesdropping she'd confront Lorenz. If she weren't such a coward she would rap on the door right now, march in and demand to know the whole story. Her racing thoughts interfered with her listening.

"...not for myself. The coffers are so low. Miners' families are starving. Our comrades! And I didn't take it all. He won't notice until they're long underway."

Dora wished she could see their faces. Lorenz's voice flowed, full of passion and purpose, defending a wrong it seemed he'd done to her sister and new brother-in-law. A sin, stealing. Where had Oskar kept their money anyway, if Lorenz was able to find it? Why wasn't it safe? She'd always thought Oskar the most careful of men. Now she wondered; would he take good care of her sister?

"You Spartakists, communist idiots." Karl's voice grew loud, then soft again. "Say what you will about Hindenburg and Hitler, the Kaiser: none of them would steal an inheritance from three good German girls, from a friend." Karl's voice deepened. "You can't justify this, Lorenz. I caught you. I won't keep quiet. You might as well just put it back."

So Karl would take care of it, tell Oskar. She could go make breakfast. Was stealing from friends and family worse than stealing from strangers? God wouldn't think so. Or would he? What about stealing for a reason, to help people who had less, who were desperate? Dora's head ached. This difficult day threatened to be even worse than expected.

"If I asked Oskar, he'd give it to me," Lorenz said.

"Well, you should have asked then."

"If it were only his money, I mean. He knows it's for a just cause. But Sofie— a woman wouldn't understand."

"They need it. It won't be easy, starting all over again in America."

"Taking that many marks out of our poor country right now isn't right. I don't care who does it." Lorenz's voice rang out, sure and strong. "America is full of money, opportunity. Isn't that why they're going?"

"Put it back, I tell you," Karl said.

If Lorenz—laughing, idealistic, sweet Lorenz—could steal from a best friend, anything could happen. Anyone was capable of anything. The door squealed, and Dora disappeared into the shadows of the stairwell as Karl exited; his wheezy breath, loud for a moment, faded as he moved in the direction of his room, or Sofie and Oskar's. Anger fluttered in her stomach like an injured bird. At first, she barely recognized the feeling. It flapped harder. How dare he steal from them? Their money, the *Gemutlichkeit* of their final hours all together, the happy memories of their friendship. Her whole sense of the world. In stories she always knew who the heroes and the villains were.

She put water and the six eggs in a pan on the stove, listening all the while for footsteps and voices overhead. The eggs sunk to the bottom and rolled against each other. She sliced a loaf of bread. After arranging the slices on a board she watched the water heat. How could an enormous ship float along on top of the ocean when an egg didn't float in a pan? Small bubbles formed along the edges of the water. The eggs began to bump and rattle as the water boiled, but they didn't rise to the surface.

Sofie burst into the kitchen, snatched her apron from the nail by the door, and tied it around herself in one continuous and efficient movement, before she even noticed Dora. Her rigid expression didn't melt into a smile when Dora smiled at her. Sofie looked at the eggs boiling and the sliced bread. Her lips tightened. Her eyes narrowed.

"I thought I'd make breakfast today," Dora explained, before Sofie could say anything. "Did Karl talk to you?"

"He's talking with Oskar alone. Why? How long have those eggs been boiling?" Sofie swept past her, seized the handle of the pan and almost splashed Dora, swinging it over to the sink. She didn't seem to know about the stolen money so what reason did she have to be angry?

"You can tell just from the smell, you've overcooked them," Sofie accused. "I don't even have to peel them to know they're hard-boiled. I always make soft-boiled eggs for breakfast. That's what people like." She ran water over them.

Dora's hands hung, useless, as she tried to stay out of Sofie's way. Sofie left the eggs and rushed around the kitchen with unnecessary zeal and clatter, making coffee, a disgusted expression stuck to her face like a mask. "I'm not the one you should be mad at," Dora said.

"I'm not mad." Sofie maneuvered eggs into eggcups. "I'm not mad at anyone. Get Amalia and the men. "Everything's almost ready."

"Sofie, Lorenz took Oskar's money, your money. Karl caught him. You wouldn't have known until—"

"Dora," Sofie smacked the counter with a spoon. "I can not listen to nonsense right now. Do you understand that in just a few minutes Oskar and I will be saying good-bye to Lorenz and Karl and this house, my home, forever? Tomorrow I say good-bye to you and Amalia and my country. Please don't make this harder than it is."

"But, I'm trying to tell—"

"Try to enjoy today—a pleasant train ride, a good meal, a night in Bremen. People say the hotel is very tall, the dining room is elegant."

Dora clamped her lips together. Heat gathered behind her eyes. Dismissed again, as always. Sofie deserved to have her money stolen if she wouldn't listen. Anyway, Karl was probably telling Oskar that very moment. She yelled up the stairs that breakfast was ready in a strident tone, full of rage, but Sofie poured coffee as if Dora had said nothing at all.

Amalia came downstairs first, sleepy and subdued. She sat at the table and without waiting for anyone, cracked the top off her egg and poked a spoon into it.

"This is hard boiled," she said.

The three men came in, one after the other, Karl, Oskar and last, Lorenz. They sat quietly across from Amalia. Dora watched them from the door to the stairs, as if from a great distance, Sofie serving, the rest of them eating. She couldn't move—pinned to the door frame by the realization that God was easier to know than another human being, even a sister or a family friend. She was suddenly terribly afraid of the secrets in the room, the things people hid from each other and themselves.

"Sit down," said Sofie. "Eat. There isn't much time."

Everyone looked at Dora as if just noticing her. She chewed her lip to keep from saying something she'd feel sorry for, and sat.

Conversation meandered, touching on the *Reichstag* elections, boxing, the May second strike and lock out. No one mentioned Sofie and Oskar leaving. No one talked about the money. No one looked upset. Dora's hard-boiled egg in its cup scorned her attempt to recognize this day as different. Everybody else seemed to be pretending it wasn't.

"You know," Karl said, pushing back his plate. "You're leaving right when things are looking up. Before you reach America, the French will be on their way back home where they belong. Only a matter of time and those of us who really love Germany will get our share of the power."

Finally, a mention of Sofie and Oskar's departure, even if it was folded neatly into the usual political talk. Time to ask about the stolen money.

"The republic is in trouble," Oskar said evenly. "We're losing the middle ground. I'm tired of extremes, fascists and Communists both."

"Oh, please," Sofie said. "Enough. We know what you think. Don't get started. We'll miss the train."

"Sofie," Lorenz pretended to swoon. "You're making a mistake. Stay here with me. Help me lead the workers' revolution. Continue the fight for the seven-hour day. Capitalist America will be so dull; nothing to do but make money." He clicked his tongue.

"Money!" Dora cried. Everyone looked at her. "Did you really take Sofie's money?" she stammered. "I heard you."

"Dora?" Sofie gave her a pitying look. "What are you talking about?"

Lorenz swung around from the table and stood to clear his plate.

"What is she talking about?" Sofie asked Oskar.

"Nothing, Sofie," Oskar said. "Nothing to worry about." He checked his pocket watch. "We should be leaving for the station."

Everyone nodded, even Lorenz—the villain, the thief. Dora looked from one to the other. With a tight and frowning nod, Oskar seemed to scold her. He had the money back, his expression said. But what kind of man would let her sister go on thinking Lorenz was one thing when he was another? She wanted to warn Sofie.

"Do you know what she's talking about?" Sofie pressed.

"What *are* you talking about?" asked Amalia.

"We don't want to miss this train," said Oskar.

Karl pushed back the bench. "Lucky you've got strong men to carry the suitcases."

"I'd better stay here." Lorenz hung back. "You go on. I'll clean up before I leave for the mine."

"I want you to come," said Oskar.

Lorenz hesitated.

"You're coming," said Karl.

Lorenz's eyes filled. He busied himself putting on a coat he didn't need.

"We'll clean up after work," Karl said to stop Sofie from clearing the table.

Karl, Lorenz, and Oskar each lifted a large suitcase. They lugged them across the road and onto the streetcar. Sofie, Amalia, and Dora carried shopping bags and their overnight cases. Their hurry, their bundles, and the crush of people around them made talking difficult.

"Will you please explain what's going on?" Amalia whispered. "Do you know something we don't?"

"Earlier when I needed help figuring out what to do, you were sleeping," Dora said. "And Sofie wouldn't listen to me. She didn't want to hear anything."

Oskar cleared his throat. Dora met his eyes, but paid no attention to the small shake of his head.

"Lorenz stole your money."

Oskar squeezed her arm. Other people on the streetcar averted their gazes.

"Not now," Oskar's voice steady and commanding.

"Everyone thinks you're so funny and kind," Dora said to Lorenz. She could feel her sisters' shocked looks.

"Please stop, Dora." Oskar said.

"No," said Amalia. "Tell us."

Suddenly aware of Sofie's stricken face and the strangers around them pretending not to hear, Dora stopped. "At the station," she said, suddenly miserable. Oskar, the most irreligious man she knew, had forgiven his friend for a terrible thing, while she simmered with bitterness and anger.

In the echoing train station—pigeons flapping up in the drafty space, dark metal beams lacy against the high, glass roof, trains coming and going—Oskar said, "No more talk of money. It's all settled. Nothing has been stolen."

"But I heard—"

"Tell us, Dora," said Amalia.

"Listen to Oskar," Sofie snapped. "This is the men's business."

This wasn't anything like the good-bye Dora had envisioned—Lorenz smoking a cigarette over by the tracks, Karl talking to him, she, Sofie and Amalia clustered arguing near Oskar.

"No need to stir things up right now," Oskar said. "Lorenz is a good man."

"He tried to steal from you!" Dora's voice rang out surprising her. She stared over Oskar's shoulder at the alternating pattern of tracks, platform, tracks, platform. People waiting, others hurrying between them. "What if Karl hadn't caught him?" she said. "Right now, he'd have your money in his pocket. You'd be on the boat in the middle of the ocean and find it was missing. Why aren't you angry?"

"Oskar doesn't get angry," said Amalia in mocking voice. Dora was gratified to see Amalia finally attentive, perplexed and irate. She'd make something happen that Dora couldn't.

Sofie stood pale and quiet, her expression unreadable. Then she linked elbows with Oskar and lifted her chin, as if daring Amalia to say another word. Dora waited. Oskar and Sofie. Sofie and Oskar. Husband. Wife. Amalia leaned out over the track as if looking for the train. Dora wanted to pull her back and encourage her to keep talking, but Amalia stared into the distance.

Their train hurtled into the station from the opposite direction to a screeching stop. Oskar, Sofie following, her hand in his, stepped toward Karl and Lorenz to say good-bye.

Dora boarded the train behind Amalia. Karl followed, lugging two of the suitcases. He helped them to their compartment and stowed the bags overhead. Dora looked out the open window to the platform where Lorenz hugged Oskar, pounding his back.

"Take care of yourself, my friend," she heard Lorenz say. "Take care of your lovely wife."

Then Lorenz held Sofie by the shoulders, and the way he looked at her made Dora shiver. It was as if he kissed Sofie all over, just by moving his eyes. "Sofie, dear…" He adjusted his tone, gave it a teasing edge. "You know I love you."

Dora wondered if he really did, and if Sofie chose Oskar over Lorenz merely because of his dreams of America. If Oskar didn't feel angry about the money, he could at least feel some jealousy. Lorenz and Sofie flirted every day, right under his nose. Yet maybe Sofie chose Oskar because he was a man of integrity and humble confidence, a gentle, reliable, steadfast man. She could depend on him. A forgiving man.

Behind Dora, out in the aisle, Karl and Amalia said their good-byes. The train whistle blew and before Dora could think any more, Sofie and Oskar were in the compartment jostling her for space at the window, and Karl was down on the platform with Lorenz, waving.

"I never want to see him again," Dora said. "He'd better be gone by the time we get back."

"Dora, wave good-bye," Amalia squeezed in tight beside her. The train began to move. Karl sprinted along beside it, grinning and waving. Lorenz stood motionless.

"*Auf wiedersehen!*" everyone but Dora called.

As the train picked up speed, Karl fell back. They lost sight of him.

"All right then," Amalia said as Dora settled into her seat, Sofie and Oskar across from them. "You'd better tell us what you know."

"It's really not important," said Oskar.

"It's important to me." Dora ran her thumb over the worn upholstery of the seat. "Stealing is a sin. No matter what."

"Lorenz really tried to take your money?" Amalia asked. "How could he?"

Oskar rubbed his chin and pulled at his lower lip. Finally, he spoke. "Lorenz is a principled man," he said.

"What?" Amalia said it so Dora didn't have to. Even Sofie turned toward Oskar, mouth open.

"He loves his friends. He loves you, but that love is small compared to his love of this crippled country, his union, justice. It has to be."

"You don't really believe that," Dora said.

"Enough!" Sofie snapped. "Enough about Lorenz."

"He wouldn't have taken all the money," Oskar said.

Dora expected her sisters, especially Amalia, to pump her for information, but no one spoke. Oskar picked up Sofie's hand from her knee, and moved it to his own, holding it there like the battered lunch tin he used to bring to work—familiar, necessary, his. After a long time, Sofie turned her hand palm up and clasped his fingers, rubbing at a blue scar on his knuckle with her thumb. Amalia stared out the window, arms crossed over her chest, hands tucked away in the crooks of her elbows.

Dora touched the wooden rosary in her pocket. She saw Sister Raphaela's forgiving face floating in the air between their seats. She didn't feel like praying, but she forced herself to beg God for a more generous heart.

As the train slowed to a stop in Bremen, Dora wondered how they would know where to go and how they would manage the luggage without Karl and Lorenz to help, but right outside the station stood the steamship company building clearly marked *Norddeutscher Lloyd*. The station platform swarmed with unemployed men eager to carry things over to the building for tips. From there a company-owned car brought the suitcases to the company-owned hotel. The busy, uniformed man behind the desk told them that dinner would be served soon in the hotel dining room, assured them that the luggage would arrive even before they did, and pointed them in the direction of the right trolley. Dora wished they could ride in a car too. At sixteen years old, she never had. All the seats on the trolley were full, the aisle crammed with people. After a series of jerks, squeaks and a short curving distance, the conductor called *"Lloydheim,"* and most everyone pressed toward the door. Dora wondered who was going places and who had come to say good-bye. She couldn't tell by looking.

The modern hotel rose before them. A green-and-gold-lettered awning stretched over the sidewalk. Dora looked all the way up the whitewashed side of the building to the roof, marveling until her neck began to ache.

In the crowded paneled lobby clusters of comfortable-looking upholstered chairs were occupied by well dressed people smoking cigarettes and pipes. Little tables and the large reception desk held vases of bright flowers.

"Tulips, from Holland," Amalia said. "Beautiful." She bent down to smell a yellow one. "No scent though. Disappointing."

In a row of luggage next to the wall Dora identified Sofie and Oskar's suit-cases, their shabbiness more reassuring than embarrassing. Another uniformed man showed the way to their room on the fifth floor.

The window looked out over the city and the river, misty and gray. Fruits and vegetables on the tiny carts down in the market square shone like bits of stained glass. Dora had never seen so wide a view. She'd always been afraid to climb the rickety stairs in the church tower in Gunstadt, though Amalia had done it many times.

"Here we are," Sofie said. "In a skyscraper. Just like in America."

"Skyscrapers have many more floors," Oskar said.

"I know that." Sofie turned her back to him and moved closer to Dora and Amalia. Their combined breath clouded the glass as together they gazed out the window.

After a big meal in the hotel dining room, Dora and Amalia wandered through Bremen while Sofie and Oskar saw the doctor for a physical and picked up their tickets. Dora didn't worry about finding their way back to the hotel; it towered above the other buildings. They walked near the piers as a heavy fog rolled in. The big ships, including the ship Sofie and Oskar would sail on, docked in Bremerhaven, but Bremen, a river town, had its share of smaller boat traffic. Beside the water, the air smelled of fish and sadness, rotting vegetables and despair. Gulls screeched and squawked. Men huddled in doorways and spilled from noisy bars.

"It doesn't feel like spring here," Amalia said.

Dora slipped an arm around her sister. "Let's go back to the hotel." She veered toward the left. "I'm tired. I ate too much."

"It's that way," Amalia pointed through fog so thick it obscured buildings just a few meters away. "I'm sure."

Too tired and cold to argue, Dora let Amalia decide. She wasn't sure of the way, and if someone had to be wrong she'd rather it was her sister. After a while, after they'd passed a long row of shops and were well into a tidy, shuttered residential neighborhood full of flowerboxes, Amalia didn't seem to know the way anymore either.

"We should ask someone. Everyone in this city would know the steamship company," Dora said.

"When we see somebody, you ask," said Amalia.

"You ask," said Dora.

"No, you."

Dora didn't bother answering. There was no one in sight.

They wandered through narrow alleys and wide squares, trying to wend their way back to the bustling streets near the train station and harbor. The cold, damp air chilled their noses and fingertips.

"Ask him." Amalia pointed at a man in a brown coat emerging from a house. Ahead of them on the sidewalk, the man looked like a bear. "Go on!" She removed Dora's arm from her shoulder and gave her a push.

"Why do I have to ask?" Dora stood her ground. The man moved on. "Why don't you?"

"Sofie would ask," Amalia muttered.

"If Sofie were here we wouldn't have gotten lost in the first place," Dora said. "We're walking in circles. I'm tired."

"I'm tired too!" Amalia slumped against the front of a house. "This is stupid. How long have we been gone? They'll go back to the room and we won't be there."

Dora wanted to cry. The day had been so long and full of strangeness. What if they never found their way back and they missed the train to Bremerhaven tomorrow and never got to say good-bye to Sofie? Like she never got to say good-bye to Mama because nobody called her in time. She prayed that someone would come along to help them.

Amalia tugged her sleeve. "Doesn't that look like a priest?"

Dora squinted through the mist at the approaching figure.

"It is," Amalia declared. "You're not afraid of a priest, are you?"

She wasn't. She'd prayed and a priest appeared. A miracle—though she kept that thought to herself. Amalia would dismiss it as coincidence.

He staggered in their direction. "Something's wrong," said Amalia. "He's limping."

"Excuse me, Father." Dora said when he was close enough to hear.

"He's drunk," Amalia whispered.

The smell of schnapps-soaked flesh gave Dora pause. Her throat constricted. She remembered *Teufelmann*. The priest was about to pass them.

"Excuse me," Amalia shouted.

The priest stopped, wobbled, then steadied himself. "Yes?" He blinked his eyes, noticing Dora. "Yes?"

"We're lost," Amalia said.

"Ah…but aren't we all?" He blinked again. "Lost…or losing…ah…life is a series of losses…to be human is to be lost…people forget that priests are human."

"Amalia," Dora whispered. "Let's go."

"Can you tell us how to get to the harbor, the *Lloydheim*?" Amalia asked.

He beamed a wide, wet smile. His gums glistened red as his face. "I can do that. Yes, I can. I might not be able to show you the way to heaven, the way to forgiveness, but I can show you the way to the hotel. Clean sheets, a good meal? Is that not heaven when it comes right down to it?" He belched. "Pardon me."

"He doesn't know the way." Dora couldn't believe Amalia wanted to follow that man. "Let's go this way. We'll ask someone else."

"Dora," Amalia said, a mocking edge to her voice. "What's the matter with you? You don't trust a priest to know where he's going? He says he'll show us."

"Ah, young lady, do not trust me as a priest. Trust me as a man." He stumbled and caught himself by grabbing Amalia's elbow. He didn't let go.

"This way, ladies," he announced, and set off arm in arm with Amalia. Dora followed a step behind.

A scandalous rescue. Dora tried to convince herself it was better than no rescue at all. Amalia was busy looking left and right, probably trying to figure out where they'd made their mistakes. What difference did it make? God willing, they'd never walk these streets again. What would people think—a drunken priest arm in arm with a young woman?

The priest suddenly veered right into a narrow alley, pushing Amalia ahead of him. "This way. Follow me." He paused to give Dora a commanding look. "Stay with me or you'll be lost in this fog."

The damp stone of the buildings on either side pressed close as Dora hurried to keep up with the priest who wasn't stumbling anymore. When she stretched out her arms she could touch the walls. When she looked up all she could see was gray mist. She had to pay attention to the wet and uneven cobblestones beneath her feet. They'd tripped her up twice already.

She bumped hard into the priest's hunched back.

"What are you doing?" Amalia's voice, full of disgust.

The drunk man whirled around and caught Dora's clenched hand. He brought it toward his crotch, pried open her fingers and wrapped them around his penis in one swift and practiced motion. No fumbling.

Dora screamed and tried to pull away, but his clammy hand held hers in place and pumped it up and down.

Everything blurred and slowed, except her hand inside the man's, moving faster, faster.

"Let her go," Amalia shouted. Dora heard the words from far away as something sticky and hot spurted over her fingers and the man made a long whimpering sound. Dora wiped her hand on her coat and stood still.

Amalia pushed at the man who fell against Dora. The three of them dropped to the ground, stuck for a long moment in a terrible knot, the man's drunk breath in Dora's ear, the heaviness of his body on her arm.

Then Dora felt the weight on her back lessen and Amalia was standing, kicking the man until he rolled over and lay curled against the wall. "Forgive me," he sobbed. "Forgive me."

"Run!"

Amalia's hands, Amalia's clean hands, helped Dora to her feet, set her in motion, pulled her back along the fog filled alley.

By the time they found the hotel, a surprisingly short distance away, Dora convinced herself that he was an evil man masquerading as a priest. There was no other possible explanation.

"Are you all right?" asked Amalia.

"That wasn't a priest," Dora said.

Amalia gave a short laugh.

"Amalia, don't tell anyone." She couldn't bear the way Amalia would try to make it funny, the way she'd imitate the false priest and insist he was real, omitting the details only Dora had experienced. "There's no reason."

"We'll tell Sofie," Amalia said.

"No."

Amalia shrugged. Dora followed her into the hushed lobby.

"I don't care what you say," said Dora. "That was not a priest."

Amalia didn't answer.

"It wasn't. Don't tell Sofie."

Outside the door of the hotel room Amalia stopped. "Do you still want to join the convent? When men of God can act like that. Who knows what goes on in those rooms behind the altar? Come to Elsterdorf with me. We'll put our money together."

Amalia's eyes blazed. Her words poured out, urgent and pleading. "We could find a piece of land. We don't have to go to Elsterdorf. We could find our old farm, Mama's farm, maybe buy it back. Together we could do it, I know."

Dora hesitated, reluctant to hurt or disappoint. Sofie's stories of the time before *Teufelmann* still warmed her insides and made her smile—cherry trees, and swings, and music.

She thought of Frau Blau and Gustav and the infection that almost killed Sofie. "Bad things happen everywhere," she told Amalia. "I know that."

Amalia bit her lip and looked as though she'd cry. "Please," she said.

Dora stood, miserable and still, unable to give her sister anything close to what she was asking for.

Amalia spun to face the closed door and banged on it. "That was a priest," she said over her shoulder as Oskar let them in.

Dora took a long breath. God was testing her.

In the room the evening wore on. There was nothing to say. Sofie grew quiet and anxious. Oskar proposed a card game to pass the time, and Amalia, Sofie and he played *skat*. They encouraged Dora to rotate in, but she crawled under the covers, feeling just like the baby they all believed she was, wanting to pray, and instead trying to make sense of everything: heavy ships as big as buildings that floated on water, friends who stole money for higher causes, drunken men pretending to be priests, secrets too shameful to tell. There were no secrets from God. Religious sisters lived together always. It was a vocation, a calling, a choice from so deep in the heart it was no choice at all. Sharing a mother and a father, sharing blood, troubles, family stories should add up to something, but what? Earthly fathers and mothers died. Natural sisters, each with her secrets and her own incomplete and inadequate version of their lives together, separated forever.

"*Passt mir nicht*," said Sofie, rejecting the first *skat* card. "It doesn't suit me." She turned up the next card, fixing trump.

They played on, cards whispering and snapping, the only words spoken related directly to the game. "I hold." "Pass." "Solo." "Diamonds."

Finally, they turned off the lights. Amalia climbed into bed beside Dora. Strange—trying to sleep with Oskar in the room. He brought a smell of sweat and metal and the sound of raspy breathing. Most of the miners breathed that way, but you didn't notice it so much in the daytime. He and Sofie whispered together. Dora coughed to let them know she was awake. She didn't want to hear them do anything. She imagined Oskar's penis and Sofie's hands and felt sick. If Oskar hadn't been there, Sofie would be in bed beside her and Amalia. They'd laugh and talk, and dropping off to sleep would be cozy and smooth.

Instead she lay rigid. A child in the next room cried. The cries escalated to howls. Sofie muttered. Oskar murmured. Beds creaked as they turned and tossed.

Dora, dry-eyed, let the child cry for her. She would need all her tears the next morning, on the too-short train ride to Bremerhaven. She would need them while admiring the cabin with its cleverly stacked beds, its folding table, a button to press to turn the lights on and off and another if one wanted to order something brought to the room. She'd need them again when the signal came for visitors to go ashore, to soak Sofie's shoulder as she hugged her good-bye, thinking *this could be the last time*. She'd need them on the long walk down the gangplank to the spot on the pier where she and Amalia would join the throng of people shouting and waving farewell as the heavy ship steamed off, and they were left with the creaking of the pilings, the splintering of hearts.

CHAPTER 14

───────▼───────

Sofie clung to the clammy metal railing as the ship cut a wide swath through the choppy sea, Oskar beside her. She had lost sight of Amalia and Dora only moments after the ship began shuddering away from the dock, long before the land disappeared. Knowing they were there, that if she had opera glasses she'd be able to glimpse them among the crowd, kept her staring in their direction. Until she shifted her gaze, the possibility of seeing them remained. Once she looked away they'd be lost. She felt incomplete and ragged, a pretzel torn in thirds.

Oskar and Sofie's hands rested side by side on the railing, strange in their plain gold rings. She'd been twisting hers constantly, wiggling it up and down between knuckles. Her crooked finger and Oskar's blue scars proved the hands belonged to them. The trembling in her body and the vibration of the ship's engines melded together where her hand touched rail and her feet met deck.

She already missed Amalia and Dora. She missed Karl and Lorenz and the streets of Tauburg and every drawer and shelf in her kitchen. When the land was out of sight and her eyes ached from staring into the wind, Sofie turned her attention to the deck and the strangers around her. A fashionable older woman standing with an equally well-dressed man gave Sofie a sad, understanding smile. She wore a bob hat, dark blue felt trimmed in a shiny white ribbon and a cluster of silk leaves. Sofie had left her own new hat in the cabin, afraid the wind would snatch it.

Oskar shoved his hands into his pockets and planted his feet wide on the deck. He turned his back to the rail.

"We'll come back, won't we?" Sofie asked.

"When we can." She had already learned that Oskar never lied, even when she wished he would, even when she needed him to.

"But when do you think that will be?" Sometimes it made sense to tell a person what she wanted to hear. Why couldn't he just say, the way everyone had, that they were sure to be back for long visits, if not to stay, once they'd made a lot of money and things in Germany had settled down. The country was still recovering from the war. Devastation of that magnitude took time to heal. Oskar was a skilled worker, and after a year or two in America he'd know English. Germany needed him. He would have a choice of well-paying jobs. They could move back to stay, if they chose to. He could work in an office, come home at the end of a day in a clean white shirt. Already she wasn't married to a miner anymore.

The older couple stepped closer to them. The man introduced himself as Max Epstein and his wife as Trudi. They looked at least forty years old and carried themselves with confident elegance. Oskar introduced Sofie as his wife. When the Epsteins said they were both doctors from Koln, Sofie knew she'd stammer and blush if she addressed them by their first names, though quiet Oskar, her husband, conversed with them as if they were mining buddies. He spoke to everyone with the same even, thoughtful interest. When the Epsteins told him they decided to leave Germany because they had nothing left to lose, nothing keeping them there, he wasn't afraid to ask for details.

"We had three children," Trudi said. "One died of the influenza. One was a Communist—injured in a skirmish with the *Reichswehr*. He died from his wounds." She ticked them off on her fingers.

"Trudi," her husband broke in.

"Wait," she said. "I'm not finished." She extended a third beautifully manicured finger. "The oldest died just last fall in a train accident they suspect was caused by a Separatist act of sabotage. We don't want to be where every street corner and building reminds us of our losses." She stared past Sofie.

"This crackpot Hitler is gaining a following," Max said. "Right-wing radicals try to take over the government and all they get is a slap on the wrist. They are as dangerous as the Communists." Trudi rested her hand on his sleeve. He ignored it. "Why don't they evoke the same kind of fear?" Max paused, examining Oskar's expression, perhaps waiting for some response.

A seagull flying low at the railing pinned Sofie with its eye and squawked. It flew even with the ship, hanging in the air as if motionless before them.

Oskar nodded and Max went on. "This last election makes things look bad for reasonable people. When times are hard and there is nothing to depend on, anyone is free to start a party. Who would have thought the Separatists could have done as much damage as they did? The Rhineland, a separate country! The French would have loved that. It's obvious to any thinking man, the French put them up to it."

"I'm tired of armies in the streets," Oskar said. He looked out over the ocean, toward Germany. "Marching, showing off their weapons, stopping traffic, so peaceful people can't get to their jobs, their homes. I'm tired of strikes."

While the Epsteins and Oskar talked politics, agreeing on all the major points, seagulls rode the wind and cried. Sofie breathed in the wet salty air, Lorenz's and Karl's contributions to the conversation ringing in her head. She knew exactly what each of them would say. Trudi listened, leaning into her husband when he spoke. She placed her hand on his sleeve to encourage him, not to suppress his comments as Sofie had first thought. People strolled the deck. Sofie wondered about her right to sadness when people like the Epsteins had suffered more. Her sisters were alive.

In the dining room they were served a sumptuous meal—soup, three kinds of meat, vegetables, potatoes, fruit—complete with white tablecloths, every piece of flatware and china imprinted with *Norddeutscher Lloyd* and a small drawing of a ship. Sofie and Oskar sat with the Epsteins, and Oskar's conversation with them continued. Still, they talked about the occupation, the best way to negotiate an end to it. Sofie tasted everything, relieved not to have to speak. She noticed that the Epsteins refused the thick pink slices of ham, her favorite. She began to urge them to try it, then remembered she'd heard that eating ham was forbidden in the Jewish religion. She wondered if the Epsteins were Jews; Epstein sounded as though it could be a Jewish name. The only other Jew she'd ever known was Frau Grunberg, but Sofie had never eaten with her; the dressmaker hadn't stayed for the luncheons after Mama's funeral or their wedding. Sofie watched the Epsteins for clues. She cut a bite of ham and chewed it self-consciously, wondering if they thought it was wrong for everyone or just wrong if you were Jewish. In America, people held their forks in the right hand. She decided to try it. The switching back and forth seemed clumsy and pointless. In America, there were people from everywhere. Even people from China who didn't use forks at all, but sticks. She'd seen pictures of Negro people and Indians. It was good practice for America to eat with Jews. Oskar leaned close to Max then to Trudi, to hear them through the buzz of conversation filling the dining room, unaware of the food and of her. She was glad when the meal ended and they could retire to their cabin.

"Nice folks," Oskar said reaching for her hand. "Would you like to take a walk? We might sleep better afterward."

Not far from the dining room they passed a line of people waiting outside what looked like a well-lit shop you'd see on the street in Tauburg. Signs advertised special deals on photographs and postcards. Heart-shaped photos of people dressed as sailors behind the wheel of a ship, surrounded by scenes of Germany, sayings like "I left my heart in Heidelberg" and poems about pursuing dreams, were plastered to the shop's window and door.

"Let's get our picture taken!" Oskar said. "We can send it to Dora and Amalia and Karl and Lorenz."

Sofie's eyes filled at the sound of their names. She berated herself for how distant and mean she'd been to them, starting with breakfast at the house on through their good-byes on board ship. Everything had been strange, like a dream full of nonsensical detail—Dora preparing breakfast when, for years, it had been Sofie's job; Lorenz's crime and Oskar's defense of him; the indignity of waiting for the doctor and the physical itself, when she should have been spending her last precious hours in Germany with her sisters; Amalia babbling about being happy to stay where she was and how she didn't have to go to America to have an adventure; Dora's continuing silence, her refusal to play cards; the baby screaming all night in the room next door; Oskar's warm, still unfamiliar body pressed against her back as she tried to sleep, her sisters stretched out in a bed big enough for three, just meters away. Amalia, who could sleep anywhere, breathing her funny little snore. No sound from Dora. She had probably been awake. Sofie had ached to go to her, to whisper in the dark, but Oskar's arm held her in place.

Sofie's stomach lurched and she wanted to lie down, but she had never seen Oskar so cheerful and animated. A good wife wouldn't disappoint him. He was right. Amalia and Dora would like a picture. They joined the line which moved quickly.

A woman with a notebook took Oskar's name and their cabin number. She pointed to a rack of jackets with big brass buttons, hats, and sailors' shirts and pants. Oskar chose a captain's uniform. Sofie couldn't decide. Her stomach churned, full of rich food. Maybe she was getting seasick. The woman, eager to keep the line moving, handed her a set of clothes and pointed her to the dressing room.

Sofie liked the way the pants made her feel. She kicked a leg up as far as she could in the small space and bent her knees deep into a squat. The sailor's hat fit snugly on her head. She adjusted the jacket and studied herself in the full-length mirror. The whole thing was silly, a lark, but the Sofie in sailor's clothes seemed better suited to the whole adventure. In thick wool pants and a jaunty cap, she could be Sofie the intrepid sailor, first mate to Captain Oskar, exploring the world.

"Next!" said the woman. She pulled back the edge of the curtain.

Oskar looked handsome and commanding. Sofie smiled and meant it.

"Over there." The woman hurried them over to a small stage. The background painting of ocean and sky had an American flag on one side and the bow of a ship on the other. A life preserver, labeled like the china with *Norddeutscher Lloyd*, stood propped against a replica of a ship's wheel. Sofie and Oskar stood as directed, gripping the wheel. The photographer counted behind his camera.

Oskar looked straight ahead, a smile twitching at the corners of his lips. Sofie glanced at him. He looked like a real captain. A bright flash and the photographer snapped the picture. Oskar paid the lady who had taken their names.

Sofie regretted having to change back into her dress, back into herself. Sofie: the wife, the homesick emigrant. At what point in the journey would she change from someone leaving Germany to someone arriving in America, emigrant to immigrant?

Oskar waited outside the little shop. He led her up to the deck. The lights from the ship glimmered on the water like stars. The stars glimmered in the sky like lights reflected on water. The darkness stretched in all directions, vast and thick.

"I bet there are sharks in this water," Sofie said.

"Sure," said Oskar. "The ocean is full of sharks. Other creatures, too. It's their home."

Home. She struggled to keep from crying. Feet planted on the deck, hands clasped behind his back, Oskar belonged here, a citizen of the world. He gazed into the dark, instead of at her, with a mild, trusting expression. She gripped the cold rail. Amalia and Dora would have noticed her silence and her sadness, asked her about it, slipped arms around her waist. If Oskar gave her the smallest inquiring look, a raised eyebrow, a tilt of his head, she'd say something. If a shadow of homesickness or longing crossed his face, she'd tuck her arm through his and lean into the warmth of his body.

Someone groaned, a loud mooing sound like a cow. A few meters down the railing a shadowy shape leaned over and vomited again and again. Sofie's own queasiness intensified.

"I shouldn't have eaten so much at dinner," she said. "I don't feel well."

"We can lie down," Oskar said. "I don't feel well either."

"You don't?" Sofie was almost glad. Maybe he didn't have the same ache in his heart, but his stomach churned like hers.

In their cabin, the seasickness knocked them to their hands and knees. They threw up in the washbasin and the water pitcher. Neither could climb into the top bunk so they lay with heads at opposite ends of the narrow bed. They vomited all night long. Even when their stomachs were empty, they heaved and choked.

A stewardess knocked on the door in the morning. Oskar's black-stockinged feet rose beside Sofie's head. The length of her body pressed against his to keep from falling onto the floor. The woman left them a basket with mineral water and rolls. She said that fresh air sometimes helped and suggested they settle in deck chairs. She told them to set their watches back an hour. They had entered a new time zone.

"Oskar," Sofie said, after lifting her head just enough to rinse her mouth. "These time zones? Now is now. How come it was eight o'clock and now it's seven? We have an extra hour. Another hour to be sick. I don't understand. Will this keep happening? More and more hours on this ship?" In her weak condition such a nightmare seemed probable.

"America is so big it has many time zones." His voice sounded weak and far away.

"But we will only live in one?" she asked.

"Yes."

She closed her eyes, relieved. She needed to be able to look at a clock and know with certainty what time it was.

Later, they helped each other up to the deck. They joined the Epsteins and others, wrapped in scratchy blankets in a line of deck chairs. Passengers retched or moaned like calves. The wind whipped the rolls from a stewardess's tray and gulls plucked them from the air. Sofie wondered if anyone was well enough to eat in the dining room; no wonder the company could afford such elegant food for the first meal. She and Oskar were not getting their money's worth out of this voyage. All that talk of movies and concerts and dances, several activities offered every night. She felt almost too weak to watch the patterns the sun made on her closed eyelids.

The next day they felt well enough to walk a little. They rested near the railing on the second deck, until vomit splashed them from above. "Not everyone's feeling better." Sofie winced and rubbed at a wet spot already staining her skirt.

"It's safer up there." Attempting a grin, Oskar pointed to the highest deck.

The stairs seemed insurmountable, but step by step they dragged themselves up. The seas grew wilder as the afternoon wore on. The crew fastened thick rope everywhere for people to grip as they stumbled and staggered toward the stairs. A huge wave rolled over the deck, then another. Sofie's new shoes squished. Her skirt hung heavy with sea water.

"We're asking everyone to return to the cabins," the stewardess said. Sofie wondered where the stewardess thought she and the clump of shivering people around her were heading. She didn't even look around for Oskar. Sailors, like hurrying spiders, webbed the deck with rope.

A loudspeaker blared, "Clear the decks. We are experiencing rough seas. Clear the decks until further notice."

The ship, enormous in the harbor, rolled and tossed in the waves like a bug. Oskar tried to reassure her by pointing out that no one in the crew looked especially frightened. They'd finished securing the deck chairs. The sea water swept the vomit from the deck, along with everything else that wasn't attached.

In their cabin, Sofie fell onto the bed. If the ship sank she would be drowned instead of sick, and she would never get to see America. Oskar squeezed in beside her, the bed too narrow for even one person.

"I thought I was getting my sea legs," he said. "I was just beginning to envy sailors their life in the sun and the salty air. I'm a bit embarrassed to admit even to you that I thought I looked good in that uniform." He curled around her back. Her muscles, strained and sore from vomiting, eased into the press of his body and hands.

When they woke, the sea had calmed and so had their bellies. Oskar peeled his body from hers and stretched. He examined his face in the mirror over the washbasin, rubbing his stubbly beard. "I think I'll shave before breakfast," he said and unpacked his razor and shaving brush. Sofie wondered if he minded her watching him from the bed. Back at the boarding house they gave each other privacy. She wouldn't mind him watching her wash her face, but she'd hate for him to see her examine a blemish or scrub her armpits. Fixing her hair in front of him would be all right. He'd helped her button her dress a few times, his fingers clumsy compared to Dora's and Amalia's. It took him more than twice as long.

As he filled the basin with water, tenderness swelled in her chest. He wet the soap and lathered his face with the brush. She'd never seen a man shave before. It felt like a wifely privilege and she spread herself across the bed to enjoy it.

He scraped along his jaw with the razor, rinsed the hair and soap off the blade by dipping it in the basin. The shaved skin looked pink and new. She wanted to lick it. When he was finished she cleaned her teeth, washing away the days of sickness. She didn't care if he watched. Her mouth tingled.

Oskar squatted by the suitcase, barechested, suspenders drooping, selecting a shirt. Sofie imagined leaping onto his back and kissing him all over his smooth face. She wondered how he would react. She'd never worn the silk nightgown after that first night. She had packed it, though.

"Oskar, we don't have to hurry to breakfast, do we?"

"I'm hungry," he said without turning his head. "Aren't you?"

"Yes, but maybe we could...maybe...I mean, we haven't..." Some things shouldn't have to be put into words. Some things couldn't be put into words.

She took the two steps necessary to stand over him and ran her finger along the row of blue scars marking his spine. She bent over him and whispered in his ear, "We have time. We have all those extra hours from all those time zones we've been moving through."

She kissed his shoulder and his chest, hesitantly at first, tasting salt. Everything tasted salty from the air, even in the snug cabin. He made a noise. She kept her eyes closed and tasted him. She covered his body with kisses. He lay on the floor and she straddled him—kissing, touching, bolder than she thought a woman should be, but it felt too good to stop so she pretended she was the sailor in the photo reunited with his wife after weeks at sea, or Oskar making fierce love to her. When it was over she couldn't look at him.

"I love you, Sofie," he mumbled, unable to meet her eyes. "I'll always love you." They dressed for breakfast with their backs toward each other.

Max and Trudi, just finishing their coffee, welcomed them to breakfast. Sofie and Oskar sat across from each other, Oskar beside Max, Sofie in the empty chair on Trudi's side of the table.

"I can see you're feeling better," Trudi said. "So are we, but then that's obvious or we wouldn't be upright at a table full of food."

"Perhaps that rough weather was a blessing," said Max. "Now, what made us seasick at first seems like nothing."

Trudi poured them coffee. The smell made Sofie gag.

"Not a coffee drinker?"

"I drink coffee," Sofie said. "I don't know what happened. Maybe I'm not back to normal yet."

Trudi carefully poured it back into the pot without spilling. She leaned close to Sofie. "Every time I was pregnant, the smell of coffee made me sick." She raised her eyebrows in a polite question.

Maybe because she was a doctor she felt she could say something so personal. Or maybe Jewish people weren't as private as Catholics. Or maybe because she was old and Sofie was young, she felt she had the right to ask.

Sofie had been married only a little more than three weeks. It did seem that she should have her monthly bleeding, but travel and sickness could have prevented it from coming at the usual time.

She answered with a slight shrug and helped herself to a slice of bread.

"Americans," said Trudi, "wear their wedding rings on the left hand."

Sofie had barely gotten used to it on the right. "I'm German," she said.

"Me too," said Trudi. "I only mention it because it's something I've been thinking about. Will I wear my ring the German way or the American way?"

Max unrolled a newspaper from Koln and held it so he and Oskar could both read it.

"What will you do in America?" Trudi asked.

"Oskar's uncle has a job waiting for him in the foundry. I'll keep house. Look for work. Study English. A lot happened just before we left..." Suddenly Sofie understood why Trudi could talk so intimately. They were fellow travelers thrown together by accident for just a short time. They would never see each other again. They could ask or tell anything. She wanted to tell Trudi about leaving her sisters. She wanted to ask her about lovemaking—how was a woman supposed to act and what about the man? A doctor might know these things. Mostly she wanted to tell about her mother's death. Maybe it was improper to talk about sickness and death at meal time, but they'd all finished eating.

"Did you ever treat patients with tuberculosis?" Sofie asked.

Trudi nodded. "Most doctors have diagnosed it. Treatment of tuberculosis is not my specialty. I'm one of those doctors who believe that, beyond rest and fresh air and good food, not much can be done. More aggressive treatment can cause more harm than good."

"My mother died of tuberculosis in March."

"I'm so sorry." Trudi took Sofie's hand, the left one without the ring.

"She didn't want to go to a sanitorium."

"Who cared for her? You?"

"Yes. My sisters helped near the end."

"That must have been difficult."

Trudi, a doctor, didn't ask why her mother remained at home. She didn't suggest that Hanna died for lack of professional care. She said *that must have been difficult.* She, who had lost three grown children, all her children, said *that must have been difficult.*

"Yes, it was," Sofie said, "very difficult."

"How many sisters do you have?"

"Two," Sofie smiled, picturing them.

"It was hard to leave them," Trudi said. She waited, her gaze steady and sympathetic.

"I want them to come to America," said Sofie. "But the youngest, Dora, is entering the convent in Gunstadt, and the other one, Amalia, acts like she's thinking about coming, but doesn't mean it at all. I'm afraid I'll never see them again."

Trudi patted her hand. "These are crazy times. There is nothing one can count on."

"Was there ever?" her husband asked, looking up from the paper. "I don't know why I'm reading this old news with such interest. My habit of reading a paper with my coffee is unbreakable. This news is five days old. I read this very paper on the train to Bremen. It was all bad news then. I suppose that's something one can count on—bad news. Every day more and more bad news. And my habit of reading it. You can count on that too." He smiled at his wife.

"Good things happen sometimes," said Oskar. He stared at Sofie until the Epsteins laughed and Sofie blushed.

"Speaking of good things," Trudi said. "I feel well enough to enjoy the sunshine. I believe I'll take a little walk."

"I'll join you, dear," said her husband.

Sofie rested her chin in her hand, elbow next to the jam jar. She loved the sound of that *I'll join you, dear. I'll join you for a walk in the sunshine.* Such a married thing to say.

Oskar buttered a piece of cold toast.

I'll join you, dear, on a journey to America. Next time she watched him shave, it wouldn't be so exciting or so strange. After many days it might be the same as watching Amalia pluck her eyebrows or Dora braid her hair.

Less than a week ago she hadn't known any women doctors. She'd never been on a ship. She'd never sat at a table with a Jewish person.

"Did you hear Trudi say that in America, they wear wedding rings on the left hand?" she asked.

"Really?" Oskar cut his toast. He balanced the knife across the edge of his plate and spread both hands in front of him, contemplating them for a moment.

He wiggled the ring off his right and put on his left, picked up his toast with his right hand and took a bite.

"Wait." He waved his toast at her. "Yours is on your right hand."

Sofie considered her fingers. "I know." She spread her fingers and laid her hands flat on the table. She watched him chew, feeling the thrum of the ship's engines, the rocking movement through the water that no longer made them sick.

"In America I want to eat in a Chinese restaurant," Sofie said. "With sticks."

"We will." He set down his crust. "But I don't know how you would eat soup with sticks." He took her hand and slid the ring off her finger. In such a short time without eating, her finger had grown thinner.

"I wouldn't order soup," she said. "I could make that at home." Home. Their home. With a stove and pots and spoons and soup. She would unpack Frau Becker's silverware first thing and polish it.

She extended her left hand, and he slipped the ring down the length of her ring finger.

"Do they speak English or Chinese in a Chinese restaurant?" She clenched her fists like a boxer's, side by side on the white tablecloth among the dirty dishes and crumbs.

"I don't know," Oskar said. He lifted first her left fist, uncurled her fingers one by one, and stroked her hand flat. He picked up her right fist and began rubbing her pinkie, then each finger in turn until he reached her crooked index finger, which he held for a long time. "We could always point at what we want." He aimed her finger at his chest and laughed.

"But how will we know what things are?" Sofie asked, touching her finger to his middle shirt button.

"We won't," he said.

She thought she might throw up again, though the seas remained calm enough that no dishes rattled, no coffee sloshed. "Then how do we know we want it?"

"We don't," he said.

He pressed the palm of his left hand against hers, his pinky to her thumb, her pinky to his thumb: an odd almost-fit. Elbows on the table surrounded by crumbs and dishes waiting to be washed, they laced their fingers together. Their rings shone sure as spoons.

CHAPTER 15

▼

In the empty bedroom of the empty boardinghouse, their furniture and dishes, featherbeds and silverware converted into the heap of money on the floor in front of her, Amalia counted it into a pile for Dora and a pile for her. One third less than the last time she'd done this, just a week ago. She'd carried it with her everywhere, in a stocking pinned inside the waistband of her skirt, even after Lorenz and Karl moved to their new quarters nearer the mine.

Lorenz's easy charm sickened her. She could hardly say good-bye. Karl offered to accompany Dora and her to the convent in Gunstadt so she wouldn't have to come back alone, but she told him she'd already made plans to go right to Elsterdorf, right to the Neufelds' and her new life. He'd rested a hand on the back of her neck and rubbed a tight spot with his thumb. Amalia remembered the night in the parlor and thought about choices. If she hadn't been so dazzled by Lorenz, might she have touched Karl the way he'd touched her, might she have married him and kept the boardinghouse, and all it contained?

She finished dividing the money. Just a year ago these bills wouldn't buy a week of food, a day of food. When hungry, better to have a loaf of bread than a stack of paper. Better to have a garden and a barn full of cows than a boardinghouse full of miners. She stuffed each roll of money into its own heavy stocking. Dora would get one, and she'd keep the other.

"Are you ready?" Dora stood perfectly framed in the doorway, a suitcase in each hand.

Amalia knew exactly what they held. She had gone over the list with Dora and made sure her sister had everything on it. She'd packed and repacked, and after

Dora was asleep, tucked a note inside. Her own trunk had been sent by train to Elsterdorf the day before. But she wasn't ready.

"I want to stop at the cemetery," Dora said.

"I don't," Amalia said.

"Because you can go any time." Dora's voice sounded whiny. "But I won't be able to. I want to say good-bye to Mama. Say a prayer."

"Doesn't God hear you from wherever you are?" Amalia stood, approached her sister and tried not sneer. "Haven't we had enough good-byes?"

"I just want to see her grave one last time."

"Go then." Amalia held out one stocking full of money. "Take this."

Dora, clutching her suitcases, didn't reach for it. "I won't have time to come back here."

"Then I'll meet you at the station."

A tear slipped down Dora's cheek and another. Amalia wanted to yell at her to put down her bags, take the money, wipe her eyes. Dora stood still, tears dripping.

"All right! I'll go with you." Amalia pinned Dora's money back inside her own waistband, Dora's stocking full of marks on one side, hers on the other. "I said I'll go with you. Stop crying."

She leaned in close to hug Dora, breathed in her sweet vanilla smell and sensed her sister's strong arms quivering with stubborn resolve or the weight of the suitcases or both.

"We should've gone with Sofie. All three of us together," Dora whispered.

"She went with Oskar, remember?"

"I know, but she should have gone with us."

"Will you put those bags down?" Amalia said. "I'm not quite ready to leave yet."

"You're packed though. I saw your bag downstairs."

"Yes."

Dora seemed to be waiting for further explanation, but Amalia didn't think she deserved one. She'd already gotten everything she'd asked for.

"Ten minutes," Amalia said. "I want ten minutes."

As Amalia closed and locked the blue door for the last time, Dora already on the other side of the street waiting for the trolley to the cemetery, she memorized the squeal of the hinges, the small lift required for the latch to click, the battered places near the bottom blackened by the clunk of miners' boots—Oskar's, Karl's, Lorenz's. In the crack of dirt where the step met cobblestone she noticed a sliver of white crockery from Sofie's *Polterabend*. She considered picking it up, but she didn't have anything to wrap it in and thought it might hurt her so she left it there.

Amalia lagged behind as Dora wove her way through the busy streets between Gunstadt Station and the convent as if her sister's overstuffed suitcase held only air. She carried her own small valise and a bulging cloth bag, full of everything that Dora hadn't been able to squeeze into the suitcase. The money chafed her skin. She should have been more careful in her choice of stockings. She never dreamed they would scratch with every step.

During the three-hour train ride Dora had done all the talking. She'd chattered and prattled nonstop about the most stupid things—Frau Becker's coffee-pot and how Sofie should have taken it and other household items to America and how Amalia should have packed more for the house she'd have one day, but at least she'd taken a few nice things full of memories like the soup tureen they'd sat around all those nights. Frau Grunberg, Dora thought, should have made Mama a dress to wear during her time with the Captain instead of a bedjacket; maybe she would have been inspired to get up. Did Amalia think Sofie was in America yet and did Oskar's Onkel and Tante Schultz have a gleaming white bathtub all their own with hot water that poured right from the faucet as Oskar had said? And, and, and…

Amalia lost sight of Dora's back, the familiar gray coat, among the throngs of people hurrying home for *Mittagsessen*. Amalia wouldn't hurry. "I'm practicing walking alone in the world," she said aloud. It sounded so dramatic she would have laughed at herself, but for the ball of tears in her throat. Crowds passed on either side of her. People packed the passing trolley and spilled out of shops on both sides of the street. But none them was Dora or Sofie or their mother. None of them belonged to Amalia. If Dora really understood what she was doing, leaving her so completely alone, would she continue to press ahead? Amalia sprinted to catch her, the scraping of the money in the coarse wool stockings telling her to hurry, to stop Dora if she could. The thick stacks of marks were all they needed to start a new life together in the country. Searching up ahead for her sister, Amalia bumped into her as she stood, suitcase at her feet, in front of a shop window.

"Watch out!" Dora took Amalia's arm, steadying the cloth bag with a protective, motherly gesture. She directed her to look in the window. "This is where they had that porcelain crèche in December. Remember, you got mad when I stopped to look at it? See what's here now!"

"I didn't get mad," Amalia said. "I was afraid we'd miss our train. I wanted to get home." Home. At least they'd had one then. Her train ride this evening would end in Elsterdorf and her hired girl's room at the Neufelds'. She wanted to grab Dora, kidnap her.

"That's crazy!" Dora said. For a moment Amalia thought she must have spoken her desperation aloud, but Dora was pointing at the window display. "Do you see?"

In the window, surrounded by pipe racks, tobacco, cigars and cigarettes, stood several stuffed animals. At a quick glance it looked like an interesting, but not unusual, assortment of birds and small mammals in various poses. Upon closer examination, however, you noticed that the fox had the wings of a hawk and the duck had the body of a squirrel—nothing right, everything twisted. Amalia's stomach churned.

"Tobacco and taxidermy, how odd," Dora went on, and then started to laugh. "Why would someone do this? Amalia, look at the goose with a...what is that...a skunk's head? And is that a rabbit? The ears don't look long enough. Are these for sale? How strange!"

"You think this is funny?" How could Dora laugh about anything right now?

"Well, yes." Dora stopped laughing. "Don't you?"

"They're hideous," Amalia pronounced. "What's wrong with a duck being a duck and a squirrel a squirrel? Who would want something this grotesque?"

"Sofie would laugh."

"Sofie isn't here." A meanness crept into Amalia's voice. "Do you think God would approve?"

"Why not? God has a sense of humor." Dora gripped her suitcase and began walking.

"Oh, yes, I forgot, you know all about God, your husband-to-be. I bet you know how he likes his coffee and whether or not he snores."

Dora paused long enough to give her a pitying look, then strode on.

Amalia rushed along after her. "I just can't believe you're laughing." Her voice sounded odd—miserable and small. "Those animals are ugly."

"Dora." Amalia struggled to catch her breath. "You can still change your mind. Don't do this. Don't leave me." Now that she'd said it, she couldn't stop. "We'll find someone to sell us a piece of their land. Please, Dora. You're making a mistake. I know it. People marry people, not God."

"Don't make this harder than it already is," Dora said. She moved down the sidewalk with long strides.

"What about lunch?" Amalia asked, hating her own pleading, whining voice. "I'm hungry."

"I think it's best if we get this over with." Dora kept walking.

Amalia panicked. "Please!" she said, loud enough that people around them paused. Dora didn't. Amalia had to chase her.

"I'm sorry," she panted, hurrying alongside Dora. She told herself to be reasonable, calm, in charge. She still had the money. What if she ran off? If Lorenz, who had been like a brother to them, could take money, so could she. Would the nuns be so welcoming if Dora arrived without a dowry? "Let's stop and eat something. I have to eat before catching the train, and I don't want to eat alone. Besides, you know what kind of food the nuns gave us. This is your last chance to eat whatever you want. We'll go to a restaurant. Please." She didn't know what she'd do if Dora refused.

"We'll buy that jellied meat you like," Amalia begged.

Dora's expression softened. She craned her neck to check the time on a clock tower. "All right. Let's just have a nice time, okay?" She tossed the words over her shoulder as they entered the nearest restaurant.

The low-ceilinged, paneled dining room was crowded, with booths along one wall and tables arranged in the middle. The dimness suited Amalia better than the bright, summery day outside. A waiter seated them and pointed out the menu written in chalk on a slate too far away to read. A man tripped over Dora's suitcase and cursed. Dora tried to push it in under the small table. The waiter came to take their order. He recited the offerings in a bored, almost resentful, voice.

Across from each other they waited for their food. Outside the bells pealed on and on: noon. The ringing stopped. A nice time? Amalia couldn't think of anything to say to lighten the heavy silence. She wanted to point out that this was their last meal together, a last meal with a blood relative. It might not matter to Dora, but it did to her. She had no one else left. No parents, no cousins, no aunts or uncles. There were probably some great-aunts and uncles somewhere, some second cousins, or were they cousins once removed? It didn't matter. She didn't know them. If she wanted to sit at a table with a relative she'd have to have children of her own or wait for Sofie to visit. Or go to America.

"Maybe I'll go to America," Amalia said. See if that made Dora nervous.

"Oh." Dora unfolded her napkin. "When would you go?"

Amalia didn't answer.

"I thought you wanted to stay here," Dora said.

"I do," Amalia said, loud enough that the couple at the next table stopped eating and looked at them. She leaned across the table and whispered, "Aren't you sad, Dora? Aren't you afraid?"

"I'm sad to leave you," Dora said. "I miss Sofie. But I'm not afraid. I want to do this. Why can't you understand?"

"But how do you *know*?" Amalia had to work to keep her voice down. "How *can* you know? You're seventeen years old. How can you decide something this big? You've never even had a boyfriend."

"I've told you before, it's not something I can explain." Dora reached across the table and put her hand on top of Amalia's. "I'll pray for you."

Amalia snatched her hand away. "Pray for yourself," she said. She adjusted the stockings bunching at her waist.

The waiter brought their plates. Amalia ordered beer. The look Dora gave her reminded her of a cow—a dumb, contented look of pity.

Dora cut bites of her jellied meat and ate it with small smacking sounds. "This is good," she said. She cleaned her plate before Amalia finished chewing her first bite. The waiter brought the beer. Amalia drank it in two long gulps to wash the slice of wurst past the lump in her throat.

"Do you want this?" Amalia pushed her plate toward Dora. "I can't eat and I can't leave food we're paying for."

"You should eat," Dora said. "You said you were hungry."

Amalia shook her head.

Dora ate the potatoes and the wurst, bite after bite, from Amalia's plate. Amalia burped without bothering to cover her mouth.

Dora laughed, but when Amalia stared at her straight-faced, she stopped. "You act like this day is all about my leaving you," Dora said. "It's not. You can visit me. We can write to each other. Why aren't you angry at Sofie? She's the one who went away. Most people are glad when someone they love is called to serve God. Mama would have been glad."

"How do you know?" Amalia asked.

"I know."

"Just don't pray for me," Amalia said.

"I'll pray for you whether you like it or not. Are you sure you don't want any of this food?"

The beer sloshed in Amalia's empty stomach. "You eat it."

Dora swallowed the last bite. "We should go now," she said.

Amalia felt for Dora's money. "I need to go to the toilet to get the money out. I'm paying with yours. Let the nuns cover two sisters' last meal together." She pushed back her chair. "I'll need all mine to survive until I find a man with a farm who will marry me."

"Are you drunk?" Dora rose. "I'll come with you."

"I can manage!" The small satisfaction Amalia felt as her words forced Dora to sit disappeared as she stumbled over the suitcase. Biting her lip to keep from whimpering or muttering to herself, she made her way to the tiny water closet. She unpinned both stockings, the right side then the left, trying to remember which was Dora's and which was hers, before recalling that it didn't matter, really, not until she took the money out. She'd divided it equally. Dora could carry her own marks the rest of the way. Amalia didn't want to be the one to hand it over to the nuns. Bad enough she had to hand over her sister. She wasn't about to pay for the privilege.

Someone knocked on the toilet door. Amalia left the pins on the high windowsill and, stockings in hand, exited past the waiting woman toward Dora sitting on the edge of her seat at the table full of empty plates and glasses. Dizzy from the beer, Amalia had forgotten to remove the money. She threw one stocking down beside Dora's plate. "You take this now," she said.

The stocking looked satisfyingly incongruous on the restaurant table. Amalia smiled.

"Should I pay the waiter?" Dora reached for the stocking.

"Never mind." Amalia opened her own. "I guess I can buy my own little sister a piece of jellied meat, her very favorite food. Her good-bye meal." What was she talking about? Why couldn't she just be quiet? She clamped her lips together and paid the bill. Maybe she was going crazy. She and Frau Neufeld would get along just fine.

"Thank you," said Dora.

Outside, the bright sun hurt Amalia's eyes. It should have been raining or sleeting. She felt like hunching her shoulders against the cold, but the air was mild. All around them people were smiling, chatting, opening up to spring after the rough winter of strikes and inflation and violence. She and Dora should be smiling too, with a pleasant walk before them, nothing to do but enjoy the sun warming their backs. After winter, spring—you could depend on it. What else was there to depend on? Dora would say God, but where had God been during the influenza, the war, the hunger? You couldn't depend on the government or money. One day a fresh loaf of bread cost a mark; next thing you knew, you couldn't buy a day-old slice with a wheelbarrow full of bills. You couldn't depend on people. One day they were there, the next they were dead, or leaving, or joining a convent. She looked around her. Dora, braids haloing her head, shoulders straight, glanced back every few moments to make sure Amalia was coming. The convent was on the next block—*Klosterstrasse*. Trees. You could depend on trees. These poor city trees with their roots trapped by paving stones. They must be suffocating and still they gave people shade and flowers; some produced nuts and fruit, even here in the city. *Gingko, linden, gingko, plum,* Amalia murmured as she passed them, to keep from screaming.

Amalia wished she knew where Frau Hollicher's shop was. She wished she could be sure of a warm welcome. She tried to think of some kind and meaningful last words to say to Dora. Busy with the money, she'd forgotten to use the toilet. She should have, after drinking that beer.

They climbed the two wide stone steps to the arched wooden doorway. They stood in the open vestibule. Amalia put the bag down.

"Ring the bell," said Dora. Her voice shook.

Amalia reached for the bell pull, then stopped. "I won't."

Dora's lip quivered. She bit it and blinked. She hesitated.

"I can't," Amalia whispered, throat aching. "Dora, let's get out of here!"

With a breath so deep Amalia could hear it, Dora moved toward the bell pull and gave it a quick tug. It echoed like an alarm.

"Don't cry," Dora said. She was the teary one. Amalia's eyes were dry.

The door opened and a strange nun stood there. Amalia had assumed they'd be greeted by someone they knew. She'd expected Sister Raphaela. The nun reached for Amalia's hand. "Welcome, we've been waiting for you."

"No!" Amalia's voice flew past the woman's shoulder, reverberated off the high ceilings and the bare marble stairs. It ricocheted off the tall leaded windows. She was embarrassed. She hadn't meant to yell.

Dora stepped forward. "I'm Dora Bauer. This is my sister. She brought me here."

"Ah," the nun nodded. "Welcome. I'm Sister Evangelista. I'll help you get settled."

The nun took the suitcase from Amalia. She shepherded Dora further into the inner vestibule.

"Write to me," Amalia said.

"Good-bye now," said the nun gently and pushed the heavy door. Amalia caught a glimpse of Dora's frightened face before the latch clicked.

It happened so fast. She imagined throwing herself against the door, beating on it until her fists were bloody, screaming Dora's name. She sat on the step.

People passed as if nothing had happened. They talked, walked arm in arm, carried groceries, rode bicycles. She should get up and go somewhere, back to the train station, but then what? Maybe if she stood and walked, the simple act of moving would provide enough purpose to make it through the next minute, hour, days, weeks.

She joined the stream of pedestrians, letting their momentum carry her along. At the *Domplatz* the sunny day had spawned an impromptu festival. People thronged around a brightly painted wooden puppet theater. Men sold nuts and flavored ice from carts.

She climbed the steps of the *Dom*, overlooking the *Domplatz*. Three little girls—gypsies, perhaps, with their olive skin, dark curly hair, and colorful layers of skirts—held hands and spun in a circle, until they tumbled in a laughing heap on the cobblestones. They brushed each other off and spun again.

Behind her, incense-tinged, marble-cooled air floated out through the open church doors. Familiar and solemn, it called her in. Here were the sad people, the lonely people, scattered among the pews like tossed crumbs. She knelt and pressed her hands together. In front of her, a young woman's shoulders shook with silent sobs. Beside her an old man muttered to himself. Somebody behind her coughed long and hard.

Amalia tried to pray, but the sobbing, the muttering, and especially the coughing only made her angry. She wandered through the church, found a toilet in the basement and thanked God for that, then continued to make her way through the shadowy aisles, avoiding the bright outdoors full of laughing little girls holding hands.

Racks of votive candles flickered along the sides of the church. People had their choice of shrines, of different saints to pray to. In an alcove dedicated to Saint Joseph, patron saint of families, a rack of green, red, and white candles twice as tall as she was angled down from a wooden statue. If you chose to light one near the top, you would have to climb a ladderlike metal staircase. She knelt before the flickering candles. Dora would have slipped a coin into the wooden box and lit one, maybe more than one, for their mother, Sofie, Oskar, for her. She considered lighting one for Dora—a white one, in the top row. From where she knelt, the bank of candles looked like a hill of colored light. St. Joseph gazed down on her with a patient and kind face.

Pray, she told herself. *It might help*. But she couldn't. The candles, the incense, the prayers, they'd stolen her sister from her, seduced her. She didn't believe in heaven or hell. She believed in compost and trees. *Light the candle for your sister anyway*, said a voice in her head. *It won't hurt. Dora would like it*. Amalia didn't want to give the church any more of Frau Becker's money, Mama's money, her money. *But Dora would love a candle. Do it for her*. The nuns already have Dora's money, her fair share. Dora should've used it for the meal. God or the nuns or Dora owed Amalia at least a small thank you. *Light the candle, Amalia, it might help. It might help you*. She would rather have a lemon ice.

For Dora's sake she dropped a coin into the locked box and lit a candle—a white one, but on the bottom, in the closest row. She hurried from the church, suddenly desperate for air.

Outside, the puppet show had started. She had a good view from the church steps. At first the puppets looked like Punch and Judy, but they were talking, not clobbering each other with sticks. A beautiful fish puppet appeared, larger than the Punch character. It sparkled in the light. "Flounder, flounder in the sea."

"The Fisherman and His Wife"—if only Dora and Sofie could be here. Amalia watched and listened, too far away to hear all the words, but she knew them so well it didn't matter.

The three dark girls now stood transfixed on the step below her. The puppeteers used large sheets of fabric for the changing water—green, yellow, purple, dark-blue, gray, darker gray, black—and shook them more and more violently each time, with accompanying drum rolls. Amalia stayed until the hat was passed. People threw in money or didn't and the crowd dispersed. One of the puppeteers announced the next show. A new crowd gathered. Amalia watched it all from the church steps.

The oldest of the three little girls caught her looking at them and approached Amalia with a shy smile. "I can tell your fortune," she said.

The younger ones giggled.

"Are you sisters?" Amalia asked.

"Cousins," the middle one said. "Like sisters."

"She can tell your fortune." The little one's voice squeaked. "Give her your hand. She'll tell you if you're lucky."

A large enough crowd had formed that the puppeteer once again moved behind his stage.

"What do you want?" the middle sister asked, smiling. She was missing her two front teeth. "Dina will tell you if you'll get it."

"Where do you live?" Amalia asked.

"We move around," said Dina. "Wherever we are is our home." She must have a caught the flicker of recognition in Amalia's face because she added, "Like you." She looked harder into Amalia's eyes. "But we have each other and you are alone."

The girl couldn't have been more than nine years old. Someone had taught her how to read people's faces, how to identify loneliness in the slump of a shoulder, the arc of a neck, the inward tuck of elbows. Fortune telling was a bunch of nonsense. Amalia felt for her money stocking. The little girls looked innocent, but she'd been warned about gypsies.

The girls began hopping up and down the steps around Amalia. "Let her see your palm."

"The Fisherman and His Wife," announced the puppeteer through a megaphone.

Amalia closed her eyes. Her head spun with flickering candles and jellied meat, puppets, girls with gold hoops in their ears, invented animals with no names. This was her new life without sisters. She'd find out if she could bear it.

Amalia held her palm out to the dark-eyed girl. "Where are your parents?"

"Over there," said the girl with a careless wave. She smoothed Amalia's fingers and examined her hand.

"Strong thumb," the girl said. "That shows great strength of will." She peered more closely. Amalia felt her damp breath on her palm.

"This is your mound of Venus," she said pointing with a grubby finger to the area just below Amalia's thumb. "See how developed it is? You are generous. You like men?"

Amalia blushed at the leering little girls and tried to pull her hand away, but the oldest girl held tight. "Look here." She pointed to a spot under Amalia's index finger. The little girls nodded and made small humming sounds full of knowing.

"A cross," the oldest girl pronounced. "Now a cross most anywhere else denotes trouble, but here on the mound of Jupiter it is a very good sign—it portends a very happy marriage."

"Her hand is all about love, love, love," said the middle girl, skipping around Amalia and the fortune teller.

"See how your life line and your heart line are tinged red?" the girl pointed, tracing them, tickling her so that a shiver ran down her back. "That indicates that you are full of emotion, overfull. Pink is a better color for the heart line. More balanced."

The little girl pulled on her earring, stretching the hole. Sounds of loud drumming from the puppet show drowned out her words. The fish was angry. The black fabric flapped.

"You will have trouble but you are stubborn," the girl continued when the noise subsided. "This mount of upper Mars is very developed. This indicates your persistence, your power of resistance, but you must watch out. You can be too stubborn, like a mule. And here, in your fate line, this scattered, fragmented place—disappointment, trouble, loss."

"There's always trouble," said Amalia.

"But you will have love," the girl said. "That is most clear."

"I saw it too," said the middle sister.

The little one frowned and scratched her belly. "Trouble," she said.

The fisherman and his wife were back in the sty. The crowd applauded.

"I told you a good fortune," the girl said, folding Amalia's fingers and patting the fist she'd made. "A good fortune deserves a reward."

Why not? Amalia gave her a mark. Dina tucked it into a beaded pouch she wore around her neck. Amalia wondered what Sofie's hands would say. What would the little girl make of the crooked finger? What about Dora? Would her hands have predicted a life of service to God? Amalia didn't believe any of it anyway. It was just a trick to make money, but as the girls waved and blended in with the crowd in the square, and loneliness set in again, she noted the redness of her heart line and thought of Tomas.

Her head ached from noise and beer. Her eyes hurt from too much movement and color. The raw spots near her waist stung. She passed the tobacco shop on the way to the station and avoided looking in the window. She was like those nameless creatures, grotesque, not one thing or another, neither here nor there. Overfull of love but alone. Aching to work the land but owning nothing. No faith in God or fortunes, but one minute she was trying to pray and the next listening to wild little girls predict her future. A walking contradiction. A walking mess. So, so tired and sore.

At the station she saw that a train that stopped in Elsterdorf would arrive in twenty minutes. She must still be traveling along the strong, well-defined portion of her fate line. She studied the map of her hand and tried to calculate how millimeters translated into days or weeks, how long it would take to come to the broken part. She remembered that she'd never felt as lonely as she had when the convent door slammed shut and decided she might well be traveling in that broken section now.

Tired as she was, she'd have to walk from the station to the Neufelds'. It would be dark. She longed for the silence of swooping bats, the quietness of plants. Her trunk could very well be there already, waiting at the Elsterdorf station. She'd ask someone to fetch it tomorrow. Tomas's bowl, wrapped carefully in her skirts, waited packed inside. She'd return it to him, tell him she loved the stew, and make him reveal the secret ingredient. She'd examine his palm.

CHAPTER 16

▼

Dora would never forget the heavy thunk of the convent door falling shut and the echo behind her as she followed short, quick Sister Evangelista. The disappearance of Amalia's stunned face threatened to undo her carefully constructed cheerfulness.

She widened her eyes so the tears would evaporate. Before her stretched a long high-ceilinged hallway, its polished marble floor full of overlapping shadows. To her left, was a row of wooden doors, each topped by a frosted transom—all the same, all shut tight, no sign of what lay behind. On her right gleamed a row of tall windows with wide stone sills, looking out on a courtyard garden with a statue of the Virgin at its center. She looked at the profusion of flowers blooming on the bushes and the ground. Amalia would know what they were called, their Latin and their common names. *Yellow, pink, white, blue.* She listed the colors and said them in her head, over and over, in the same order, like beads on a necklace. She thought she should pray, but strangely all she could do was list colors and follow the nun, a syllable for every step, as she turned right down a hallway exactly like the first, and right again down the opposite side of the square. Now, when she looked out at the garden, Dora could see the Virgin's back. *Yellow, pink, white, blue.* The reverberation of the clicking latch followed her. She clung to the handle of her suitcase; her bag bumped against her thigh.

Sister Evangelista stopped at a door. Dora wondered how the nun had distinguished it from all the others. Perhaps she'd counted, third door after the third turn. Perhaps it didn't matter and behind every door lay exactly the same thing.

A knot of three whispering girls loosened and grew quiet as Sister Evangelista and Dora stepped into the room.

"Dora Bauer has finally arrived," the nun announced. "Now we can begin. Please sit." She motioned to a row of high-backed carved chairs, against the wall. The 'finally' made Dora feel as though she should apologize for being late, but the girls looked more anxious than annoyed, and she was afraid to say anything for fear it would be wrong.

The girls dragged their suitcases along with them, over to the chairs. Dora moved her chair and her bag forward a few centimeters so they lined up evenly with those of the girl beside her.

The girl, who later introduced herself as Claudia, had a set of three shiny, expensive-looking leather valises—small, medium, and large. Claudia herself wore an embroidered crepe de chine blouse, sheer stockings, and a soft wool skirt. She had dark red hair that glowed from attention or fancy hair products or both. She had a wide, nervous smile and a sprinkling of freckles.

"I'm Petra," said the girl sitting next in the row. Her suitcase was the smallest, scuffed and tied shut with a piece of twine. Like her luggage, Petra was small and shabby-looking. Beneath a cap of short blonde hair her thin, sharp-featured face looked tough and tired. At the end of the row slumped Anneliese, a large, dark-haired girl with pasty white skin and a missing front tooth. She had a round case with a broken handle and a huge rectangular trunk that looked too heavy to lift. They all kept a hand or foot pressed against their belongings. Dora waited for Sister Evangelista to notice and tell them to sit straight, hands in lap, feet on floor, but she didn't. She wondered when she'd see Sister Raphaela or any other familiar face.

The nun went over the schedule for the rest of the day and then for the following. The next day's schedule would be the schedule for every day after that: 5:15, a knock on their doors would wake them; 5:30, chapel; 6:00, meditation; 6:30, Mass; then breakfast and either religious studies or assigned duties; examination of conscience; noon, dinner; afternoon duties; community meeting; meditation; supper; recreation; daily instruction on religious life by Sister Evangelista; prayers. At 8:00, began the Great Silence, kept until after Mass the next morning.

"There is never any talking in the dormitory," Sister Evangelista finished. "You will quickly grow accustomed to it."

Already Dora couldn't remember much of what she'd said. Recreation—she liked the sound of that and wanted to ask what it was. Great Silence—that sounded lofty and grand.

"But today, today I will take you to the Postulantship where second-year novices will help you change into postulant dresses. You will have the opportunity to unpack and store your things. Late this afternoon we will have the hooding ceremony, during which you will receive the postulant veil in church. Then supper, prayers, and bed. No time for recreation today."

Sister Evangelista stood and motioned for them to follow. "Dora, Anneliese, Claudia, Petra. This is how you will line up—oldest to youngest." With their suitcases they merged into a straight line. Anneliese couldn't move her trunk alone and Sister Evangelista didn't seem to notice. Wordlessly, transferring her bag to the same hand as her suitcase, Dora lifted the front end of Anneliese's trunk. First in line, arms aching, Dora heard the girls behind her struggling with their luggage, breathing heavily. Sister Evangelista skimmed across the floor in front of them carrying only a clipboard.

Now I'm the oldest, Dora thought. *The oldest sister. Dora, Anneliese, Claudia, Petra.* She adjusted her hold on the trunk, hefted it a bit. She would have felt more comfortable in Petra's place, but a whole new life was beginning and now she was first.

Sister Evangelista opened a door at the end of the corridor that led into a dim hallway, no tall windows overlooking the garden. The ceiling was lower, the floor of wood instead of marble, but polished just as bright. Doors lined both sides.

The muscles in Dora's arms quivered. She didn't know how much further she could go. She wondered why Sister Evangelista hadn't called for people to help them or why the Postulant Mistress herself didn't carry something. This was an order dedicated to helping the sick, the weak, the unfortunate. At least she was helping Anneliese. Sofie would have spoken up, asked Sister Evangelista for help. Amalia would have complained until someone offered.

Just when Dora was about to ask for a rest they arrived at the postulantship. Sister Evangelista waved them into the dormitory. It looked just like the room she and Amalia had stayed in while working in the hospital. Six iron bedsteads, with bright white spreads and flat pillows, protruded from the white walls like teeth, three to a side. Each bed had a narrow wooden cabinet beside it. The three small windows of frosted glass let in a vague, watery light.

"Unpack your things. The novices will be along soon to help you dress for the hooding ceremony." She left them standing in a clump near the doorway, among their luggage.

"Why six beds?" asked Claudia. "There are only four of us." She chose the bed at the end on the right by dumping her suitcases on it.

"Who are the two that didn't come?" asked Petra. "We'll never know."

Dora giggled, more because she wanted to be friendly than because she found Petra's comment amusing. Petra and Anneliese chose their beds on the opposite side from Claudia, leaving an empty one in the middle. Dora saw she should take the one closest to her on the right. She supposed she should be thankful for the space between them. The other girls seemed to like it that way. If she'd chosen before Petra and Anneliese set their example, she would've selected the bed next to one them. She didn't like the separating emptiness. She imagined Amalia in the bed beside her, Sofie across the room. Her sisters. The two who didn't come.

"Maybe they know something we don't," Anneliese said. It wasn't until she grinned that Dora realized she was attempting a joke.

Claudia pulled a pair of sheer stockings from her red valise and held them up. "Maybe one of them could use these," she said. "I know I won't, but I couldn't bear to leave them behind."

"One of them?" asked Dora, still thinking of Sofie and Amalia.

"One of the two who didn't come. The two who'll be out dancing in the beer garden while we're praying in the chapel." Claudia crumpled the stockings into a ball and threw them across the room. "What am I doing here?" She sat on her bed and buried her face in her hands.

Anneliese moved two pairs of shoes from her trunk to her cabinet. Petra worked to unknot the twine that held her suitcase shut. Dora wanted to respond, to sit beside Claudia on the bed, place a comforting hand on her back, but in her throat mounted a surge of fierce laughter or wild sobs, she wouldn't know which until it escaped. Determined to keep a calm exterior, she pressed her lips together and removed a bar of soap from her suitcase. Next to the stack of soap she'd packed, rustled a thin sheet of paper she hadn't.

Though the paper was folded in half, it was so thin she could see writing on the other side. Amalia had bought that paper before they left for Bremerhaven. She'd given a third of it to Sofie, a third of it to Dora, kept a third for herself, and had extracted promises of letters, though none of them liked to write much. Amalia had started already. Had she also written to Sofie in care of Oskar's uncle? Right now, in America, was Sofie receiving mail? No, a week wasn't long enough. Sofie wouldn't even be there herself.

"I wonder if my parents have arrived home yet," Anneliese mused. "They were so sad leaving here. They were acting as if I'd died, as if they'd never see me again."

"Mine couldn't wait to see me go," whispered Petra. "One less person eating."

Dora moved the soap to the top shelf of her cabinet. She didn't let herself touch the note.

Claudia said, "What if I liked the idea of being a nun more than the actual life? What if I've made a mistake?"

Dora swallowed and managed to speak. "That's why there's a postulant period. During the next six months you can leave if this isn't the right life for you. Any of us could." She looked from Claudia to Anneliese to Petra, all looking back at her. She was sure she wouldn't leave. She slammed her suitcase, hiding the letter. "Do you think they bring us water for washing? Is there a washroom somewhere?"

"There must be." Petra strode toward the door at the opposite end of the room from where they'd entered. "You would think that after all our traveling, they might have shown us where it is." She flung the door open, almost hitting two young nuns in long white veils, arms loaded with folded, dark clothing.

"Oh!" Petra stopped, bowed her head, bending her knee in a kind of curtsey. "Excuse me." She shrunk back into the space between Claudia's bed and the wall.

"Hello, Sister," the first nun addressed Petra. "Here are your clothes. I am Sister Hermine. This is Sister Greta." She placed the stack of clothing at the foot of Claudia's bed. The other nun placed hers on Petra's. They neatly split their piles in half. Sister Greta brought Anneliese hers, while Sister Hermine approached Dora. "The washroom is through that door and to the left." Sister Hermine pointed in the direction that Petra had been going. "We're here to help you dress. Notice that all your items of clothing are numbered." Dora flipped through her pile—dark wool stockings, long bloomers, a long-sleeved undershirt, a long petticoat, a black skirt and blouse, a short black cape, all numbered—172. She wondered who had been 172 before her, or was the number all her own? She almost giggled again, remembering Amalia asking her to be sure to tell her about nuns' underwear. Amalia said she just couldn't imagine it.

"You won't be needing your suitcases or anything that wasn't on your list of required items," Sister Greta said. "Please unpack only the things you were told to bring. and leave anything else..." She stooped to retrieve Claudia's balled stockings and held them at arm's length between her thumb and index finger as if they smelled bad. Noticing Petra's empty suitcase, she dropped the stockings into it. "Leave anything you were not asked to bring in the luggage. We will find a use for it or dispose of it. From now on, all your needs will be provided for by the community." Frowning in the direction of Dora's open cupboard, she pointed at the neatly stacked soap. "There's a cabinet in the washroom for soap and toothpowder and other toiletries you were asked to supply. All are for communal use."

Dora blushed.

Petra looked as though she wanted to say something. Maybe she wanted to disclaim any connection to the stockings. Dora snatched the note from her suitcase before Sister Hermine could inspect it. She crumpled it way down into the toe of her extra pair of sturdy black shoes, while the nun exchanged quiet words with Claudia.

The washroom looked a lot like the dormitory, with a row of sinks instead of beds. There were no mirrors. Sofie and Amalia wouldn't have liked that.

"I guess they don't believe in privacy," Anneliese whispered to Dora.

Dora wasn't bothered much. After years of dressing and sharing beds with Sofie and Amalia she was used to constant company. If she had to be alone in a cell tonight with no one breathing beside her, God forgive her, she'd feel lost. Being with the three other postulants-to-be kept her from crying.

She stripped to her camisole and petticoat and scrubbed her face and body. At the next sink Anneliese did the same. Dora's head came to Anneliese's shoulder. Her sidelong glance took in the taller girl's huge pale arms with long thatches of dark hair in the armpits. She was very white and very dark at the same time—white, white skin, black, black hair. Dark circles under dark, dark-browed eyes. Dark space between white teeth. Black and white like the postulants' dresses and the veils they'd soon be wearing. Dora remembered the blue of her own eyes, and, with a sharp pang, realized the thought as a fault against humility. She would have to be vigilant.

Claudia and Petra joined them. They slipped off their underclothes. Dora concentrated on the smell of soap and the splashes of water. Everyone took pains not to look at anyone else directly. With her peripheral vision she noted Claudia's slender neck and long torso and Petra's scrawny shoulders and flat chest. These girls seemed wrong. For the first time she saw how she, Amalia, and Sofie had, with only the minor variations of Amalia's ample breasts and her own few extra inches in height, the same basic form, the same sturdy body. Anyone could have identified them as sisters.

Sister Hermine and Sister Greta had finished emptying the girls' suitcases. Anything they would be keeping rested on their beds in a few sparse piles. The suitcases and even Anneliese's huge trunk had disappeared.

Wrapped in a thin scratchy towel, holding her dirty underclothes, Dora tried not to think about her missing suitcase and looked forward instead to putting on her postulant's dress. As long as she could remember she'd waited for this moment, when clean and expectant, she'd put on the clothing of a nun. Finally someone could look at her, just the briefest glance at her external appearance, and understand her deepest desires and intentions, her heart.

She looked up from fumbling with the strings of the petticoat and saw Petra and Claudia and Anneliese all in various stages of dressing in the same clothes. Under the same skirts and blouses and caps, their bodies were different, but look deeper and you'd find they were more the same where it mattered than she and Sofie and Amalia were. These were her true sisters, sisters in God. It might take time, but she would come to believe this.

Sister Hermine helped her slip the heavy blouse over her head and for a disorienting moment Dora felt Amalia's hands dressing her for the part of Rapunzel— the sense of excitement, the sense of being cared for—but it wasn't the same at all. That was pretend and this was real.

Sister Hermine and Sister Greta made sure the caps with the attached veils fit each girl's head. They pinned names to the fabric. Dora tried to tie the simple white cap over her pinned-up braids, but it wouldn't fit. Everyone else was able to tuck her hair inside. They weren't expected to cut their hair until they took the habit, when they became novices, six months from now. With sweaty hands Dora pressed at the thick lumps under her untied cap, willing them to disappear. The other three caps and veils dangled from Sister Greta's hand. Sister Hermine hovered near Dora, holding her veil and several straight pins. Claudia, Petra, and Anneliese stood fully dressed, heads covered with the scarves they'd been instructed to bring from home.

Sister Greta and Sister Hermine exchanged a significant glance. Sister Greta lay the three pinned veils across the foot of Dora's bed and slipped out of the room. Dora kneaded and pounded her lumpy hair. She began to sweat.

Sister Hermine tugged at the front edge of the cap, urging it forward, attempting to stretch fabric that had no give. The other girls put away their things and smoothed their beds to avoid staring at Dora's mounting agitation.

"Maybe if I unbraid it…" She tore off the cap and began fumbling with hair pins. Her braids tumbled free, almost to her waist.

Sister Hermine stopped her. "No, Dora, that won't be necessary. Sister Greta has gone to fetch the scissors."

Someone gasped. "But her hair is so beautiful," Claudia blurted. "So long."

Dora stiffened her shoulders. "It's only hair," she said. She wouldn't fail this test.

Sister Greta brandished a pair of gleaming silver scissors. She clicked them open and closed as she circled Dora. Dora squeezed her eyes shut.

The cold edge of a scissor blade touched her neck, just behind her right ear. One snip and the severed braid flopped in Sister Greta's hand. The nuns kept their scissors sharp. One of the things Dora liked best about them and their way of life was this very close attention to detail, the care put into daily tasks, everything done right in the service of God. She winced when the tip of the scissors grazed the other side of her neck and cut through her second braid with a light crackling sound like bacon frying. She imagined sending one to Sofie and one to Amalia, but Sister Greta had already tucked them into the black cloth pouch hidden away in her skirts. Dora wanted to send them to her sisters, a part of her to hang onto.

Sister Hermine adjusted the cap, running her hands over Dora's head. "That fixed it," she said. She pinned on the veil. "Much better," she pronounced, stepping back for a better look.

Dora stood completely still. They would do whatever they wanted with her. She had to learn obedience. Obedience, chastity, poverty. She had a lot to learn. She wondered what Sister Greta would do with her braids.

Sister Hermine removed the cap and veil. Sister Greta pinned a name tag to it. Dora chose a small dark scarf from her pile of things and covered her shorn head in preparation for church.

After consulting her watch, Sister Greta announced that in twenty minutes they would line up and proceed to the chapel for the hooding ceremony. Sister Evangelista would return to lead them there. She and Sister Hermine left, the scissors glinting silver against Sister Greta's dark habit. The white veils, each labeled with a name, floated from Sister Hermine's hand.

The girls stood still in the milky light. Dora felt everyone's eyes on her. She pushed a ragged lock of short hair under her scarf and wanted to weep. From far away a single bell clanged the quarter hour.

"What a shame!" Claudia exclaimed. She, Petra, and Anneliese approached in a cluster of concern as if the bell had given them permission to move and speak.

"Oh, you must feel terrible, so sudden like that," Petra said.

Anneliese put an arm across Dora's shoulders.

Dora continued to stare at the play of light and shadow on the polished floor. Girls dressed in black with dark head covers, comforting and grieving, reminded her too much of her mother's funeral. Their sisterly concern threatened the resolve she'd built since then, brick by brick, prayer by prayer. Many things had chipped away at it, but it had never wobbled like it was wobbling now. If she didn't get Anneliese's arm off her back, extricate herself from the suffocating circle of comforting murmurs, she might faint or run away. She didn't care about the haircut. She really didn't. But the braids were hers.

Even when, on the farm, all the kids had lice, old Frau Neufeld had spent hours combing through Dora's long, long hair with kerosene and a fine-tooth comb. The rest of the children had theirs shaved off, but Frau Neufeld thought Dora's was too beautiful. All those hours when the old lady could have been making her crocheted cloths, she combed instead. And for Dora, aching for her mother and her sisters, those were the happiest times on the Neufelds' farm. Frau Neufeld would give her a piece of looped crochet thread to keep her settled, and with her nimble fingers Dora created string figures for Frau Neufeld to admire between strokes of the comb. All her life she'd grown those braids. Her mother and her sisters had touched that hair.

The girls drifted away during her long hard silence, yet she felt their concern even as they talked among themselves of other things. Anneliese continued to glance at her every few moments.

"It's all right," Dora said. "Please, it's really all right." *Worry about yourselves,* she wanted to scream. *I've had too many people worrying about me for too long. Stop looking at me. You'll all have shorn heads soon enough.*

She scolded herself for such uncharitable thoughts, only moments before the hooding ceremony, but as soon as she stopped berating herself, she thought them again. She closed her eyes and began to pray, right where she stood. In the middle of a Hail Mary, she remembered Amalia's note.

Sister Evangelista opened the door. "Line up, sisters, it's time."

Dora took her place at the front of the line.

They entered a door at the front of the church. Dora breathed in the church smell of incense and immense stone space. The sounds of an organ filled the sanctuary with an unfamiliar music, hauntingly beautiful. The evening sun shone through the stained-glass windows, splashing pew after dark pew of nuns with swatches of colored light. Dora scanned the rows for Sister Raphaela, but the nuns all had their heads bowed. It was impossible to tell which one she was, yet knowing she was there somewhere calmed her. She remembered looking into the wrinkled nun's blue, blue eyes, the touch of Sister Raphaela's finger on her chin.

The four girls knelt at the wooden altar rail. Candles flickered. Jesus hung on a giant crucifix, his face peaceful and sad at the same time. Dora listened to the prayers of the nuns behind her and felt her panic subside into a peaceful sadness like his. The Reverend Mother placed the cap and veil on her head, smoothing it over her cropped hair. It fit tightly over her ears. For a moment she couldn't distinguish any individual words, only a rising and falling hum, like a lullaby. The Reverend Mother moved along behind them—Anneliese, Claudia, Petra—each with the veil of a postulant. She couldn't see herself, but she could look at them and see how they'd changed. Here, at the altar, name tags removed from the fabric, they were part of the community, part of that great sea of nuns behind them. She prayed.

After the hooding Sister Greta brought them back to the postulants' community room to wait until supper. "This is where you'll receive religious instruction from Sister Evangelista and have recreation. Once a week, on Sunday, except during Lent and Advent, you will be permitted to write letters to close family members. You will also be permitted to receive letters from close family once a week, on that same day. In your letters we ask that you never write about what happens inside our community. We also ask you to refrain from expressing any personal feelings. Sister Evangelista will collect all letters, unsealed, at the conclusion of the letter writing time. Any letters you receive will be opened and read first."

Again, Dora thought of Amalia's note, crumpled in the toe of her shoe. She prayed God would forgive her. Maybe she should throw it away without reading it or hand it to the Postulant Mistress to read first. What did anyone write about? She could see that the other postulants were wondering the same thing. Sister Greta did not invite questions.

"You all know that you are here, secluded from the many distractions of the world, to develop a deep, personal relationship with God. Everything you do is in service of this goal. Even the smallest daily acts are a means of worshipping God. In just a few minutes we will have supper. Eating is an act of devotion. We eat everything on our plates with conscious appreciation and awareness, attention to every bite. All meals are eaten in silence while a sister reads from holy texts."

Dora realized that she was starving. It seemed weeks ago that she and Amalia had eaten the jellied meat. In the spareness and hush of the postulants' community room it was hard to believe that several blocks away stood a bustling restaurant—many bustling restaurants, and trains and rushing people buying things, shop windows, all the distractions of the outside world.

"Follow me to the refectory," Sister Greta was saying. The girls stood.

Once they passed through the door the time for speaking would have passed. "Excuse me, Sister?" Dora heard herself say.

Sister Greta stopped. She looked surprised.

"Forgive me for asking," Dora began.

The girls seemed to be holding their collective breath. Dora plunged in.

"My braids...what have you done with them?"

"That is not your concern," said Sister Greta, voice firm though not unkind.

"Oh," Dora said, "but it is...I mean, I am...I'm just wondering because..."

"You will examine your conscience twice a day, at noon and night. Ask yourself these questions to stop yourself from asking others. Have I been grateful for the favors I have received from God, my trials as well as my consolations? Have I lived up to my commitment to trust in God's love? You may find it helpful to practice this more frequently. Resolve with the grace of God to lead a better life." Sister Greta smiled.

Dora's head ached. She wondered if her cap was too tight. She prayed to slow the pounding in her temples. As last in line, she would have been able to see the others, to judge from their postures, their steps, what they thought of Sister Greta's response to her feeble attempt to speak up. She followed Sister Greta through doors and corridors to the refectory. The nun's back told her nothing.

The room loomed around them, no sounds of pots or crockery, no cooking smells. "Tonight the four of you will be eating alone. There will be no reading. There will be silence. You will keep your eyes on your plate."

Long rectangular tables ran along all four walls of the room, benches on the outside so that when people sat, everyone faced in toward the center where another square of tables, benches along the outside, was arranged. In a corner of the room, on a raised platform, stood a podium, where Dora assumed the reader would stand. She wondered when the other nuns had eaten or would eat, but knew better than to ask.

"Tomorrow you will have regular meals with the community. The inner tables are for postulants and novices. The outer tables are where the professed sisters sit."

Sister Greta paused at a place setting near the corner of a table, gestured to the four set places nearest to her, and bowed her head in what Dora guessed was a silent grace. The girls stood in order, heads bowed. They sat when Sister Greta sat.

A novice appeared with a tray of covered dishes. She placed a platter of sliced bread, a tin of lard, and a bowl of watery soup in front of them. It was strange to be sitting in a row, no one across the table to smile at, to converse with. Dora thought of the noisy meals at home. Karl, Lorenz, and Oskar, the other mining students, and always her sisters—Sofie bustling, Amalia laughing, both of them flirting. She felt the emptiness at her back. Would it feel more or less strange to be surrounded by benches filled with nuns? In a full dining room someone had to click her spoon against a bowl or make a slurping sound.

Sister Greta served the soup. Five strands of cabbage floated in Dora's bowl. Her stomach gurgled. Eating this so-called soup would only make her hungrier. Sister Greta passed the bread. Dora counted the pieces and calculated that she could take two. She slid them off the plate. The lard tin followed. She helped herself to a generous portion, approximately one-fifth of the whole. Out of the corner of her eye she watched each of the others follow suit. Relieved, she began to eat.

The moment their plates were empty, the novice reappeared with a large pail of soapy water in which she indicated they were to wash their dishes. They dried them on the towel provided and rearranged them for the next meal. Anneliese splashed. Petra clanked. Claudia dropped her fork. Dora willed herself to move deliberately. *Every act is an act of devotion.* Washing lard from a knife in tepid water. Drying it. Setting it down, dull blade toward the soup plate. Everything clean and waiting to be used again, all in the service of God.

They followed Sister Greta back to the dormitory. They wouldn't have found it without her. All the hallways, the closed doors, looked very much alike. The whole time Dora had worked at the hospital, she'd yearned to know what mysteries hid behind the convent doors. Now, inside, it still seemed full of secrets.

"Soon you will hear the eight o'clock bells indicating the beginning of the Great Silence. You'll want to prepare for bed now. Good night and God bless you." Sister Greta shut them into the dormitory. Lavender-tinged light filtered through the opaque windows. This close to the solstice, the days were long. They'd be in bed before sunset.

Dora pushed at the window latch. She wanted to see the sky.

"I tried to open that earlier," Anneliese said. "It wouldn't budge."

Dora struggled for another moment before giving up.

"I never go to bed this early," Claudia said. "I'll never fall asleep."

"You'll get used to it," said Petra, heading for the washroom, clutching her nightgown and toothbrush. "People can get used to anything."

"Even things they shouldn't get used to," Claudia said. "Like the French and Belgians during the occupation, but that didn't make it right that they were here."

"Or empty shelves at the markets," Anneliese agreed. "But being used to that didn't fill our bellies."

"We got used to seeing wounded men begging. The more we got used to it, the easier it was to ignore them," Claudia went on.

Be quiet, Dora thought. She waited until all three left for the washroom. She pulled Amalia's note from the shoe and read it standing half-hidden by the cupboard door.

Dear Dora,

By the time you read this you'll know what nuns' underwear looks like. Or you will soon enough. Do they, or I guess I should say you, sleep with your veils on? Write to me as soon as you can, care of the Neufelds. I hope that old lady isn't as crazy as she seemed, but if she is I suppose I'll get used to it. You can still change your mind, right? You're not officially a nun yet. There are all kinds of ways to love and serve God. If you miss the breeze in your hair and squelching mud between your toes, if you miss the sound of dance music or men laughing, you can always leave. So what if they have your money. I'll share mine with you. We will be all right.

Love,

Amalia

PS I think there's a rule that says they have to give the money back if you leave before you're professed.

That's all. Dora ached with disappointment. What had she expected the note to say? If the note had arrived in the mail, if Sister Evangelista had read it, what would she have done? Would she have torn it up, blackened out sentences, or passed it along with a whisper of warning? What should Dora do with it now? Amalia didn't understand. True, there were many ways to love and serve God, but for Dora there was one and she had chosen it, or it had chosen her. She felt homesick, lonely, disappointed. But none of that meant she had made a mistake. She missed Amalia and Sofie, her second test, much bigger than the loss of her braids. Tests came in threes. What would the next one be?

Somewhere under the convent roof Sister Raphaela worked and prayed and breathed. Dora had to remember that. The other girls returned in whispered conversation. The bell began to chime. Dora peeled off her clothes, reminded herself to fold and hang them neatly. She climbed right into bed, afraid to use the washroom once the Great Silence had begun. She wasn't sure it was allowed. She lay in bed, needing to use the toilet, Amalia's note crumpled in her hand.

Someone opened the door and stopped at her bed. The graying light revealed Sister Evangelista. She made the sign of the cross and nodded before moving on to Claudia. She stopped at Petra's bed, then Anneliese's, then she was gone. The note burned in Dora's hand. She wondered if she should have given it to the Postulant Mistress. She'd never sleep if she didn't get up to use the toilet.

After waiting to make sure no one else floated in to say good night, she tiptoed to the washroom, heart pounding so that she thought the other girls must be able to hear it. The high-ceilinged rooms so amplified sound that she half expected nuns throughout the convent to hear it beating like a drum, summoning them. Come see the disobedient postulant sneaking to the toilet with an illicit note.

Dora peed with great relief and appreciation. Nothing like peeing when you really have to, Amalia would have said. She remembered Amalia scandalizing her by peeing behind a gravestone in the church cemetery long ago, when they'd hidden so well it took the other kids forever to find them. As a postulant, was urinating an act of devotion to God? She stifled a laugh, and read Amalia's note again. Breezes, mud, music, men laughing. She didn't care about any of that. She missed her braids and her sisters, but she'd get used to it. She tore up the note and dropped the pieces between her legs, into the bowl. She pulled the flush chain over and over until they disappeared.

PART III

▼

1924–1925

CHAPTER 17

▼

"Business as usual," Oskar read in English from the front page of *The Rivertown Sentinel*, "is motto at White House as Coolidge continues duties. Election causes stocks to climb." Sofie made no effort to understand the string of unfamiliar syllables. Every evening except Saturday, no matter how tired she was, Oskar read to her from the newspaper. He tried to convince her to read to him, but she didn't like the way the words tricked her tongue and clogged her mouth.

On Saturdays they danced at the German Hall. Even with her baby growing heavy in her belly she preferred dancing to English lessons, but today was only Wednesday. She settled her swollen feet on Oskar's lap, and rotated her ankles.

He continued to sound out words, his forehead creased with the effort. Occasionally he would frown and thumb through the already-tattered German-English dictionary he always carried in his pocket. He'd bought one for Sofie too, but she kept hers on top of the Frigidaire the landlord had installed just before they moved in, and touched it only to wipe underneath. "President expresses his 'simple thanks' for reelection—issues Thanksgiving proclamation."

Thanksgiving—Sofie recognized that word, like *Ernte Dankfest* back home. She remembered celebrating the harvest festival in Elsterdorf. Even during the war when most crops were eaten or preserved the moment they were picked, Heinrich and Herr Neufeld hitched the horse to the wagon, and invited Sofie and Gustav Blau—Tomas was away at the front then—to help Dora and Frau Neufeld decorate both the horse and wagon with flowers. All of them paraded through town with their meager load of potatoes and turnips, followed by Amalia with the Muellers and all the other townsfolk. They built a fire in a field and roasted potatoes on long forks. Flames licked away the stars and illuminated people's faces. They sang and told stories, lips sooty from the blackened potato skins.

The past few days she'd noticed signs advertising Thanksgiving specials papering the Five and Ten and the grocery store on Main Street. There were special foods Americans ate on this holiday. Tante Eva, who had been in the United States for eighteen years, told her they ate turkey meat—the male, not the hen, something called cranberry sauce, and, instead of fruit torte, a pastry called pie. Oskar would want to eat the American food too, but Sofie didn't know how to make it, even with the recipes Tante Eva had given her—one for mincemeat pie, another for cranberry relish. Back home everyone loved her cooking. The only familiar dishes Tante Eva mentioned were the potatoes which, here in America, lacked flavor, and turnips—which Sofie wouldn't eat again unless she were starving, and she would never starve in America. If she ever had to be hungry like that, she'd be hungry in Germany among people she could understand.

"Oskar, we should go mushroom hunting. Mushrooms grow here too." She had a sudden craving for the woodsy taste of *boletus badius* fried with onions.

"No time, Sofie. The season for the best mushrooms is already past. Can't you buy some at the market?" Oskar laid the newspaper down. "Elections and no violence," he marveled. "True, Coolidge has been president for more than a year, since Harding died, but still…When I listen to Americans talk it barely makes a difference what party they belong to. Certainly, no one seems ready to pick up a gun or march in the streets."

"Why should they?" Sofie said. "No one starved during the war. They haven't had to live in occupied territory. No one ordered them to give their bedrooms to strangers, to enemies." The baby moved. She pulled the fabric of her dress tight over her round belly. "Can you see him rolling around in there, Oskar?"

He shook his head. No one could see. The baby was still too small, but she could feel its silent sloshing, like summer plums in their heavy syrup, the ones Amalia and Frau Mueller canned. Her mouth watered. She could see herself lifting the dark jar from the pantry shelf, feel the textured glass.

"Onkel Ludwig and Tante Eva have invited us over for Thanksgiving Day," Oskar said. "We'll bring something for the dinner, of course." He leaned toward her and absently stroked her abdomen. "Sofie, you have to work harder to learn English. This is our home now. Our baby is American. We will be Americans."

Was her baby American when it wasn't even born yet, the way it was already a boy or girl? How could a German woman have an American baby growing in her womb? Sofie moved her stockinged toes between Oskar's thighs. Renate Wald, the midwife Tante Eva had found for her, said dancing and passion in moderation were good for the mother and wouldn't hurt the baby.

Oskar folded the paper. He lifted her feet and set them on the floor. After the warmth of his lap the shock of the cold linoleum curled her toes. He had to leave soon for his job as a night watchman at American Brass, and she'd be alone again in the attic apartment. A nice apartment with conveniences—a bathtub, a Frigidaire. It didn't take long to clean two rooms inhabited by two fastidious people. The red-and-gray patterned linoleum floor shone like a tabletop. The white ruffled curtains hung stiff and bright over the two small windows, one overlooking the street and one over the grassy back yard they weren't allowed to sit in. The porcelain sink and gas stove gleamed white. Each stack of old newspapers under the sink stood exactly the same height as the one beside it, the knot in the twine resting in the exact center of each top page. Even the makeshift workbench Oskar set up in the corner, to build furniture out of scrap wood they collected, was immaculate. It didn't take long to count the money they kept in a coffee can at the back of the low cupboard under the eaves, as she knew exactly how much was in there at all times, but she tallied it every evening anyway.

She noticed a browning leaf on her well-watered geranium. Good, something to do. She would pluck it when Oskar left for work. She'd never liked caring for plants, that was Amalia's job, but another flower or two would give her more to do and more to look at. She'd ask Tante Eva for some cuttings.

"I'm sorry I have to leave early today, Sofie," he said. "But the extra money will be good."

Eleven PM to seven AM was long enough. She hated the days when he added another four hours.

"The harder I work, the sooner we'll have money for our own house." Eyebrows raised, he grinned and gently tweaked her nose. She willed herself to smile.

For three months they'd lived in Onkel Ludwig and Tante Eva's tidy garage, but the autumn weather combined with Onkel's fussiness over his car being left outdoors, forced them to locate an apartment of their own. Onkel and Tante gave them a table and chairs and, on their first visit, brought the traditional bread and salt. "Bread so you'll never go hungry. Salt for flavor and luck," Tante Eva had said. They weren't suffering hunger—that was for sure—but luck? Salt for tears might have been more accurate.

She was glad to be away from Onkel's drunken passes and Tante's constant talk about the baby. You'd think Tante Eva was the pregnant one. Yet Sofie had never lived with just one other person. She'd never been alone, night after night.

Onkel and Tante gave her something to complain and joke about. They'd play *skat* with her in the hours before bed, when Oskar was at work.

In the same way she hadn't unpacked the few photographs she'd brought, she wouldn't let herself look at her loneliness when Oskar was there. If she cried to him or told him how she'd come to see that homesickness, like hunger, made a belly ache, she'd never be able to stop her tears. Best keep it to herself.

Oskar shaved, angling his head to fit in the scrap of mirror he'd hung from a nail. He rinsed his face and wiped the sink. He buttoned the gray shirt she'd ironed. Sofie took his paper-wrapped sandwich from the Frigidaire and put it into his lunchbox along with a thermos of coffee.

She followed him to the door to hand him his lunch. When he kissed her good-bye she kept her lips shut.

Leaning against the door, listening to his receding footsteps, the tears came. First, they collected in her throat in a huge throbbing lump. Not tonight, she thought. It had been six months and two days since she left home. Enough. Didn't time heal all? Still, the tears came. All that crying couldn't be good for the baby, but to her it felt like peeling off layers of clothing on a sultry summer day in Tauburg. Every evening she cried and cleaned and reread letters from Dora and Amalia. She kept them in a cracker tin. She knew them by heart, but liked to hold the paper that her sisters had held. Their handwriting, so strange at first, had grown familiar.

Dear Sofie,

I am Sister Gabriele now since taking the veil one blessed week ago. It would have been nice, especially for Amalia, if you could have been at the clothing ceremony. The flowers, the music, the prayers—all were beautiful. I am truly happy. I pray that you and Amalia will come to see that I am living the life I am called upon to live. I pray for you and Oskar and your unborn baby. Amalia says she tries to imagine what you look like pregnant, but she can't. Be well. God bless you.

Sister Gabriele

Sofie smoothed the letter on the tabletop. When she'd received it three days ago, she'd crumpled it and thrown it hard across the room. Better no word at all than such antiseptic, shallow drivel. It would have been nice for Amalia, if Sofie had been there? Dora wrote as if Sister Gabriele were already above the realm of human feeling. The next day Amalia's letter had arrived, a thick, substantial envelope that cost a lot to send.

Sofie,

You should have been beside me when Dora took the veil. Just like a bride she marched down the aisle, only the groom was in her head. She had some nerve com-

plaining that your wedding wasn't a real one. What about a wedding with no groom? What is that? I was alone among mothers, fathers, brothers, sisters, grandparents, aunts, uncles, cousins, friends, even former boyfriends—everyone watching a girl they loved marry God and change her name. Not to Frau something but Sister something. Dora already was a sister. Ours. Now she's Sister Gabriele. Where did that name come from? I asked her and she said she prayed and the voice of God whispered it in her ear. You wouldn't recognize her. When I visited with her just after the ceremony, she'd begin to gossip with me about Sister Monika and some of the other nuns I knew when we worked at the hospital, then suddenly stop herself, right in the middle of a sentence. I asked how she spent her days. She said, "Scrubbing stairs." Relieved to hear a trace of complaint in her voice, our old Dora, the girl who hated housework and never could do it right, I said, "You didn't have to become a nun for that!" I could see her struggle to smooth her face and change her tone. As mild as milk. She smiled as if she pitied my ignorance and said, "Every act is an act of devotion to God. Be happy for me, Amalia." I wanted to slap her and hug her at the same time. Our little sister, in a habit. She complained about the wimple forcing her to look straight ahead, no distractions from the sides, but when I began to sympathize, she caught herself and said again how happy she was. She said that as a novice she'd be allowed to receive mail only once a month instead of the weekly letters we exchanged when she was a postulant. Her letters are still read before she receives them. I think she reminded me so I wouldn't write any jokes or rude comments about the nuns and their underwear or their frustrated desires for real men. Be warned! The letters she writes to us are put unsealed in a leather mail pouch on the novice mistress's door. How can we be sure she's telling us how she really feels?

I go to church. Dora would be glad. I have to if I want to see friends. It's my time to relax. Sometimes I fall asleep. Afterward, standing in a circle with the other women, I'm surprised to discover I'm grown up. I look over to the graveyard and I remember us hiding behind the gravestones, the priest yelling at us to get out, flapping his arms like a big magpie. The other day, I could swear I saw your little shaved head. Remember how Dora kept her hair, thanks to Frau Neufeld's patient combing? Frau Mueller was just too busy to do that for me, but at least she didn't shave mine. Frau Blau...what makes a person so mean-spirited? She would have made Teufelmann *a perfect wife. You should see her now, still inspecting Gustav's hands before dinner as if he's a small child, then swatting him across the palms with a horse whip she's shortened just for that purpose. A whip! I ask Tomas why he doesn't stop her and he only shrugs. He's afraid of her too. I know I can't say anything. You would make her stop. Dora and I would never have dared to hide in the graveyard if it hadn't been for you. You were always the brave one.*

Sofie put the letter down so the tears that had begun to run down her face wouldn't fall on the paper and smear the ink. Brave, ha! She looked around her. Amalia wouldn't think she was brave now. She hardly left the apartment. She hated how stupid she felt, not understanding the language, how scared whenever she saw a colored person. What happened to that girl on the boat, determined to eat with chopsticks? The only places in Rivertown, in the whole United States, as far she knew, where she felt happy were at the German Hall on Saturday nights or in bed with Oskar's arms around her. But they were in bed at the same time so rarely.

She wiped away her tears with her sleeve and continued to read. *I have my work cut out for me here. Poor Heinrich Neufeld with no one but his crazy old mother. When I feel lonely for Mama or you or Dora, I look at him and count my blessings. At least Mama is at peace. At least you and Dora are living the lives you wanted to live.*

What had she imagined when she'd pictured herself in America? She tried to remember. Cowboys and Indians. Having a lot to eat. Loving Oskar. She hadn't seen any cowboys or Indians and wouldn't know what to do if she did. She saw Negro people. They lived mostly on two streets of houses near the river and the men worked in the foundry along with everyone else. The women shopped along Main Street and perched on delicate wire chairs to eat ice cream from fluted dishes Saturday afternoons at Marino's ice cream parlor like any other women. Their church stood just across from the German Hall and on Saturday nights they played bingo. Sometimes on Sunday mornings when it was her turn to clean the hall she'd see whole families arriving dressed fancy for church and marvel at the power of their singing to shake the building. But she'd never seen an Indian. Or maybe she had and just didn't know it. She'd never seen a Chinese person either, or a Chinese restaurant. Tante Eva said they had them in New York and that they'd go sometime on the train, but what she'd seen of New York after landing, the crowds of noisy people in a hurry, the traffic, overwhelmed her. Until she could make herself understood in English, she didn't want to go.

Food, they had plenty of. She'd gained more than a few kilos and it wasn't just the baby. She still registered a thrill when she entered the grocery store and the shelves lay before her fully stocked, the glass cases loaded with meats and cheeses. She had to fight the urge to hoard, her tendency to think of Brady's Market as the witch's candy house—tempting, illicit, dangerous, her desire to take all she could carry and run.

Loving Oskar. She did love him. But she didn't know him much better than she had in Germany. He was a dependable, honest man. She trusted him. On his workbench lay pieces of the cabinet he was building. He'd suggested she find a hobby—knitting, crocheting, sewing. All her life she'd had enough to do, running a household, cooking, cleaning. She wanted a job, but who would hire a pregnant woman who couldn't speak English? Perhaps, once the baby came, she'd have enough to keep her busy.

Sometimes I believe I am falling in love with Tomas Blau, but I'm worried that it's his land that makes him so attractive to me. How can I tell? I try to imagine him without it, but it is impossible. The land is so much a part of him and he is so much a part of it. And then again, his mother makes poor, crazy Frau Neufeld seem like an angel and Gustav will be Tomas's responsibility for as long as they live. Anyone who married him would inherit those two as well as the land. Those disadvantages weigh heavy and, I suppose, cancel out any advantages, so if I am thinking about marriage, maybe I do really love him. I don't know how he feels about me. When we're having coffee with his mother and she's studying every move I make with judgment in her eyes and Gustav is rocking back and forth in his chair and Tomas is scurrying around trying to make everyone comfortable, I only want to run away. In the evening, if Heinrich will stay with his mother, I help Tomas with the milking. My hands and arms ached at first, but I've grown strong and they don't bother me at all anymore. I peek under the cow at Tomas's back, his strong neck, his long legs folded so he fits on the milking stool. The cow's teats are warm in the cold barn. The milk is warm. Her flank is warm. And I think to myself this must be happiness. The sound of the first squirts of milk hitting the bottom of the pail. The breath of cows. Their chewing. Cows may be dumb, Sofie, but there is something slow and warm and wonderful about them, don't you think? These days we always have milk and cream and butter. When we are there in the barn, the light fading outside, and I look at Tomas's back, I want to sneak up behind and wrap my arms around him and stay forever between those warm and stupid and smelly cows. Do you think that means I love him? He has never kissed me or acted as though he wanted to. I wonder what he would do if I kissed him first.

Sofie was no expert on love, but if Amalia did love Tomas Blau, for his land or not, she would never come to America. Oskar told Sofie he loved her. He told her in English and in German, in whispers when he came home from work and woke her to prepare his meal. She believed him. She loved him back. But he didn't know how little she slept, how often she cried, and she didn't—couldn't—tell him. He worked so hard. He hoped for so much from America.

Sofie stood at the window, staring down at the quiet street. People hadn't had their suppers yet, and it was already growing dark. To her baby she whispered stories of standing at Frau Becker's window with Amalia and Dora, feeding the birds, waiting for Mama to come home to tell them stories and braid their hair. She told the baby Mama's stories too—the ones in the red book, the ones they begged her to tell them. By the time the baby was born he or she would know all the stories by heart. She imagined the baby's first words: *Mama, Amalia, Dora. Once upon a time.*

Dora and Amalia still lived on the same round earth. Right now—she looked at the clock—Amalia was probably putting supper on the table and Dora having her hour of recreation. No. For them it was later in the day. Hours later. Why was it still so hard to remember which way those time changes went? She leaned her head against the wall and began to cry again. If she could sleep the time would pass more quickly. She curled on her side, under a stack of thin blankets, wishing for a featherbed. She'd wanted to bring one, but it hadn't fit in the suitcase. You didn't see them here and, if you did, Oskar wouldn't buy one. He wanted a house. They had to save their money for that.

She imagined her mother, pregnant with Dora, receiving word of their father's death. What if Oskar died now in this strange place? Sofie would surely go back to Germany. For a moment she let herself imagine an accident at the foundry, flames and molten metal, then in a wave of panic and guilt pushed the thought aside and hugged her belly. She would try to be strong like her mother. She would be resourceful like Gretel who, even when forced to live deep in the forest, in the witch's sweet and terrible house, never gave up. But Gretel had her brother, even though he was in a cage. And Mama, she hadn't really been alone when their father died either, surrounded by neighbors, people who had known her all her life.

Still, when Hanna Heller Bauer lost her land to *Teufelmann*, she never went back and never complained. She carried on. On Saturday at the German Hall, Sofie and Oskar would dance to the familiar music. They'd speak German. Sofie would try to make friends she could call on during the week. She'd bring something made from one of Tante Eva's American recipes. During the war, at the Blau's, she'd waited with this same longing for Sundays when she'd see her sisters. Now strangers who spoke her language substituted for sisters and dancing had taken the place of hide-and-seek. You're brave, Sofie Bauer Schmidt.

Sofie always dressed carefully for her morning trips to Brady's Market—every narrow pleat in her wool crepe skirt pressed with precision, the bow at the neck of her blouse neatly tied, shoes polished until they shone. Last, her red wool coat. Amalia wouldn't believe how beautiful it was—a deep red, just like the cover of the book of fairy tales from which they'd learned to read. After she'd admired it in Isaacson's window, Oskar bought it for her—just three weeks ago when the weather turned crisp. He'd spent part of his pay before he even brought the money home and wouldn't tell her how much the coat had cost, but she guessed at least twenty dollars. Elegant dark fur trimmed the collar and sleeves. The bottom buttons just reached over the baby. Soon they wouldn't close. She smoothed her hair in front of the mirror. She needed the critical eye of a sister now, not this inadequate reflection. She needed Amalia to adjust her collar, pick off a bit of lint, then tell her she looked beautiful, or at least as stylish as any American woman in Rivertown.

Into her handbag she slipped the list of American ingredients dictated to her by Tante Eva. Sofie had translated pounds and ounces and cups to grams and kilograms and back again, milliliters to teaspoons, confident she was learning the relationships. She practiced the words: *cranberries, raisins, suet, oranges. Mushrooms.* She must remember to look for mushrooms. She eyed the dictionary, considered taking it along just in case, and decided not to. She'd be too self-conscious to use it.

On the few blocks to the market, she nodded to her neighbors—the mother of all those children, Oskar said they were Irish; the old lady with the little white dog; the young man who sat all day on the bench in front of the market waiting to help people with their groceries. He reminded her of Gustav. She practiced her "good morning" on him. He said something back that she didn't understand, but she smiled and pushed open the glass door.

At the meat counter, Sofie's downstairs neighbor chatted with the butcher, pointing into the case. Sofie longed to be able to ask for exactly what she wanted, to ask what was fresh, debate with him the pros and cons of various cuts of meat, ask his advice on how to prepare it. He seemed nice. At the cash register, a clerk rang up another woman's purchases, talking the whole time. Near the produce a grocer weighed three oranges on a shiny scale and handed them to a little boy. "Oranges," she whispered to herself, and moved toward them.

"May I help you, Miss?" the grocer asked. Sofie understood and nodded. She pointed to the oranges and held up two fingers. The grocer spoke again. Sofie could tell he was asking what else she wanted. She consulted her list. "Raisins," she said. "Five hundred...um, one pound." She almost said grams. Hundred was almost the same in English as it was in German, easy to say. Was the grocer laughing at her? He scooped the raisins into a small paper bag. She watched as he weighed them to make sure he didn't cheat. "Cranberries?" she said. "One pound." He turned toward a bin of gleaming, dark red berries. He gestured toward her. What was he saying? He pointed to her coat. The color matched exactly. He smiled. Everyone in the store seemed to be smiling. So far, so good, as the Americans said. She went on to the meat counter. Under her coat she was sweating.

After she obtained a small piece of fish and some butter, the man at the cash register rang up her purchases. Instead of giving her the receipt he held it just out of reach and said something. Oskar wanted to keep all the receipts. She liked to go over them herself, to make sure she hadn't been cheated. No one had ever tried to keep one from her before. "Please, give," she stammered.

The man talked on and on. He shook a box at her—a small wooden box with a slit in the top and a lock on the side. She thought he said *drawing*, but she must not be understanding right because the receipt had no picture on it. She heard the word *turkey*, but she hadn't bought a turkey and didn't want to. Tante Eva was making the Thanksgiving turkey. "Oskar Schmidt, right?" the man asked and wrote something on the receipt. Everyone knew she was Oskar's wife, but no one knew her name. Why was he writing on her slip? Had she done something wrong? Something the man would report to Oskar. Something that would get Oskar in trouble at his job. Everyone in the store was looking at her. His hand with the receipt hovered above the slit. Why did the box have a lock on it? "No," she said. Her heart pounding hard, she reached for the receipt and knocked the bag of cranberries off the counter. They rolled across the floor in all directions like pearls from a broken necklace, hundreds of them. The woman behind her in line muttered something nasty. Suddenly frantic, Sofie bent to pick up cranberries. She'd already stepped on some of them. They stuck to the soles of her shoes. Everything spun around her, a ringing began in her ears, people speaking long tangled strings of English. Sweating and dizzy she thought she might faint. She began to crawl around in the narrow aisle, kneeling on cranberries, bursting them with her weight, hurting her knees, ruining her new coat, pushing cranberries into the bag, scattering and squashing as many as she saved, trying to clean the mess she'd made.

The grocer who had helped her with the produce leaned down beside her and said something reassuring. He tried to help her to her feet. If she stood people would see that she was crying. She was not the kind of person who cried because she spilled something, but all of these American people she saw every day would think she was and she couldn't tell them otherwise.

"We're ready early again." Oskar laughed and picked up his mandolin. He looked handsome in his band uniform, his bright white shirt and embroidered cummerbund.

Sofie buttoned her cranberry coat. She didn't like thinking of it that way but, since the grocery store incident the day before, couldn't help herself. The berry stains didn't show unless you looked closely and knew they were there. Lucky the colors matched so well; a white coat would have been ruined. She'd gotten the receipt back after she made sure Mr. Brady subtracted the cost of the cranberries. She understood numbers. Thank heaven they were the same in English and German even if the money and measurements weren't. It could be worse. In China they used a whole different writing system. It didn't occur to her until later that the shopkeeper could have charged her for the damaged fruit. On Monday she would have to go back, unless she walked more than a kilometer to the other market, which people told Oskar was more expensive. She'd have to find a way to thank him, to look him right in the eye and apologize. Yesterday blurred in her mind. She remembered clutching the corrected receipt and her purchases, rushing from the store, head down. Once home, she spent the afternoon cleaning her coat and fixing Oskar's dinner, when she realized she hadn't even looked for mushrooms. They would have tasted so good with the bland fish. She didn't tell him about her humiliation, even when, especially when, he read from the paper about Brady's Market giving free Thanksgiving turkeys to the lucky winners whose receipts were drawn on Monday, Tuesday, and Wednesday of next week.

The cold night air nipped her nose, but inside her coat she was warm and well-fed. One gloved hand curled in a pocket, the other held Oskar's arm. She enjoyed walking beside him as much as she always had in Germany. He looked unwaveringly ahead of him and walked with a steady, comfortable stride. The mandolin never seemed to bump his leg. The stars sparkled in the clear cold. An occasional automobile passed them. People in pairs and groups, an occasional single man, headed for the speakeasies at the bottom of Main Street and along the River Road. Here in America drinking schnapps or beer was illegal, yet people laughed at the law and drank it anyway. Many familiar faces, speaking unfamiliar languages—English, of course, and Italian, Polish, and Russian. Oskar greeted men he knew from work with a nod and a 'good evening' in English. She'd smile, mute. What would he do if she decided to go back to Germany? She couldn't imagine him begging her, chasing her, forcing her to do anything against her will. He'd let her go. He hummed a few bars of a waltz. He'd let her go. That simple truth contained all she loved, and all she hated, about him.

They crossed the river on Bridge Street. A gust of wind swept Oskar's hat from his head, over the railing, toward the water.

"Oh, no!" Sofie wailed, leaning out to reach it. "That's your good hat!" It rode the wind a moment, inches from her fingertips, before dropping into the river.

"We have to climb down and get it." She rushed along the sidewalk, back the way they'd come. "I think there's a way down the bank, over there."

"Sofie, Sofie." Oskar, hurrying behind her, put a hand on her arm. She shook it off.

"It's your good hat. From home!" It couldn't have gone far. The river was moving slowly, even icing up at the marshy places near the banks. She'd get a big stick and wait for the hat to pass.

"Sofie!" Oskar caught her arm with both of his. "Sofie, let it go. We can't even see it. It's too dark. Come on, we'll be late."

"Don't you care? Aren't you upset?" Sofie's voice squeaked in her effort not to shout and make a scene. People passed on the opposite side of the street. Beside Oskar his mandolin stood in its black case. She wanted to kick it over.

"What would be the point?" Oskar asked. "It's gone. I'm sorry to have to spend money on a new hat, but that one is gone. Now come on, my head is cold!" He smiled.

Sofie ran across the bridge and squinted downstream. There was no way she could make out a dark hat in the dark water. He was right. He was always right. She laid her cheek against the icy railing, wondering for a moment if her skin would stick, then realizing it wasn't cold enough.

Oskar came up behind her and enveloped her in a hug. "Sofie, don't cry. We're going dancing."

Saturday. The day she waited for all week. She turned and pressed herself against him, the fluttering baby inside her safe between them.

"The homesickness will fade," Oskar whispered. "And we'll go back to visit."

"When? When will we have money for that?" Sofie asked. "So many expenses. The baby. A house. The hat."

"Not for a while. But we will. You'll see."

"Maybe if I got a real job, more than cleaning the German Hall once a week."

"You'll have a job. Taking care of our baby." He reached down for the handle of the mandolin case, as though everything was settled. "Really, Sofie, we're very late now. Come on."

Homesickness, *Heimweh*—did people die from it? It lived inside her, growing like a disease. No, not a disease, more like the baby. *Heimweh*, a constant companion, a true sort of sister who would always be with her. She let Oskar lead her across the bridge. The lights of the German Hall beckoned from blocks away. She thought she heard the music start.

CHAPTER 18

▼

Amalia rubbed Frau Neufeld's cold, gnarly feet, as she did every other night once she'd helped the old woman into bed. On alternate evenings Heinrich took responsibility for the bedtime ritual. She pressed her thumbs into the thick skin of Frau Neufeld's heel. The woman's little moans of pleasure did nothing to dilute the resentment Amalia felt when her turn fell on a Saturday night. Heinrich bicycled into town to his card game and the dance. Tomas would be there. Everyone who could go went. Frau Neufeld blinked her papery eyelids and smacked her lips. Tomas would be arriving at the Three Kings, shaking hands with neighbors at each table he passed, installing Gustav in a corner with a stack of cardboard coasters to play with and a pig's foot to chew. Tomas sat at the younger farmers' *Stammtisch,* Heinrich with the older men, but the conversations at both tables were the same: taxes, farming, prices, and politics. They wouldn't be talking about her. She remembered serving the miners. Did men ever talk to each other about women except to make jokes and lewd comments? Maybe one of the women would ask where she was, forcing Tomas to think of her.

Outside the moon silvered a crust of old snow. Frau Neufeld hummed a tuneless song. Anyone would think she was drifting into sleep, but Amalia knew from long experience that after the foot rub came soup sipped from a cup to warm the stomach, then the toilet one more time and the five to twenty-five adjustments of the pillow and the covers, and the countless times she popped up to warn Amalia to hide the food from the soldiers or remind her to barricade the door with the heaviest furniture.

Amalia slipped thick stockings onto Frau Neufeld's feet, then placed them side by side and tucked the featherbed over them. The old lady breathed evenly. She couldn't be sleeping already. Tiptoing close to the head of the bed, Amalia leaned over to scrutinize her closed-up face. A scrap of paper stuck out from under her pillow, an envelope. Amalia peered closer. A foreign stamp, an American stamp, like the ones Sofie used. Focused on Frau Neufeld's turtle-like features, Amalia pinched the corner of the letter, easing it from under the pillow. The paper rustled as she drew it toward her. She winced.

In black ink, her name in Sofie's careful writing. Enraged, she snatched the envelope all the way out. Frau Neufeld's eyes blinked open and, with fingers still strong from decades of crocheting, cuffed Amalia's wrist. The letter flapped.

"Don't open that!" Frau Neufeld shrieked. "We must burn it." She grabbed the letter with her other hand. If Amalia pulled it would rip, and she'd been waiting months for a letter from Sofie. Maybe there were others hidden around the house. All the days Amalia had been with Tomas and Heinrich in the field or the barn when the postman came. He should have known better than to give precious mail to a crazy woman. She would ask him on Monday how many times he'd done so. "Let go. Don't touch!"

Reason never worked with Frau Neufeld. "All right. I'll burn it. You let go. I'll put it in the stove."

"You are not to be trusted." Frau Neufeld answered. "No, not with these letters, not at all. I know what you are up to." She glared at the wall. Amalia fought the urge to slap her. Frau Neufeld was a pathetic old woman, out of her mind. The envelope had been handled until the edges were worn, but hadn't been opened. Inside might be news about Sofie's baby. She tried to read the postmark. Frau Neufeld, with Amalia holding fast to her end, tried to push the letter into the folds of her nightdress, between her scrawny legs. Amalia flipped back the covers.

Frau Neufeld squeezed her legs together, curling forward. "Don't!" She screamed. "Don't touch me. I'll tell my father. He'll fix you like he fixes little boy pigs. You'll squeal like they do too. They'll hear you at the Blaus'. I'll tell my husband."

Amalia gave the letter an experimental tug. Frau Neufeld held tight. "What do you want?" She stared into Amalia's face. "Who are you? How much do you know?"

Amalia tickled her under the arm that held the letter. Frau Neufeld yelped and released it. Amalia slipped it into her pocket.

The old lady's toothless mouth opened in a strange wail, like a rabbit caught on barbed wire. She shrieked louder and louder. Amalia tried to pat her shrunken, twisted back. Frau Neufeld jerked her shoulders and continued to scream.

"Shh, it's all right," Amalia murmured around the surge of panic in her throat. What if the woman never calmed? She'd been this upset before, but never without Heinrich to settle her. Amalia tried to remember what it was he said or did, but she didn't know. He always emerged seeming embarrassed, and she went along with him in pretending the screaming hadn't happened. Why hadn't she imagined it might occur sometime when he was in town? "It's all right." She could take her letter into the other room, close the door, let Frau Neufeld cry herself out like a fussy baby. Besides, there were all the other letters to find.

"It's not safe," Frau Neufeld sobbed. "Never trust an American. They're as bad as the French." She moaned and moved to climb out of bed. Amalia grabbed the old woman's upper arm too hard. So little flesh surrounded the bone that the tip of Amalia's middle finger touched her thumb.

"Can I help?"

Amalia whipped around. Tomas. Had he seen how rough she'd almost been?

"You didn't hear my knock." He stooped a little, stepping through the door. At the sight of his kind, weathered face her rage melted to relieved tears.

Still moaning, Frau Neufeld looked from Amalia to Tomas with wide eyes.

"Guten abend," Tomas approached the bed. "Are you feeling lucky tonight? Amalia, go get her dice. Do you know where Heinrich keeps the schnapps, on the low shelf, behind the tins of lard?"

Away from Frau Neufeld and her noise, the rest of the house seemed full of air and moonlight. Amalia passed through the kitchen to the dirt-floored room connecting the house and barn. Moving a heavy tin canister of lard, she found the half-full bottle and, behind the bottle, in a crack between two boards, a scrap of paper. Even in the dimness she knew it was another letter, more than one. Three envelopes. Plucking them loose she squinted at the addresses, walking toward the circle of lamplight in the kitchen. As she suspected, they were hers—two from Sofie and another from Dora. Furious, she paced the kitchen.

"Amalia!" Tomas called. "Frau Neufeld's feeling lucky! Let's celebrate." *Hurry up before she starts screaming again* said his tone. She slipped the letters into her pocket beside the first. She grabbed the forgotten bottle, then found the leather dice cup on the sideboard in the parlor. If she hadn't been so upset and excited about the letters she could have thought of the dice herself. Tomas's soothing words grew louder as she made her way back to Frau Neufeld's room. "It's your lucky day. You'll see." Frau Neufeld whimpered, then giggled.

Tomas took the dice from Amalia and rattled them temptingly before handing them to Frau Neufeld. He splashed schnapps into the empty teacup on the nightstand and held it to her mouth. She drank and smacked her lips, shaking the dice the whole time. He poured her another shot.

He looked over his shoulder at Amalia. "This should settle things down."

Amalia felt the letters in her pocket. She had to read them but leaving the room felt wrong. It wasn't Tomas's job to care for Frau Neufeld. It was hers, and she'd failed.

Frau Neufeld slumped against her pillow. Tomas clucked and hummed to her as he eased the dice cup from her hand. He adjusted the covers around her neck and patted her sunken cheek. Amalia watched, afraid to move.

"She's asleep," he whispered after an impossibly few moments. "Come." He touched Amalia's shoulder. "Let's go sit. We'll visit for a while."

"Why aren't you in town?" Amalia asked as they entered the parlor. She adjusted the tablecloth and shifted the surrounding chairs.

He blushed. "Why would I want to be there when you're here?" He sat on the sofa and patted the cushion beside him. She touched her letters. Interesting question. Why would Sofie want to be in America and Dora in a convent, when she was here? But then she was here, and she could have been in America. She could have been a nun, for that matter. "When was the last time you missed a Saturday night? People will worry about you." Amalia sat, smoothing the crocheted doily on the armrest.

"They'll guess where I am." His look held her.

"She's been hiding my letters." She slid the four envelopes from her pocket and fanned them like a hand of cards. "Three from Sofie, one from Dora. I've been waiting and waiting for mail. There may be more hidden around the house. Why the postman gave them to her I don't know."

"You haven't opened them yet? You must want to read them. Go ahead. Please." At her hesitation, he went on. "I can leave, give you some privacy." He lifted a hip to reach a pocket, and pulled out a pipe and a pouch of tobacco from his best pants. He wore them to church and out on Saturday nights. He was wearing them to call on her. She didn't want him to leave. His preoccupation with filling the pipe, lighting and smoking it, gave her all the privacy she needed. The rich, fruity smell of tobacco permeated the room. She slit the first envelope with her fingernail. Beneath her eagerness to read Sofie's words she savored the easy feeling of solitude in the company of another person. She hadn't felt it since her sisters left.

February 11, 1925

Dear Amalia,

You are an aunt! Martin Georg Schmidt was born on February 4th. He is one week old today. He is a scrawny thing—five pounds, six ounces—how many kilograms? I don't understand how he can be so skinny when I grew so huge I could hardly move at the end. I couldn't see my own feet. When we danced, Oskar couldn't reach around me. I wish you could see this boy. I'm surprised you can't hear him all the way over there across the ocean, he screams so loud. Every day from five to nine he screams. Wait, in your time that is more like the middle of the night. Do you hear him in your dreams? If only you were here to walk with him awhile.

"I am an aunt," she told Tomas.

"*Tante* Amalia," he laughed. "It suits you. How is Sofie?"

"She sounds all right." Amalia skimmed through more of the letter. *I'm so tired. The neighbors downstairs bang on the ceiling with their broom handle when Martin cries. If they came up to help me he might be quiet. Banging only makes me nervous which makes him cry harder. Oskar is working two jobs so we can save money for our own house. Oskar doesn't want the baby baptized. Don't tell Dora, please. Even though I don't go to church here, I would baptize him, just to be safe, but Oskar thinks it's hypocritical and I suppose he's right.*

Oskar thinks. Oskar wants. Oskar, working hard to provide for her sister and her nephew. Still, she pictured Sofie alone in her apartment, no, with a baby—was that better or worse than being alone? Were a baby's screams worse than Frau Neufeld's? Five to nine, every day? Frau Neufeld fussed for ten minutes and Amalia couldn't think. That relief she'd felt when Tomas appeared. Her sister had none of that, trapped up high like Rapunzel: Rapunzel with short hair in an American apartment.

Tante Eva says the colic comes from the derangement of my liver, that I am not eating properly. She tells me to eat bread and fruit and fish and give him catnip tea. I am tired of advice. All I want is someone to hold him for a while, to laugh with me while Oskar is at work. I wish I knew English better. I try to speak and read it, but the words come so slowly. Oskar still practices with me by reading the newspaper.

"She's lonely, I think," Amalia said. "Even with the baby. Learning English sounds hard." She folded the letter and slipped it back into its envelope. Sadness pressed her into the sofa. She couldn't read any more.

"Are you going to read the others?"

"Later. I've waited so long. I don't want to gobble them up. Sofie taught me that. She always made sure she had something hidden away for later, for an emergency." Amalia shuffled the envelopes, peering at the postmarks. "I should have read this first."

"An aunt," said Tomas around the stem of his pipe. "Amalia, have you thought about having children of your own?" Even his good eye was staring off somewhere. What was he thinking?

"Of course, doesn't every woman?" she asked, though, picturing Sofie's exhausted pacing, she would make sure she had her children among friends and real neighbors who helped each other.

"Dora doesn't," Tomas chuckled.

He had no right to laugh about her sister, even though she'd giggled about the nuns herself. Suddenly the room seemed as stuffy as Frau Neufeld's bedroom. "I should be with Sofie," Amalia said. "That baby will be a man before I see him." She stood.

Tomas frowned. He seemed about to apologize or ask a question. She felt sorry for him, so she forced a smile and an invitation. "Let's go for a little walk. It's a beautiful night and this room is stifling. Frau Neufeld won't wake up. That schnapps put her out. She's not used to it."

"It's cold out there," Tomas said.

"But the moon is bright," Amalia said. Now that she'd said it, she realized she wanted to walk and she wanted his company. "Then we can come back, have a warm drink, and you can help hunt for more letters, if you want to."

They bundled themselves into their coats without talking or meeting each other's eyes and strode through the moonlit fields without discussing a destination. When Amalia stumbled on one of the frozen ruts concealed by the snow, Tomas grabbed her arm to steady her and didn't let go. "Do you mean it? About being with Sofie in America?" he asked.

Amalia considered his question as they walked on toward the creek, making a dark trail of bootprints. Did she mean it? Could he be worried about her leaving? How much did it matter to him?

She clenched her fingers in her coat pockets. His hand on her sleeve must be freezing. They approached the creek. Water gurgled beneath a thin layer of ice, slurping, tinkling, reminding her of Frau Neufeld eating soup. She'd never thought of it as a pretty sound, but in the silvery light, in the wide silence where Tomas waited for an answer she didn't have, the stream sang a song as sweet as the one the band, no doubt, was playing that very moment at the Three Kings.

"You don't want to cross, do you?" Tomas asked, as they stood on the bank. "The rocks could be slick and there aren't many places the ice would hold us. I wouldn't want to get wet feet in cold like this."

"Sounds like you want to go back," she said, stepping away from him.

"Not at all." He gestured toward the sky. "It's beautiful. Look, the moon is so bright, you have a shadow."

Amalia waved her arms and stomped her feet to make her shadow dance. "You do it too," she said. As the words slipped from her mouth she regretted them. She couldn't imagine him doing such a silly thing. She shimmied her shoulders, turning so she wouldn't have to see him uncomfortable. Lorenz would have taken her hand, twirled her around, cartwheeled along the creek, even in the snow. He'd enact an entire shadow play. She remembered skating. "Have you ever ice skated, Tomas?" she asked, still twirling and waving her hands above her head. Perhaps this question would erase her reckless request. She stared at the big, fat, glowing moon to avoid his face, the awkward smile she imagined he wore.

"We never had skates, but we'd pretend, in our shoes," he said.

"I skated once." She rolled her shoulders and leaned into a backbend. If her hair had been long it would have tickled the ground. Eyes closed, swaying her torso, feeling her muscles, moving to the music of the brook, she realized she no longer felt silly or regretful or angry but rather beautiful, an exotic dancer in the spotlight of the moon. She opened her eyes to see Tomas upside down, watching her with an unreadable expression. She straightened up so quickly she felt dizzy.

They stood a meter apart and stared at each other. She readied herself for a kiss. One long stride toward her, he'd take her in his arms. Or they'd each take a step and meet in the middle. Tomas stood in place, raised his arms high overhead and wiggled his fingers and jerked a little from side to side, lifting first one foot then the other. Amalia laughed. She tried to catch her breath, but Tomas's struggle to keep a serious face set her off again, and then they both collapsed, surrounded by clouds of their combined laughter, visible in the bright, cold night.

Side by side, breathing hard, they sat on the snowy ground, legs stretched out in front of them, leaning against each other. Surely, he'd kiss her now. The creek burbled by under its skin of ice.

With stiff fingers Amalia pried a stone from the frozen earth and tossed it toward the creek, where it broke through the thin layer of ice with a satisfying crunch. Tomas did the same. For the next few moments, with the steady unspoken purpose they had when pitching hay from the hayloft, they picked up rocks and threw them one after the other, breaking and sloshing. Why wouldn't he kiss her? They'd have to go back soon. What if Frau Neufeld woke up and wandered away? What if Heinrich came home and found his mother left alone? She flung a heavy stone with all her strength.

"Amalia?" Tomas said.

Now, now he'd touch her throat with his cold fingers and she'd shiver as he pressed his hot lips against hers. She could feel a tightening in her belly and between her legs. She pulled her knees up closer to her body and angled toward him.

Instead of pulling her close, he held out a white stone, the size of a peach pit and shaped like a heart.

"Nice," she said. A rock? If he hadn't kissed her yet, he wasn't going to, and she wouldn't kiss him first.

"Do you want it?" he asked.

"Just throw it," she said. "It only looks nice because it's wet from the melted snow. Sofie and Dora and I would pick pretty rocks from this very stream, only to bring them home and find once they'd dried they weren't pretty at all. We were always disappointed." Still they'd collect them, somehow unable to believe that colors that vibrant would grow dull. Even though they'd experienced the phenomenon countless times, it was easier to believe someone had switched stones in the night than to think the nondescript rocks on the window ledge were a version of the same treasures they'd carried home in their apron pockets.

She buried her hands in her armpits. "I'd better get back."

He scrambled to his feet and held out a hand to her. She wanted to ignore it, but her toes ached, her hips and thighs creaked with cold, and a friendly hand was better than struggling up on her own, snow melting through her stockings to her knees.

She let go of his hand as soon as he pulled her up. They walked back to the house, following their footprints. Amalia carefully placed her toes in the heel print of her boots, concentrating to keep from thinking about the kiss that never happened. It would be all right as long as he never knew how much she'd expected it.

"Do you want a drink?" she asked at the door. "Warm milk with schnapps?"

"Would you like me to check on Frau Neufeld?" he asked, moving toward the front room and the stairs.

"I don't hear anything, thank heaven." Amalia unbuttoned her coat. Tomas had come to visit when he could have been at the Three Kings complaining about the government and playing cards. She wasn't a fool for thinking he was interested in her, though she felt like one. If only she knew what he'd been thinking as she danced. She poured milk into a pan, heating it slowly. Milk burned so easily; you had to be patient. She stirred it round and round, the heat warming the hand on the spoon. She held her other hand over the pot.

"She's sleeping," Tomas reported. "I'll get the schnapps."

Amalia took two cups from the shelf, filled them with milk, and set them across from each other on the small cloth covered table. Sofie did this kind of thing every day for herself and her husband. The letters rustled in Amalia's pocket when she sat down. She'd scour the house for more, after Tomas left. Heinrich would have to help her. He might know the old lady's hiding places.

Tomas hung up his coat and splashed schnapps into each of the cups. He set the bottle on the table between them. "*Prost,*" he said, raising his cup and taking a long swallow before sitting down. He moved the nearest chair so that it was beside her, and sat on that.

Amalia's fingers, wrapped around her cup, warmed to the bone. She and Tomas sat in silence, surrounded by the dingy kitchen walls and the big cold world outside. If Tomas wasn't going to talk or take her hand or kiss her, she wished he'd leave so she could read her letters and feel her disappointment in peace. Instead he sipped his drink and lit another pipeful of tobacco. She watched him, the sweet milk and fiery schnapps inscribing a hot fuzzy line from her lips to her heart. She could say something. She could grab his hand. She could kiss him. All this time she'd waited; maybe he was waiting too. She rested her cup in its saucer with a sharp clink. His hand lay on the lacy tablecloth less than twenty-five centimeters away.

The door opened, startling her, and Heinrich stepped in, flushed from drinking and the ride home. "Ahh!" Tomas greeted him. "Can we offer you some of your own schnapps?"

"So here you are," Heinrich said. "We wondered. This is a cozy scene."

"Hope you don't mind our drinking some of this?" Amalia held up the bottle to show Heinrich they hadn't drunk much and was surprised to see how the level had dropped.

"We had to sedate your mother," Tomas said. "Then once we had the bottle out, we couldn't resist a taste ourselves."

"It's fine." Heinrich carefully removed his coat and hung it on a peg. Now there was no reason to wait any longer to read her letters. She pushed her chair back.

"Don't go." Tomas placed his hand over hers. Another hot line rushed from his fingers through her hand, up her arm and down her spine.

"What a cozy scene," Heinrich said again. With his foot he nudged back the chair across from them and dropped into it with long sigh. "I need a wife," he said.

Amalia almost giggled. Heinrich must be drunk. He barely talked and when he did it was usually to thank her for work she'd done in the house or barn.

She felt happy, her hand pressed between Tomas's palm and the lace of the tablecloth. She wished it were her whole body under his, with the crocheted lace etching patterns into her naked skin. Blushing, afraid they'd guess her thoughts, she concentrated on her empty cup.

"But I'm too old," Heinrich went on. He drank schnapps from the bottle. "And who would marry someone with a mother like mine, God forgive me for saying so."

She's not as bad as Frau Blau, Amalia almost said. *Better crazy than mean.* It was Tomas's turn to say something about wanting a wife, but he didn't.

"A man needs a woman, a wife." Heinrich slurred his words together. "I look at you two and I think, how have I survived without one? It's time for a change. Maybe I should have asked Amalia to marry me before you did."

"Heinrich, you're drunk," said Amalia. "Tomas, help him to bed, please." She yanked her hand free.

"I haven't asked her," Tomas said. He lowered his gaze the way he used to when Frau Blau scolded Gustav. Amalia remembered how much she'd hated his refusal or inability to stand up to her meanness, to stop her.

"So I can?" Heinrich laughed. "I'm old enough to be her grandfather. I was joking. You know I was only joking, Amalia. You're a nice girl. Like a daughter, a granddaughter."

He rested his forehead on the table. "You're right, I should go to bed." He began to breathe deeply, then snore.

"Have you ever heard him talk so much?" Amalia whispered.

"Only when he drinks," Tomas said. He placed the heart-shaped rock on the table.

"I thought you threw that away," Amalia said. "See, now, how it's so bleached out. If it looked like that you'd never have picked it up."

"Maybe I would," he said. "The shape is nice. See, a heart."

"If only there were a way to keep it shiny," she said. "Sofie used to put them in a bowl of water, but the water would evaporate and we'd lose interest anyway."

Heinrich moaned. Maybe he would adopt her, somehow make her his heir. She remembered the day he'd insisted on holding the ladder when she climbed into the cherry tree, how cared for she'd felt, how safe. He'd shouted to scare away the bold, cherry stealing crows, and even when he waved his arms at them, his foot held the ladder in place, like a father might have done, had he lived.

Amalia wanted Tomas to speak, to move, to do something, but he sat at the table as if waiting for her orders. "You really should help him upstairs," Amalia said, clearing the cups and saucers with a vehemence that disquieted her.

After Tomas had dragged Heinrich to bed and gone home, she sat at the table with her letters. She made sure to open them in the proper order. Sofie's first, since there were more of them.

December 25, 1924

Dear Amalia,

We celebrated Christmas with Onkel and Tante. I missed you and Dora so much. I received a sort of Christmas letter from her, sent before Advent when she was still permitted to write once a week, but all it did was make me sad. I suppose Christmas is all about the birth of our savior. If I saw it that way I might feel better, but to me it is about being with family, and without you, I feel alone.

Christmas had been the last time Amalia had really cried. She'd received no letters. She'd gone to church and chatted with people and made a nice enough dinner for Heinrich, Frau Neufeld, and herself, but lying in bed that night, remembering the day, it had no color at all. That had never happened before—a memory, and such a recent one, devoid of any color. She knew she wore a green dress, she could climb out of bed and look at it hanging in her closet, but when she remembered herself kneeling in church or spooning potato onto Frau Neufeld's plate or slipping out of the dress to help Tomas and Heinrich in the barn, it was a dark shade of gray.

I'm slow to learn English. Oskar and I read the newspaper every day. Remember Mama teaching us to read? That was much more fun. Even though I am almost twenty years old I would rather read stories than news articles. In the paper is a story called Little Jack Rabbit, little bunny boy, he's called. I like trying to read that even though it's meant for children.

You wrote that you planned to spend Christmas with the Blaus.

That's right. Tomas had invited and then, at his mother's insistence, uninvited her, contributing to the disappointment of the day. He'd given several explanations for his mother's chilly unsociability—her delicate nerves, her belief in Christmas as a day for family, Gustav's tendency to get overexcited—but Amalia suspected she was punishing Tomas for daring to invite someone without asking his mother's permission first.

Do you remember the time when the Muellers returned me to Frau Blau, after my finger began to heal and Mama had gone back to the city? She'd made that nice meal, the chicken with potatoes and even the apple pancake for a sweet. She felt guilty, I think, about my finger and the Muellers feeding me while it healed, wanted to make at least a gesture of appreciation. There sat all that delicious steaming food, the smells of warm butter, no, it couldn't have been butter, but lard, anyway, so heavy in the air that just breathing went a little way toward satisfying hunger. Frau Blau ruled over the table with her frowning face. Even Frau Mueller looked uncomfortable, shifting in her seat, barely speaking, like a small child. Gustav stared at his plate the whole time, even after he'd wiped it clean with a piece of bread. I was afraid Frau Blau would hit him for bad manners right there at the table. She never even scolded him, yet the whole time I waited, my shoulders hunched, face tight in a wince. I think we all did. Do you remember that? I never relaxed in that house. It seemed she was always watching, waiting to find fault. I hope your holiday is better than that. Perhaps Frau Blau is friendlier once you get to know her or when you are no longer a child. She certainly was frightening when I lived there.

Glad she'd waited until Tomas left to open it, Amalia finished the letter and folded the tissue-thin sheets. She inserted a knife under the flap of the next.

January 26, 1925

Dear Amalia,

I was waiting to write until the baby was born, but an amazing thing happened. I have to tell you about it. Two days ago we experienced a total solar eclipse, the first in 119 years and we were here to see it! Maybe you heard about it. I don't know how far news like that travels. People filled the streets as the morning light turned purple. Waves of light flickered over the snow banks, the roads, and the sides of buildings. Cars, trolleys, everything stopped. All the colors in the world seemed to burst outward from a dull reddish rim around the moon. No one paid attention to the cold. "The perfectly clear sky made conditions for observation perfect," Oskar read from the newspaper the next day. Mercury, Venus, and Jupiter shone as clearly visible as at night, but it was 9:11 in the morning. Oskar would normally be at work, but he planned it so he could go in late. That's when I knew an eclipse was something special. Oskar doesn't like to miss a chance to add to the money in our can. I don't sleep. I can't get comfortable. I just lie in bed waiting for morning, wishing for the baby to be born. So I was happy to have Oskar there, keeping me company. I have never seen him so excited. This is history, he kept saying. It was, to be sure, a sacred moment, celebrated afterward by Oskar bringing me chocolate in a china cup—sweet and thick and hot. Remember how the Captain would make chocolate for Mama in the days before she died? I hope it tasted as good as mine.

Amalia licked traces of warm milk and schnapps from her teeth. She wondered if the same big moon streaming light on the ground outside, illuminating Heinrich's bicycle where he left it lying on its side, the wagon full of milk jugs, the footprints she and Tomas made heading to the river and back, streamed down on Sofie and Oskar and her new nephew. If Sofie looked out her window right now, would the moon be as close to full as it was here, or did it look different from other parts of the earth? Maybe it was daylight in America, so Sofie wouldn't see the moon even if it was bright.

The baby showed even more pleasure than I did, bumping around in its tight space after I'd drained the cup. I even licked the drops that had splashed onto the saucer. I am huge. You can't imagine. My belly passes through a doorway minutes before I do. I want the baby to come, but I'm scared of the birth. I do have a German midwife to attend me. Wish you could be with me too. I keep thinking of cows calving, how I couldn't stand to watch, how calm you were beside Herr Mueller and the others, even as a little girl of nine or ten. If you were here, I know I could have this baby. Without you...I am terribly frightened. I tell myself this beautiful astronomical event is a good omen. I tell myself Dora is praying for me. If God doesn't listen to her, whom would he listen to? Your sister, Sofie

Well it had all worked out, hadn't it? If Amalia had read this letter when she was supposed to, she would have worried. Worrying, a terrible waste of time. She set the heart stone on top of Sofie's letters, then opened Dora's, the last one until she searched out more.

November 20, 1924

Dear Amalia,

I hope this letter finds you well. Is Elsterdorf beginning to feel like home?

We neither write nor receive letters during Advent so don't be worried when you don't hear from me. Save all your news for a Christmas letter. I pray for you every day.

Substitute America for Elsterdorf and Sofie must have received the same letter. Where was Dora in those stilted words? She fought the urge to crumple the page and smoothed it instead, then folded it exactly in half. She lifted the stone to slip Dora's note underneath, with Sofie's.

"Why would I want to be there when you're here?" Tomas had said. Her sisters were there. She was here. He was here. Or could be at a moment's notice. If he opened the door, accompanied by the winter wind, now or tomorrow morning or the next day, the heart stone would keep her sisters' words from blowing away.

Amalia could have ransacked the house the next day, searching for hidden letters, but it was Sunday; there was church, and she visited the Muellers afterward. On Monday, she decided to be practical and clean as she looked, lifting every cushion, emptying cupboards and drawers, and moving furniture. She lined the shelves and drawers with new paper, swept behind the sofa, beat the upholstery, but uncovered no more mail. Late in the afternoon, just before Tomas Blau usually arrived, she dropped onto a chair at the parlor table where Frau Neufeld shook her dice cup. The old lady sat with perfect posture and a vacant stare. Amalia always positioned her so she could look out the window.

Disappointed and exhausted, Amalia wondered where she'd find the energy to fix supper. It was her turn to put Frau Neufeld to bed, but perhaps Heinrich would trade nights. He'd been even more silent than usual, more distant, since coming home drunk Saturday night, as if embarrassed to face her. She thought she heard a bicycle and leaned forward to peer out the window. When the post-man came she wanted to ask about the mail. When Tomas came she wanted to…what? Whatever she thought she'd heard, she didn't see anyone.

She folded her arms on the table and rested her head on them. The dice clicked gently in the leather cup. Frau Neufeld made an occasional sound, a whimper or a chuckle, triggered by something inside her head—not the throw of the dice because she never rolled them out across the table, just shook them, over and over and over until Amalia wanted to scream.

"What is Tomas thinking?" she said aloud. "What does he want? There I was, so sure he wanted me. He's acted like it. Do I even love him? Tomas Blau. How does anyone know they love someone."

"Hilda," Frau Neufeld said in a gossipy whisper. "Those boys are afraid of their mother. Children should respect their parents, but that woman has the elbows of a witch and feathers in her infected mouth and the pear tree is full of lice. Someone is sure to die."

Amalia didn't bother to raise her head. Frau Neufeld wouldn't care. The old lady talked when she felt like it and, alone with her, Amalia indulged herself the same way.

"I'm finished with Tomas Blau," said Amalia. "He gave me a stone instead of a kiss? And his mother? Hey, you're making some sense, aren't you? You're talk-ing about her, Frau Blau. What a witch! You're right." She peeked up at Frau Neufeld, who stared into the depths of her dice cup, hypnotizing herself with the shaking motion.

"You know, not that you're listening, but what I believe I really want, more than a husband, is a home. Some land of my own. You own all this and you don't even realize it. Not many farms have a stream running through them. My mother's did, a river! Imagine, if you could just give this farm to me. I'd plant every field. We'd get some pigs and make our own sausage to sell. You know, cows are really a lot of work—maybe too much—with fewer cows we'd need less pasture, less hay, we could plant potatoes and—"

Behind her someone cleared his throat. If Tomas Blau had sneaked up on her and overheard what she had said about his mother…she couldn't convince herself to turn around. What else had she said?

Nothing moved except Frau Neufeld's dice cup. No one spoke.

She tried to concoct a benign and plausible explanation for calling Frau Blau a witch, before looking over her shoulder; the impossibility and sheer embarrassment of the moment made her snicker through her nose. Her eyes watered. All right, Tomas, time to be honest. With a sudden swoop of Frau Neufeld's arm, the dice flew through the air and scattered.

Heinrich. He began scrambling on hands and knees, locating dice. Amalia's initial relief that Tomas hadn't heard her insult his mother turned to new anxiety as she tried to reconstruct what Heinrich had heard. The part about Frau Neufeld giving her the farm was awkward, but at least she hadn't called the old lady any names. Besides, she and Heinrich understood each other. They ran the farm. He'd never fire her. No one else could mind his mother, keep house, and help with the milking.

"There's one, under the lamp," she said to his back. He added the die to the ones in his hand without looking at her. "Have you seen the postman today?"

"Tomas mentioned the letter problem," he said, voice raspy. "Why didn't you tell me about it?" He counted the dice in his palm, then labored to his feet. "You could have told me."

"Is Tomas here?"

"Out in the barn."

He usually stopped at the house to say hello. He must be avoiding her too.

"So," said Heinrich with his characteristically long pause. "The vet said the cow will be all right."

"That's good." Amalia had been able to get more cleaning done than usual, as Heinrich had been dealing with a sick cow and hadn't come home for the midday meal. "The postman…" she prompted.

"I met him on the road. No mail."

"Did you ask how many letters of mine he'd given to her?" Amalia took the dice from Heinrich, marched back to the table, and dumped them into the waiting cup. "Here," she encouraged Frau Neufeld.

"He couldn't remember, two or three. I told him to give the mail directly to me or you from now on."

"Thank you." So there weren't any more letters. At least she had a clean house to show for her trouble. Amalia wiped a little spit from the corner of Frau Neufeld's lip. "I'll start supper," she said. "You must be hungry, out all day."

"I ate in town." Heinrich hadn't moved since he'd stood up. "Amalia, I want to say, about Saturday night…I had a lot to drink."

"That was clear!" Amalia laughed. "Don't worry about it. I've seen you drunk before. Do you want to stay here with your mother and I'll start dinner? Once it's on the stove I can help Tomas scald the milk buckets and jugs. You didn't have a chance to do them today, did you?"

"Actually, I want to ask you something." He shifted his weight and nodded.

Amalia figured they still had plenty of the green beans she'd canned last summer—she'd open some of those—and ham and that mild cheese from Frau Mueller.

"I don't know how to begin," he said. He stared past Amalia, out the window. He rubbed the back of his neck.

Frau Neufeld flung her dice again and screamed, "Take that!"

Heinrich ignored her.

"Just say it," said Amalia. "What?"

"Lousy French!" Frau Neufeld began to bang her dice cup and sing *Oh Hindenburg*.

Heinrich continued to stand speechless.

"Take care of her," said Amalia. "I need to start dinner."

"Times were good!" Frau Neufeld intoned. "And then came the war."

In the refuge of her kitchen Amalia groaned aloud. Poor woman.

Heinrich would put Frau Neufeld out with the chickens for a little while. She liked to feed them. Their fluttery dust baths delighted her. She couldn't run away or get into much mischief in the chicken yard. Amalia set the table for four, in case Tomas wanted to join them.

Heinrich appeared in the doorway, face pale and resolute.

"Is something wrong?" Amalia asked. "She's fine with the chickens, isn't she?"

"Yes, she's fine." He pulled at his earlobe. Heinrich had long ears, with hairs sprouting from them. Strange, since his head was completely bald. "I have something to ask you. A deal to propose."

"Yes?" She handed him the jar of green beans to open.

"I don't want to offend you."

"Heinrich, come on, out with it, say what's on your mind. We don't have all night." She banged the silverware drawer harder than she meant to.

"I talked today with Tomas."

"Yes?"

"I asked him why he hasn't married you yet."

"What?" Amalia froze midstep.

"I told him he was a fool."

"You told him as much the other night, too, when you were drunk. Do you remember?" Amalia slammed a pot on the stove.

"I am sixty-two years old. You are seventeen. I have no children to take over this farm."

"I'm almost nineteen." Amalia's heart pounded. She felt for a chair and sat down. Could it possibly be that Heinrich Neufeld would really make her his heir? She could marry Tomas Blau some time in the future on her terms, or not marry him, or marry someone else. She'd fix up the outside of the house first thing, then build a pigpen.

"We would draw up the papers to make it all legal," Heinrich said. "Please don't think badly of me. I'm old, and old men have earned the right to ask for what they want."

"Badly?" Amalia asked.

"I'm old enough to be your grandfather. People will talk."

She watched his face wondering what people would talk about. Everyone knew Heinrich as a kind and honorable man.

"If you have my child."

"Child? What?" He couldn't be saying what she thought she heard. "Wait a minute. Please. Let's go over this again." Amalia rose from the chair, more to feel her feet on solid ground than to move the bubbling pot of beans from the stove, though she did that too. "What about Tomas? What did he say?"

Heinrich took her hand and ran his thumb across her palm, his voice full of quiet dignity. His yellowed thumbnail rubbed over the creases in her skin as if erasing them, yet they remained, as distinct as when the little girl read her fortune. "We would work here together. The farm would belong to us, to you when I'm gone. We could try to have a baby. If it happened, we'd marry right away; if not, we'd go on as we are now." His voice trailed off.

She pulled her hand away. "It? What do you mean, it?"

He blushed and stammered. "A baby, a pregnancy. I, uh, if you want to get married anyway, baby or no, I'd like that. It would be more correct. I'd been thinking, perhaps..."

Baby? she thought, but she said, "Tomas?"

"He can't marry you until his mother dies."

"Until his mother dies?"

"I told him if he didn't ask you on Sunday, yesterday, I would ask you myself." Heinrich punctuated his words with a sharp nod.

A marriage proposal. So many nights before falling asleep she'd anticipated the moment a man would ask her to marry him—Lorenz, Karl, Tomas. She studied Heinrich's dear, old face, imagined licking the wrinkles with the tip of her tongue, like a kitten. Then what?

What would Sofie say? Or Dora/Sister Gabriele? How could she tell them she married such an old man? Old. With a prosperous farm. Acres of rich soil. A herd of cows. A flock of chickens. An orchard. Old. Dependable, hard working. Old. Kind. Old. He wanted her. He wanted to have a baby. A scene like this, thought Amalia, belongs in a dream, in which images from life tumble together and develop in ways that make you wonder. She didn't say no.

C H A P T E R   19

▼

Sister Gabriele forced herself awake toward the end of the Great Silence to reread the mail she'd received the day before. After months of hearing nothing from Amalia, a letter finally arrived, with one from Sofie enclosed. Sister Gabriele cared too much about the letters. She hated throwing them away after just one or two readings, though she always had until yesterday. At the end of recreation Sister Greta stood just outside the door holding a metal trash receptacle. She dropped in the envelope, minus the pages hidden in her sleeve. Back in her cubicle, she folded them small and stuck them deep into the toe of a shoe in her cupboard, the same dark space in which she'd hidden Amalia's note back at the very beginning of her postulancy. Now, six months into her first year as a novice, she knew better. She had no excuse. She would throw them away today, flush them down the toilet as she'd disposed of Amalia's note her first night in the convent. Without making the slightest sound, she opened her cupboard, removed the letter from deep in the shoe, closed the door, tiptoed to the washroom, and, leaning against the end sink, unfolded the pages under the dim glow of the nightlight. She read them slowly, trying, as she had the evening before, to memorize them, the curve of her backside warming the cold porcelain of the sink edge through her thin nightdress and bloomers.

May 15, 1925

Dear Sister Gabriele, (Will I ever get used to calling you that?)

Since there are no opportunities for visiting, I am enclosing the baby photo Sofie wanted me to bring to show you. I decided to enclose her letter too, as I have been so busy I don't have to time to copy it over or even copy out the important parts. You might as well have the whole thing. Please send the photo back if you are not allowed to keep it. I have hired a man to replaster the Neufelds' house. Heinrich bought four handsome pigs that are fattening nicely and I've decided to raise a flock of geese. I always wanted goose for Christmas dinner, like the rich people had, with applesauce.

It won't be long until the trees are thick with cherries. Heinrich helps to can them. You asked about Tomas Blau. He's not about to marry me or anyone else. His mother won't permit it and I think she will be around for a good while yet. Even death will have nothing to do with her. Gustav loves to shine our shoes—Heinrich's, Frau Neufeld's and mine—and brush lint from our Sunday clothes. Every Saturday he comes over and I pay him a pfennig. It saves me some time as I do all the housework, most of Frau Neufeld's care, and some farm work as well. Heinrich consults with me whenever there is a major decision to be made. He is a good man. We are partners. You know, sometimes the most unlikely people bring out the best in others, like water on stones. A funny little story about Heinrich and stones. He remembered us, you especially since you lived with them, collecting rocks from the river and sorting them by color, shape, and personality. I mentioned how disappointed I'd always been by how dull they grew when they dried out and, as an example, held up a white stone I happen to have on the windowsill. He didn't say much; he never does. Then later, as I was doing the dishes, he got a strange look in his eye, picked up the rock, left the room, and came back holding it in the palm of his hand. He'd coated it with lard and it gleamed! Why didn't we think of that when we were girls? I suppose there wouldn't have been any lard to spare for such foolishness. My stone is still shiny these many months later, the whitest of whites, but I have to keep it on a saucer or it leaves a grease spot.

Sofie's letter had gotten mixed up with Amalia's. Sister Gabriele kept reading, without reordering the pages, hoping the words would fasten themselves to her heart like the field burrs that stuck to her thick stockings.

Dear Amalia,

Please bring this picture when you go to see Dora, I mean Sister Gabriele, on visiting day. Isn't Martin nice and fat? You can't tell in the picture, but the coat I'm wearing is the most beautiful red, just the color of that book we had when we were girls. I wish I knew what happened to that. Oskar and I have already saved enough money to buy a piece of land no one else wants. Years ago it was the town dump so it will take some work to clean it up, but you know I don't mind work and cleaning is enjoyable when it serves such a clear purpose. It lies next to a large strip of woods where we like to wander on Sundays. We have found some delicious mushrooms there. Remember, in Tauburg, how Oskar would bring them home for me to cook? They were the tastiest thing we had to eat then. Now we have all the food we want, but they are still the tastiest thing. Oskar and I will build the house. I keep thinking how happy Mama would be to know that one of her daughters has land. What about you? Have you agreed to marry Tomas yet? If you wait for Frau Blau to die, you might be too old to have children. Why don't you and Tomas come here? So von Hindenburg is now president of Germany? Oskar thinks this is a terrible development. The old man is nothing but a pawn. We read in our paper that the Communists protested. Was Lorenz there, do you think? Wherever he was, we can be sure he was unhappy, while Karl is surely smiling. What about Tomas? Do you like his political views? Our poor country. So tired and beat up from the war. There is none of that here; this is a nation of people who win. They expect to have full bellies and paychecks that cover the rent and more. Everyone wants a car and, you know, it won't be long until we have one ourselves. It is a nation of Fisherman's Wives, wanting, wanting, and getting! They stop just short of wanting to be God, so they don't lose it all. Did Germany not know enough to stop? Is that why we were punished? I'm afraid of this crazy Hitler and his party. On Saturday nights, between polkas and waltzes, people talk about German politics and worry. American politics are not as interesting. Now that I am learning English I am much happier. Anyone can learn faster than I did. I spent too much time resisting. I think I believed that as long as I couldn't speak the language I was still a German. I wasn't settling here with my heart. But now we have been here almost a year. Martin Georg Schmidt is a US citizen. His parents will be US citizens. I would be happy here if you and Dora were with me, but I must accept that will never happen. I try to speak English to the baby even though he is so small. But when I talk about you, when I sing him lullabies or tell him stories, I speak German. Sofie, Amalia, Dora, I say over and over, like a nursery rhyme. Once upon a time, always in German, the language our mother loved us in, the language we share. Yours, Sofie

"I'm glad she's happy," Sister Gabriele whispered, as if Amalia were in the washroom with her, sitting on the edge of the next sink, skirts hiked up, swinging her legs. "She sounds happy, doesn't she? Not as lonely as she used to sound. And the baby looks cute and healthy."

She switched back to Amalia's more rounded, careless handwriting. *I tell Heinrich stories about Tauburg, the miners and the boarding house. He helps me remember the years we spent in Elsterdorf during the war. He reminded me about you and the rocks and Frau Neufeld combing nits from your hair while teaching you to crochet. It's hard to imagine her teaching anybody anything but forbearance. He felt sorry for us, three small girls separated from our mother, but he says he was always envious of how we took care of each other. He says we were lucky, he's spent so much of his life alone. But we sisters don't really have each other anymore, do we? That's over. Sofie is thousands of kilometers away, and you might as well be. When I have trouble falling asleep at night I tell myself other stories about us. Stories help me sleep at night and the urgency of the cows' full udders gets me up in the morning. I depend on those things the way you must depend on God.*

The bells clanged. Claudia, or Sister Clara, the caller, would be rolling out of bed to wake the rest of the novices for chapel. Sister Gabriele turned on the faucet, let it run for a moment, and, passing Sister Clara's curtained cubicle, scurried back to her own. The letters, folded around the picture she was careful not to crease, burned in her hand. She vowed to herself and God she wouldn't keep them much longer.

"Blessed be God!" Sister Clara said, grabbing the foot of Sister Gabriele's metal bed frame through the curtain and shaking it.

"Now and forever more, Amen!" Sister Gabriele, sitting on the side of her bed, made her voice sound sleepy then, remorseful over this small deception, fell to her knees for a moment before dressing.

They gathered in the chapel for meditation and Mass. Sister Gabriele loved the Gregorian chant, the familiar beauty of the prayers, the intimate union of her soul with God through Holy Communion. In one of their weekly talks, Mother Franziska, the Novice Mistress, had emphasized the few moments after receiving sacred Host as a time to converse with God, to ask for graces and pray for relatives. Sister Gabriele prayed for Amalia to marry Tomas so she'd have a home. She prayed for Sofie, Oskar, and especially the baby to be healthy. She tried to stop herself and pray for their salvation instead, as she'd been instructed. So many rules. Sister Gabriele followed most of them with little trouble. Sister Raphaela had told her, even before she became a postulant, that the first year as a novice was the most difficult for any nun, though every individual had her own struggles, different faults, aspects of her wordly self needing to be shattered, so that at the end of the two years in the novitiate she could offer her brand new, pure self to God.

Sister Clara committed faults against humility over and over. She was vain about her looks. In the garden Sister Gabriele had more than once seen her pick a blossom, tuck it under the edge of her veil, and squint to sharpen her reflection in a window. Petra, or Sister Paul, seemed to have the most trouble with obedience. Sister Gabriele had watched her eyes narrow, nose twitch, and lips move in a disgruntled mutter after Mother Franziska instructed her to sweep the walk by whisking the broom in the opposite direction from the way Sister Paul moved it, accomplishing the same thing as far as any of the novices could see. Anneliese, Sister Lucia, couldn't seem to contain her generous body and spirit. She dropped things wherever she went, laughed when she wasn't supposed to, and tore her clothes. Sister Gabriele caught herself, remembered the letter in the shoe, the times she'd faulted Sister Lucia for not maintaining custody of the eyes. She couldn't have seen the raised eyebrow, the wink, the questioning stare if she hadn't failed to maintain custody of the eyes herself.

Just before she entered the refectory for breakfast, Mother Franziska stopped her. "I would like to see you in my office right after morning chores." Her face was stern. Their weekly appointment wasn't until Wednesday, two days from now. She had to be in trouble. Up until now, all through her postulancy, Sister Gabriele had never been reprimanded for anything serious enough to warrant a summons. The past week rolled through her head. She'd already done penance for listening to Sister Clara complain about scrubbing the Virgin Mary's stone pedestal with a vegetable brush. Sister Gabriele hadn't minded spending the afternoon in the sunny courtyard garden working silently, side by side with Sister Clara. She didn't care about efficiency. The sun felt nice on her back, even through the habit. Sister Clara had complained about the size of the brush just as Sister Greta passed through the garden. Consequently, both Sister Gabriele and Sister Clara were assigned to scour the toilets with even smaller brushes. She'd been prompt for everything without rushing. All in all, she was making progress in her conduct toward God, others, and herself. Of course she slipped now and then, and she did miss her sisters more than she should.

After breakfast she picked up her basket of cleaning supplies, the morning's bread an indigestible lump in her stomach. The feeling of dread wouldn't be prayed away. All four novices were to wax the floor of the refectory. Sister Clara and Sister Paul lifted the benches and set them upside down on the tabletops. Sister Lucia swept up the few morning crumbs. On her knees in the far corner, Sister Gabriele pried open the tin of wax, smeared her rag, and began applying it to the floor. The other girls picked rags from the basket, dipped them in the wax, and on hands and knees in a jagged row, worked their way across the room, under the heavy tables. When they finally reached the doors to the kitchen and the hall, Sister Lucia stood and groaned, rolling her shoulders. Sister Clara giggled. Sister Gabriele began to furiously buff the floor, making her way back to the platform where the reader's podium stood. That still needed waxing. She was in too much trouble to get caught laughing. She wanted to ask the other girls, all of whom had been called to Mother Franzika's office more than once, what happened behind that closed door, but she wouldn't risk talking now. A loud "oops" echoed through the cavernous room, then a cacophony of stifled giggles. She peeked around the podium to see Sister Lucia on her bottom, Sister Paul and Sister Clara helping her up. The moment she stood upright, she took off twirling, rags under her feet. Sister Clara slid after her, waving her work-reddened hands above her head. Sister Paul spread her cloth and stood on it, twisting her feet and wiggling her hips. Their eyes full of silent laughter lit the cavernous room. The three of them skated across the refectory, twirling, dancing, throats gurgling with giggles, buffing the floor as they went. Behind the reader's podium Sister Gabriele clutched her waxy rag, too afraid to join in. When Sister Lucia reached for her hand she shrunk away. She could hear Amalia and Sofie's teasing voices calling her a saint. She wasn't a saint, just afraid of being scolded. The wood under her hands shone.

When she'd finished polishing the platform and moved back to the main floor, the other girls had returned to working on hands and knees. Disappointment edged Sister Gabriele's relief. You would think the skating, the laughing had never happened. Amalia would have polished the floor that way. Sofie would have pretended disapproval, but when Amalia refused to stop, Sofie would have joined her. Finally, when it looked like fun, Sister Gabriele, Dora, would have joined in. How had she always managed to avoid the housework? Her sisters had spoiled her.

The four novices repacked the cleaning supplies. Sisters Paul, Clara, and Lucia had more chores to complete. Sister Gabriele turned the opposite way toward Mother Franziska's office alone.

She rapped on Mother Franziska's door as she'd been instructed—twice lightly with the knuckle of her index finger. She enjoyed the weekly talks with the Novice Mistress. Mother Franziska listened the way Sister Gabriele believed God listened when she prayed with true devotion, humility and confidence. If only this was a regular talk and not a summons.

"Come in." The voice rang out sharply, not the gentle invitation Sister Gabriele had come to expect. She obeyed.

"Good morning, Mother," Sister Gabriele said.

Mother Franziska gestured to a spindly, straight-backed chair without looking up from the small piece of paper in her hand. Sister Gabriele seated herself and waited. She had grown used to quiet, appreciated the stillness as full of the presence of God. But this charged silence which hurt her ears and made her sick to her stomach was as loud as the bells and sirens announcing an accident at the mine.

The polished expanse of table spread between them, empty of all but the older nun's small white hands holding the scrap of paper. Mother Franziska, a medium-sized woman, sat dwarfed by the back of her elaborately carved wooden chair—a gift from the Kaiser, Sister Gabriele had been told. Not a speck of dust hid in the intricacies of the designs; Sister Gabriele had cleaned it herself the day before with a special rag on a pointed stick.

Mother Franziska sniffed and continued to stare at the paper. She must be reading the same words over and over as it couldn't take that long to read such a small amount of writing. The waiting, the plain white walls, the simple crucifix, the rays of sunlight angled across the gleaming table all reminded Sister Gabriele of the room at Frau Becker's. She, Sofie, and Amalia had all memorized the shifting progression of light across the polished wooden floor. She scolded herself. Why did even the most universal, everyday things, nothing particular about them, remind her of her sisters? After all this time of study, prayer, and practice, she shouldn't remain so attached. The struggle with the guilt of attachment to wordly affairs complicated and intensified the ache of simply missing them.

Mother Franziska finally looked up, frowning over her glasses. A tapping sound broke the silence—Sister Gabriele's foot.

"I'm sorry, Mother." She placed her hands flat on her thighs to keep her legs quiet.

Mother Franziska cleared her throat, flattened the scrap of paper on the table, folded her hands, and leaned forward. "Sister Gabriele, we are concerned about you."

Sister Gabriele looked past the Novice Mistress's disapproving face. During weekly appointments Mother Franziska always began by asking how she was doing. They talked about the importance of the different spiritual practices and the obligations of religious vows. With Mother Franziska, Sister Gabriele could raise doubts and questions. Last time they'd discussed the daily examination of conscience. "Too often," Mother Franziska had said, "we forget to begin by thanking God for all the favors he has bestowed upon us. When thinking so hard about our sins we tend to forget God." Sister Gabriele liked that. Other sisters, Sister Greta for instance, seemed to focus on the sinning, and terrible old Sister Monika! Dora and Amalia had been so scared of her. Stop. Again, thinking about the past.

"Why are you concerned, Mother?" Sister Gabriele asked. She looked toward Jesus on his cross for help. She wouldn't forget God, not for a moment, even as she panicked inside about whatever she'd done wrong.

"The letter." Mother Franziska spit the word, making it sound like sin itself.

Blood pounded in Sister Gabriele's temples. She couldn't breathe. No one knew about the hiding place. No one but God.

"You are encouraged to dispose of them, if not immediately then after recreation. Sister Greta reports that she found an empty envelope in the trash can."

Sister Gabriele's stomach jumped. *That tattletaling snoop.* No. That was an unkind thought. She had to do better.

"Mother, I know I am guilty of keeping the letter. I pray to God to help me stop missing them so much. It hasn't gotten any easier." She prayed for the strength not to cry.

"Perhaps we should curtail your correspondence," Mother Franziska said.

A sob escaped Sister Gabriele's throat. "No, that won't be necessary, Mother."

"Where is the letter you've neglected to discard?"

"In my cupboard, Mother."

"You must get it now, and bring it to me. Go."

"Yes, Mother."

Her eyes itched with tears. She told herself to move with quiet grace through the corridor. She was a novice, not a homesick postulant. This was a lesson, a real test of her devotion to God.

She passed Sister Clara perched on a ladder like an awkward bird, dusting the tops of the frosted transoms. She passed Sister Paul polishing door handles. She passed Sister Lucia washing windows. She felt their questions at her back.

In the empty dormitory she pulled the curtain around her bed and sat. She wanted to obey, knew she had to obey, and quickly, but her legs refused to carry her another step. She slipped yesterday's fat letter from the shoe, remembering her excitement when Mother Franziska had handed it to her. She had gone such a long time without mail. She'd expected the infrequency from Sofie all the way across the world, but Amalia lived less than a day's train ride away. Sister Gabriele ached to read the letters one more time, but Mother Franziska waited in her office.

The improbability of being alone in the dormitory in the middle of the day underscored the seriousness of her crime. With shaky fingers she slipped Sofie's photo back into the toe of the shoe. She'd send it back to Amalia. There would be more letters.

She raced back through the echoing corridors to the Novice Mistress, heels slapping carelessly. She slowed a bit, concealing the pages in the sleeve of her habit as she passed her fellow novices at work. At the office door, she paused for a breath before knocking.

Mother Franziska stood silhouetted by the window. She came around the table to meet Sister Gabriele hand outstretched. Sister Gabriele placed the letter on Mother Franziska's open palm and bowed her head, trying not to flinch as she waited for the scolding she deserved for having taken so long to obey her superior. The letter disappeared into the Novice Mistress's pocket.

"Sister Gabriele."

Sister Gabriele looked at the floor. She wouldn't cry.

"As Saint Teresa tells us, if a sister's heart is occupied with temporal affairs, she is 'seriously ill in spirit.' If you concern yourself with anything other than your relatives' eternal salvation you will have little peace and no devotion at prayer. Worrying about their temporal affairs returns you to your family; you are no longer a part of our community. You're in danger of losing your vocation."

"No!" Sister Gabriele yelled, startling them both. "No, Mother." She quieted her voice. "Please."

Mother Franziska reached out with the same hand she'd used to take Amalia and Sofie's words away. She held Sister Gabriele's clenched fist, uncurled the tight fingers, rubbed the knuckles with her thumb.

"It's natural to miss your family. It grows easier. You must pray." The light reflecting off Mother Franziska's glasses made it impossible to see her eyes.

"Mother, I'll try harder. There is no need to stop my mail. My sisters will worry if they hear nothing from me."

"I had no intention of stopping the sending of letters. It is the receiving of them that concerns me."

Sister Gabriele swallowed her intemperate protest. "Whatever you think best, Mother." God had put the right words into her mouth! Mother Franziska smiled.

"Pray hard. Examine your conscience. You've spoken to me of your love of the Rosary. Immerse yourself in the mysteries—the joys, the sorrows, the glories. They have so much to teach us. Make the Rosary your own. God will help you understand why limiting written contact with your sisters is necessary."

Mother Franziska examined the letters. "Wasn't there also a photograph?"

Sister Gabriele's breath came hard and fast. She swallowed, eyes downcast. "Yes, Mother."

"And why isn't it in this envelope?"

"Because...because my sister asked me to send it back to her if I couldn't keep it, Mother."

Mother Franziska looked at the clock. "I expect to see that photograph right here." She tapped the desk. "Before vespers. I will return it to your sister and let her know that at this time it is not in your best interests to receive family pictures."

"Thank you, Mother."

"Sister Gabriele, we are very disappointed. As you well know, the call to religious life is an invitation, not a command."

"Yes, Mother." Sister Gabriele knew she should listen without answering back, but desperate to explain herself she spoke. "I've wanted to be a nun as long as I can remember. You've said before that such a natural inclination, present from a young age, is a clear mark of vocation."

"*Often*, Sister Gabriele. *Often* a clear mark. Search your heart and soul. There are any number of ways to lose one's vocation. Undue intercourse with the world is one of them. Go directly to the chapel and remain there as long as you feel necessary. Pray."

On the short walk to the chapel Sister Gabriele had to remind herself twice to slow down. She remembered Sister Raphaela's words from long ago, when she and Amalia argued about going home for Christmas. "Love for our relatives doesn't stop with our separation from the world. Quite the opposite. Instead of a transitory, worldly love based on something as temporary and material as the body, that love is transformed to a pure, spiritual, eternal love." Even then Sister Gabriele had known that her place was in the convent.

She would pray for her sisters. She would pray for herself to stop missing them, or to accept that she did. All her life God had helped her accept and understand. She must keep faith that He would help her now.

The bank of candles flickered red in the small chapel. The one stained-glass window above the altar let in lozenges of blue and yellow light. She knelt in the last pew, her rosary wound between her fingers. She prayed.

Three girls born from the same man and woman within three years. They shared beds and dreams and fears and hunger and food and chores. And stories. Candy houses, magic fish, hair strong and long enough for princes to climb. They shared a life until they chose different ones, or different ones chose them. Sofie had America and a baby. Amalia had pigs, a flock of geese, a barn full of cows to milk. Sister Gabriele—Sister Gabriele had a vocation. She would pray daily for her sisters' true welfare, their eternal salvation. She fingered the beads—every life had its joyful, sorrowful, and glorious mysteries. You had to immerse yourself in them, be a wet stone, let love be the water that brought out the best in you and others. *Stories help me sleep at night,* Amalia had written.

Once upon a time there were three sisters. The oldest had gray eyes, the color of a stormy ocean. She would travel far. The middle sister had eyes like her mother, the brown of freshly dug earth. She would do whatever was required to establish roots. The youngest sister had eyes as blue as heaven. She would know God.

When they were small, waiting for their mother, they used to end their story *now the girls are safe and happy.* Who was ever safe in this dangerous world? What was happiness but a transitory and subjective thing? But love. Love mattered. All love.

In her excitement Sister Gabriele's elbow slipped from the back of the pew. Her beads clattered against the wood. She didn't need letters to feel her sisters' presence. On steady knees she breathed in the soothing smell of incense and candle wax and closed her eyes to assimilate the biggest revelation of her almost eighteen years. In the holy quiet, Sister Gabriele knelt, drenched and radiant and sure. She didn't need photographs to know that her sisters walked the world, shining too, drenched in love.

Acknowledgments

Many thanks to:

Maxie Chambliss and Susan Fehlinger, intrepid cover designers, who know what I really want before I do;

my companions and teachers in the writing life: Hallie Touger, Maggie Bucholt, Pat Rathbone, Carolyn Heller, Donna Tramontozzi, Anne Meirowitz, Tracy Winn, Nancy Tancredi, Judith Hert, Patty Smith, Joanie Grisham, Nathan Long, Bessie Blum, Candace Perry, Judith Felsenfeld, Anne Walsh, Eileen O'Toole, Marjorie Saunders, Brooks Whitney, Mark Ford, Laura Brown, Samantha Schoech, Grace Paley, Tom Jenks, Michael Cunningham, Dick Bausch, Anne Bernays, Allan Gurganus, and Marie Howe;

research helpers: Brigitte Giber, Jane Thomas, Hannelore Biewald, Shirley and Ed Biewald, Gunter and Christel Biewald, Rudi and Anneliese Laumeier;

colleagues and families at the Fayerweather Street School;

the Fine Arts Work Center, Vermont Studio Center, Millay Colony, Massachusetts Cultural Council, and the Wesleyan Writers Conference;

my family and friends, especially the people who lived with me through the many years of writing this book: Jeannie Ramey, Bruce, Lukas, Mollie, Georgia, Izaak and Emmett Biewald, and Jeff, Jake and Owen Thomas;

and my grandmother and great-aunts: Wilhelmine Hulsken Biewald, Agnes Hulsken Laumeier, and Schwester Uriele, for their stories.

978-0-595-36267-7
0-595-36267-2

Made in the USA
Lexington, KY
25 November 2013